DANCE WITH ME

080 6 0.40 6062

Somerset was desperately aware of Isabel in his arms. As the music lilted them across the polished parquet flooring, he decided that she belonged there always, as if God had intended this pairing.

Glancing down at her, he noticed her eyes had drifted shut and she had a dreamy expression on her face. "Isabel?" he said softly.

With a small start, she opened her eyes and glanced up at him. She licked her lips, as if her mouth had gone dry. He knew his own mouth was longing for a taste of hers, but he didn't suppose her problem was the same as his. Unfortunately.

"There," said Isabel, giving herself a tiny shake that Somerset barely felt. "See? You dance beautifully. Gloriously, in fact. But you need to lift your chin and look down at me as if we were the only two people on earth."

BOOK YOUR PLACE ON OUR WEBSITE AND MAKE THE READING CONNECTION!

We've created a customized website just for our very special readers, where you can get the inside scoop on everything that's going on with Zebra, Pinnacle and Kensington books.

When you come online, you'll have the exciting opportunity to:

- View covers of upcoming books

- Read sample chapters

- Learn about our future publishing schedule (listed by publication month *and author*)

- Find out when your favorite authors will be visiting a city near you

- Search for and order backlist books from our online catalog

- Check out author bios and background information

- Send e-mail to your favorite authors

- Meet the Kensington staff online

- Join us in weekly chats with authors, readers and other guests

- Get writing guidelines

- AND MUCH MORE!

**Visit our website at
http://www.kensingtonbooks.com**

A PERFECT STRANGER

Anne Robins

ZEBRA BOOKS
KENSINGTON PUBLISHING CORP.
http://www.kensingtonbooks.com

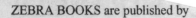

ZEBRA BOOKS are published by

Kensington Publishing Corp.
850 Third Avenue
New York, NY 10022

Copyright © 2004 by Alice Duncan

All Kensington titles, imprints and distributed lines are available at special quantity discounts for bulk purchases for sales promotion, premiums, fund-raising, educational or institutional use.

Special book excerpts or customized printings can also be created to fit specific needs. For details, write or phone the office of the Kensington Special Sales Manager: Kensington Publishing Corp., 850 Third Avenue, New York, NY 10022. Attn. Special Sales Department. Phone: 1-800-221-2647.

Zebra and the Z logo Reg. U.S. Pat. & TM Off.

First Printing: July 2004
10 9 8 7 6 5 4 3 2 1

Printed in the United States of America

Prologue

April 14, 1912

"Eunice! Mrs. Golightly!"

Isabel Golightly recognized that voice, although she could scarcely credit her ears. "What the bloody hell. . . ?" Holding on tightly to her daughter Eunice, she tried to see over the throng of pushing, shoving passengers. It was no use. She was too bloody short, and everyone was in a tearing panic.

"I believe that's Miss Linden, Mama," Eunice said. Eunice, of all the people aboard the ship's steerage-class deck, seemed calm. She would. A most unnatural child, Isabel's daughter Eunice. And thank God for it, at least for now.

"I know, sweets." What's more, Isabel couldn't imagine what that rich and privileged young lady, Loretta Linden, was doing down below with the riffraff at a time like this—or any other time, for that matter. Miss Linden belonged with her set, abovestairs among the other first-class passengers. Steerage-class and first-class passengers weren't supposed to have anything to do with each other. The White Star Line's rule booklet said so.

That hadn't mattered to Miss Loretta Linden, who had made Isabel and Eunice Golightly her business since the ship left Southampton. Isabel bitterly imagined that most of the first-class passengers were already in lifeboats. Not Miss Linden, who had been kind enough to come looking for Isabel and Eunice.

This wretched ship was supposed to have taken Isabel and Eunice to a new life in America. It wasn't supposed to end their old lives by sinking.

"I think Miss Linden wants us to follow her," Eunice pointed out.

Isabel was having a fight of it to keep upright. The notion of her six-year-old daughter dying before she'd had a chance to live made Isabel's entire body throb with grief, fear, and outrage. She wouldn't let Eunice witness her despair. "Yes, dearie, but I don't know where she is. I can't see anything but backs and shoulders."

"I believe she's over there, Mama." Eunice pointed.

Incredulous, Isabel looked and realized Eunice was right: there was Loretta Linden, clinging with one hand to the service stairway railing, her wire-rimmed spectacles sliding down her nose, the lenses winking in the electrical lights that would probably go out any minute, frantically waving a white handkerchief in their direction. Isabel ought to have trusted her daughter, who was smarter than any other five people she knew, including herself and Eunice's father, although, admittedly, that didn't take much.

"Yes, I see. But I don't know how to get to her." She was being squished at the moment, and finding it difficult to keep her footing. And if she fell, they'd both be trampled to death in the melee. It was impossible to aim herself in any particular direction. The water was up to her ankles now, too. Damned unsinkable ship. Like hell. She tried to look around and get her bearings, but encountered only a sea of shoulders and chests.

Something bumped her hard from behind, and in spite of everything, Isabel found herself shoved forward and to her left, toward the service stairwell.

"Eunice!" Loretta screeched. "Mrs. Golightly! Come here! We must get to a lifeboat!"

Another shove, and Isabel landed on her bottom on the third step of the service stairs, Eunice plopping onto her lap with a grunt. Loretta reached down, grabbed Isabel by the arm, and yanked, nearly wrenching Isabel's shoulder from its socket.

"Ow! Be careful!"

"I think Miss Linden is trying to rescue us, Mama," said Eunice, panting slightly.

Isabel almost laughed as she stumbled up the stairs, realizing for the first time that Miss Loretta Linden, wealthy spinster, first-class passenger, and an American to boot, might just be saving the lives of Isabel and her daughter. She also didn't understand why the rest of the steerage-class passengers hadn't already stormed the service stairs but were, like sheep, trying to exit through the regular passenger corridor. She cast one last look back at the frantic mob and wondered, with a sharp pang, how many of her fellow passengers would drown that night.

After what seemed like millions of stairs and many hours later, Miss Linden shoved a door open and stumbled out onto the tilted upper deck of the *Titanic.* "Hurry, Mrs. Golightly. There's a lifeboat being filled only feet away from us. I see it, and they look as if they're going to lower it to the sea before it's even filled!" She raced toward the lifeboat, flourishing a fist in the air. "Stop! *Stop!"*

Isabel tried to hurry after her. She was exhausted, though, after carrying her daughter all the way up from steerage class, and her tiredness made her clumsy. Catching her foot in a coil of rope, she felt her ankle give way, and she screamed, *"Eunice!"* as she went sprawling. Terror claimed her when her daughter slipped from her grasp. "Eunice! Where are you!" Her daughter had disappeared into the milling throng. Isabel's terror soared.

"Here," a deep masculine voice said. "Let me help you."

"No!" she shrieked, scrambling forward on her hands and knees. "I have to get my daughter!"

"Go to the lifeboat, ma'am. I'll carry your child."

"Where is she? Oh! Where is she?"

"I have her, ma'am."

Feverishly peering into the multitude, trying to spot her daughter, Isabel beheld a large man standing before her. Miracle of miracles, he held Eunice in his arms.

"I'm here, Mama," Eunice said calmly.

"Thank God." Her whisper was ragged.

"Hurry, ma'am. You need to get into the lifeboat."

Grabbing the man's arm for fear of becoming separated from Eunice again, Isabel stumbled madly in the direction of the lifeboat. The man shoved others out of the way as he steered a straight path ahead. Thinking of Loretta, Isabel called out, "Miss Linden?"

But Loretta had vanished. Isabel could only pray that she'd made her way into the lifeboat. Then she heard her voice, loud and commanding. "Don't you dare lower this lifeboat until it's filled! If you do, you'll be guilty of murder!"

A sailor grumbled, but Isabel imagined he would obey that imperious voice. Loretta Linden was only about five feet tall, but she possessed a positively massive presence. Isabel was grateful for it when they reached the lifeboat, which had been prevented from being lowered until filled by the tiny Miss Loretta Linden.

The man holding Eunice said, "You get in first, ma'am. I'll hand you your daughter."

She didn't want to do it, afraid of being separated from Eunice forever. But she understood the sense of the stranger's directive, so Isabel obediently climbed into the swaying craft. Instantly, she reached for Eunice. Only then did she see the face of the man who had saved their lives. She wasn't surprised to observe that it was a good face, and a handsome one. "Thank you," she said. "God bless you."

His smile was kind and full of perfect white teeth. "You're very welcome, ma'am." And he turned and shoved his way back through the people fighting for seats on lifeboats.

"Why doesn't he get into our boat, Mama?" Eunice asked. She clung with a grip of iron to her mother's hand.

"He's probably going to try to save others, Eunice. They load the women and children first." A sob caught in her throat.

"Mrs. Golightly! Eunice!"

It was Loretta Linden's voice, and Isabel actually managed to smile. She called out, "We're here, Miss Linden!"

"Thank God!" Loretta's voice wavered, as if she were fighting tears.

And then the sailors on deck swung a divot attached to the chain carrying their lifeboat over the side of the ship, and the boat began its swaying trip into the icy Atlantic.

"Where's that man?" Eunice cried. "He needs to get into the boat, too, Mama!"

"I don't know where he is, sweetheart." She hadn't

even asked his name so that she could pray for him. The thought of that noble, brave man going down with the unsinkable *Titanic* was the last straw. In spite of her strength and her determination, Isabel Golightly burst into tears.

Chapter One

April 25, 1912

"There are too many bodies for the rescue boats to carry, and they didn't bring sufficient coffins. I fear many are being buried at sea."

Isabel, her left foot propped on a stool, looked up from the *New York Times* she'd been scanning and saw that Loretta Linden had entered the hotel room—and without a single squeaking hinge to announce her entrance. Money could even buy silence; how amazing.

"They don't have enough coffins?" Her heart squeezed, and her mind instantly pictured the wonderful man who had handed Eunice to her in the lifeboat. Had he died in that awful, freezing, black water? He and Loretta had saved their lives. And he'd probably perished for his kindness.

"They've found several hundreds of bodies. I presume there were more than they expected. It's difficult to take in the enormity of the tragedy. The casualty list keeps growing." Loretta looked at her sadly as she took off her scarf and threw it on the sofa.

Isabel was unused to people treating fine clothing and fine furniture in so cavalier a manner, but she held her tongue. She'd known from the cradle that the rich and the poor were different in every way.

Loretta went on, "So far, they've only ascertained for certain that a few more than seven hundred of us survived. That means over fifteen hundred are gone." She shook her head. "What a catastrophe."

"But why weren't more saved?" Isabel asked, refusing to allow the lump in her throat to turn into tears. Her mind's eye kept picturing Eunice's savior. She didn't want to think of him as one of those who had died. She couldn't bear it.

Marjorie MacTavish, who had entered the room after Loretta, frowned briefly at Loretta's back, then picked up Loretta's scarf and hung it and her own in the closet beside the front door of the suite. "Because they didna bring enough lifeboats," she said, her burr more pronounced than usual. "It's wicked, is what it is. I understand that Mr. Ismay was one of the survivors, too." She gave a meaningful sniff, as if to say she believed someone more deserving ought to have been saved and Mr. Ismay, chairman of the White Star Line, allowed to drown.

Miss MacTavish, a Scottish lass and one steeped in the traditional class distinctions of her homeland, had been a stewardess aboard the *R.M.S. Titanic*. While she never said so aloud, Isabel sensed that she didn't approve of Loretta consorting with Isabel and Eunice. Isabel didn't, either, if it came to that, but she wasn't going to offer herself as a sacrifice for anyone—save, perhaps, her daughter.

Eunice, who had been drawing quietly at a table in the

corner, stuck an oar in. "Why aren't there rules about how many lifeboats are carried on ships? I think there should be enough lifeboats to save everyone in case a ship hits an iceberg. If Mr. Ismay was responsible, I think he ought to be persecuted." Eunice's little brow wrinkled. "Or do I mean *prosecuted?*"

Isabel, who tried always to encourage her brilliant daughter in the conquest of the English language, smiled wanly and said, "Prosecuted, dearie."

Eunice nodded, pleased to have added another word to her vocabulary.

Miss Linden and Marjorie had swivelled to stare at the girl. Unlike Isabel, they weren't used to Eunice.

"*I* think he should be persecuted," muttered Marjorie.

"I think you're right, sweetie," Eunice's mother said, still fighting her lump.

"You're absolutely correct, Eunice," Miss Linden said firmly. She had taken quite a shine to Isabel's daughter, and Isabel appreciated her for it. "And I intend to write to our elected leaders about the matter."

"Aren't *Titanic* and her sister ships British, Miss Linden?" Eunice asked. "Will your leaders be able to do anything about British boat-builders?"

"No, but after this miserable event, they'd better pay attention to our own shipyards and do their utmost to avert future disasters of a like nature. Since most of the passengers were Americans, the British had better pay attention, too."

"Most third-class passengers, like us," Eunice said in her piping, albeit matter-of-fact voice, "were Europeans headed to America in search of a better life."

"Yes. I suppose that's true." Miss Linden looked uncomfortable.

Isabel knew why. It was because she was rich, and Isabel and Eunice, not to mention most of the people who had died, were poor. Isabel hadn't known Loretta Linden long, but she'd already discovered that the young woman, who had been born into wealth, possessed a social conscience big enough to rival that of the fellow who had established the Salvation Army. There weren't many people like Loretta. Isabel wasn't sure if that was a bad thing or not.

After thinking over the matter for a few moments, Eunice nodded and turned her bright-eyed gaze upon her mother. "Why don't you write to the prime minister, Mama? He ought to know about the *Titanic*, too."

"I'm sure he already knows about it, sweetie. They're calling it the worst ocean-liner disaster in history."

"Well, I'm not going to write to anyone," said Marjorie.

"How come?"

Although Eunice was only curious, Isabel winced inwardly. Marjorie MacTavish was extremely conventional, and not the sort to appreciate curiosity in children.

The edges of Marjorie's mouth turned down a little, but she only said, "I may go back to being a stewardess one day, and I don't want any black marks against me."

"Would a letter be a black mark?" Eunice asked incredulously.

Loretta sniffed. "The men who run things don't like to hear women speak the truth, dear. It upsets their tidy little world."

"Well, I wouldn't put it exactly that way," said Marjorie in a strained voice. Isabel felt rather sorry for the woman because she reminded her of an overwound watch. Isabel feared she might blow up one day, and her mental gears fly off in all directions.

Eunice, who had been following the conversation avidly, although Isabel wasn't sure how much of it she understood, said, "*Do* men run things, Miss Linden?"

"They do," said Loretta firmly.

"How come?"

"Because they're the oppressors of females, dear. It's how they maintain their power."

Marjorie rolled her eyes.

Eunice looked puzzled, but Isabel decided not to step in and explain. This was mainly because she wasn't sure herself what Loretta was saying. Isabel's life to date hadn't had much room for political and social philosophy.

"Did they run the *Titanic?*"

"My goodness, yes!"

"Well, then, they should get lots of letters telling them what happened. Especially about the lifeboats." Eunice nodded, as if satisfied with her own opinion, and went back to her picture.

Loretta offered Isabel a small, lopsided smile. "One can always trust the young to tell the truth. Before society's rules get in their way and they learn to lie."

Having had more experience with children than Loretta, Isabel might have contradicted her on that point, but she didn't As strange as Isabel found Loretta Linden, still more did she like her, in spite of the differences between their nationalities and social positions. It was curious to her that she might consider a woman from the upper classes of society a friend, even if she was an American, but that's exactly what Loretta seemed to be becoming. She was so bloody friendly. And she was so bloody *honest.*

Blooming. She was blooming friendly and honest. For Eunice's sake—and for Loretta's—Isabel had vowed to clean up her language. She didn't want Loretta ever to regret her generosity to the two of them. More, she didn't want Eunice ever to be ashamed of her mother.

Besides, if she managed to make a success of life here in America, she more than likely wouldn't even *want* to swear anymore.

At any rate, Loretta Linden was both friendly and honest, and Isabel liked her a lot, even if she did support approximately six thousand special causes. She was about to add another one, if her recent comments about letter-writing were anything by which to judge. And then there was her promotion of women's rights and suffrage. Loretta was *always* talking about women's suffrage.

As if Isabel had the time or inclination to give a fig about women's rights. She only wanted to figure out how to earn a living for herself and her daughter in this new country.

She returned her attention to the *New York Times* she'd been looking through. The primary problem with securing employment now that she was in New York was that she didn't understand the wording in the advertisements. Everything was so different here in America. She was accustomed to doing char work in England, which was abysmal labor, but respectable. She'd rather do something else, but she wasn't sure what. It was inevitable, therefore, that she'd end up doing drudge work. What a depressing thought.

What she *really* liked to do was dance, but even if she could find a dancing job that paid well, she supposed it wouldn't be considered respectable. And since her primary aim in coming to the United States was to create a new and respectable life for herself and, especially, Eunice, that left out dancing for a living.

No one here in America knew or needed to know a single thing about Isabel's past. All they needed to know was that Isabel was a widow, and that Eunice was her daughter.

Anyhow, none of the ads in the *Times* mentioned needing a woman who could dance. None of them mentioned char work, either. Isabel suspected Americans called it something else. Perhaps she could apply at a domestic employment agency. She couldn't find one of those, either. With a sigh, she shoved the newspaper aside, knowing she'd have to call on Loretta's kindness yet again to explain the vagaries of the American language as used in employment advertisements to her.

Standing up, Isabel limped over to Loretta. "Here, let me help you, Miss Linden." She reached for Loretta's beaver-skin coat, a lovely item Loretta had purchased at Bloomingdale's the day before. Isabel had never seen anything so fine.

"Nonsense," said Loretta stoutly. "I am perfectly capable of hanging up my own coat, and you shouldn't be walking on that ankle."

Eyeing the scarf she'd just hung up, Marjorie, ever the tidy one, sniffed. Loretta tossed the coat over the sofa as she had the scarf. Before Marjorie could do so, Isabel snatched it up and headed for the closet.

"Will you two stop that?" Loretta sounded peeved. "I hate having people wait on me. I'll try to be more orderly, but if I'm not, please don't pick up after me."

"Yes, ma'am," said Marjorie, sounding as if she didn't mean it.

Isabel finished with her small chore and turned back to Loretta. "You've done too much for us already, Miss Linden—"

"For heaven's sake, will you stop calling me Miss Linden?"

Isabel started slightly, because Loretta sounded honestly irked. She looked it, too, although it was difficult to tell because her countenance didn't lend itself to ill humor. Isabel had always assumed that women who wore spectacles were not attractive, but she thought Loretta was cute as a bug.

Short and well-rounded, Loretta had the thickest, glossiest dark brown hair Isabel had ever seen, and the biggest brown eyes. Loretta's eyes were almost as pretty as Eunice's, but not quite. Isabel would like to have big brown eyes herself, but she'd been born with big blue eyes, and there wasn't much she could do about them at this point. She was glad Eunice had inherited her father's eyes, although she couldn't help but pray that was all she'd inherited from him.

"My name," Loretta continued, "is Loretta. I can't *stand* it when you kowtow to me."

Oh dear. As Isabel had grown up kowtowing to people with money, this was certain to get complicated. It was one thing for Isabel to know in her heart that she was just as good as anyone else in the world. It was quite another to live as if she was. Her entire upbringing screamed out against such effrontery.

"Try it," Loretta insisted. "Say *Loretta*. It's not a difficult name." Loretta yanked a hat pin out of the confection that sat atop her lovely hair and flung her hat at the sofa. She missed, the hat landed on the floor, and Marjorie pounced on it.

Isabel knew she was blushing and hated herself for it. Nevertheless, she laughed softly. "Loretta. I'll try to remember."

"See that you do." Loretta shook a finger at her in the parody of a disciplinary gesture. She saw Marjorie with her hat. "Marjorie MacTavish! Do I have to speak to you by hand?"

Marjorie appeared to be as puzzled as was Isabel.

"Spank you," said Loretta patiently.

Marjorie said, "I've been trained to be tidy. I canna help myself."

Loretta aimed a quelling glance at her. "You may have earned your living as a stewardess with the White Star Line for a few years, Marjorie MacTavish, and you might have had to clean up after other people as part of your employment, but your ship sank. It has become painfully obvious that you won't be able to go back to that kind of work any time soon, and that you're probably going to remain in the United States for a good long while. I want you to get it through your head that you're not my servant. You're my friend."

Marjorie blushed, probably at the mention of her inability to perform her duties as a stewardess. She said, "Thank you," in a stifled voice.

Isabel felt a pang of sympathy for Marjorie, who had developed an absolute terror of the ocean. She hadn't been able even to look at it when the three of them and Eunice had taken a cab to the harbor. Poor Marjorie had turned white and begun trembling and crying as soon as the ocean hove into view. Then she'd remained in the cab with Isabel, who couldn't walk because of her ankle injury, while Loretta had taken Eunice to visit the famous Statue of Liberty.

Marjorie was ashamed of this newly developed problem and considered it both an embarrassment and a grievous flaw, although Isabel didn't blame her for it. Loretta called Marjorie's problem a phobia, but Isabel wouldn't know about that. She herself wouldn't mind if she never saw an ocean again, but Marjorie wouldn't take any comfort from Isabel's weakness. Isabel was pretty certain that Marjorie, although she attempted to disguise her opinion, considered Isabel below her on the evolutionary scale—if such a thing existed—and wouldn't care to claim any similarities if they existed. Class distinctions, and all that.

"So please," Loretta said once more, "call me Loretta."

Marjorie said, "Yes, ma'am."

"Ma'am?" Loretta made a moue with her rosebud mouth. "I'm going to have to have you two practice saying my name, I guess."

"I don't think Mama is used to calling people from your station in life by their Christian names, Miss Linden."

Again, all three women turned toward Eunice, whose huge, chocolate-brown eyes observed them soberly. "In Great Britain, class distinctions are quite pronounced. Calling you Loretta would be considered impervious." Her brow furrowed and she glanced at her mother. "Is that what I mean?"

"I believe you mean impertinent, dear," Isabel said softly, amused but not wanting to show it.

Loretta and Marjorie exchanged a glance, then looked at Isabel. Loretta asked—and Isabel wasn't sure she was joking—"Are you sure your daughter is only six years old?"

Isabel was sure, although she understood Loretta's doubt.

A knock and a brisk, "Room service!" came from the hallway. Isabel started for the door at once but, because she couldn't move very fast, Marjorie beat her to it. A uniformed boy pushed a cart laden with covered dishes—they looked as if they were made of silver, but Isabel wasn't certain—cutlery, plates, and glasses into the room. Uncertain and a trifle overwhelmed, Isabel limped over to assist in any way she could. Eunice, too, gazed with wide-eyed wonder at the groaning board.

Not Loretta, who was used to such opulence. Rubbing her hands together, she said brightly, "Oh, good! I'm simply famished." Glancing at her companions, she added, "I hope you don't mind that I ordered for all of us."

Marjorie made a noise signifying approval. As for Isabel, she'd never experienced the glories of room service before in her life—indeed, she hadn't even known such a service existed on earth. She and Eunice were so delighted by the prospect of eating food neither of them had prepared, they wouldn't have caviled if Loretta had ordered snails, which Isabel understood some French people considered a delicacy. They would.

"The doctor is coming to call on you after supper, Isabel."

Distressed, Isabel said, "Oh, dear, I wish you hadn't gone to the bother of calling him in again, Miss Linden." She'd sprained her ankle when she'd tripped over that coil of rope during her mad dash to the lifeboats.

"Loretta, if you please," said Loretta. "And fiddlesticks. You injured your ankle, and it needs to be tended. How's it doing, by the way?"

"Quite well, thank you," Isabel lied. Her ankle hurt like the devil, but she didn't feel comfortable saying so.

She knew she'd never be able to pay Loretta back for her many kindnesses. Not only had Loretta, with the help of that angelic and unknown male benefactor, saved Isabel and Eunice from the terrors of the deep, but Loretta had established them in a suite in this top-of-the-trees New York hotel, and she'd also paid for a doctor to tend to her ankle. Here. At the hotel. She wouldn't even allow Isabel to go to the doctor's office, but had *him* call on *her*, as if she were as rich as Loretta herself and was accustomed to having doctors call on her every day. Isabel had never heard of such a thing.

Besides all that, Loretta had bought clothes for Marjorie, Isabel and Eunice, all three. She also checked the casualty lists every single day, searching for names of people they knew. Since the name of Isabel's hero remained unknown, there was no finding out about him.

The knowledge made Isabel want to cry, so she tried not to think about it, which never worked.

"Let's dig in," said Loretta. "Eunice, dear, will you fetch that covered dish we kept over from luncheon and give it to the bellboy so he can return it to the kitchen?"

Eunice's eyes opened wide, her mouth opened, and she stood up from her table, but she didn't speak or rush to do Loretta's bidding. Rather, she stood still, clasping her hands behind her back, and her glance slid from the bellboy to Loretta and back again.

Isabel gazed searchingly at her daughter. It was unlike Eunice not to do Loretta's bidding instantly. She suspected perfidy of one sort or another, but hoped she was wrong. While Eunice was a very well-behaved child, her curiosity sometimes led her to do unusual things. "Eunice?" she said. "Go on and get the dish."

The little girl licked her lips. "Um . . . may I give it back later? At our next meal?"

"Why?" Isabel's voice was a trace sharp. Her suspicion grew stronger.

Eunice's gaze wavered between her mother and Loretta. At last she sighed. "I'm afraid you won't like it, Mama. I'm sorry, Miss Linden."

"Good Lord, child, what did you do?" Isabel took a step toward her daughter, but she'd forgotten about her ankle and stepped out with her left foot. Her ankle shrieked, and she had to grab onto the back of the bloody chair to keep from falling over. The blooming chair, was what she meant.

"It's nothing bad, Mama. It's only that I found a . . ." Eunice looked to see where Marjorie existed in the room. Marjorie was more apt to disapprove of things than were her mother or Loretta.

"A what?" Isabel was becoming seriously annoyed.

She and Eunice owed Loretta *everything*, and Isabel didn't like this evasiveness on her daughter's part.

"It's only a little one," Eunice said, her tone placating.

"It's only a little what?"

Loretta began to laugh. "Oh, my, did you find a sweet little froggie or something in the park, dear?"

Isabel's horrified gaze flew to Loretta's face, then back to her daughter's. "Eunice Golightly, if you dared to bring a frog—"

"Oh, no, Mama, it's not a frog. It's only a teensy little snake."

Marjorie screamed. So did the uniformed bellboy. Loretta laughed harder. Eunice limped over to Eunice and gave her a gentle swat on the behind. "You go fetch that dish right this instant, young lady. I can't believe you brought a snake into this hotel!"

With the assistance of her mother's hand clamped to her arm and with her mother's force behind her, Eunice headed to her bedroom, protesting as she went. "But we didn't have any snakes in England, Mama! I didn't think it would matter! The doorman said it wasn't poisonous or anything. I thought maybe I could keep it. I wanted to look up its Latin name and study it!"

"Well, you were wrong." Mortified, Isabel didn't let go of Eunice's arm until the deed was accomplished and the covered dish presented. Then, since the bellboy wouldn't take custody of the dish as long as the snake remained inside, Loretta and Eunice carried it downstairs and let it loose in the park across the street.

They returned a few minutes later, Loretta grinning, Eunice chastened. "I'm sorry, Mama and Miss MacTavish," she said.

Isabel figured Loretta had coached her in the apology. With more sternness than she generally used with her daughter, mainly because she seldom needed to, she said, "You'd better apologize to Miss Linden, too, Eunice. It's only because of her kindness that we're alive and here today."

"Fiddlesticks," said Loretta.

But Eunice, turning her big brown eyes gaze upon her mother's mentor, murmured, "I'm very sorry, Miss Linden. Thank you for not killing my snake."

Isabel rolled her eyes. Marjorie made a noise of disapproval—or perhaps it was disgust.

"It really was rather a nice little snake," Loretta said. "For a snake."

"I'm sure," said Isabel, who thought Loretta Linden might possibly be some kind of saint.

A maid had made up the fire in their suite's sitting room, and Loretta, Isabel, and Marjorie were reading peacefully. Isabel had been thrilled to discover that Loretta enjoyed Jacques Futrelle's *Thinking Machine* stories—Futrelle was another who had perished when *Titanic* sank—and had bought several of them. "To keep us amused on the journey to San Francisco," Loretta had said. Isabel couldn't help but think how nice it must be to be able to buy books any old time you wanted to.

Be that as it may, she was engrossed in one of Futrelle's stories when she heard Eunice's muffled sobs. She put her book down and stood abruptly.

Loretta said, "Oh, dear, do you think she's having another nightmare?"

Marjorie clucked and said, "Poor wee bairn." Her sympathy rather surprised Isabel, who had suspected heretofore that Marjorie didn't care for children or the disturbances they caused.

"I'm afraid so."

Eunice's nightmares worried Isabel almost as much as they worried Eunice, because the little girl had never been troubled by bad dreams before. Like Marjorie, however, the *Titanic* disaster had affected Eunice adversely. That made sense to Isabel, but her heart ached for her daughter. She rushed into the bedroom as fast as her limp allowed, sat on the bed, and took her daughter in her arms.

"There, there, dearie, it's all right. Everything is all right. You're safe now."

"B-but the man isn't," sobbed Eunice, wetting her mother's shoulder with her tears.

Kissing Eunice's head, her heart aching, Isabel said, "What man is that, dearie?"

"That man. The nice one."

Isabel thought she understood. "You mean the man who carried you to the lifeboat?"

Miserably nodding her head, Eunice sniffled. Her tears seemed to be drying up, although her unhappiness remained. "I saw him in the water. He was all frozen. Like all those other people."

Closing her eyes and trying not to bring the images to mind, Isabel hugged Eunice more tightly. "He wasn't there, dearie. It was only a dream." She hoped she was right.

"I know. I know it now," the little girl explained. "But I didn't know it in my dream."

Isabel sighed. "Dreams can be very frightening, sweetie. I hope that man is safe, just as we are."

Eunice knuckled her eyes and nodded. "Me, too."

"Perhaps we should pray for him, dearie."

"If he's dead, it won't matter what we pray," the ever-practical Eunice pointed out.

Isabel's heart hitched. "Let's pray that he's safe—wherever he is."

"But we don't know his name."

A shaft of pain shot through Isabel. "I know, sweetheart, but God will know who we mean."

"Oh. That's so." After a moment, Eunice said, "I guess we can do that."

So Isabel knelt next to her daughter beside the bed, and they both folded their hands and prayed. Sharing her daughter's confusion on the subject—if the man was already dead, they couldn't very well pray him back to life—she nevertheless asked God to bless the fellow. Wherever he was.

Chapter Two

The train whistle sounded mournfully through the thick evening air. It had rained all day, and it looked as if it aimed to rain all night, provided the droplets could find their way through the fog. Isabel and Eunice stared out the train window as New York slipped away from them. They couldn't even see it anymore.

Actually, they hadn't seen much of it during their brief stay. The dock, the hotel, a few shops, the hotel's restaurant—where they'd eaten better than either one of them had ever eaten in their lives until that point—and Grand Central Station. Loretta had taken them on a whirlwind tour of a few interesting spots, but Isabel's ankle had hurt and they'd all been upset because of the recent tragedy. No one had been in much of a mood for sightseeing.

The final death tally was staggering. Over fifteen hundred people had been confirmed dead. The dead who had been fortunate enough to be incoffined had been taken to Halifax, Nova Scotia, and authorities were attempting to identify the bodies. Isabel's heart hurt as she thought of loved ones anxiously waiting to hear what had happened to their kin.

When the rescue ships had run out of coffins, or when the corpses were too damaged to be recognizable—a notion that made Isabel shiver—the dead had been buried at sea. Before the crew had let them slide into the deep, they'd searched pockets for any kind of identifying evidence. Every night Isabel prayed that those people had been identified so their loved ones could know their fates. Not knowing would be awful.

She prayed every night for the man who had reunited her with Eunice, too. Why hadn't she asked him his name? But it had been a terrible night; she guessed it wasn't surprising that, in her panic, she'd neglected the courtesy. She regretted it now, for she'd never know if he was alive or dead. As she and Eunice watched New York slip away into the distance, her heart and throat both ached, and she silently prayed once again that her hero had survived the tragedy.

Her hand ached, too, because Eunice held it so tightly. Isabel sighed. Until the *Titanic* disaster, Eunice had been a self-possessed, virtually fearless little girl, and almost more independent than Isabel liked, mainly because Isabel herself craved human companionship and didn't understand her daughter's pleasure at being by herself.

Since the catastrophe, Eunice had been clinging to her mother like a limpet. She continued to be plagued by nightmares, as well. Isabel couldn't criticize her for her newly developed night terrors any more than she could criticize Marjorie for her fear of water. She was surprised her own dreams weren't more often filled with scenes from that dreadful experience. She knew she'd never forget them.

She remembered watching through that hideous night and feeling the waves created by the sinking ship rock the lifeboat she, Loretta, Marjorie, and Eunice had occupied. She'd scarcely believed it when the ship split and its two halves sank under the black, black surface of the water. Such a gasp had gone up from those watching, and so many tears had been shed as they'd shivered there in the dark. Isabel had kept thinking she must be dreaming. But it hadn't been a dream, more's the pity.

And the bodies. There had been so many bodies floating or struggling on that dark sea, their life preservers holding them up. People from her lifeboat had tried to drag others into the boat with them, but it was too small to hold many people. She recalled with horror the terrified shrieks and cries. With even greater horror she recalled the cries fading into moans and then dying out altogether. The water had been too cold for anyone to survive in it for very long. Being in that frigid water would have been akin to being buried in a snowdrift. In fact, she wished her mind would stop dwelling on it. Then she decided that was too much to expect. Perhaps, in time, the images would fade.

"Maybe we can come back to New York City someday, Mama, and visit the museums." Eunice sounded wistful.

"I'm sure we shall," Isabel said in order to cheer her daughter up. It would be a cold day in hell—August—before Isabel Golightly would be able to pay the fare back to New York City in order to visit museums, although she'd love to give her daughter the opportunity. It had become painfully clear before Eunice's first birthday that the girl was smarter than her mother and father and all the rest of her relatives combined. It grieved Isabel that she couldn't provide more enriching opportunities for her child.

"Miss Linden said that San Francisco is an interesting city with quite a few museums and nice parks. I'd like to visit them."

"We'll do that, sweetheart," Isabel promised. Now *that* was a promise she could probably keep, since museums and parks didn't generally cost anything to visit. She still didn't know how she was going to earn a living.

She and Loretta had talked about it, and Loretta didn't seem concerned—but Loretta didn't have a six-year-old daughter to provide for. Even if she'd had a dozen children, Loretta had the money to support them.

Isabel felt glum and wasn't sure why. She supposed it was natural for a woman who had left her home on one continent, headed to another, encountered an iceberg along the way, been one of a very few people rescued from the catastrophic sinking of an unsinkable ship, and now faced an uncertain future, to be slightly melancholy, but Isabel wasn't accustomed to giving in to adversity. She was accustomed to facing adversity head-on, fighting it tooth and nail, and then, whether bloodied or untouched, rising above it.

Now she felt stupid for having been such an optimist all her life. Here she was in America without a penny to her name, with a daughter, without skills, and with a tremendous need to earn money, and she didn't know what to do.

"I think Miss Linden will help you get a job, Mama," Eunice said. "I'm sorry I'm not old enough to help."

Isabel hugged her daughter to her side. She knew she should be the one offering comfort to the little girl and not the other way around, but she appreciated Eunice right then more than she could say. "I'm sure she will, sweets." Again, Isabel's mind boggled at the prospect of paying Loretta Linden back for all her kind offices.

"She must have a lot of money," Eunice mused. "She hired a whole train carriage for the four of us."

"I guess she does."

Eunice sighed. "It must be nice."

"Must be." Isabel sighed too, deeply.

Somerset FitzRoy frowned at the stalk of *Panax quinquefolius L.* It was an interesting specimen, and one he'd not encountered anywhere but in the eastern United States. He'd have liked to compare it to the specimen he'd found in Ireland. That option was forever lost to him, however, since all of his specimens, as well as all of his notes, drawings, and books had gone down with the *Titanic.*

This specimen of *Panax quinquefolius L* looked a good deal like the Asian variety. Somerset wondered how it had come to this continent.

He'd read that there might once have been a land bridge connecting Asia with the continent of America. He conjured a mental image of hide-clad Asians marching along with sacks full of the stuff. He might make mention of the alleged land bridge in his book.

He set the specimen on the table before him, turned his sketchbook to a clean sheet, and picked up a charcoal pencil. Squinting harder—he was going to need spectacles before long, he feared—he began quickly drawing the leaves of the plant. It was the root that people were primarily interested in, but Somerset intended his book to contain the whole plant, no matter which part of it was used for medicinal purposes. At least he didn't have to do much research on the usage of this one. People had been employing it in various concoctions for different ailments for hundreds of years.

A slight feeling of uneasiness at his back made him

twitch his shoulders. He kept on sketching. He'd managed to pick some of the plant's berries, too, and he'd draw those to the side of the picture of the whole plant, so that people who bought his book would know exactly what to look for if they ever attempted to find a specimen of their own.

Again, his shoulder blades twitched. Irritated, thinking he was being pestered by an insect, Somerset flapped his left hand in order to scare the critter away.

"Why are you drawing that weed?"

The chirping voice startled him so badly, he jumped in his chair and let out a cry. Perhaps he'd not been as unaffected by the recent catastrophe as he'd believed. His charcoal pencil slid across the page, making a line through the five-leaved stem he'd just drawn. Spinning around, he was astonished to behold a little girl standing behind him, eyeing his drawing quizzically. She reminded him of someone, but he couldn't think of whom.

"Who are you?" he barked. Belatedly, he realized the child hadn't meant to alarm him. Somerset knew he could become totally lost to outside influences when he was involved in his work. It wasn't the child's fault she'd startled him.

"I am Miss Eunice Marie Golightly," the child said.

Again a faint memory tugged at Somerset's mind, although it vanished instantly. She was the soberest little thing he had ever seen. He took a deep breath and endeavored to be polite, knowing how sensitive children could be. He even managed a smile. "How do you do, Miss Eunice Marie Golightly?"

"I am well, thank you. Chamomile tea might help your nerves, sir, although it tastes nasty. My mother puts a sprig of basil or mint in it, but it doesn't help much."

Chamomile tea? Nerves? Basil? Mint? Was she a figment of his imagination? Somerset stared at the small girl, trying to put the words that had just sprung from her lips together with the tiny frame, tidy blond braids, and big brown eyes staring at him so earnestly.

He, too, was serious by nature, but he enjoyed a lively sense of humor, and this little sobersides tickled it. "Thank you very much, Miss Golightly. I shall keep that in mind. However, in mitigation of my startled reaction to your question, I was deeply involved in my work when you spoke."

"I beg your pardon."

"Think nothing of it." Somerset waited, but Eunice didn't say anything. She was certainly composed for such a young child. She made him a bit nervous, actually.

That being the case, he stuck out his hand. "My name is Mr. Somerset FitzRoy, Miss Golightly." Recalling her own introduction, Somerset elaborated. "Mr. Somerset Anderson FitzRoy. I'm pleased to meet you."

Eunice took his hand and shook it gravely. "How do you do, Mr. FitzRoy? I'm happy to meet you, too. You have three last names."

Somerset uttered a short crack of laughter. "I suppose I do."

They stared at each other for several more seconds, and then the little girl repeated, "Why are you drawing that weed?"

Somerset glanced at what had been a lovely drawing of *Panax quinquefolius L.* before the advent of Miss Eunice Marie Golightly into his life. "It's not a weed," he said ruefully. "Its botanical name is *Panax quinquefolius*. I'm drawing it for a book I'm writing."

"On weeds?"

"On the medicinal and traditional uses of various common plants. They're only weeds if you don't know what they're good for and how to use them." He scowled at his picture. It looked great except for the black line running through it. Turning back to Eunice, he said, "Where did you come from?"

"The village of Upper Poppleton in the county of Yorkshire, in the north of England. We came over on the *R.M.S. Titanic,* which sank. We were rescued."

"Good Lord." Somerset stared at the girl with new respect. No wonder she was behaving a trifle oddly if she'd survived the *Titanic* disaster. What a terrible experience, especially for such a young one. It had been bad enough for him, an adult.

And then it struck him. This girl, Miss Eunice Marie Golightly, was the tyke he'd handed to her mother right before the crew lowered one of the too few available lifeboats into the ocean. Good God. This girl was the one with the ravishing mother, the woman Somerset hadn't been able to get out of his mind since the damned ship sank. Thank the good Lord they'd survived the disaster.

Eunice's eyes thinned and her gaze sharpened. Somerset thought she was annoyed with him for not saying anything immediately, but she surprised him.

"Weren't you aboard the ship, too, Mr. FitzRoy? Aren't you the gentleman who rescued me after my mama dropped me?"

Somerset swallowed. It was still hard for him to remember that hideous night. He'd worked so hard to save lives, only to be sucked down into the fathomless depths of the freezing Atlantic Ocean when the ship finally slipped beneath the surface of the water. He'd thought for sure he was a dead man, but he didn't give up. Kicking like mad, and fighting through a field of debris floating down, down, down, he'd aimed for oxygen. His lungs had almost burst before he broke the surface and gasped in huge breaths of air.

And cold? Lord, it had been like ice in that water. Somerset had managed to remain afloat, although his teeth were chattering, his fingers were numb, and he'd feared that he'd become a victim of hypothermia before help arrived. He'd been close to unconsciousness when a small boat—not one of the large lifeboats, but some kind of collapsible craft—pulled up beside him. He'd gazed hopelessly at the boat, and then received the shock of his life when four brawny arms lifted him from the water and heaved him aboard. Then he found himself grinning like an idiot at two muscular sailors. He tried to thank the men, but his mouth and tongue wouldn't coordinate to form words. A lady in the boat threw a blanket over him.

Great God, what a night. Somerset supposed his conscience would trouble him for the rest of his life because he'd been of so little help.

After clearing his throat, he spoke to the child. "I believe I am, Miss Eunice. I'm very happy to see you again." He attempted a genuinely friendly smile, but he was under the influence of severe emotion and feared his result was puny. "Under more pleasant circumstances."

Again she nodded. "Yes. The train's much nicer than that awful ship."

Suddenly, the door to the sitting-room car was flung open and the woman herself erupted into the carriage. Somerset, who had been mooning about this woman for more than a month, stood, knowing he ought to have done so for the little girl, but having forgotten, undoubtedly owing to his nervous condition. Chamomile tea, indeed. His lips twitched as he suppressed a grin, then any hint of amusement faded altogether when Eunice's mother hurried up to her daughter.

She was still lovely, although daylight, and probably a less heated emotional climate, indubitably colored his impression. She appeared worried at the moment.

"Eunice!"

Both females were small and had thick blond hair and beautiful eyes, although the daughter's were as dark as polished mahogany and the mother's were . . . Somerset contemplated them. They weren't quite the color of *Cichorium intybus,* and they weren't as deep a purple as *Lavandula officinalis* or *Delphinium ajacis,* but . . . Somerset shook his head to clear it of irrelevancies. In his daydreams, he'd not given the woman's eyes any particular color. Now his dreams could be more complete.

Their complexions were fair, although the mother's face was flushed. The daughter's braids boasted blue ribbons, and the mother's head sported a small blue hat. Both were clad in white shirtwaists and blue calico skirts and matching jackets that looked new.

"Hello, Mama," Eunice said, turning to face the newcomer. Somerset was glad to see her smile. He'd begun to wonder if he might encounter a key in her back if he were to tip her upside down and look. "This is the gentleman who rescued us aboard the *Titanic.* He's drawing a weed."

Mrs. Golightly—he assumed her name was Golightly—stopped short and stared at Somerset, her mouth slightly open and her eyes growing large and luminous under the influence of shock. She whispered, "Oh, my." Then, with a gasp, she rushed over to him and grabbed both of his hands, which had been resting on the table.

"Oh, my!" she cried again. "I can't believe it's you. But it is!"

"Er . . . yes." Somerset, delighted to see her again,

was nevertheless a trifle uncomfortable with her raw emotions.

"I can't begin to tell you how happy I am that you survived that dreadful accident." Tears stood in her eyes. "I've been praying for you every night, and was so sorry that I never asked your name."

"This is Mr. Somerset Anderson FitzRoy, Mama," Eunice supplied helpfully.

"Mr. FitzRoy." Mrs. Golightly swallowed hard. "I can never, ever thank you enough for saving us." She bowed her head over his hands, and Somerset decided the Golightlys were an odd pair of females, although the mother appeared slightly more normal than the child. A tear splashed the back of his hand.

Ill at ease at having her gratitude showered upon him—he'd only done what was right, after all—he said, "Please, Mrs. Golightly—your name is Golightly?"

She nodded, almost too choked up to speak. "Isabel Golightly."

"Please don't thank me. I felt it was my duty to help. Under the . . . well, under the circumstances and all." He attempted another smile. "And you did spill your daughter practically at my feet, you know."

When she lifted her head, tears had made silvery trails down her perfect cheeks. Somerset had a mad impulse to kiss them away. Naturally, he did no such thing.

She gave him a tremulous smile that nearly broke his heart. "I know better than that, Mr. FitzRoy. You saved our lives."

"Well now, I wouldn't go that far." This was becoming downright embarrassing.

"You did. I'd never have climbed into that lifeboat without Eunice, and I never could have found her again in that mob."

Eunice nodded. Somerset felt the back of his neck

get hot and wished Mrs. Golightly would let go of his hands so he could run his fingers under his collar and loosen it. "Well, it's over now, thank God. I'm only sorry so many of our fellow passengers perished."

"Yes. It was such a horrible night." She cleared her throat and seemed to pull herself together. She also let go of his hands. They felt strangely cold after she withdrew her warm essence. "I'm sorry my daughter bothered you, Mr. FitzRoy. We'll leave you in peace now." Snatching a hankie from a pocket, she wiped her tears away and offered him a tremulous smile.

Somerset didn't want her to go. He wasn't sure how to say so without appearing to be the kind of man he wasn't. "She didn't bother me . . . not much, anyway. I was drawing this plant and she asked me why." He waved at the drawing, then blurted out, "Thank you for praying for me." Then he felt stupid.

"Oh, I'll pray for you for the rest of my life, Mr. FitzRoy. You're the reason we're both alive today."

Good God. He would have waved away her effusive thanks, but he couldn't bear to do so. He discovered within himself a severe disinclination to do anything that might in any way upset Isabel Golightly. An extraneous and irrelevant notion entered his head, and he had to bite his tongue before he could ask her if her husband had survived the disaster. What was the matter with him?

"And thank you for putting up with Eunice. She likes to walk through the carriages, because it's a long and tedious trip, but I've told her not to speak to strangers." This time her smile was spectacular. "I must say, though, that I'm glad she spoke to you. We'll be going now."

She turned to go, and Somerset experienced a mad impulse to grab her and make her stay. As ever, he resisted the impulse, which he knew to be irrational and totally unlike him. "Any time, Mrs. Golightly." He feared he had a sappy smile on his face. "Any time at all."

But Mrs. Golightly had already dragged Eunice almost as far as the end of the carriage. Somerset sighed deeply, wishing he'd paid more attention when his mother had tried to teach him how to woo women. He hadn't been interested in women at the time. His interest and attention had always centered on the world's flora. There was nothing he could do about it now, he guessed.

Turning to eye his drawing, he decided it was ruined. With an abrupt and irritated jerk, he tore out the page of his sketchbook and turned over a clean sheet. This time, he sat on the other side of the table, with his back against the carriage wall, so nobody could sneak up on him.

"I know I've told you never to speak to strangers, Eunice, but I'm glad you spoke to that one." Isabel had almost suffered a spasm when she'd gone looking for Eunice and found her talking to the hero of her very life.

"I wasn't sure at first, Mama, but I thought it was him." Eunice frowned and corrected herself. "I think I mean he."

"I'm so glad he didn't go down with the ship," Isabel whispered. "So, so glad."

"I am, too, Mama. He seems to be a nice man."

Isabel glanced sharply at her daughter. "Yes, he did. However, I don't want you to bother him anymore, Eunice. Even though he saved our lives, he's still a stranger, and he seems to have work to do."

Eunice frowned, but Isabel knew what she was talking about. Mr. Somerset FitzRoy was a big, muscular, tanned, and very handsome man, with lovely dark hair and gorgeous brown eyes, and Isabel, while she'd worship him for the rest of her life, didn't want anything to do with him. She knew too well that big handsome men were nothing but trouble.

"I think Mr. FitzRoy is a real gentleman, Mama."

"Possibly," Isabel said under her breath.

"And he did rescue us," Eunice reminded her.

"Indeed, and I'll be forever grateful to him, but we . . . we mustn't bother him, Eunice."

After pondering this possibility for a couple of seconds, Eunice said, "He didn't seem to be awfully bothered."

Bloody hell. Isabel meant blooming daffodils. She said, "He's an American, Eunice. The standards are different. Until we figure out how people live here, and until you're given permission from me, you are not to speak to *anyone*. Do you understand me?"

"Yes, ma'am."

Isabel glanced sharply at her daughter. But Eunice, as usual, had no expression on her face.

Every now and then, Isabel wished she'd given birth to a normal child.

Chapter Three

It was late when Somerset entered the dining car. He'd meant to go to dinner earlier so that he could find a good table, but he'd become so involved in his drawings—and, he was annoyed to realize, in thinking about Isabel Golightly—he'd lost track of time.

Losing track of time happened to him quite often. Mooning about a woman didn't, although he found the phenomenon interesting. For the first time, Somerset wondered if he should marry somebody—Isabel Golightly sprang to mind—if only to keep him fed on a timely schedule. Of course, Mrs. Golightly might have something to say about that. Not to mention *Mr.* Golightly.

Don't be an ass, he advised himself.

"How do you do, sir?" A white-coated dining-car waiter smiled at Somerset, who had lost track of time yet again. He snapped to attention at once.

"I don't suppose there are any empty tables." Somerset scanned the car without hope. It looked mighty packed to him. His stomach took that opportunity to growl. He couldn't remember, but he thought he'd forgotten to eat luncheon.

"I'm afraid not," the waiter said. "But our passengers are congenial." He chuckled in a manner Somerset supposed he'd practiced until it came almost naturally. "May I find a table for you?"

"I suppose so." Somerset repressed a sigh. He hated having to make small talk with people he didn't know. Nobody ever shared his interests, and most people considered him eccentric, which wasn't true. Well, except for his one tiny little interest in horticulture, which *might* be considered an eccentricity, but only by illiterate bumpkins. Anyhow, Somerset endeavored to read at least one daily newspaper so that he could converse about politics and baseball with the odd passing stranger with whom he might come in contact—though he usually forgot.

"Here we are. You don't mind sharing a table with several lovely ladies, do you, sir?" The Pullman waiter grinned as if he was doing Somerset a favor.

Somerset noticed the three women and the little girl sitting at the table, all of whom peered back at him uncertainly, and decided the waiter was correct. This truly *was* a favor.

He was overjoyed to find Miss Eunice Marie Golightly and her mother seated with two other ladies, both of whom appeared formidable enough to give Somerset hives, but whom he would endure for the sake of Mrs. Golightly. Fortunately, his digestion was sound, so even if the two alarming ladies turned his meal to vinegar in his bowels, he probably wouldn't suffer much. Anyhow, it would be worth it in order to deepen his acquaintance with Mrs. Golightly, even if he had to do so while being scrutinized by a couple of strangers.

Determining to make the best of the situation, he

smiled, removed his hat, bowed politely, and said with somewhat forced heartiness, "Greetings, ladies. We meet again, Miss Golightly. Mrs. Golightly."

"Hello, Mr. FitzRoy." Eunice smiled up at him.

"Oh!" said the lady with the brown hair and the grim expression which lightened considerably, "Are you the gentleman who rescued Eunice and Isabel the night of that terrible accident? We're so happy to meet you! They told us all about your kindness and about meeting you on the train this afternoon."

Bother. If there was one thing Somerset didn't want to endure, it was being lauded for doing something as basic as trying to save the lives of a woman and her child. Hoping to turn the subject, he said, "Indeed. Miss Eunice and Mrs. Golightly and I introduced ourselves this afternoon."

"He was drawing a weed," Eunice said, the ends of her mouth turning downward. "I still don't know why."

"A weed?" The brown-haired lady blinked at Eunice. Then she turned abruptly toward Somerset. "But I'm forgetting my manners. Please, allow me to introduce the rest of our party. My name is Miss Loretta Linden. This lady"—she indicated the redhead seated next to her—"is Miss Marjorie MacTavish. It's so good to meet you and to know that you, too, survived the tragedy."

Somerset bowed generally at the ladies. "It's a pleasure to meet you all under much more pleasant circumstances." He smiled at Miss MacTavish, who gazed up at him like a scared rabbit and didn't smile back. After sighing and wishing he were more of a ladies' man, he sat and gave his order to the waiter.

"Why were you drawing that weed, Mr. FitzRoy?" Eunice asked after a short and awkward pause. "I should genuinely like to know."

Somerset decided this was as good a topic for con-

versation as any other, and it was much better than baseball. "It wasn't a weed, in particular, Miss Golightly. Its
botanical name is *Panax quinquefolius L.* It's an American
species of an Asian plant that has been used for hundreds of years in a variety of medicinal and ceremonial
purposes."

"That's very interesting, Mr. FitzRoy. Why were you
drawing it, though?"

Somerset gazed at Eunice, wondering if there was
something wrong with the child. She couldn't be much
older than six or seven, but she sounded like an elderly
and excruciatingly refined gentlewoman.

"I intend to publish a compendium of flora native to
various regions in the North American continent, Miss
Golightly. The book will detail traditional and medicinal uses of the different plants. I had wanted to compare the specimens with some I gathered in Great
Britain, but I'm not sure I'll be able to do that."

Eunice's eyes grew even larger than they had been.
She appeared to be curious, although Somerset couldn't
credit such a reaction from so young a child. "That's
very interesting, Mr. FitzRoy. Thanks awfully much for
telling me about it."

Puzzled, Somerset murmured, "You're more than
welcome, Miss Golightly."

"My mother made me let my snake go." Eunice went
on. "I had wanted to study it because I want to be a biologist when I grow up, but perhaps I should study
plants instead."

Somerset swallowed a laugh, perceiving that Eunice
hadn't meant her comment to be funny. "Er, yes, I believe plants might be more acceptable to most mothers
than snakes." He glanced at Isabel, who was looking at
her daughter in mild reproof. "Er, I should be happy to
give you a lesson or two."

"Really?" Eunice's lovely eyes sparkled with excitement.

"I'm sure you don't want to be bothered by my daughter," Isabel said, and a faint color crept into her cheeks.

"Oh, but, Mama, I—"

Somerset interrupted them both. "Nonsense. I enjoy sharing my interest in botany and horticulture, Mrs. Golightly. Miss Eunice won't be a bother at all." He looked at Mrs. Golightly, hoping she'd volunteer to attend her daughter's botany lessons.

"Well . . ." Isabel cast a searching look at Somerset, who attempted to appear friendly and helpful, and not as if he were a man who wanted to get to know her better. "If you're certain you won't mind having Eunice pester you."

"I won't pester him!" exclaimed an indignant Eunice.

"She won't pester me," Somerset agreed. "I'd be pleased for the diversion." He paused, took a deep breath, and dared add, "Perhaps you would care to join us, Mrs. Golightly. I'll be happy to teach you about plant life here in the United States."

"Oh, do, Mama!" Eunice said, enchanted with the idea.

"What a lovely offer," said Miss Linden, smiling at everyone at the table in a narrow-eyed, short-sighted sort of way.

"Oh," said Isabel in a faint voice. "How kind of you."

She was utterly charming. Even if she didn't care a rap about plants—and he could tell she didn't. Somerset thought her accent was wonderful, too. It wasn't at all akin to the broad, strange accents of the farmers he'd met when he'd visited Yorkshire; he couldn't even understand half of what they'd said to him. Her accent was much more refined than theirs.

"What a delightful way to spend a long and tedious train trip," Miss Linden said. Somerset noticed that she seemed quite eager to promote camaraderie between himself and Mrs. Golightly. He hoped she wasn't one of those match-making females. Somerset preferred to do his own courting. Not that he ever had. "After all, you're from the north of England and Mr. FitzRoy"— she smiled myopically at Somerset—"is an American." He noticed a pair of eyeglasses resting on the handbag in Loretta's lap.

"That's right," Somerset said. "I'd be interested in comparing American plants with those you remember from Yorkshire, Mrs. Golightly. You see, I spent three months in Great Britain on a specimen-finding expedition, but all my specimens and my notes were lost with the ship. If you're willing, I'd appreciate any help you can give me in reconstructing my lost research."

Doubtfully, Isabel said, "Well, I'm sure I can try, although I don't know how much use I'll be, since I don't know much about plants."

"Thank you." Somerset gave her a bright, friendly smile, which seemed to embarrass her. Her color deepened, at any rate. "Perhaps you can help me with common British names of various species."

Isabel took a sip of water from her glass, squinting at him over its rim as if she were stalling for time, although Somerset didn't know what he'd said that could be considered the least bit complicated. He feared her intelligent child got her brains from her male parent.

But that was unkind. Somerset didn't even know Isabel Golightly. Perhaps she was merely uncomfortable around people she didn't know. He could understand that. Didn't he read sports news for that very reason?

"I can tell you one thing," Isabel said at last. Then she didn't tell him.

Somerset prodded. "And what's that?" Hoping to poke a hole in her resistance to his charms, if he had any, he smiled what he hoped was a winning smile.

"I don't know any plant called panax—whatever you said." She turned a vivid shade of crimson.

Somerset stared at her for a second, then burst out laughing.

It was clearly the wrong thing to do. Isabel thumped her water glass on the table and glared at him, even as her cheeks glowed with color. He checked his laughter, not having intended to embarrass her, of all people. He wanted to impress her, not humiliate her. "I beg your pardon, Mrs. Golightly. I tend to forget that not everyone knows Latin."

She smiled. It was a chilly smile. "Fancy that. I'm afraid my Latin is a trifle rusty."

Miss Linden gave a trill of laughter. "Nobody uses Latin nowadays," she said hastily, as if she wanted to iron out the burgeoning strain between Somerset and Isabel. "Only physicians and professors." With a glance at Somerset, she added, "And botanists, of course."

"I wasn't laughing at you, Mrs. Golightly, but at myself. I've become so accustomed to calling plants by their Latin names that I forget not everyone is familiar with them, you see."

"Ah," said Isabel. He sensed she wasn't ready to forgive him quite yet.

So, apparently, did Miss Linden, who said in a rush, "That plant you were drawing, Mr. FitzRoy. What is that in American?" Her smile was almost pleasant enough to make up for Mrs. Golightly's.

Somerset appreciated her a lot. He directed his answer at her, since Mrs. Golightly still looked as if she intended to stab him with her butter knife as soon as he turned his back. He got the impression she was sensitive about something, perhaps her education or class or something else. The British were so touchy about those things.

"It's very much like the Asian species of ginseng. I suppose it might be called American ginseng. In New Hampshire, where I found my specimen, the people I spoke to called it five-fingers, although one old farmer called it Tartar root, which I found interesting."

"Oh, my, yes," said Eunice, climbing into the conversation as if she belonged there. Somerset had never met a child who seemed so at ease among adults. "That's *very* interesting, Mr. FitzRoy. The adjective 'Tartar' might harken back to its Oriental origin. You know, like the Tartar hordes." She looked uncertainly at her mother. "Or were they Tartan hordes? I don't remember."

"I believe they were Mongol hordes, actually," said Isabel, easing up a bit for her daughter and offering Eunice a small smile.

Eunice's little nose wrinkled. "Where'd I get Tartar hordes?"

"I'm sure I don't know." Isabel sounded as if she were having trouble not laughing.

Because he remembered what it was like to be a curious child who sometimes got things wrong, Somerset said, "I believe many of the Mongols were Tartars, Miss Eunice."

"Ah," said Eunice, her troubled expression clearing. "That's probably it."

"Probably," Isabel said. She relieved Somerset's worry by smiling at him, probably because he'd saved her daughter from embarrassment.

Very interesting family, the Golightlys. And there didn't seem to be a *Mister* Golightly anywhere in sight, a circumstance that vaguely gratified Somerset. Maybe dinner wouldn't be unpleasant after all. When he glanced at the other two ladies, he encountered the same blank, unfocused expression he was accustomed to seeing on the faces of people who didn't share his horticultural fascination.

Only slightly dismayed by the disinterest of his audience, he cleared his throat and went on. "Yes. It's as if somehow, lost in the mists of time, a Chinese root was being acknowledged by the old farmer, who hadn't a clue that there's another plant in the Orient that people have used for hundreds of years as a virtually magical cure-all."

"My goodness," said Miss Linden politely.

Miss MacTavish gave him a vague smile. Somerset suppressed his sigh.

It was Isabel who saved the conversation, much to Somerset's surprise. Her porcelain brow wrinkling slightly, she said, "I think I've heard of ginseng, Mr. FitzRoy. Mrs. McNally, the old witch who taught me what little I know about plants and which ones were good for what, had a supply of it that she'd got from a gypsy woman, but she only used it in dire emergencies."

"Ah," said Somerset, wondering what to say to *that*.

"She wasn't really a witch," said Eunice, as if to reassure Somerset.

Isabel smiled—really *smiled*—for the first time, and Somerset blinked. She had quite a smile when she chose to use it.

"Of course she wasn't," Isabel said with her soft lilting accent that made Somerset's toes curl. "That's just what she wanted people to think. It gave her a certain status in Upper Poppleton. The gypsy woman was a real gypsy, though. In a caravan and everything."

"There aren't really any such things as witches," Eunice pronounced. "Although there are lots of gypsies in England."

"True," said her mother.

"What constituted a dire emergency?" Somerset asked, curious.

"Oh, if a woman . . ." Isabel stopped speaking, caught her breath, and shot a glance at her daughter. "Uh . . . well . . ."

"I think the root was used by ladies who wanted babies," said Eunice.

Everyone at the table stared at her. Isabel, whose cheeks had again bloomed bright red, put a hand over her mouth, as if she was trying not to laugh. Loretta appeared both shocked and amused. Miss MacTavish gasped. Somerset wanted to laugh, too, but knew if he did, he'd never get to chat with Eunice's mother about herbs and plants and the British and American common names thereof. Or ask her if she'd marry him.

Stop it!, he bade himself silently.

"I've heard that," he said.

Then something good happened. The waiter returned with everyone's dinner. Somerset couldn't have planned the scene better if he'd had control of the entire Pullman empire.

After they were served, Somerset made an attempt to salvage the conversation. "Speaking of dire emergencies, Mrs. and Miss Golightly and I were survivors of the recent *Titanic* disaster. Were you ladies aboard the ship, too?"

Marjorie MacTavish's fork paused halfway to her mouth. Somerset might be imagining things, but it looked to him as if she had paled, too. He hoped he hadn't just put his foot into something smelly.

Stillness settled over the group, and Somerset could have kicked himself for his inattention to social amenities. Of course, the ladies wouldn't want to talk about the tragedy during a meal. He knew better than to bring up unpleasant subjects at the dinner table. His strict old grandmother, if she were watching from above, was undoubtedly shaking her head over him in dismay.

"I beg your pardon," he said quickly. "I didn't mean to bring up an unhappy topic. I'm sure it's one you aren't eager to talk about."

Loretta took up the conversational gauntlet. "Oh, no, Mr. FitzRoy. Please don't be embarrassed." She leaned closer to Somerset. "People who weren't there can't understand the horror of it all. They don't realize how deep an impression something like that can have on a sensitive soul." She tilted her head slightly to her right, and Somerset noticed that Miss MacTavish had set down her fork with a hand that shook.

"Yes indeed," he said. "I'm so very sorry, ladies. It was clumsy of me to bring up the topic."

Miss Linden and Isabel murmured soothing noises intended, Somerset was sure, to put him at his ease and to let him know that they didn't consider him a bumbling idiot. It didn't work.

Eunice, gazing at each adult in turn, finally said, "Maybe we ought to talk about plants. They seems to be a safe topic."

"Yes." Somerset nodded gravely and decided he was beginning to really like the kid. "Plants do seem a very safe topic."

So they talked about plants, a subject that kept Somerset amused, although he sensed that he occasionally lost his audience. Except for Eunice, who was rather like a sponge and who drank in everything he had to say.

But even though the ladies weren't horticulturists, they seemed to like his being with them. That pleased Somerset immensely, and not merely because he wanted to know Isabel Golightly better. For some reason he couldn't understand, it was a comfort to be with others who had shared the *Titanic* disaster. He didn't know why, unless Miss Linden's theory was correct, and it was simply soothing to be with others who understood.

The small group of newfound friends confabulated all through dinner, into coffee and dessert, and were still nattering when it became clear that the dining car was about to close. That being the case, their discussion spilled over into the sitting room of the private carriage Loretta had secured for them.

Isabel had placed the man who'd saved her and Eunice from a certain and horrible death on a pedestal even before she knew his name. She'd not expected ever to see him again, much less meet him and talk to him and take meals with him.

And he was a horticulturist.

Isabel wasn't sure how she felt about that. It seemed so . . . so . . . She chided herself even as she admitted that horticulture seemed a mighty unmasculine profession for her hero to be involved with.

Although she hadn't really thought about it before meeting Somerset FitzRoy—and she did like his name—she believed that the hero of her life, especially since he was an American, ought to be something like . . . well . . . a cowboy. Or one of those rugged Western sheriffs one saw when one went to the motion pictures. Or even a wealthy New York financier. Or a motion-picture actor. Isabel wouldn't have pegged her hero as a horticulturist if she'd been given a million years and two million guesses.

She knew that was silly thinking. Mr. FitzRoy was

what he was. And he'd saved her daughter's life, and undoubtedly Isabel's as well, because Isabel never would have climbed aboard the lifeboat without Eunice.

Besides all that, he seemed a very nice gentleman and a man of character and principal. A genuinely noble man. How often did a person meet one of those? In Isabel's life, not often.

And so, for the sake of her genuine gratitude, and for the sake of her child, and for her own sake, Isabel enjoyed the evening, even if Somerset FitzRoy didn't exactly fit her idea of a knight in shining armor. She hadn't given a thought to plants other than perhaps to cabbages, carrots, and potatoes, before in her life until she met Mr. FitzRoy. She'd felt neither the need nor the desire to do so. Fortunately, the subject of plants and plant life gradually eased into other topics.

"So you've been to some of the great English estates?" Somerset asked, after the chitchat had slid away from individual plants and into the more general subject of English country gardens.

"One or two, yes. Many members of royalty hold open-house days," Isabel said. She glanced at Eunice, bringing her into the conversation. "Do you remember when we visited Belvoire Castle, Eunice?"

"Um . . ." Eunice's face crunched up in thought.

"You were *very* young, sweetie. We went with your great-uncle Charlie."

Eunice's expression brightened. "Oh, yes! Now I remember. It was pretty. And windy."

"Very windy," Isabel agreed.

"It was fun." Eunice's tone was wistful, and Isabel's heart wavered a trifle. She'd been able to offer her daughter too few educational experiences and amusements in her short life.

She discovered to her surprise that it was quite pleasant to speak with a man again, even if much of the conversation centered on plant life. Isabel hadn't spoken to a man, except for those in her immediate family and those whose houses she scrubbed, since before Eunice was born. The circumstances of Eunice's birth and Isabel's own folly and shame had caused Isabel to do everything she could to redeem herself, and that meant she'd had nothing to do with men socially.

"I didn't visit Belvoire," said Somerset. "Wish I had. There were some lovely gardens in Kent and Kew."

" 'Go down to Kew in lilac time,'" quoted Miss Linden dreamily. "It was lovely, wasn't it?"

"Indeed," said Somerset. "And Cambridge had some beautiful plantings."

Loretta, who had been everywhere, including Cambridge, said, "Oh, my, yes. Along the canal and the river. I remember being so impressed with some of the topiaries."

"Ah, yes, the topiaries. I created a topiary figure in my own garden back home," said Somerset.

Isabel gazed at him, amazed, although she knew that most of the gardeners she'd known in Upper Poppleton were men and, therefore, that she shouldn't consider Somerset's interest in plants unusual. Besides, a botanist probably made more money than a cowboy. Not that money mattered—well, not as far as Somerset FitzRoy went, anyhow.

And he *was* writing a book. That signified that he was a serious-minded gentleman. Or she supposed it did. Isabel mainly listened as Somerset and Loretta talked about the beautiful estates they'd visited, and Eunice asked questions. Isabel popped into the conversation occasionally when Eunice needed to know the correct word to use in a sentence.

Then, a couple of hours into the evening, when

Somerset was showing Eunice some of his plant sketches, Isabel decided that it didn't matter if Somerset was a horticulturist. Not even a cowboy or a sheriff or a motion-picture actor could have been more noble than he when she'd needed him. She was certain no New York financier would have bothered to save Eunice's life. Rich people didn't give a hang about poor people.

Not that *that* mattered, either, of course. It's not as if she was ever going to see the man again after this train trip . . . although it was odd that they'd run into each other after the *Titanic* disaster. Perhaps it was a sign. An omen. Perhaps God had meant for them to meet again. Perhaps . . .

Perhaps Isabel Golightly was a fool and an idiot who hadn't learned from her own experiences. She was disgusted with herself.

Too soon, Somerset said, "But I'm keeping you ladies from your rest. Perhaps we can resume this discussion tomorrow."

Knowing she shouldn't, but unable to resist, not because she gave a hang about plants, but because she wanted to be with him some more, Isabel said, "That would be lovely."

"May I draw some of your plants, Mr. FitzRoy?"

Regarding her daughter keenly, Isabel saw Eunice with her hands clasped in front of her, staring up at Mr. FitzRoy with fierce concentration. Isabel had taught Eunice never to beg and never to be a pest. Rich people didn't appreciate the children of chars getting in the way or putting themselves forward. She experienced an impulse to shush the little girl.

Somerset preempted her. "Absolutely, Miss Golightly. In fact I have some colored pencils you might enjoy experimenting with."

Eunice's eyes gleamed and her cheeks went pink.

"Oh, that would be bully, Mr. FitzRoy. Thank you ever so much!" "Bully" was a word Isabel had never heard Eunice use before, and it tickled her so much she forgot to fret about her daughter's audacity.

"Thank you very much, Mr. FitzRoy," Isabel said. "That's awfully kind of you."

"Nonsense. I'll enjoy it."

Isabel doubted that, but she didn't say so. Besides, she was as eager as Eunice to meet Somerset again. *It's only for the duration of the train trip,* she told herself, and wished it weren't so.

"It was so nice to meet you, Mr. FitzRoy," Loretta said, standing and holding out her hand for Somerset to shake. Not for Loretta Linden the shy, shrinking ways of a blushing maiden. Now she, unlike Isabel, not only knew she was as good as anyone else, but had no trouble acting like it. Then again, she had money, and money always seemed to give a person confidence.

"The pleasure was all mine, Miss Linden." He glanced at Marjorie, who had tucked her knitting into a bag on the floor and had stood up, her hands clasped loosely in front of her, her expression remote. "Good night, Miss MacTavish."

"Good night, Mr. FitzRoy," said Marjorie in her vaguely stifled voice.

After the door closed behind him, Isabel had a shocking impulse to hug herself. And it wasn't only that she found Mr. FitzRoy, the hero of her life, attractive. Not that he wasn't, but . . . At any rate, it was because it had been so terribly long since Isabel had allowed herself or, indeed, been able, to hold a conversation with anyone of the opposite sex. Not that she'd said much tonight, but it had still been thrilling, even if they'd only talked about plants and gardens.

And she'd better put a clamp on *that* emotion instantly. She'd allowed herself a thrill once before, to her everlasting regret, and she aimed never to do so again.

"My goodness," said Loretta, bestowing a broad smile upon Isabel. "What a nice man. And to think that he actually saved your lives. I'm so glad you found him for us, Eunice."

"Loretta!" Marjorie was, naturally, shocked by this flippant remark.

Isabel laughed and ignored Marjorie. That was much the best thing to do with the poor woman when she displayed her devotion to convention. "Yes, Eunice, Mr. FitzRoy was a fortunate find. I had been wanting to know his name ever since that awful night. And he's even going to let you use his colored pencils. That should be fun for you."

"Oh, yes," Eunice breathed, as if she weren't quite sure the promised treat would come to pass. Isabel's heart suffered a sharp pang.

"But you need to wash up now and take off your day clothes." Isabel remembered with a secret thrill that both she and Eunice now had more than one set of day clothes, thanks to Loretta's generosity. She could meet Mr. FitzRoy tomorrow with the confidence that came when one knew one looked respectable, even if one really wasn't.

"Yes, Mama." Eunice actually skipped to the wash basin.

"He's a handsome man, too." Loretta cast a significant look at Isabel, who felt her cheeks get warm.

"Tosh. That has nothing to do with anything."

"If you say so, Isabel dear. But he *is* handsome." Loretta grinned like an imp.

"I thought you didn't approve of men," Isabel said, feeling uncomfortable and a trifle annoyed. She didn't want to think of Somerset FitzRoy as a handsome man.

She didn't want to think of him as a man at all, if it
came to that, because men always complicated things.
She wanted to think of Somerset FitzRoy as a savior and
a friend, to Eunice—oh, very well, and to herself—and
that was all.

"I don't disapprove of all men," Loretta said. "Only
the ones who want to oppress our sex."

"Honestly!" said Marjorie, her lips twitching as if she
were trying to suppress a gurgle of mirth—heaven forbid that Marjorie MacTavish exhibit a sense of humor—
"The two of you shouldna talk like that in front of a
bairn!"

"I don't mind," said Eunice, who clearly didn't.

Isabel decided Marjorie might have a legitimate
point, although it would probably be the first time.

"Fiddle," said Loretta. "Children are never too young
to learn the truth."

Marjorie and Isabel exchanged a glance. Isabel
thought Marjorie's looked approximately as helpless as
her own probably did. When Loretta Linden began
talking about what she termed "the truth," they both
tried not to encourage her.

"Here, Eunice," Loretta went on. "I thought you
might enjoy a new nightgown for your trip to San
Francisco." She reached into a drawer and pulled out a
pretty white flannel nightgown with pink embroidery
decorating the yoke, sleeves, and hem.

Eunice's already large eyes went as round as platters.
She didn't reach for the confection, but only stood at
the wash stand, shocked. Isabel's heart suffered another spasm. Eunice had never seen such a glorious
nightgown, much less worn one. She probably didn't
believe it was truly meant for her.

"That's so very nice of you, Loretta. But you must
stop giving us things. We'll get spoilt." She smiled at her

daughter to let her know she didn't believe it of Eunice.
And she didn't. She wasn't so sure about herself.

"Fiddlesticks." Loretta walked over to Eunice, who
had finished with her washing-up and had stripped out
of her shirtwaist and skirt and now stood in her knick-
ers, gaping at the nightgown. "Here. Let me help you
put it on." She slipped the nightgown over the little
girl's head.

When her head emerged from the fabric, Eunice was
gazing at the new nightie as if she'd been transported
to a magical kingdom and been assigned the role of
princess. Isabel had seldom seen her daughter look so
much like a normal little girl.

"Oh, ma'am," Eunice whispered. "Oh, Miss Linden.
Thank you *ever* so much."

"It's no more than you deserve, Eunice. I've never
met a better-behaved young lady." Loretta's eyes glittered suspiciously.

Isabel hadn't suspected her new friend of being a secret sentimentalist under her surface veneer of invinci-
bility. "Thank you very much, Loretta," she said, truly
touched by the woman's kindness.

"And that's enough of *that.*" Evidently through with
mawkishness for the day, Loretta bent and gave Eunice
a quick peck on the cheek. Eunice surprised everyone
by throwing her arms around Loretta's neck and hug-
ging her hard. Isabel found herself lifting a hand to her
cheek to remove a slight bit of moisture there.

Marjorie sniffled, and when Isabel turned to see why,
she saw Marjorie dabbing at her own eyes with a hankie.
When she saw Isabel watching, she turned away and
blew her nose. Her emotional display—as minor as it
was—surprised Isabel, who hadn't suspected that Marjorie
would give way to sentiment, since a proper lady never
did so.

How much her life had changed in the past few weeks! Before she set out for Southampton with Eunice in order to sail on the *Titanic,* Isabel had never even dreamed of traveling to San Francisco in a private railroad carriage with two brand-new friends she hadn't met before boarding the ocean liner.

After she finished with her own ablutions and donned her night dress, Isabel lay down in the cot next to Eunice's—another thing she was unaccustomed to: a bed of her own—and tried to empty her mind so she could rest.

Sleep didn't come easily. She couldn't stop thinking about Somerset FitzRoy and how they'd first run into each other. The terror of that night plagued her, waking and sleeping. And the mental images of the steerage passengers, herded together like sheep and trying like mad to reach the spurious safety of the upper decks, haunted her.

She should have tried to bring others with her when she escaped up the service staircase with Loretta. If she hadn't been so panic-stricken, she might have thought of someone besides herself and Eunice. Now she felt guilty and ashamed of herself.

She supposed she should try to emulate Loretta Linden. Loretta didn't allow anyone or anything to get her down. If Loretta hadn't been a superior sort of person, she never would have tried to find Isabel and Eunice on that dreadful night. She'd have saved herself and forgotten all about them. If she had, Mr. FitzRoy wouldn't have had the opportunity to rescue them, because they'd have been trapped and would have gone down with the ship.

Of course, neither Loretta nor Somerset knew the

full story of Isabel and Eunice, or neither would have bothered with them in the first place.

When she finally got to sleep, Isabel dreamed about the night of April 14. In her dream, she was looking for Eunice. In her dream, Somerset FitzRoy didn't appear like a miracle out of the chaos and confusion to reunite them and lead them to safety. Instead, Isabel ran like a madwoman, searching for her daughter. But she never found her, and the ship sank, and the frigid water climbed up her body until it threatened to cover her head. And still, she couldn't find Eunice.

She woke up once and discovered she'd been crying in her sleep. Sheepishly, she slipped out of her bed and tiptoed to her handbag, where she removed her handkerchief, wiped her eyes, blew her nose, and told herself that it was way past time for bathos and bad dreams. She had a daughter to rear in a bold, new world, and she couldn't afford to get sloppy about something that was over and done with.

Chapter Four

The train chugged through the woods toward the station in San Francisco several days after it left New York City. The tangy scent of pine trees and redwoods kissed Somerset's nostrils and made him remember why he'd moved from Chicago to the west coast in the first place. *The forest primeval,* somebody had called it. He couldn't remember who. He should probably ask Eunice Golightly, who seemed to know everything.

"Smell that bracing balsamic scent, ladies!" Loretta thumped herself on the chest and sucked in air, then let it out in a whoosh. No wilting lily she.

"It's wonderful," Isabel murmured, as if her mind were elsewhere. Which it probably was, mused Somerset, who'd been thinking a lot about Isabel Golightly in the past few days. He probably should be ashamed of himself for being grateful to learn she was a widow, but he wasn't.

"The scent reminds me of the Caledonian hills."

Somerset turned his head but he couldn't see Marjorie MacTavish, who had uttered the last sentence, because she was hidden behind Isabel. It didn't seem in character for Miss MacTavish, who seemed to him to be a most silent and withdrawn individual, to be voicing any kind of nostalgic sentiment, but her tone had sounded wistful. He was probably wrong.

"I love the smell of the woods," he said, in order to be saying something.

He stood with his newfound lady friends—the designation included Eunice, who didn't act all that much like a child—on the observation deck at the end of the train. No matter how much he loved the redwood forest and found the aroma refreshing and all that, Somerset wasn't especially looking forward to seeing San Francisco heave into view, although he adored his adopted city. Slanting a glance to his right, he surreptitiously eyed Isabel Golightly's profile. She was gazing out over the giant redwoods, bushy ferns and tall fir trees, and he acknowledged the reason for his own lack of enthusiasm for disembarking from the train.

His problem was that he didn't want to lose touch with Isabel. Or Eunice, either, for that matter, although the little girl kind of spooked him. He'd never encountered so serious and intelligent a child. Not that he saw many kids on a regular basis. Still, his sister's two boys seemed awfully normal compared to Eunice, always punching each other and playing baseball and catching mice and that sort of thing.

Somerset couldn't imagine Eunice touching a baseball bat, much less hitting another child. As he thought about it, however, he recalled Isabel telling him about Eunice's encounter with a snake in New York's Central Park. Now *that* seemed normal for a child her age. Or it would have seemed normal, if Eunice had been a little boy, or if she hadn't voiced her intention of looking up its biological name and studying it.

Face it, he told himself. *The child is strange.* Not in a bad way, but . . . Bother.

Eunice and Isabel were holding hands, and Loretta held Eunice's other hand. Somerset felt left out, and he didn't like it. "What are your plans now, Miss Linden?" he asked, hoping to discover Isabel's plans, too, by stealthy means.

He didn't have a clue why he felt shy about asking Isabel straight out, except that he wanted to so much, yet didn't want to pry. From everything Somerset had gathered about the Golightlys, Isabel was a hardworking young mother whose husband had died before Eunice was born, and Eunice had spent most of her young life searching out books from which she'd gleaned her amazing store of knowledge.

He tried to recall if he'd been reading books like *Treasure Island* and *Moby Dick* when he was six years old, and almost laughed. When he was six, his literary taste had run toward McGuffy's Readers, if he remembered correctly.

The thing that really puzzled Somerset was that Isabel kept pulling away from him. He should have thought that a woman in her circumstances, which couldn't be comfortable, would be doing her level best to snare him. After all, he was far from an ugly fellow, and he was well fixed in the world. It made no sense to him.

"Oh, I expect I shall go back to my old life."

Peering at Loretta speculatively and noticing the devilish gleam in her eyes, Somerset decided she enjoyed her old life. "And what does that old life entail?"

"Work at the San Francisco Ladies' Benevolent Society, campaigning for women's suffrage, demonstrating for temperance, agitating for unionization, particularly for those poor women who have to work in factories and sweatshops. All those things. I'm no shrinking violet, Mr. FitzRoy." She said it proudly—and unnecessarily.

"No. I can tell you're not." Somerset liked her for it, too, although he imagined she'd be rather a handful to live with, providing a man ever dared to try it.

Loretta sighed happily. "I am particularly interested in the Chinatown clinic run by a friend of mine, and in the Ladies' Benevolent Society's soup kitchen near Chinatown. The misery of the people who come to us cannot be overstated."

"Really?" Somerset knew he ought to care more about the underprivileged members of San Francisco's society, but he didn't, other than to throw the odd coin at a beggar from time to time. He'd never let on about his lack of interest to Loretta, mainly because he didn't want to hear a long lecture on the subject.

"Absolutely. Why, did you know that most of the men we serve in the soup kitchen have serious mental problems, Mr. FitzRoy?"

"Er, no, I didn't know that."

"It's the truth. Most of them are merely confused, and very few of them are violent, but they all need help, not condemnation. Understanding and, perhaps, hospitalization, not incarceration."

"I'm sure that's true." Somerset wouldn't have been surprised if she'd started pounding on the railing and orating to the pine trees they were passing.

"People don't *know* what poverty does to people, Mr. FitzRoy, and they don't know what kinds of conditions lead to poverty. It's a crime." This time she *did* pound on the railing.

"I see." Somerset was taken aback. He hadn't realized Loretta Linden was quite such a militant young woman, although she'd given him enough clues to have figured it out before now.

"I can tell them all about poverty, if they really want to know," muttered Isabel.

That stopped Loretta's rhetoric cold. She turned to Isabel. "I know, dear, and it's a shame. But we'll fix that." She sounded as if she meant it. Somerset wished her well. He'd even help, if he were allowed.

Everyone was silent for a moment, until Eunice spoke to him, peering around Loretta's skirt in order to do so. "What will you do in San Francisco, Mr. FitzRoy? Do you have a regular job?"

"Indeed, I do, Miss Eunice. I've been on an extended holiday in order to do research for my book, but I write a weekly horticultural column for the *San Francisco Chronicle.*" He also collected royalties on several books that were being used in various colleges throughout the nation, but he didn't mention those.

"Oh, you're a journalist!" Eunice seemed to find this discovery a delightful one. "I should like to be a journalist one day."

He smiled at her. "I thought you wanted to be a biologist, Miss Eunice."

"Well . . . yes." Eunice frowned. "I have lots of different interests."

"That's the truth," murmured Isabel, as if she were well acquainted with her daughter's many and diverse interests, and found them rather wearying.

"I have a feeling you'll be able to do anything you want to do, Miss Eunice," Somerset said. "You have the equipment for it." He tapped his head meaningfully.

The little girl's cheeks turned pink. "Thank you."

"She certainly does," Loretta agreed. "I aim to see the child educated, too."

This comment caught Isabel's full attention. She'd been staring beyond the observation carriage and into the forest as if her thoughts were miles away from where she stood. She turned toward Loretta, and it looked to Somerset as though she had to give herself a mental shake to bring her attention back to the present. "You've done too much for us already, Loretta. What I need to do is find a job of work so that I can support my daughter and myself."

Aha. A subject he might be able to help with. Grasping at it with energy, Somerset said, "I should be pleased to assist you in your search, Mrs. Golightly. Ah, you've mentioned a little difficulty with understanding American employment ads." He grinned to show her that he was teasing. "I should be more than happy to interpret for you."

"Thank you, Mr. FitzRoy." She didn't return his grin. In fact, she seemed downhearted today. Somerset couldn't blame her for that. She faced a daunting task, although it wasn't as daunting in San Francisco as it might have been in England, or even New York City. The American west had long been a haven for independent females. "I expect Loretta will be able to help me with the newspapers." She managed a wan smile for Loretta's sake.

Marjorie MacTavish, on Isabel's right side, said, "Miss Linden has been a godsend for all of us." Miss MacTavish seemed pale and drawn, as if she weren't looking forward with anything even approaching optimism to her a life in a new city. Somerset had learned to expect as much from her. A gloomy individual, Miss Marjorie MacTavish. She could put a damper on dashed near any occasion without half trying.

"Indeed. We need to discuss employment possibilities for both of you when we're settled in." Loretta, on the other hand, was perfectly serene, even faintly bubbly. Well, why shouldn't she be? It hadn't taken Somerset long to determine that it was she who had the money in this odd quartet of feminine pulchritude.

"Will you all stay together in San Francisco?" Was that too bold a question to ask? Somerset silently told himself not to be an ass. If he wanted to keep in touch with Isabel, he *had* to ask where she'd be staying.

"The four of us are going to my home, yes," Loretta answered, speaking for all of them. Which was natural, since she had the money. And the house, apparently. Not to mention determination enough for all four of them. "I'm hoping to persuade Isabel and Marjorie to remain there."

As unpaid labor?

Somerset told himself not to be cynical. He didn't think Loretta Linden was any sort of tyrant. She was undoubtedly only being helpful.

"After we settle in, we'll have to sort ourselves out, of course, but I don't believe that will be too difficult. I know several people who will be able to help in finding work for Mrs. Golightly. Miss MacTavish is considering the possibility of becoming my secretary."

"Ah, it's fortunate that you have such a position available."

"It's fortunate for me," Marjorie muttered. She looked scared to death, poor thing, attempting a smile that quavered pathetically. "I'm glad I took a typewriting class the last time I stopped in Edinburgh."

"On the contrary, it's fortunate for *me*," Loretta said bracingly. "I shall try not to be a hard taskmaster."

The three women laughed, Loretta heartily, the other two in a perfunctory manner that confirmed Somerset's impression that they were more worried about their new lives than they wanted to admit. As for Eunice, she was as composed as ever. The little girl was amazing.

But that didn't solve his problem. With greater daring than he usually demonstrated around women, he said, "Whereabouts is your home, Miss Linden?"

"On Lombard Street."

"Ah, the Russian Hill district."

"Yes."

"That's a lovely neighborhood."

"It serves the purpose." Loretta smiled. "Thank God for inherited wealth, Mr. FitzRoy." She gave a peal of laughter that sounded to Somerset as if she were struggling not to apologize for being rich. He didn't think she had anything to apologize for. If every wealthy person in the world used his or her money to do good works like Loretta Linden, the world would be a better place. He wouldn't embarrass her by telling her so.

"It must be nice," he said instead, grinning to let her know that *he* knew she was a peach, even if she didn't want anyone saying so aloud. "May I attend you ladies to your home? You'll probably need help dealing with all your luggage and so forth."

"We don't have much luggage," Isabel said, dashing his hopes. "It was all lost when the ship sank."

"Pooh, Isabel!" Loretta shot her a look that told her to keep her depressing remarks to herself and turned back to Somerset. "Your help would be very much appreciated, Mr. FitzRoy. Thank you for offering."

Well, thought Somerset, it was nice to know *someone* valued him. Eunice let go of her mother's hand and circled around Loretta's skirt to gaze up at him with her huge, somber eyes. She made a pretty little curtsy and said, "Thank you for helping me with my drawings, Mr. FitzRoy."

"You draw beautifully, Miss Eunice," he said honestly. "You have genuine talent, and it was a joy to help you."

"Thank you. You were a very good teacher. I think my mother needed someone to help divest me."

Somerset stared at her. "Um . . . I beg your pardon?"

Isabel chuckled. "I believe you mean that he helped to *divert* you, sweetie."

"Divert," said Eunice, filing the word away in her mental dictionary. "Yes, that's what I meant. Thank you, Mr. FitzRoy."

"You're welcome, Miss Eunice. It was my pleasure."

Isabel turned to Somerset. "Yes, thank you very much for diverting Eunice, Mr. FitzRoy." She held out her hand to him. "It was good of you to keep the dear little imp out of my hair during the trip. And for saving her in the first place so that she could still be alive to annoy us all."

Eunice grinned up at her mother.

Perceiving that it was either go along with the joke or make a fool of himself, Somerset took Isabel's hand and bowed over it in feigned seriousness. "It was nothing, ladies. In fact, it was my great pleasure to play the knight in shining armor. And it will be my continued pleasure to serve you until you're settled in Miss Linden's house."

"Thank you, sir knight." Loretta laughed and clapped Somerset on the back as if they were all old cronies.

San Francisco was a much bigger city than Upper Poppleton. It was bigger than York or Southampton, as well. But what Isabel found more disturbing than its size was that San Francisco was so *different* from any-place else she'd ever been. Not that she'd seen much of the world, other than the huge, black ocean that had swallowed up most of the passengers aboard *Titanic*. A shudder caught her by surprise, and she told herself to stop brooding about the tragedy. She had to forge onward and forget the past.

As if she could ever do that.

Nevertheless, she did her best to suppress unhappy memories and hold tight to Eunice's hand as the two stepped from Loretta's private railroad carriage onto the platform at the train station.

Lord in heaven, what was she going to do? Isabel's heart felt as if it were being squeezed in a giant's fist. Could someone die from fear? She'd heard the expression "frightened to death," but had always supposed it applied to people higher on the social ladder than herself. People in her station in life weren't supposed to possess feelings, much less succumb to them. Unfortunately, she had feelings anyway. And she was scared.

"Look, Mama," Eunice whispered.

Isabel knew where her daughter's attention had stuck, because she'd just spied the same scene: a group of Chinese people in blue coats and trousers and black skull caps and with long pigtails hanging down their backs, greeting each other farther down the platform. "Yes, dearie. I see."

"And look over there, too," Eunice persisted, gazing in another direction.

When Isabel looked, she saw a group of dark-skinned people, also greeting each other. She had no idea where they were from. Africa? India? Arabia? South Carolina? Lord on high, this was *such* a new land to her. She knew that people from many countries and of many races mingled in London, but she was from Upper Poppleton, where everyone looked like her.

"This is going to be quite an adventure, Eunice," she murmured.

"Yes. It surely will be." Eunice sounded excited.

Isabel didn't think her own heart's thunderous pounding had much to do with excitement. She was just damned bloody scared. Dashed blooming scared, was what she meant.

"Mrs. Golightly."

She turned and found that Somerset had spoken to her. "Yes? I'm sorry, Mr. FitzRoy. I didn't mean to ignore you." She felt stupid for having become so engrossed in her surroundings that she'd forgotten about the people who were trying so hard to help her.

He had such a charming smile. Isabel liked his smile a lot; in an odd and totally irrational way it gave her comfort. Or perhaps it wasn't irrational. He had, after all, saved her life and that of her daughter. That was a comforting thought all by itself. Small wonder she should have put him on a pedestal of honor in her mental memorial hall.

"Think nothing of it," he said, still smiling. "But we need to stay together in a group. It won't do to become separated."

"Right." She and Eunice left off staring at the new and fascinating rainbow of people surrounding them and went over to where he had indicated the luggage lay. Marjorie and Loretta, each of whom carried a small parcel, hurried up to them.

"We're here!" Loretta announced in a joyous voice. "It's so good to be home."

Isabel had been happy to leave her homeland, but right this minute, she was sure she'd feel more comfortable back in Upper Poppleton. While she hadn't been particularly happy there, she had at least fit in, although she'd always wanted more. Much, much more—for Eunice, if not for herself. But none of that mattered now. She'd made her decision, and she'd made her move.

She and Eunice would survive. No. They would *flourish* here, damn it. Dash it.

Somerset took the parcels and set them down on top of Loretta's one suitcase. Neither Isabel nor Eunice had ever possessed a suitcase. In Upper Poppleton, Isabel had wrapped their possessions in a canvas sack for their trip to the United States.

Now their few belongings were rolled up into one of the two parcels recently carried by Marjorie and Loretta. Loretta had decreed that Isabel had enough to do keeping track of Eunice, although the reverse was probably true. Isabel feared that Eunice was better equipped to keep tabs on her mother and to deal with their new surroundings than the other way around.

Isabel had no idea why she'd been blessed—cursed?—with such a brilliant child. It was just one of those quirks of nature, she supposed. Or a joke God had decided to play on her. As if she didn't have enough to deal with. How was she ever supposed to offer Eunice the educational opportunities she deserved? Maybe with Loretta's help . . .

Oh, Lord, she couldn't be worrying about that now.

"Where is your baggage, Mr. FitzRoy?" she asked, surveying the small pile of possessions at his feet.

"I sent it along to my home by cab. I can devote all my attention to you ladies." He smiled broadly.

"Ah, I see. That's very kind of you."

"It's my pleasure," he assured her.

How nice he was. Isabel wasn't accustomed to men being nice to her. She told herself not to get used to it, because it wouldn't last any longer than it would take a wagon to get them all to Loretta's house.

"And now," Somerset said, briskly rubbing his hands, "I'll go and hire a taxicab to take us all to Miss Linden's house."

"Thank you very much, Mr. FitzRoy," said Loretta, beaming. Her gaze greedily took in the railroad station, churning with people and raucous with noise. "It's *so* good to be home again."

Isabel's heart, which had been aching terribly, eased and softened a little as she watched Loretta. It was nice to know at least one of them was glad to be in San Francisco. Loretta was home. Isabel hoped she and Eunice would feel at home again someday, somewhere. A glance at Marjorie, white and gaunt, told her that Marjorie, too, was worried—as well she might be, although at least she had only herself to worry about.

Somerset took himself off, his step jaunty. Eyeing him critically, Isabel decided he truly was quite a well set-up young man, even if he was a botanist and not something more . . . well . . . masculine. His profession didn't matter one little bit. Besides, it wasn't only her gratitude that had raised him to the stature of a saint in her life; he was a genuinely good man. Good-looking, good-natured and kind, as well, qualities that she had come to value greatly since her experience with Eunice's father, whose good looks had gone only skin deep. Inside, he'd been a rat.

And Somerset FitzRoy was writing a book about plants. Fancy that. Isabel couldn't imagine writing a book about plants. She could conceivably write a novel if she ever had the leisure, but a book about plants? Although she hated to admit it to herself, since it seemed a betrayal of her hero, Isabel, who could recognize a cabbage growing in a garden when she saw one, couldn't think of too many subjects more boring than plants. Somerset himself wasn't boring, true, but . . .

She decided not to think about that, either. She had plenty enough important thinking to do; she shouldn't waste time on irrelevancies.

A heavy sigh escaped her. What she really wished was

that she could stop reflecting about her past. It was dead and gone. And good riddance to it. She was better off here, in America, where nobody knew her story. Eunice was better off here, too, where no one could hold the accident of her birth against her. As if anything was Eunice's fault.

A sudden sob caught her by surprise, and she slapped a hand over her mouth. Instantly, Loretta's avid expression turned into one of concern, and she rushed to put her arms around Isabel. "It will be all right, dear," Loretta said soothingly. "Everything will be all right."

Feeling like a bloody-blooming-idiot, Isabel nodded, swallowed another sob, and tried to smile. "I know it will. Thank you. I didn't mean to be stupid."

"Don't be ridiculous, Isabel Golightly. You've endured terrible horrors, and you've done a brave thing in coming to a new country. You must be frightfully confused and lonely, and you deserve to cry all the tears you have in you. But you needn't do it alone. We'll face your new life together." Loretta glanced at Eunice and smiled. "Won't we, Eunice?"

The little girl nodded gravely. "Yes. Thank you, Miss Linden. If you and Mr. FitzRoy hadn't helped us, we'd jolly well be in the suds."

Both Isabel and Loretta laughed, Isabel rather moistly, Loretta as if she were having to force her good humor. "In the suds, indeed," said Eunice's mother as she furtively wiped her eyes with the back of her hand. "And that's God's honest truth."

She gave Loretta one last hug and released her, wishing she'd kept better control over her feelings. She couldn't afford to be emotional. She was poor, for the love of God. Poor people weren't even supposed to *have* emotions—for good reason, since they were seldom allowed to express them.

She heard a suspicious sniffling noise and turned to see Marjorie MacTavish blowing her nose. That made her feel better in an odd way. At least she wasn't the only one worried about beginning a new life so far away from home.

Somerset trotted up to them a few minutes later, smiling as if he hadn't a care in the world. Isabel envied him. "All set, ladies. Please allow me to carry your baggage—"

"Such as it is," interrupted Loretta.

"Such as it is," agreed Somerset. "And I'll guide you to the cab."

Isabel, once again taking Eunice's hand, followed Somerset, glad that Loretta and he could joke about their circumstances.

She and Eunice stopped dead still in the middle of the milling throng when they saw the taxicab towards which Somerset was leading them.

"I believe that cab has no horse, Mama," Eunice breathed. "It is propelled by an infernal combustion engine."

"Internal, sweetie." Then Isabel took note of the machine chugging noisily at the curb in front of the train station, and she made an effort to close her gaping mouth.

This, she reminded herself, was America. It was San Francisco, a city even Oscar Wilde had deemed outrageous. She ought to have anticipated that horseless carriages would be in vogue here, where people were so eager to fasten onto new ideas. It was 1912, after all, and the fact that she'd seldom even seen such a vehicle, much less ridden in one, only emphasized the fact that she was unworldly. In some ways.

"My goodness," she said, striving to keep her voice steady. "It *is* a horseless carriage."

"Here we go." Somerset waved to them, urging them forward. Obviously, *he* thought there was nothing strange or unusual about riding in an automobile.

Not wanting to be perceived by him as unsophisticated, Isabel hurried the two of them forward. Eunice needed no prompting. After she'd come to grips with her shock, she all but dragged her mother the last several yards, so eager was she to experience this novel and innovative means of transportation.

"I probably should have wired my housekeeper," said Loretta, nibbling a gloved fingernail as she waited for Somerset to toss the luggage into the cab's rumble seat. "She could have met us here. But she hates driving the motorcar." She cast a critical eye over her three new friends and Somerset. "Anyhow, I don't think my own machine could hold us all."

"You have a motorcar, Miss Linden?" Eunice whispered, awed, gaping at her hostess.

Isabel clamped her jaws together so that her mouth wouldn't drop open again, and didn't speak.

"I certainly do," said Loretta. "It's much the best way to get around in the city." Then she laughed, as if at her own pretensions. "That's not really true. San Francisco has a wonderful cable car system, and it's almost all back up and running. Many of the lines were damaged during the 1906 quake. Truth to tell, I just wanted an automobile. It's my one indulgence."

"Ah," Isabel managed to say. Her last indulgence had been the purchase of a bar of lavender-scented soap, and she'd had to think long and hard before spending the money for that.

"I've never ridden in one of these before," Marjorie said. She sounded stunned. When Isabel glanced at her, Marjorie looked stunned, too. Again, Isabel took an odd sort of comfort in knowing she wasn't the only grown woman around who was finding San Francisco a strange place.

With a dramatic bow, Somerset opened the door and ushered the ladies into the tonneau of the cab. Eunice had to sit on Isabel's lap, and Somerset rode up front with the driver. Loretta gave him the direction and, with a tremendous growl, the machine rumbled into traffic. Isabel and Marjorie gasped and Isabel's arms tightened around Eunice, who stared at the passing scenery with fascination untainted by fear.

The trip wasn't too alarming. There were certainly a lot of people in San Francisco but overall, the streets seemed less crowded than those of Upper Poppleton. Perhaps that was because there weren't so many people walking and there were many fewer horses and wagons. So many people, even those who appeared to number among the working classes, were in motorized vehicles or cable cars. Eunice squealed with delight, sounding almost like a normal six-year-old, when she saw her first cable car.

"Look, Mama! Those people are hanging onto the poles! They aren't even sitting down. I want to do that!"

Loretta laughed.

A sense of desperation nibbled at Isabel's self-confidence. She felt as if she was losing control of *everything*. "I don't know, dearie. I think we'd best sit down if we ever ride on one of those things."

"They aren't really dangerous," Loretta said.

Somerset turned around, slung his arm over the back of his seat, and grinned at Eunice. "I'll take you for a ride on a cable car, Miss Eunice. You'll like it. I promise. And I won't let you fall out of the car." He winked at Isabel, who blinked, startled, unused to being winked at by gentlemen. The winks she was accustomed to receiving were from men who thought they understood her moral fiber, and who learned their mistake sometimes painfully.

"Oh, I'd like that, Mr. FitzRoy," Eunice exclaimed in delight. "I think San Francisco is bully!"

Chuckling, Somerset turned toward the front of the cab again. "It's bully all right. It's a great place."

So was Loretta's neighborhood. Loretta grew more chatty as the cab drew closer to Lombard Street. Isabel and Eunice, on the other hand, grew more silent.

Eunice scrunched closer to her mother and whispered in her ear, "I've never seen so many big houses, Mama."

"Nor have I," Isabel whispered back.

"Do you think Miss Linden lives around here?"

"I don't know, sweetie." She cast a quick glance at Loretta and Marjorie, glad to see them both staring at the city from the other side of the cab. Isabel knew it was impolite to whisper. So did Eunice. But since she figured Eunice was suffering from the same sense of intimidation that had begun tormenting her, she didn't scold her daughter.

Rather, she decided to put on a show of bravery for Eunice's sake and courageously asked a question. "Is your home nearby, Loretta?" She was proud that her voice didn't crack in the middle of the sentence.

"Yes," Loretta said happily. "We're almost there. I can't wait to get home. I loved my stay in England, but there's no place like home."

Right. There was no place like home for Isabel, either, and this wasn't it. It wasn't even close.

"Oh, I'm so sorry," Loretta said, suddenly stricken. "That was thoughtless of me. I know you three are *from* Great Britain, and this is very far away from your own homes, but I promise that I'll try to make you feel as though you belong here."

Fat chance of that, if this was Loretta's neighborhood. Isabel hadn't even *worked* in homes this grand back in Upper Poppleton. "Please don't think you were thoughtless, because nothing could be further from the truth."

"Indeed," muttered Marjorie. "You've been the saving of all of us."

"Fiddlesticks."

But Loretta was pleased by the tribute; Isabel could tell. And she didn't begrudge her a sense of satisfaction, either. If Isabel could, she'd rescue the whole world. Right now she'd be happy if she could just provide a decent life for her daughter. And herself, of course.

Somerset again turned to speak to the ladies in the tonneau. "My own home is just over the hill there." He pointed. "You can't see it from here, and it's nowhere near as grand as these houses, but it's mine, I built it just the way I wanted it, and I'm fond of it. I have a wonderful garden. It's full of plants native to California. I hope you'll come over and inspect it one of these days, Miss Eunice. And you, Mrs. Golightly. I think you'll find it interesting."

"Yes. I'm sure we'd both enjoy that," Isabel mumbled. She hadn't been paying attention, although she thought he was talking about plants again. She couldn't quite grasp anyone having a garden containing anything other than vegetables necessary for sustaining life, but perhaps Mr. FitzRoy was able to buy his food.

"And you, too, ladies." Somerset nodded at Loretta and Marjorie.

Marjorie looked at him blankly for a second. "Oh," she said. "Yes. Thank you."

Isabel would have bet that Marjorie had no better

idea than Isabel herself as to what she'd just agreed to. Marjorie seemed bewildered at the moment. Isabel felt sorry for her, which made her feel more hopeful about her own uncertain future.

Somerset went on, "I'll have to host a garden party and invite people from the newspaper. You need to meet people in your new city."

Good heavens. "How nice," Isabel murmured. If there was anything she wanted to attend less than a garden party, she couldn't think of what it could be. Anyhow, she wouldn't know how to behave, since she was unused to being a guest. She's probably pick up the platters, start serving the other guests, and embarrass herself.

"I should like to meet some of the *Chronicle* people, Mr. FitzRoy," Loretta said eagerly. "And see your garden, too, of course."

If she, Isabel Golightly, had said such a thing to a man who was nearly a stranger, she'd have been totally embarrassed for having been bold and brassy. The comment didn't sound at all out of place coming from the enthusiastic and progressive Loretta Linden. Isabel sighed. How long would it take her to get used to American manners? Perhaps she never would. Now there was a discouraging notion.

"Are those tall trees we saw when the train went through the forest native to California, Mr. FitzRoy?" Eunice. Of course.

"Indeed, they are, Miss Eunice. They're California redwood trees, and they're the tallest trees in the world, according to current understanding."

"My goodness," Eunice said, impressed. "Things in general seem to be very 'normous in America."

He laughed. "I suppose they might seem that way."

"America itself is very 'normous," mused Eunice. "Ever so much larger than Great Britain. I didn't think the train would ever get here."

"Mercy, nor did I," Marjorie said under her breath.

Loretta, who had been closely scrutinizing her fellow passengers, suddenly reached out and touched Somerset's arm, which he'd slung over the seat back again. "Mr. FitzRoy, are you interested in landscape design?"

Mr. FitzRoy seemed startled. "Landscape design? Why . . . yes, I am. Actually, that's one of my business interests. I designed my own home garden, and I've helped my sister and her husband plan out a wonderful garden on their property. I've also designed gardens for several others, and have been hired by the City of San Francisco to help with renovations on Golden Gate Park. Why do you ask?"

"Because I've been wanting to consult with someone who knows something about landscape design ever since I bought my home from my aunt. It's huge, and the grounds are huge, and I'm hopeless when it comes to gardening and plants and so forth."

A huge smile bloomed on Somerset's face. "I'd be more than happy to assist you, Miss Linden."

It might have been Isabel's imagination, but she could have sworn Somerset glanced at her before declaring his gratification with Loretta's question.

He withdrew his wallet and was pulling out money to pay the driver, when Loretta stopped him. "I'll take care of this, Mr. FitzRoy. After all, you're only trying to help us. You shouldn't be put to the expense of delivering us."

"But . . ."

There were no "buts" in Loretta Linden's life. She withdrew a wad of bills, and Somerset replaced his wallet with a sigh. Isabel thought how nice it would be if *she* were so rich she could afford to transport her friends all over town.

But that was silly thinking. She would make her way here in this new land. Indeed, she had a good start, what with Loretta's help and all. Why, she and Eunice had friends here already, and that was a big step in the right direction. Certainly life here couldn't be any more complicated than life had been in Upper Poppleton.

"Look!" Loretta cried suddenly. "There it is! Home, sweet home."

Isabel's mouth fell open before she could stop it.

Eunice's eyes opened wide.

Marjorie gasped, "Och!"

"That's your house?" Somerset's voice held awe.

"That's it," Loretta said happily.

Isabel shut her mouth and gulped.

Eunice said, "Um . . . it's quite big, isn't it?"

"I'd say so," Somerset agreed dryly.

Loretta only laughed.

Isabel stared at Loretta's beautiful, daunting mansion; glanced at her own daughter, who deserved the best education money could buy even though Isabel didn't have any; and at the horseless carriage in which she'd been transported to her new lodgings; and Somerset FitzRoy, the good angel of her entire life even though he was absolutely fascinated by plants, of all the tedious fields of study in the universe—and she decided America would take some getting used to.

Chapter Five

Somerset gazed through the isinglass side window of the cab and up into the blue, blue sky, miraculously unmarred by fog or smoke on this, the day of his homecoming. He took in the unique scent of the city he loved, and decided he was glad to be in San Francisco again, even if Loretta Linden had slightly unmanned him by insisting she pay the cabbie.

It was particularly pleasant to be here with his two new and charming acquaintances, Isabel and Eunice Golightly. He'd wager they'd never even seen, much less lived in, a neighborhood like this before.

As the cab chugged through the massive iron gates and putted up the long drive to Loretta Linden's house on Russian Hill, Somerset realized that the word *house* didn't do the structure justice. In reality, her home was a mansion of impressive proportions. He couldn't help but wonder why a woman as young as Loretta had bought so large a home.

Then again, Loretta Linden was an unusual woman who espoused many causes. Perhaps she made it a habit to take in strays, like the Golightlys and Miss MacTavish, and needed the room in which to house them.

"It was my aunt's house," she said, as if she'd been reading his mind. "I bought it when she decided to move in with my cousin Andrew."

"Ah." That explained it. Kind of. He decided to ask. Loretta didn't seem the delicate type of female that would shrink from a nosy question—and he *was* a newspaperman, after a fashion. "Do you utilize all this space?"

She laughed. "Of course not. However, I have plans for the place." She said no more and gave him a teasing look that told him he'd get no further answers that day.

"Aha. I trust your plans involve no nefarious activities."

"That depends on who's judging them," Loretta said with another laugh.

Her companions weren't nearly as jolly as she. Marjorie MacTavish, staring out the cab's windows at the mansion looming closer and closer, looked as if she might be sick. Isabel seemed both pensive and slightly downcast, and Eunice gawked at the house as if she suspected dragons lived inside.

"Oh, my," the little girl said in a tiny voice as she turned on her mother's lap and stared fixedly back at the massive entryway, laden with lions, they'd just driven through. "Is this really your house, Miss Linden?"

"It really is, Eunice."

"Do you have a large family?"

With a chuckle, Loretta said, "I'm afraid I don't, dear. Except that it's now your home, too, and I'd be pleased to call you my family."

"Oh," whispered Eunice. "How nice."

Somerset understood instinctively what Eunice and her mother were thinking: they'd never even seen a house as grand as this one; how could they ever be comfortable living here? "Big place, isn't it?" he said, smiling benevolently upon the child, who was so different from most children but who was still only six.

The two of them must be overwhelmed. According to Eunice, who had become quite chatty on the train, Isabel had earned money cleaning other people's houses in their village of Upper Poppleton. He wondered if any of the people for whom she'd worked had owned homes as large as this one. From the expressions on their faces, he doubted it.

San Franciscans were noted for their flamboyance, and the man who'd built this house had been one of the flashiest. Somerset wondered if Loretta's aunt had been married to him, or if her aunt had bought the place from him. Maybe Loretta came by her outspoken ways naturally.

"It is extremely tremendous," Eunice said, stepping from the cab and holding her hand out to assist her mother. "Even huge."

Somerset smiled as he watched Isabel exit the cab. She was staring at the grand house with the same awe her daughter exhibited. "My word," she said, and swallowed.

Loretta had left the taxi on the other side, assisted by the driver. "It's only a house," she called over the top of the cab. Then she chuckled. "Larger than most, I must admit."

"Ah," said Isabel. "Yes, of course. Somewhat larger."

Somerset knew she didn't believe it. He didn't, either, although he could understand Loretta's point of view, too. He didn't want to abandon Isabel and Eunice, but knowing he should offer his aid to the other passengers, he walked around the cab to see if he could help Loretta or Marjorie. "It's a grand one, though, you must admit," he said to Loretta.

"Indeed it is," Loretta acknowledged. "I love it."

Her household staff were coming at a run. Out the massive double doors, across the huge marble porch, down the polished steps, and across a well-tended expanse of grass, they hurried: three women in uniforms. Somerset guessed Miss Linden didn't employ a butler. No surprise there, as she was an admitted feminist. Somerset imagined she didn't want employ a *man* in her home, because *men* could get jobs anywhere.

It might be true that men could find employment more easily than women, but Somerset didn't necessarily think that was a bad thing. After all, it was the men in the world who had to support the women and children.

His glance returned to Isabel and Eunice, and he realized how stupid his last thought had been. However, he didn't want to contemplate the injustices of the world at the moment.

Loretta didn't stand on ceremony with her staff. She hugged them all as if they were long-lost friends, and she the prodigal daughter returning to the fold. Which might not be too far from the truth. He hadn't asked her what she'd been doing in England, but he wouldn't be surprised to learn she'd been agitating. He could envision her in a suffrage march with a band of like-minded women, waving a placard, or attempting to chain herself to the gates surrounding 10 Downing Street. The picture his mind conjured up made him smile until he thought about it some more.

Women with the vote. Imagine that. He mulled it over for a second or two, and his mind's eye presented him with a vision of Miss Eunice Golightly as President of the United States addressing the Congress. Good

God. He shook his head, dislodging the picture, and forced himself back to the present.

The taxicab rattled off, leaving everyone on the drive in front of Loretta's front porch, most of them staring around in awe and wonder. Somerset picked up the one piece of luggage before anyone else could snabble it, allowing Loretta's household help to grab the rest of the bundles. He might not be any better than a woman, but he was damned well going to act like a man, whether they liked it or not.

He noticed that Isabel and Eunice had left off staring and were now walking very closely together, and that Eunice held tightly to Isabel's hand. Or vice versa. He couldn't tell which one appeared more cowed by this ostentatious show of wealth, but neither one of them looked comfortable. A glance at Marjorie told him that she wasn't comfortable, either. In fact, her face had gone dead white and she was standing still as if she didn't dare to move. As he watched, she swayed slightly and he feared she might faint.

Alarmed, he plopped down the suitcase and caught her before she could collapse on the hard concrete drive. "Miss MacTavish!" He glanced around. "Somebody, open the door." Relinquishing his suitcase to a maid in favor of a more chivalrous and manly duty, he lifted the woman in his arms and dashed up the steps.

"Marjorie!" Loretta cried out, too, and darted after Somerset.

Isabel and Eunice, dismayed and wide-eyed, exchanged a worried look. "What happened to Miss MacTavish, Mama?"

Somerset caught the little girl's question as he hurried inside the house, and he almost grinned. Imagine that: at long last Eunice Golightly had encountered something she didn't understand.

* * *

Although she was sorry for Marjorie, Isabel was glad to have something useful to do now that the other woman had fainted. Isabel knew how to nurse people. She didn't have the least idea in the world how to live as a poor person in a rich person's house. As a guest. She could perform like nobody's business as a housemaid.

Kneeling beside the sofa upon which Marjorie lay, she fanned Marjorie's pallid face with a fan Loretta had discovered in the drawer of a writing table—and a lovely ivory fan it was, too. It had probably come from China or Spain or somewhere else equally exotic. Glancing up, she asked, "Do you know if the tea is almost ready?"

"Mrs. Brandeis is in the kitchen making it right now, I believe, Mama."

Wherever the kitchen was. Mrs. Brandeis, Isabel had learned, was Loretta's housekeeper. Mrs. Brandeis's niece Molly was one of Loretta's housemaids. The other housemaid, a Chinese girl named Li, was obviously unrelated to the Brandeis clan. Loretta had bustled off after seeing that Marjorie was comfortable on the sofa and, since Isabel didn't know her way out of this room much less around the house, she hoped someone would come back and rescue them soon.

"Gi' a lady rest, canna ye?" Marjorie, whose Scots accent was ruthlessly subdued under normal conditions, sounded both fussy and intensely Scottish.

The fussiness was normal, a fact that made Isabel glad for Marjorie's sake, since it meant she was feeling better. For her own sake, she'd be just as happy if the woman would remain laid up for a while—at least for as long as it took Isabel to overcome her immense feeling of inferiority.

This *house*. It might as well be a palace, for the love of

God. Isabel would never, ever, in a million years, be able to repay Loretta for everything she'd done for her and her daughter. In truth, Isabel was beginning to feel the tiniest bit oppressed by her kindness.

But that was silly. She needed help, and it would be the height of stupidity to refuse help when it was offered. For Eunice's sake, if not for her own, she would accept Loretta's offers of assistance.

If she ever saw Loretta again. Gazing about the room in which she, Marjorie, and Eunice presently resided, she realized it was larger than her entire home in Upper Poppleton. Not to mention better furnished.

Was that real gold decorating the picture frame over the fireplace? And was the picture of the snobby-looking woman that was framed in gold a relation of Loretta's? Painted by a real, honest-to-goodness artist? Was the fireplace itself really crafted of black marble? Were those Chinese lions rampant on the mantelpiece carved out of real jade and ivory? And was this sofa presently holding Marjorie MacTavish's recumbent form truly covered in forest-green velvet? Sweet Lord in heaven.

Damnation, but she wished she'd been born somebody else. Somebody with money. Not lots of money, perhaps—she was neither greedy nor selfish—but it would be ever so wonderful to have enough for once. Enough wasn't too much to ask for, was it? Enough would be wonderful, and more than she'd ever had so far in this bloody life. Blooming life. Isabel mentally chastised herself for her many profane lapses of thought in recent hours.

"Och, don't bather me," grumbled Marjorie, drawing Isabel's attention from her surroundings and back to her patient. "I feel enough of a baffin already."

"It's perfectly natural that you should be overwhelmed, Miss MacTavish," she said in her most soothing voice, deducing from context what a "baffin" was. The tone of voice was one she'd cultivated while taking care of old Mrs. Finchley in the village. Now *that* was a job she'd actually enjoyed, until the old lady died. Then she'd had to go back to cleaning houses.

"Call me Marjorie, canna ye?" Isabel's patient said vexedly. "For the love of Christ Jesus, we sank on the same ship together."

The brusque words startled a short laugh from Isabel. "True, true. Very well, Marjorie. In that case, you just lie there and rest for a few more minutes. You fainted, and you had every reason to, given everything that's happened to us all. But we'll fix you right up."

Marjorie uttered an unhappy sound that might have been a huff or a sigh, but that Isabel decided not to pay attention to. She was being useful; that was what was important at the moment. When Marjorie recovered, Isabel would just find something else to do in order to be helpful in this alarming house.

Maybe she could assist with the mending. Or with the mopping and dusting. Eyeing the gleaming furniture, she ruefully acknowledged that Loretta's household staff seemed to be doing quite nicely without her. Still, she was used to doing that kind of work. It didn't matter that she hated it; it would be one way, if a small one, of paying Loretta back for her tremendous kindness.

"Here's the tea. I brewed it according to a recipe I found in New England, with some feverfew I got out of Miss Linden's garden. I hope you don't mind that I added a sprig of lemon balm and a pinch of anise seed to the feverfew. Feverfew is pretty powerful all by itself."

Isabel jumped at the sound of Somerset's voice. She hadn't expected him to be assisting her in the nursing of Marjorie. None of the men she knew had ever helped her nurse sick people. In fact, if memory served, when faced with illness they generally ran the other way as fast as they could. Isabel had assumed all men did the same.

Peering up at him, she gave him a tentative smile. "Thank you. That's fine. I'm sure the concoction will taste better for the lemon balm. I'm not sure about the anise." She also wasn't sure about the feverfew, whatever that was, but she didn't say so. She took some comfort from his sudden reappearance, though, and not merely because she liked him. If *he* could find his way around in this monolithic mansion, certainly *she* could. Eventually.

Somerset grinned as he gently deposited the silver tray holding a lovely flowered China teapot, cup, and saucer on the table. "It smells good, anyway."

"Yes, it does." Isabel was impressed and entertained the frivolous notion that perhaps Somerset could cook, too, as well as brew tea. What a useful man he seemed to be.

"Miss Linden's housekeeper is bringing some regular tea and some sandwiches for those of us who aren't ill."

"Ah, good." And now she was going to be waited upon. Would wonders never cease? "Here, Marjorie, let me help you." She slipped an arm under Marjorie's shoulders to help lift her into a seated position.

Marjorie was having none of it and shook off Isabel's arm. "I can sit up by meself," she snapped. "And I can hold my own teacup."

"Very well." Marjorie MacTavish had no reason to bark at her; she was only trying to help. Nevertheless, Isabel didn't bark back. She drew away from the sofa upon which Marjorie had been lying and watched the other woman push herself to a sitting position. Then she poured out some tea and handed her the cup and saucer.

"Thank you." Marjorie took a sip of the concoction and grimaced. "Och, my, that tastes as if it will cure anything."

"It's good for what ails you," Somerset said heartily. "No matter what it is."

"Nothing would dare stay in t'same body with it," Marjorie murmured after swallowing another sip. "Is there any sugar to put in it?"

"I'm sorry. I didn't think to bring any, but I'm sure Mrs. Brandeis will bring some with the regular tea." Somerset laughed. Isabel didn't. She was annoyed with Marjorie, the ungrateful prig.

Marjorie reached out and touched Isabel's hand. "I'm sorry I'm so cankersome, dearie. It's only that I'm so worried, you know." Her Scottish burr gave the words a pleasant lilt, and her face was intensely sincere. "I dinna know what to make of America. I've never worked as anyone's secretary. I'm fleefu', Isabel, dreadly fleefu'."

Isabel deduced that "fleefu'" meant worried, and her heart melted at once. She could understand frailty much better than she could incivility. "It's all right, Marjorie. We're all frightened about what to expect in America." She glanced at her daughter, who didn't look upset or scared in the slightest. "Well, most of us are, anyway."

Marjorie peered at Eunice, too, and sighed. "It mun' be nice to be young and eager for new things."

"Yes." As Isabel gazed at Marjorie, she pondered how old the other woman was. She didn't look very old, although she often acted as if she were a hundred and ten. How sad and bleak Marjorie's life seemed to be. At least Isabel had experienced the joy of having loved a man—briefly—and she had a wonderful daughter.

Poor Marjorie had been employed as a stewardess. That might have been interesting work, and it must have been entertaining to travel the world, but now she seemed to have nothing and no one. Isabel decided she ought not allow herself to lose her temper at the poor woman, even when Marjorie was ill-natured.

Somerset, who had been watching from a chair nearby, said, "Can I get you anything else, Miss Mac-Tavish?"

Marjorie's cheeks went from pasty white to bright pink, Isabel presumed with embarrassment. "Nay, thank you, Mr. FitzRoy. I feel like a gudgeon for having fainted."

"Don't be ridiculous. You ladies have been through an amazing series of events, tragic and otherwise. You have every right to faint if you want to."

"I didna want to," Marjorie said with a sigh.

"Such is life." Somerset gave Marjorie one of his wonderful smiles, and Isabel considered having a faint of her own.

They all stiffened as a bell sounded in the house. "Is that a doorbell?" Isabel asked. "Who could be visiting Miss Linden so soon after her return from abroad?"

She didn't expect an answer, which was just as well since she didn't get one. She did, however, see the Chinese housemaid scurry down the hall outside the room and felt better for having espied a human being belonging to the household. She felt even better when Loretta, following Li down the hall, turned into the parlor in which her guests tarried.

"How's our patient?" she asked, smiling.

"Much better, thank you." Marjorie's color remained high. "Mr. FitzRoy's tea is . . . fortifying."

Somerset grinned. "It's less fortifying than it would have been if I hadn't added the extra ingredients. Feverfew by itself would have curled your hair."

Eyeing Marjorie's pretty red hair, Isabel said wistfully, "Not that you need it."

"I'm so glad, Marjorie." Loretta smiled upon them all. "I've been giving cook instructions for dinner, and Mrs. Brandeis is bringing tea." She turned to Somerset. "I expect you to stay and dine with us, Mr. FitzRoy. A meal is the least I can offer you, after your many kind services."

"I'd be more than happy to take dinner with you ladies." Somerset bowed and appeared genuinely glad to have been offered the invitation.

"What's that I smell?" came a booming voice from the hall. "Have you taken to concocting poisons in your spare time, Loretta Linden?"

Loretta whirled around with a squeal. "Jason!" She pelted to the door, clearly elated, and when a young man entered, she threw herself into his arms. Isabel, Marjorie, Somerset, and Eunice all stared, astounded.

After letting the newcomer go, Loretta grabbed his hand, and dragged him into the room. "But I must introduce you to my new friends, Doctor."

This she proceeded to do, and Dr. Jason Abernathy bowed politely to each of them. He was a nice-looking man, tall and lean, with curly dark hair and twinkly blue eyes. "How do you do? Don't let Miss Linden bullyrag you." He spoke the last words to Isabel and Marjorie.

Marjorie gaped at him and her mouth dropped open. Isabel didn't go that far, but she didn't quite know what to make of Dr. Abernathy. Loretta smacked him on the arm and giggled, indicating to Isabel that the two were long-time friends, at the very least. Could they be lovers? Scrutinizing the pair, she decided they acted more like brother and sister. Not that you could really tell about such things.

Pretending to be severely wounded by Loretta's light smack, Dr. Abernathy staggered across the room, clutching his arm, until he seemed to recall that he held something in his hand and stopped, straightening up. "Oh, I forgot. Who wants this . . . this . . ." He squinted at the colorful bottle he held. "Um, I'm not rightly sure what it is, but I think it's a soothing lotion intended to cure chapped hands or whatever else ails you. Probably from an old Chinese recipe, smuggled into this country by an old Chinese medicine woman." He twinkled at Marjorie and Isabel. "*Are* there Chinese medicine women?"

"How in the world would we know?" Marjorie asked shortly, then her face bloomed crimson when Dr. Abernathy grinned directly at her.

"Don't badger my friends, you beastly man." Loretta snatched the bottle from Dr. Abernathy's hand, opened it up, and sniffed. "Oh, it smells divine. You took it in payment for your medical services, I presume." She heaved an exaggerated sigh. "If you don't start charging your patients, you're going to go broke, you know."

"Pooh. I have enough money to run six hospitals, let alone my little clinic."

How nice, Isabel thought, wondering where all these rich people had been earlier in her life. Then she wondered if she might have a chance with Dr. Abernathy, who was rich enough to operate six hospitals. But no. He was probably married with seventeen children. Besides, he seemed to be Loretta's property.

Anyway, she needed a man like she needed a second head. She was better off alone. Or perhaps with Somerset FitzRoy.

Her last thought brought her to her senses, and she chided herself as an idiot.

"Aha!" Somerset said suddenly. "I thought your name was familiar. You're the Dr. Jason Abernathy who's trying to get them to revoke the Chinese Exclusion Act, aren't you?"

Dr. Abernathy bowed again, this time at Somerset. "I have that distinction." He straightened abruptly. "If you can call it that."

"And you run the clinic on Sacramento and Grant. Of course." Somerset strode up to the doctor and held out his hand. "You are performing a valuable service to the community, Dr. Abernathy. I salute you."

Isabel watched all this with growing interest. If Somerset liked the doctor, he must be a good man and not a bounder.

Instantly, she asked herself how she'd come to that conclusion. For all Isabel knew, Somerset himself had performed only one good deed in his entire life by saving herself and Eunice. Granted, that was a highly exceptional thing to have done, but it might have been an anomaly.

"But to whom should I give this delightful . . . uh . . ." He sniffed the bottle's contents. "Well, whatever it is, who wants it?"

"I believe," said Loretta, "that Miss Eunice would benefit from a rare Chinese lotion."

"I believe you're right, Miss Linden. For once."

She smacked him again, grinned, and went to Eunice, who was staring at the adults' antics as if she were watching a rare and unusual dramatic performance. Her mouth fell open when Dr. Abernathy bowed over her and held out the bottle. "For you, my dear. Wear it in good health."

"Thank you, sir," she whispered. She sniffed the bottle's contents, as had Dr. Abernathy and Loretta. "Oh, my, it smells heavenly." Her glowing smile made her mother's heart leap.

Isabel decided that Dr. Abernathy was a good man, even if he was a bounder. Anyone who could make her daughter happy was all right with her.

Mrs. Brandeis entered the room, bearing a tray laden with tea things, followed by Molly with another tray, this one piled with sandwiches, and Somerset hurried to assist them. They set both trays on the table next to Marjorie's medicinal pot, and Loretta began pouring.

"Now sit yourself down, Doctor," she commanded. "And you, too, Mr. FitzRoy. Perhaps you can help us, Jason."

"Gladly." Dr. Abernathy, first snatching a sandwich from the top of the pile, plopped down on the sofa next to Marjorie, who bounced once and then scooted over to the other end, as far away from him as she could get. He grinned at her discomfiture. Isabel decided she *did* like the man, and that he definitely wasn't a bounder.

Somerset took the chair next to the one Isabel occupied. They smiled at each other, and Isabel felt her heart get warm and her cheeks get hot, which was ridiculous for a woman of her age and with her experiences, not to mention a daughter. She was too old to blush and to get heart-warming palpitations. She pretended she wasn't aware of Somerset's nearness and watched Loretta as if riveted.

"As you know," said Loretta, sitting in a chair facing the sofa and, as usual, not noticing that Marjorie was embarrassed and Isabel blushing furiously, "Miss Mac-Tavish, Mrs. Golightly, Eunice, Mr. FitzRoy and I were all aboard the *Titanic*. I wrote you about it."

"Made my blood run cold," agreed Dr. Abernathy with an eloquently theatrical shudder. Marjorie squinted at him nervously. Isabel thought he was darling.

"Now," continued Loretta, "since Mrs. Golightly and Miss MacTavish have decided to remain in the United States, they both need employment. Miss MacTavish has agreed to be my secretary."

"Poor lady!" the doctor exclaimed. "Brace yourself, Miss MacTavish. Miss Linden is brutal with the whip."

"Och, now, really!" said Marjorie.

Loretta threw a small embroidered cushion at him. He caught it and threw it back, and both he and Loretta burst out laughing. Isabel stared, enthralled. She'd never seen horseplay like this before. It charmed her. A glance at her daughter showed her that Eunice, too, was spellbound and enjoying the show. So was Somerset. His delighted smile made Isabel's heart turn a back flip and pitter-patter in her chest. Stupid heart. Only Marjorie seemed perturbed by the jolly goings-on. No surprise there. A remarkably conventional woman, Marjorie MacTavish.

"To return to what's *important,*" Loretta said loudly, "we need to secure employment for Isabel. She has to support herself and Eunice now. Of course, they will both remain here for as long as they like." She smiled at Isabel and Eunice, both of whom smiled back, Eunice with unmitigated pleasure, Isabel with appreciation mingled with uneasiness.

"Ah." Dr. Abernathy turned his twinkly blue eyes upon Isabel. "What sort of work are you accustomed to do, Mrs. Golightly?"

Chapter Six

He would have to ask, wouldn't he? Embarrassed by her lack of marketable skills, Isabel nevertheless spoke up. She had nothing to be ashamed of, after all. She'd never done anything the least bit underhanded or illegal, and if char work wasn't elegant, it was paid employment, and she'd done it well.

"I used to do char work in Upper Poppleton." Encountering a blank stare from the doctor, she recalled their lack of a common language and expounded. "I cleaned houses."

"Ah." The edges of his mouth turned down a bit.

Isabel's heart fell. She was so bloody useless. Blooming useless.

"But Isabel is capable of so much more. Why, she's got a real knack with words, and she's a whiz at being a mother." Loretta smiled brightly at Isabel, who still felt lower than dirt. Few people cared if a woman of her class could read and write, and still fewer cared if a woman was a good mother.

"She's got other skills, too. Important skills that could and should be put to use."

This unexpected commendation was plunked into the conversation by Somerset FitzRoy. It silenced the doctor and Isabel. Everyone turned to look at him, Loretta and Dr. Abernathy with interest, Marjorie with disbelief, Isabel with extreme misgiving. She knew herself to be talentless. Unless Somerset was going to make something up out of whole cloth, which would be nice but unlike the person she believed him to be, she couldn't understand why he'd spoken thus.

He went on, "Mrs. Golightly is quite gifted at handling ill people. Witness Miss MacTavish here." He gestured at Marjorie, who looked as if she wanted to crawl under the sofa cushions. "With only a little training, she'd make a superior nurse. She certainly has a way with people who are under the weather."

Marjorie, after clearing her throat and twining her fingers together nervously for a second or two, nodded. "Aye, that's so. She was quite efficient with me." Staring at the empty cup in her hand, she sounded surprised when she added, "I feel quite the thing now."

"Ah." Turning his gaze in Marjorie's direction, Dr. Abernathy asked, "And what, pray, happened to you that required Mrs. Golightly's nursing skills, Miss MacTavish?"

Her frown returning along with her heightened color, Marjorie said under her breath, "I fainted."

"Hmm. Fainted, did you? Odd. You don't look the fainting type."

Marjorie puffed up in outrage like a hen who'd fluffed her feathers. "And what, pray, is the fainting type?"

Dr. Abernathy ignored her question. Turning to

Isabel, he asked, "Have you ever considered being a nurse, Mrs. Golightly?"

Astounded by the turn of the conversation, Isabel shook her head. "No. I mean . . . I never . . . I mean . . ." She stopped babbling and took on a cargo of air. "What I mean to say is that I've never done anything but char work. Cleaning houses, I mean."

"That's not true, Mama."

This time, everyone in the room turned to stare at Eunice. As usual, the little girl's composure remained unaffected by this concentrated attention. "You nursed Mrs. Finchley and Mr. Potter, Mama."

"Oh." Isabel had forgotten all about Mr. Potter. "That's right, I did, but . . . well, I wouldn't exactly call it nursing."

"I don't know why not," said her daughter. "Because that's what it was."

"Ah," said the doctor.

"And they both praised you highly." Eunice nodded at Dr. Abernathy, as if to confirm the judgments of Mrs. Finchley and Mr. Potter. "Mrs. Potter said that if it hadn't been for Mama, she would have killed Mr. Potter for being a cantankerous old curmudgeon."

A few muted chortles issued from the observers. Isabel had forgotten about Mrs. Potter's declaration, just as she'd forgotten about Mr. Potter, whom she'd have liked to kill, too, the crotchety old bastard. Buzzard.

"Aha," said the doctor. "So you *do* have nursing experience."

"Well, not to say *nursing* experience. Not really. I've not been trained or anything. I only helped out a few people in the village when they needed it. I can't really say that I've ever wanted to be a nurse, but I'm willing to do anything." She thought about Somerset and said brightly, if mendaciously, "I like plants, too. I wouldn't mind working in a nursery or for a florist." It wasn't a lie, exactly, since she truly had nothing against plants except that they made for boring conversation.

Loretta shook her head. "Nobody would hire you for either job, I fear. It's totally unfair, but nurseries only employ men, and florists only hire women to sell their bouquets on street corners. You'd not make enough money to keep a gnat alive, much less yourself and Eunice."

"Oh." How discouraging. Isabel chewed her lower lip and thought some more, even while knowing it was pointless to do so. No amount of thinking would make her skilled at some kind of employment that would pay her well. Which left the sweatshops and factories and other people's houses. "I suppose I could operate one of those electrical sewing machines."

"No!" cried Loretta.

"No!" echoed Somerset.

"That's terrible work," said Dr. Abernathy.

Marjorie sniffed.

"In fact," announced Loretta with vehemence, "some enlightened women in San Francisco, among whom I happen to number, are agitating for unionization for the female sewing machine operators in the city. It's a crime, the way those poor women are treated."

Isabel appreciated Loretta's soft heart and willingness to work for causes in which she believed, but at the moment, Isabel was only really interested in employment opportunities. She guessed sewing was out, especially if there was labor unrest in the various shops.

A space of silence followed Loretta's last comment.

"You can dance, Mama."

Again, all eyes turned toward Eunice. Isabel felt herself flush.

"Dance?" said Somerset.

"Dance?" Dr. Abernathy's right eyebrow lifted.

Marjorie regarded Isabel with bemusement.

"That's right! You can!" said Loretta, as if Eunice had brought to mind something wonderful that she'd forgotten.

Nodding, Eunice said, "Mama's aunt and uncle, my great-auntie and great-uncle Chesterfield, ran the Palais de Dance in London for many years before they retired to York. Uncle Charlie taught Mama how to talk like someone from London and he taught her all the popular dances. He said she was a naturalist. Mama's always said that dancing is the only thing she's any good at, but that's not true." She offered her mother a glorious smile.

"I think you mean a *natural*, sweetie, although . . . well, it doesn't matter." Wishing she'd taken the time to glue her daughter's mouth shut before this conversation began, Isabel added, "Thanks, dearie, but no one needs a dancer, I'm sure."

Isabel could recall very few times in her life when she'd been this mortified. Now everyone would think her to be no better than she was, and she'd been pretending so hard. She'd finally told Loretta her black secret, because she'd felt she must. But Loretta didn't count, because she was . . . well . . . Loretta.

"What kind of dancing?"

When she squinted at Somerset, expecting to encounter an expression of severe disfavor on his handsome face, she was surprised that he only appeared interested.

"What kind?" Isabel gestured helplessly. "Oh, waltzing, fox-trotting. The polka. The schottische. Ballroom dancing. Social dancing." She omitted mentioning ragtime, which was lots of fun, but was looked down upon by some. Or the tango, which was positively shocking—but fun. Oh, so fun.

"I've seen Mrs. Golightly dance, and she's wonderful. She dances like . . . like . . . well, like Vernon and Irene Castle, only without Vernon. If you know what I mean. She is simply exceptional." Loretta's tone was one of awe and absolute approval.

When Isabel glanced at her, she appeared awed and approving, too. How strange. Or perhaps it wasn't. It had been Loretta who had bullied Isabel into donning one of her own ballgowns and accompanying her to the magnificent ballroom on *Titanic's* first-class deck. Isabel had never seen anything so grand, and she'd been terribly unnerved. For one thing, she was a little taller than Loretta and the gown was rather short for her. For another thing, Loretta's bosom was quite a bit larger than Isabel's. But the main thing that caused her to feel inferior and afraid was the sheer grandeur of the ballroom and its dozens and dozens of swells. Never, in all her days, had Isabel seen anything to rival that crowd.

And then gentlemen had begun asking her to dance, and she'd forgotten all about being poor and unworthy and had succumbed to the sheer fun of dancing to a sophisticated orchestra. That night beat any dance Isabel had ever attended in Upper Poppleton, where they were fortunate if a couple of the neighbor children could play the fiddle. She'd remember dancing aboard *Titanic* with wistful pleasure for the rest of her days. That didn't help her at the moment, however.

"Er . . . yes. I'm not as good as Irene Castle, of course." She gave a self-deprecating smile—and she lied. She was every bit as good as Irene Castle, actually, but she knew better than to say so since that would be boasting, and nobody liked a braggart. "And I don't have bobbed hair." She attempted a laugh, but it came out thin and tinny.

"Ah." Somerset.

"How fascinating." Dr. Abernathy.

"She's spectacular. Truly, she is." Loretta. With her hands clasped at her bosom.

Marjorie said nothing. Her face spoke for her, and Isabel felt like hiding when she received the message. Marjorie was shocked, both by Isabel's lone talent and by the fact that she and Loretta must have conspired to allow a third-class passenger to dance in a first-class ball-room, or how would Loretta ever have had a chance to judge Isabel's skill? Bloody hell. Blooming heather.

Nobody spoke for a moment. Dr. Abernathy sat on the sofa, tapping his chin with his forefinger, and staring at Isabel in a way that made her squirm. *Why* had Eunice brought up her colorful, but inelegant, relatives and her totally useless, although refined, terpsichorean skills?

But it wasn't Eunice's fault. Isabel should have thought to tell her daughter not to mention dancing or her aunt and uncle Chesterfield. She hadn't, Eunice had, and now they were in the soup. People all over the world looked down upon theatrical folks. Peeking at Loretta, she noted that this universal sense of condemnation didn't apply to her. Well, of course, it wouldn't. Loretta was a true original.

Perceiving that she'd dropped a bomb of sorts into the conversation, Eunice swivelled to gaze at her mother. "Is there something wrong with dancing, Mama?"

"Well . . ." Isabel didn't know what to say. She couldn't bear the thought of crushing Eunice's feelings for having inadvertently caused her mother embarrassment.

"No. There's not a thing wrong with dancing."

Somerset smiled sympathetically at Isabel, who wished he hadn't. His benevolence made her want to cry.

"Heavens no," said Loretta with a laugh. "I wish I could dance as well as your mother. When I watched you on the—" She broke off suddenly and shot a glance at Marjorie, having realized that Isabel's visit to the *Titanic's* ballroom wasn't something she ought to talk about. The anguished expression she saw on Isabel's face probably reminded her. As, in all likelihood, did Marjorie's horrified squeak. "Ahem. In any case, I don't know how much being able to dance will help your mother in securing employment, however."

"Oh." Clearly disappointed, Eunice subsided onto her chair.

"But don't despair!"

Dr. Abernathy's sudden outburst made them all start. Afraid to hope, Isabel offered him a tentative smile.

"I have an idea." The doctor leaped up from the sofa, making Marjorie bounce again. Isabel got the feeling he did it for that very reason. What a strange man he was. But pleasant. Very pleasant.

"It's about time someone got an idea," muttered Marjorie, glowering at the doctor's back.

"What is it, Jason?"

The doctor turned to face Loretta, who had asked the question. For the first time since he'd entered the room, he appeared serious. "Do you remember Joseph Balderston?"

Frowning as she sought through the files in her mind for the reference, Loretta said slowly, "Joseph . . ."

"Lived down the block from us. We grew up together. You must remember him. Shortish. Fattish. Family's richer than Midas and all his kin. In the hotel business."

Suddenly, Loretta's countenance cleared. "Of course! Why didn't I think of that?"

"Because you never think," the doctor said with a wicked grin, sitting down hard on the sofa. Marjorie, bouncing, frowned at him. He paid her no mind.

Naturally, Loretta, leaning way out of her chair, smacked him on the arm. "That's not true. It's because I didn't remember that Isabel was so talented until Eunice reminded me." She bestowed a happy smile upon Eunice and Isabel.

Talented? Because she could dance? Isabel wished someone would explain this to her, because she was totally confused. She did manage to return Loretta's smile, but feared it was a feeble effort.

"Balderston owns the Fairfield Hotel now, you know, Loretta."

"That's right. He does." Loretta sat up straight, as if stricken with a dazzling notion. "What a brilliant idea!"

Feeling dazed, and because they were, after all, discussing *her* future, Isabel ventured faintly, "Um . . . what's a brilliant idea?"

"The Fairfield! It would be perfect, if he needs someone."

Isabel licked her lips and didn't speak again, praying that all would be made clear soon.

"I'll talk to him," declared Dr. Abernathy. "I'll make him need someone."

To do what? Dance? Isabel didn't ask because the concept was so bizarre, and she didn't fancy being laughed at. Perhaps Mr. Balderston needed housekeeping help in his hotel.

"In fact, I'll telephone him right this minute," the doctor cried, again leaping from the sofa and again making Marjorie bounce. She grabbed a sofa arm and clung on as if to a life preserver.

Isabel swallowed hard. A telephone? Good God.

There was a telephone in Loretta's house? Well, of course, there would be. Loretta was rich, after all. Isabel had never used a telephone in her life.

"Marvelous!" cried Loretta, clapping her hands. "Mrs. Golightly won't be able to begin work until next week, however. We have things to do first."

They did? Isabel blinked, wondering what those things could be.

"Be sure to tell him that," Loretta called after Dr. Abernathy as he hurried from the parlor.

"I will."

After a moment of silence, Isabel cleared her throat. "Um . . . what is Dr. Abernathy going to ask Mr. Balderston?"

"Why, if he needs a dancer, of course." Loretta beamed at Isabel.

"But—" Oh, dear. This was so confusing. "But I've never danced professionally, Loretta. I'm not a . . . a ballerina or anything."

"Of course not! But oftentimes hotels hire people to dance with guests in the evenings. It's perfectly respectable. San Francisco has become a favored spot for holidays. And we always have businessmen visiting and staying in town for business purposes. Hotels do the same thing in London. Why, when I was staying at the Clarendon—"

Isabel's mind fastened on the name for a second and she lost a couple of Loretta's words. The Clarendon was probably one of the most expensive hotels in the entire world. Oh, my. She was truly in exalted company now.

"—had a gentleman and a lady hired to dance with the guests. They also performed an exhibition dance once or twice an evening. They were wonderful, and they were applauded by all. I believe a dancer would earn much more than a cleaning lady, too, and their clothes are ever so much nicer. I wouldn't be surprised if that's how Vernon and Irene Castle got their start."

"Um . . ."

"Or perhaps they started in vaudeville, but I don't suppose you have that kind of experience, and you'd probably need to have a partner already. But the hotel would be just the ticket. Oh, this is so exciting!" Unable to contain her enthusiasm, Loretta popped up from her chair and twirled around the parlor a couple of times to the tune of an imaginary waltz before stopping in a flurry of skirts in front of Isabel's chair. "I'd *love* to learn to dance better. Could I talk you into teaching me?"

Dumbfounded, Isabel whispered, "Of course."

This was incredible. It was probably a figment of her imagination. She was most likely dreaming and would wake up and discover that she was going to go to work in some rich lady's house, cleaning out the scullery and sweeping floors. Maybe she could work her way up to parlor maid if she tried hard enough. It wasn't possible that she, Isabel Golightly, might actually be hired to *dance,* of all things.

Why, she loved to dance. How wonderful it would be to get paid for doing something so jolly . . . .

"Done!"

Isabel had no sooner turned to see Dr. Abernathy, who had shouted the word, before she discovered herself lifted from her chair and hugged soundly by the much shorter Loretta Linden.

"Marvelous! Oh, Isabel, I'm so glad. What a wonderful job!"

It would be, if this weren't a dream, which it was, so she wouldn't celebrate yet. Released by Loretta almost as suddenly as she'd been plucked up, Isabel sat with a plop onto her chair.

"I should have said it's almost done," amended Dr. Abernathy.

Aha. Isabel knew it had been too good to be true, even for a dream.

"Mr. Balderston wants to meet you, Mrs. Golightly. And I expect he'll want you to perform a dance or two with the male dancer he has on staff."

"Oh," said Isabel, feeling numb. "Of course."

"Who is it?" Loretta giggled. "The man dancer, I mean."

"I think his name is Jose something-or-other. Or maybe it's Jorge. He's from the Argentine."

"Oh, my," whispered Isabel, thinking of the tango. The only man she'd ever done the tango with was her uncle Charlie, and he was so old and fat and merry, besides being a relative and so bowlegged that their bodies didn't touch. She couldn't *imagine* dancing such a sultry dance with a stranger.

"You'll do wonderfully," Loretta assured them both.

Isabel wished she were that confident.

"So." Dr. Abernathy rubbed his hands together. "Mr. Balderston would like to see you tomorrow afternoon, if you can manage to be at the Fairfield then, Mrs. Golightly."

"I'll be happy to escort you, Mrs. Golightly."

Isabel started, having almost-but-not-quite-forgotten about Somerset. Her mouth opened, but since she couldn't think of anything to say, she shut it again. She'd like him to escort her, but she wouldn't say anything so brassy.

"There's no need for that," Loretta assured him. "I can drive her there. I'd love to see the dance demonstration."

"So would I," declared Eunice.

Somerset frowned more seriously than Isabel had

heretofore believed him capable of. "I don't think either of you should appear at the Fairfield without a male escort, Miss Linden."

It was the wrong thing to say to Loretta, as Somerset ought to have learned by that time. She straightened up to her full five feet and a little and glowered at him. "If there's one thing neither Isabel nor I need, Mr. FitzRoy, it's a male escort. *Anywhere.* We"—she pounded herself on the chest—"can take care of ourselves."

Somerset huffed.

Dr. Abernathy, lips twitching with what Isabel felt sure was a repressed smile, said soothingly, "Nobody thinks you can't take care of yourself, Loretta. But to assuage everyone's feelings, we'll *all* go. I want to see the dance demonstration, too." He turned a devilish squint upon Marjorie. "And I'm sure Miss MacTavish is dying to see it, as well."

Without allowing Marjorie to utter the words teetering on the tip of her tongue, Loretta cried, "Perfect!"

Eunice went so far as to clap her hands.

Somerset smiled as if he approved of the turn of events.

Marjorie gave the room a general, all-purpose frown once she quit bouncing after Dr. Abernathy again sat, hard, on the sofa.

Isabel wasn't sure, but she thought she was happy.

Somerset found himself reluctant to go back to his own home after Loretta's "simple" dinner, which had been nothing of the sort. His reluctance caught him off guard. As a rule, he loved the house he'd built on Chestnut Street and would have been eager to return to it after his long sojourn in Europe and the eastern states.

But he'd enjoyed the light, bantering tone of conversation between Loretta and Dr. Abernathy during dinner. More, he enjoyed talking to Isabel and Eunice—between whom he'd been seated, bless Loretta Linden for a saint—even though any other hostess in San Francisco would have fed little Eunice in the kitchen.

The one good thing about leaving his new friends was that, after taking dinner and then coffee in the parlor, the night was too dark for him to make an adequate survey of Loretta's very large grounds and garden areas with an eye to landscaping. Ergo, he had to make arrangements to visit the house again soon. And he made sure to extract a promise from Isabel that she would assist him with the rehabilitation of Loretta's garden, even though she'd told him she knew nothing of gardens, thus assuring himself of her company for a good long while. What a sly devil he was, to be sure.

The guests congregated in the enormous hall before the front door as they took their leave of each other. Isabel appeared to be in a state of numbness, which made sense to Somerset. After all, her life had changed drastically in the past few weeks and she was facing a trying day tomorrow.

Marjorie, too, seemed bewildered. She also seemed to have taken a dislike to the doctor, who had teased her a good deal during dinner. Somerset hoped she'd get over it. He thought Dr. Abernathy was swell.

Eunice, unlike his sister's children, had thoroughly enjoyed herself with the adults during dinner. He hoped that she'd be given sufficient opportunity to increase her education now that she was in San Francisco and under the wing of the generous Loretta Linden. He'd like to help her, too, but it would have been outrageous of him to offer his assistance on so short an acquaintance.

"Would you like Mrs. Brandeis to call a cab for you?" Loretta asked him as he gathered his hat and coat from the mahogany hat rack beside the front door.

"That's not necessary, thank you. My house is only a short walk away."

"Pooh. I'll drive you home," Dr. Abernathy said in his booming voice. "I've got to return to the clinic tonight anyhow."

"You have to work tonight?" Marjorie was appalled.

"Alas! A doctor's work is never done." Dr. Abernathy put the back of his hand against his brow as if suffering a spasm. He was a comical fellow. Somerset was pleased to have made his acquaintance.

Marjorie narrowed her eyes and peered at the doctor as if she suspected he was *really* going off to an opium den or had some other nefarious scheme in mind.

"Thanks." Somerset tugged on his coat. "I'll gladly accept a ride, Dr. Abernathy. I have a proposition for you."

Dr. Abernathy gave Somerset a quizzical look. "A proposition, have you? Hmm. I'm not sure I like the sound of that." He laughed.

"It's a good one," Somerset assured him. "I'm writing a book, you see." It had occurred to him during dinner that Dr. Abernathy might be a good source of information. Somerset was never one to pass over a source without giving it a try first.

"A book, you say?" Dr. Abernathy's right eyebrow lifted.

"A book about plants and their medicinal properties."

"Is that so?"

"It's so. Most of my notes sank with the *Titanic,* and I'd like you to help me replace them."

The doctor nodded and took Somerset's arm in his as they strode toward the doctor's automobile. "Aha, I see. You'll have to tell me all about this book of yours."

So Somerset did.

The next day began a whirlwind of activity that lasted the week Loretta had predicted that they'd need. Isabel hadn't overcome her awe at the suite of rooms Loretta had assigned to her and Eunice before Loretta whisked them and Marjorie off to a seamstress to be fitted for skirts and shirtwaist. Loretta deemed such garb more practical than more elaborate day wear, a decision with which Isabel concurred, although she'd rather have made their clothes herself than pay someone else to do it. She made the mistake of saying so.

"Don't be silly, Isabel," Loretta told her, flapping her hand in the air. "You don't have time for that. You'll certainly need formal gowns too, for your new job."

"Formal gowns," Isabel whispered, her mind having mislaid the information relating to her dancing audition, probably in the interest of self-preservation.

"Besides," Loretta went on happily, as she bustled them all down the porch steps, "sewing is so boring, and we all have many other things to do."

Not for the first time, Isabel, Eunice, and Marjorie chorused, "We do?"

Loretta, who had led the march downstairs and out of the house, into the fog, and up to her automobile, merely contemplated them for a moment, shook her head, then flung her arm out in a gesture of inclusion, and said, "Everybody in!"

Without further questions, the three of them piled into Loretta's automobile, a bright yellow Oldsmobile Runabout that made Isabel nervous at first. But Loretta knew how to drive the machine, and she did it with flair. If she drove a teensy bit faster than Isabel deemed absolutely necessary, she chalked it up to her own inexperience, although she did notice that Marjorie kept her eyes clamped shut and looked like she was praying during most of the drive.

Eunice, sitting next to her mother in the tonneau, was delighted with the motorcar ride. Eunice, unlike Isabel, was not intimidated by new experiences. Or speed. Or traffic.

"Eeee!" cried Isabel at one point, hunching in the seat with her heart hammering painfully, and squeezing her eyes shut.

Deftly jerking the steering wheel to the left, Loretta swerved around a milk wagon being pulled by an obstinate and extremely slow horse. "There's nothing to worry about," sailed back to Isabel's ears from Loretta's mouth.

Isabel felt foolish for having given voice to her terror and vowed to remain silent from now on, no matter what. She tried to concentrate, instead, on all the new and interesting sights and sounds available to her in San Francisco.

Nannies in white aprons and caps pushed babies in perambulators. Fashionably dressed women chatted and minced along in their narrow hobble skirts. They were probably going to the vaudeville theater past which Loretta's automobile roared. How nice it must be to be able to go to an entertainment in the middle of the day.

Merciful heavens, there went another one of those cable cars, whizzing down the street, its bell clanging loud enough to deafen a person, men in suits with newspapers folded under their arms clinging like barnacles to the poles. How in the name of heaven did the conductors collect tickets? Surely, people must have to purchase tickets before they rode the dangerous things.

The fog started to lift, and the air smelled of fish and salt air, with a hint of creosote and some odd sweet aroma, like that of incense. Looking around, Isabel realized she could catch glimpses of the ocean through gaps between buildings. The Pacific Ocean. Imagine that. The ocean on the other side of her former world. She suddenly felt shaky and unsure of herself.

"It's all right, Mama," Eunice whispered, taking her mother's hand.

Feeling foolish, Isabel kept her daughter's hand in hers. It made her feel safer somehow.

Thus it was that Isabel and Eunice Golightly and Marjorie MacTavish were taken to meet Mrs. Gonzales, Loretta's seamstress, and were measured for a wardrobe of skirts, shirtwaists, and warm coats. Isabel felt a compulsion to object, or at least to apologize to Mrs. Gonzales for not being Loretta, but she kept her mouth shut.

As they prepared to leave Mrs. Gonzales's shop, Loretta said, "And now for shoes! You'll need dancing shoes as well as everyday shoes, Isabel."

Isabel gulped.

When Marjorie said, "I expect the cost of these clothes to be taken from my salary," and Loretta objected, and Marjorie insisted, Isabel decided Marjorie had a good idea.

"Yes. And I shall pay you from my salary as . . . as . . . well, whatever work I do." It was probably silly, but she was reluctant to speak openly about being hired as a dancer. Because she was accustomed to the pittance earned by a charwoman, she added, "I may have to pay you over time."

"Fiddlesticks! You two are absolutely *ruining* my gesture of goodwill!"

Marjorie, her worried frown in place, said, "Codswallop. No one in my family has ever accepted charity, and I willna be the first."

"Likewise," said Isabel, although she wasn't sure about that.

"And I," said Eunice, as usual causing all eyes to turn to her, "would appreciate being given chores to do so that I may earn my own keep, please, Miss Linden."

"But you're only six years old!" Loretta's protest was vigorous.

Eunice didn't buy it, a fact that made Isabel proud. "Nevertheless, Mama and I are doubtfulous about accepting so much from you, Miss Linden. We both know that you are a generous lady and don't look for payment, but we would have squeams if you were not to accept it, even if you don't need or want it."

"Squeams?" Isabel, who generally understood her daughter's intentions, was puzzled this time.

Eunice looked up at her fixedly, her little brow wrinkled up like an old man's. "Squeamish. Squeams. Don't there have to be squeams, Mama?"

"Oh. Um, I don't think so, dearie. But we would be squeamish. That's very true."

Lifting her chin in a manner Isabel knew she'd learned from her mother, Eunice said, "I am sure there will be something I can do for you, Miss Linden, even if it's only helping the cook." With a grin that transformed her back into a little girl, she added, "And I should very much like to learn to cook."

Loretta gazed at Eunice for several seconds, then shrugged. "Very well, if it will make you all feel better, you can pay me back, but I'll be hanged if I'll accept more than you can comfortably spare. And I don't like doing even that much."

"We'd feel better, however," Isabel said.

Marjorie nodded.

Eunice tilted her head to the side and said, "Being poor is simply vexifying."

As usual, after one of Eunice's odder comments, they all stared at her.

"Um . . . I believe you mean vexing, darling," said Isabel. "And you're right. It is."

Chapter Seven

Loretta allowed Eunice to watch her crank the automobile, although she cautioned the child about getting her arm caught should the crank spin out of control. "People break their arms all the time that way."

"Yes, I can see how that might happen."

Since Eunice wasn't strong enough to operate the crank by herself, Isabel supposed she wouldn't have to worry too much about her daughter taking it into her head to break her arm. Anyhow, Eunice was an obedient child, and she'd never touch something that didn't belong to her.

Another glimpse of her daughter, watching eagerly as Loretta dealt with the Runabout's crank, gave Isabel pause. This was America. Life could be wild in America. It probably wouldn't hurt to give Eunice a little lecture on the behavior expected of her. Isabel surveyed the street scene going on around her and sighed. She had more faith in Eunice's ultimate survival here than in her own. She'd never let on.

"And now," Loretta called over the racket of the automobile and the traffic after they got going again, "we're off to visit Dr. Abernathy's clinic. It's in the middle of Chinatown, so we will have luncheon there. Is that all right with everyone? Chinatown is quite an experience, and all visitors to our wonderful city by the bay must see it."

"Oh, yes! Thank you, Miss Linden!" Immediately, Eunice clapped a hand over her mouth and muttered, "I beg your pardon."

Isabel gave her daughter a stern look.

Loretta laughed gayly. "Excellent!"

Marjorie, seated in the front seat next to Loretta, transmitted a sidelong glance of disappointment at Eunice.

Isabel didn't resent Marjorie's stuffy attitude. In fact, she renewed her determination to have a good long talk with her daughter. Eunice had been taught never to put herself forward. She was a child, and children were supposed to be seen and not heard, although, because of Eunice's ability with the language, Isabel made allowances. But to offer an opinion before the adults in the group did, as Eunice had done, was as disrespectful as it was unusual. Even though Isabel was far from strict, she was unhappy with Eunice's outburst. A glance at Eunice assured her that the little girl felt properly chastened.

With a sigh, Isabel went back to observing the sights. San Francisco was *so* different from what she was used to. In Upper Poppleton, most travel was still accomplished by horse or by foot. Here, motorized vehicles abounded. Why, Loretta had told them that San Francisco was installing electrical stop lights specifically to regulate automobile traffic. Isabel had never heard of such a thing.

Cable car bells split the air what seemed like every

second or two, and the cable cars rumbled uphill and down at a frightening pace. Isabel knew that Eunice would give her eyeteeth to ride on one of the clanking monstrosities, and she also knew that it would be unforgivable of her to refuse to honor her daughter's desire. After all, they were now San Franciscans—saints preserve them both.

Everywhere Isabel looked she saw hustle and bustle and people rushing hither and thither. Men in suits, carrying attaché cases and wearing tall hats that seemed constantly in danger of being blown off their heads, strode purposefully down streets. Chinamen carrying long poles on their shoulders with buckets hanging from each end darted through traffic. Children who, according to Loretta, carried messages for the city's large population of attorneys, ran through the streets or bicycled furiously up and down the hills. Women dressed in fancy clothes strolled along sidewalks. Automobiles were *everywhere*. Isabel was surprised they could maneuver as well as they did, given the amount of construction going on. Although much of the city had been rebuilt or restored, it was still recovering from the disastrous earthquake and fire of six years earlier. Isabel didn't look forward to enduring an earthquake and prayed such natural disasters were rare.

And then there were all the hills. Just looking at them made Isabel dizzy. When Loretta's Runabout groaned up one hill and started down on the other side, Isabel's stomach pitched and rolled as it had when they were at sea. She hoped she wouldn't be sick. How embarrassing that would be.

"We're almost there," Loretta sang merrily from the front seat.

Thank God. Isabel tried to smile, but couldn't. It didn't

matter since Loretta couldn't see her, but she felt as if she'd let the side down.

A few minutes later, the streets became narrower, and Isabel's nostrils quivered with the advent of strange odors. Her eyes widened when she saw dead ducks hanging in rows in front of storefronts. Bins full of strange vegetables sat on sidewalks, and men with push-carts shouted in Chinese, presumably hawking their wares. Small, dark shops held merchandise she couldn't identify. Most of the pedestrians were Chinese now. Where were the women? Isabel saw only men, most of them wearing dark blue coats, baggy trousers, and skull-caps, and shuffling along in black slippers. They all had long braids hanging down their backs. Eunice stared avidly. For that matter, so did Isabel.

"Oh, Mama, look! They're wearing pajamas. I've read about pajamas."

"Is that what they're called?" Isabel thought they looked mighty comfortable.

"They're marvelously comfortable," Loretta shouted into the tonneau as if Isabel had magically transferred her thoughts to her own head. "I think they'll become all the rage soon."

"But they're trousers," protested Marjorie.

"Trousers for women," declaimed Loretta, "are the coming thing. Why should men be the only ones who are comfortable in their clothes? Women are oppressed enough as it is. Why should we be the victims of our clothing, too?"

Evidently Marjorie couldn't think of an answer. Neither could Isabel.

"We'll have to get you some pajamas, Eunice. And the rest of us, too."

Good Lord. Isabel and Eunice shared a glance.

Eunice's expression was almost as gleeful as Loretta's. Isabel feared hers wasn't. This country was so strange, and Loretta was so determined to direct her new friends' lives. Isabel appreciated her help a lot, but wasn't sure she could ever get used to her ways. Or pajamas.

Suddenly Loretta let out a loud gasp of outrage. The Runabout screeched to the curb and stopped with a shudder, and Loretta's door flew open.

Isabel was sure something catastrophic had happened. She opened her door in order to jump out and be of service if Loretta had inadvertently, say, run somebody down or knocked someone over.

Once she exited the automobile, however, she was unable to ask Loretta what was wrong because Loretta wasn't there. She was racing away from the machine and her friends, waving a fist in the air and shouting, "Stop that! Stop that this instant!"

"What's Miss Linden doing, Mama?"

For once, Eunice seemed just as puzzled as Isabel. "I . . . don't know, dearie." Glancing around, she saw no dead bodies on the roadway, but Loretta was manifestly upset about something. "I suppose we should see if we can be of help, though."

Eunice, game for anything, slid out of the machine after her mother. Isabel took her hand and glanced to see if Marjorie planned to join them. Since, at that moment, Marjorie was occupied in burying her face in her hands, she decided not to.

"I think Miss MacTavish feels unwell, Mama."

Isabel nodded. She'd been thinking the same thing for some time now. Marjorie hadn't seemed to take to automobile travel. She didn't voice her thought but said, "Let's see what we can do for Miss Linden." It would help if she knew what had happened.

However, puzzled but amenable, she grabbed

Eunice's hand and took off running after Loretta. When they were halfway down the block, Isabel realized what had riled Loretta. "Oh, dear."

Three ragged white boys were taunting an elderly Chinese man, who was trying to shoo them away and not having any luck. He was either crippled or injured because he was unsteady on his feet. He'd been using a cane to help himself walk, but had started batting at the boys with it. The hooligans dodged the weapon with agility, jeering and laughing.

By this time Loretta had reached the scene of the melee and had begun flailing at the boys with her handbag. She shouted as she swung. "Brutes! Ruffians! Stop that this instant!" She caught one miscreant on the ear with her handbag, and he danced away, holding his reddened ear and swearing.

"Aw, he's just an old Chink," retorted one of the boys, a dirty specimen in bare feet and a torn cloth cap, ducking a stab from the Chinaman's cane.

Turning upon him with violence, Loretta took a hard swing at him with her handbag. "Don't you *ever* use that derogatory term again!"

The boy tried to duck, failed, said "Ow," and cast Loretta a baffled frown as he cupped his cheek with his hand. Stumbling backward, he said, "What's that mean?"

Eunice, out of breath but stouthearted, grabbed the boy by the tail of his dirty shirt. "That means the word *Chink* is an unseemly one for a child to call an adult."

"Huh?" The boy, startled at being lectured by a six-year-old, tried to tug himself out of Eunice's grip. She lifted her foot, kicked him behind the kneecaps, his legs gave out, and he fell to the ground with a grunt.

Isabel, wondering how and where her daughter had learned *that* trick, reached out and took him by the arm before he could get up and escape or attack Eunice. She snatched another junior felon by the waist of his too-large trousers and held the boys away from her so they couldn't hit or kick her. Loretta had managed to nab the third one by that time. Eunice stood guard, her fists clenched, her lips set, ready to fell another scoundrel if need be.

She said fiercely, "If any of you hurts my mother or Miss Linden, I shall retort you to the authorities."

"Report," corrected Isabel, but her heart wasn't in it.

The boys gawked at her. Loretta grinned, panting. "You're a girl after my own heart, Eunice."

"Thank you, Miss Linden." Eunice again spoke to the three boys, her frown ferocious. "It's not nice to make fun of another person. It's perfectly shocking to try to injure someone who is elderly and has to use a cane. I'm surprised your mothers didn't teach you better manners."

The boy she'd kicked behind the knee, plainly the most verbal of the lot, said, "Huh?" again. The other two boys only stared at her. They stopped struggling.

"Miss Golightly is correct," said Loretta. "You boys should be ashamed of yourselves."

"But he's just an old Chink," muttered the vocal boy, then cringed. "I mean he's only a Chinaman."

"Desist!" came a roar from behind the fracas.

Isabel started and whirled around, carrying the boys with her, various articles of clothing flapping in the wind thus created. Dr. Abernathy, looking like an avenging something-or-other, strode toward them. Even better, from her point of view, Somerset FitzRoy was with him. He, too, appeared rather like an avenger, albeit a slightly absentminded one. She couldn't repress her smile. He smiled back, as if he and she were the only people on the street. Her heart fluttered madly for a few seconds.

Dr. Abernathy removed the boy from Loretta's grip, and Somerset relieved Isabel of her two burdens.

"What do the three of you mean by this outrage?" Dr. Abernathy asked in a earsplitting voice. "I'm ashamed of you. I thought you were supposed to be helping your father, Gerry O'Banyon."

One of the boys hung his head. "I was helping him, Dr. Abernathy."

"Badgering another person isn't helping anyone," the doctor said seriously. "And you, Jimmy Dallas. What ever possessed you to tease Mr. Fong here?"

Jimmy, the vocal one, mumbled something Isabel didn't hear.

The doctor huffed. "And *you.*" He shook the third boy by the scruff of his neck. "Sam Billings, I'm ashamed of you."

The third boy's face went scarlet under its smears of dirt. He didn't speak.

"Did you bring the pencils? I won't pay for services not rendered, you know, and your parents won't be pleased if you lost the goods in favor of persecuting a fellow citizen of San Francisco."

"We have 'em," a shamefaced Jimmy said. Reaching into his pocket, he withdrew a bundle of five pencils. "My pa'd skin me if we'd lost 'em."

"And well he should," declared Dr. Abernathy. "I should skin you anyway. You certainly don't deserve this money." He removed a nickel from his pocket and held it between his thumb and his finger before of the three boys. "However, I made a deal, and I keep my bargains. See that you do the same from now on, and that you don't get sidetracked into doing vicious things to innocent people. Now get out of here, and don't let me see you ever doing anything like that again."

Dr. Abernathy propelled the villainous minors down the street and bent to speak to the elderly Chinese man. "Are you all right, Fong?"

The man nodded. "All right."

"Do you need my help?"

"No, no. Go on way now." He hobbled off.

They all watched his back for a moment as he hot-footed it up the street as fast as his cane and his limp would allow, then Loretta punched Dr. Abernathy lightly on the arm, a form of communication Isabel had already deduced was normal for the two of them. "You need pencils like you need a hole in your head, Doctor."

"A fellow can always use a few more pencils," he said, laughing.

Somerset grinned at his new friend, Dr. Abernathy. "I get the feeling the good doctor is supporting every bum in San Francisco."

"You're right, Mr. FitzRoy." Loretta nodded. "He acts tough, but he's a softie underneath."

"Balderdash," growled Dr. Abernathy. "I'm mean and rugged and make it a point to beat up at least three young thugs every morning before breakfast. And I see someone who can probably use these pencils!" He bowed to Eunice, whose eyes grew large.

"Oh, my goodness, Dr. Abernathy." She clasped her hands behind her back as if she were afraid they'd get away from her and snatch the pencils out of his hand. "Don't you need them yourself?"

Isabel smiled at her daughter, who had never seen five brand-new pencils at one time in her life.

"Nope," said Dr. Abernathy. "But I suspect you do. Mr. FitzRoy here told me that you're quite the artist."

Eunice went pink with pleasure and bestowed a glorious smile upon Somerset. "Oh, *thank* you, Mr. FitzRoy. And thank *you*, Dr. Abernathy. I shall take very good care of them."

"I'm sure of it." Dr. Abernathy stood up, grinning like a benevolent giant at the little girl.

"Would you like me to keep them in my handbag, Eunice?" Isabel knew she was being silly when she felt tears prickle her eyes. But people were being so kind to them here in the wild western city of San Francisco, California, U.S.A. She hadn't anticipated such benevolence—or that she and Eunice should need it.

"Yes, thank you, Mama." She handed over the bundle of pencils and Isabel dropped them into her handbag.

Somerset's smile turned upside down as he gazed at Isabel and Eunice. "Where's the third musketeer?"

"Who?" Loretta looked around as if she expected swordplay to break out on the street.

Eunice said, "I think Mr. FitzRoy means Miss Mac-Tavish, Miss Linden."

"Ah. Of course." Loretta shook her head. "I don't know. We were all together in the Runabout, and then I saw those nasty boys and . . ." She shrugged.

"I'm here," came a small voice from several feet away.

When they turned, they saw Marjorie, wan and shaky, coming down the roadway toward them. Because she appeared to feel poorly, Isabel went to help her. "Are you all right, Marjorie?"

"I felt a wee bit sick back there," admitted Marjorie. "I think it was the ride in the machine."

"I know it, dearie. You aren't accustomed to automobile travel."

"Aye," said Marjorie, her voice faint but fervent.

As she and Isabel slowly approached the group waiting for them, she observed the expression on Dr. Abernathy's face and couldn't put a name to it. She feared it boded ill for Marjorie, however.

She was right.

"I see you let your friends clear the way for you, Miss MacTavish. Very intelligent decision, although I'm not sure sending a child into battle is a particularly humane choice."

Marjorie stopped walking, thereby jerking Isabel's arm. With a sigh, Isabel stopped walking, too, and braced herself. She noticed the doctor's eyes were twinkling alarmingly, and she peeked at Somerset, who grinned back at her and winked. Mercy, she wished he wouldn't do that. When he winked she felt warm all over, and Isabel knew that was an inappropriate reaction to a man she barely knew, even if he was the most wonderful man in the world and had saved her life and her daughter's.

"I beg your pardon?" Icicles might have coated Marjorie's vocal cords.

"I think Dr. Abernathy was only teasing, Miss MacTavish," Eunice said consolingly.

"Of course he was," said Loretta with haste.

Marjorie, glowering at the doctor, said, "Och, yes. I suppose."

"Your health seems a bit rocky, Miss MacTavish," Dr. Abernathy went on, still twinkling. "Perhaps you need a complete physical examination to determine what the matter is."

"Codswallop," growled Marjorie, straightening up and looking a bit stronger.

Sighing, Isabel watched the pair and waited for the fireworks. One of these days, she expected Marjorie would tire of the doctor's teasing and bop him one, or try to. Hoping to prevent a violent scene, she again glanced at Somerset.

"But we need to take luncheon!" Somerset declared jovially, anticipating her and Marjorie and preempting the comment poised on Dr. Abernathy's tongue. "I don't know about anyone else, but I'm starving and need my daily ration of chicken with almonds. I almost died from the lack of good noodle dishes when I was back east."

Dr. Abernathy's mouth snapped shut, and Isabel breathed more easily. She silently blessed Somerset, even as she silently cursed Marjorie and the doctor. What was the matter with those two? The doctor seemed to delight in making Marjorie uncomfortable, and poor Marjorie already felt like a fish out of water; she didn't need his help.

"My goodness, yes," said Loretta. "I could use some chop suey. It's been a long time since I've had good old San Francisco food." She rubbed her hands together.

"What's chop suey?" asked Eunice.

"Some heathen Chinese fare, I imagine," said Marjorie, who, Isabel had learned, was a staunch Presbyterian.

Dr. Abernathy took her by the arm. Isabel held her breath, but Marjorie didn't belt him. "Heathen or not," said the doctor, "you need to learn to eat it, Miss MacTavish. If you refuse to eat Chinese food in San Francisco, you're beyond hope."

Somerset and Isabel exchanged a glance, and Somerset leaned over to whisper in her ear. "I'm afraid she might be beyond hope."

With a giggle, Isabel said, "I'm afraid you might be right." She put her hand on his proffered arm and was pleased when he offered his other arm to Eunice, who smiled, delighted to be treated like a big girl. Then she spoiled her sophisticated image by skipping down the street to the restaurant.

* * *

The light in the restaurant was low, and the place smelled like Somerset's idea of heaven. He had missed this so much while he'd been away. He loved San Francisco. It amazed him that the atmosphere of the city he adored should be enhanced so greatly by the company he kept.

During luncheon, which consisted of rice, chicken with almonds, chop suey for Eunice and plenty of fragrant tea, he began to experience a feeling so strong it might be called a compulsion if he suffered from such things, which he didn't. But the urge to keep this group together forever clamped onto his heart and clung there. Such an urge was unlike him, and he couldn't quite account for it. He'd always been something of a lone wolf—or a lone beetle, anyhow—and this need for friends was new to him.

Perhaps he was coming down with something. Influenza, maybe. Could influenza cause emotional symptoms? He remembered his sister crying a lot when she was sick. Maybe such afflictions ran in families.

He was relatively sure that the intense pleasure he derived from Isabel's company didn't signify anything bad, such as mania, insanity, or neurasthenia. He truly didn't think he was crazy. On the other hand, he supposed it wouldn't hurt to check the family records for documented cases of derangement just in case. After all, he *had* thought about her constantly between handing her daughter to her in that lifeboat and their providential meeting on the train.

In any event, and with time and luck, he expected he'd get over it. And in the meantime, he would merely keep company with his new friends and take pleasure therefrom. And if time and luck didn't help cure his symptoms, he'd just have to marry the woman.

He liked that thought.

* * *

After luncheon, Somerset offered to accompany the three ladies and Eunice to the Fairfield Hotel on Nob Hill, where Isabel was scheduled to dance with an Argentine stranger in front of Joseph Balderston, another stranger, and one who would decide her future. Isabel pressed a hand over her heart and willed it to stop pounding so hard.

"I'd love to see the audition and I had intended to go, but I must return to my clinic. I have to perform an operation this afternoon that I hadn't anticipated."

"Come over some evening this week, Jason, and we'll tell you all about it."

Isabel wasn't accustomed to men and women being so free and easy with their invitations and assignations, although she'd certainly never noted anything the least bit unsavory about Loretta and Dr. Abernathy's friendship.

Over lunch, she'd learned that the two had grown up together, and lived next door to each other until they both graduated from college, he from Stanford, and she from the San Francisco Seminary for Young Ladies. Isabel had never known a female with a college education before. Loretta and the doctor remained friends after Dr. Abernathy had gone on to medical school and Loretta had gone on to irritate her parents by espousing a variety of radical causes.

Although she considered the idea a trifle disloyal, Isabel wondered if the fact that Loretta's parents objected to her political and social views was one of the reasons she clung to them so tenaciously. It must be nice to have wealthy parents to rebel against. Isabel chided herself for disloyalty. Her parents had both been saints.

She thought it was both typical and splendid that

Loretta had chosen to express her rebellion in so many useful ways, however, instead of sinking into some form of degradation. She was assuming, of course, that women's suffrage was a useful cause. She was pretty sure the soup kitchen Loretta spoke about so often was performing a valuable function in the world.

"I'd be delighted to. What day?"

Loretta's pretty brow furrowed. "Oh, Thursday would be a good day. I guess."

"You guess that, do you?" With a grin, Jason asked, "And what time?"

"Oh, about seven-thirty or eight, I suppose," said Loretta, sounding distracted. She opened her handbag and peered at an undoubtedly expensive gold watch on a chain contained therein. "But we have to dash now, Jason. We don't want to be late to the Fairfield."

"Right. Good luck, Mrs. Golightly." Dr. Abernathy smiled winningly at her, took her hand, and shook it heartily. Then he wheeled abruptly, grabbed Marjorie's hand, lifted it to his lips, and kissed it.

Poor Marjorie turned a brilliant scarlet, stuttered a few incomprehensible syllables, and stared, dumbfounded, after the doctor as he strode jauntily away. Accosted by what looked like a beggar's child hawking posies, he bent, offered the waif a coin, received in return a shabby bouquet, and reentered his clinic.

Pondering the doctor's bizarre behavior, Isabel murmured softly, "I do believe he's rather taken with you, Marjorie."

She knew she'd misspoken when Marjorie swirled around and stared at her incredulously. "You *what*? I canna believe you! Why that man is the most baneful, pernicious, awful, clamjamphried . . ." She ran out of adjectives and subsided into irate splutters.

Loretta smacked Isabel lightly on the arm, the first

time Isabel had been the recipient of Loretta's favored form of expression. Leaning close to her ear, Loretta whispered, *"Wrong* thing to say."

It certainly had been. Feeling like an idiot, Isabel tried to smooth the waters. "Of course, I may be mistaken."

"Aye," said Marjorie, her bosom heaving, her cheeks a remarkably becoming pink. "You're mistaken."

Isabel, Loretta, and Eunice—her expression all too comprehending—exchanged a meaningful glance. Then Loretta grinned and said, "Well, we'd best be off."

"Please," said Somerset, who'd been watching with amusement, "allow me, Miss MacTavish." With a twinkle for Isabel, he took Marjorie's arm and began leading her up the street.

"Will you come with us to the Fairfield in my Runabout, Mr. FitzRoy?" Loretta trotted behind Somerset and Marjorie.

Taking Eunice's hand, Isabel did the same, amused that Marjorie, in her righteous rage, was leading the way and causing Somerset himself to trot a little. Full of good Chinese food, Isabel was puffing a bit when they reached the Runabout.

"My machine is parked just across the street," Somerset told Loretta, gesturing at a large, imposing automobile. "I'll meet you ladies there."

"I'm so excited about this," exclaimed Loretta.

Isabel was glad about Loretta. As for her, her tummy felt slightly jumpy. It didn't help that Loretta squealed into the oncoming traffic on two wheels, as if she were steering a racing automobile through an obstacle course.

Marjorie closed her eyes as soon as the engine roared to life, and she covered her face with her hands as soon as the machine left the curb. Poor Marjorie.

Fortunately, neither Isabel nor Marjorie had the time to become seriously ill. It wasn't long before Loretta sang out, "This is Nob Hill. We're almost there."

Isabel's heart sped up as Loretta guided the Runabout—at a furious rate—up another one of San Francisco's steep hills.

Fabulous mansions lined the street. Isabel noted signs that the neighborhood was changing, although not for the worse. The mansions appeared to be giving way to mammoth hotels and businesses, maintaining the same level of luxury, but not in single-family residences. From what Isabel had seen so far, the single-family residences might have housed entire neighborhoods where she came from, but where she came from people didn't have so much money to fritter away.

The landscaping everywhere was magnificent. The entire hill breathed lavishness and extravagance. It boggled Isabel's mind that a mere six years earlier, most of the city had been demolished during that tremendous earthquake and fire. Once again she hoped she and Eunice would be spared earthquakes.

"Here we are!" Loretta called out cheerfully.

She turned the wheel sharply, sending everyone in the automobile sliding sideways, and the Runabout screeched into a long, curved drive and pulled to a stop under a portcullis. A uniformed attendant darted to the automobile and opened first Loretta's door, then Marjorie's, and then Isabel and Eunice's.

Taking a last big breath for courage and silently praying that the audition would not prove to be too humiliating, Isabel stepped out of the machine. Smiling, she took Eunice's hand and helped her with the big step down.

Chapter Eight

Isabel peered up at the building they were about to enter and knew she didn't belong there. Well, perhaps if she were a member of the cleaning staff, she might, but . . . The Fairfield Hotel was perfectly fabulous. And Loretta knew the man who owned it. Isabel wondered if she'd ever get used to traveling in such lofty company.

Loretta, of course, suffered no such qualms as those afflicting Isabel. She fitted in here, as she'd fitted in among *Titanic's* first-class passengers. "Joe's office is on the top floor," Loretta said, as if she visited the man all the time. "But let's wait for Mr. FitzRoy, and we can all go up together."

It wasn't a long wait, and as Isabel watched Somerset's shiny black automobile pull up behind Loretta's, she noted that it was a Maxwell sedan. Unfamiliar with American motorcars, she didn't know if it was as expensive as it looked. Newspapermen must make more money in San Francisco than they did in Upper Poppleton.

Eunice's soft voice wafted up to her, and Isabel bent

slightly to hear her better. "Do you believe this hotel might have electrical lifts, Mama?"

"I don't know, sweetie." Electrical lifts. Good heavens.

"I hope it does."

When she glanced down at her daughter, Isabel recognized the symptoms of extreme excitement. Although Eunice seldom behaved like an ordinary child, because she wasn't one, when she became especially interested in something, she nearly vibrated with energy. She was vibrating now, and Isabel hoped the Fairfield Hotel wouldn't disappoint her.

It didn't. Not only did the four ladies and Somerset get to ride up the entire eighteen floors of an unbelievably posh hotel in an electrical elevator operated by a uniformed young woman with a snooty air about her, but they were all treated as if they belonged there.

Isabel knew that was because they were in the company of Loretta Linden, daughter of a well-known and wealthy San Francisco family, but Eunice thought it was just because people were nice. Isabel hoped she'd never have to learn otherwise.

Mr. Joseph Balderston jumped up from the chair behind his mammoth mahogany desk when his secretary—a female, Somerset noted with interest—announced their arrival. He hurried to greet them with hands outstretched, a broad smile on his smooth-shaven face. His greeting was much more informal than his office, which was furnished in the height of elegance, with crimson brocade wallpaper and an expensive Persian carpet covering the floor from wall to wall.

Somerset was curious to see that Balderston wore no

chin whiskers. A few years earlier, if a man wanted to be taken seriously in the business world, he'd have had to wear a beard. Whiskers were considered old-fashioned nowadays among those who strove to attain a place in society.

Somerset shaved his own face because beards itched and he didn't need to prove anything to anybody, but he had a feeling it was otherwise with Mr. Balderston, who owned and managed the most expensive hotel on the west coast of the United States. Perhaps Mr. Balderston thought it was in his best interest and that of his hotel to follow current modes.

A portly, jovial-looking man in an expensive suit, Balderston left a costly Cuban cigar smoldering in the tray on his polished mahogany desk. Although he didn't indulge in cigars himself, Somerset could detect the differences in tobaccos, as he could recognize different varieties of many other plants. Mr. Balderston smoked only the best, it would seem.

"Come in! Come in! Loretta, it's good to see you again. It's been years."

"Not that long, surely. My parents came here for my father's birthday party last month. I saw you then."

Balderston laughed merrily. "Making a liar of me, are you, Loretta Linden? Why, if that isn't just like you, I don't know what is!"

"Fiddlesticks." But Loretta laughed.

They shook hands all around, and Balderston gestured them into several deep, plush chairs facing his desk. "And which one of these young ladies is our dancer?"

Somerset thought he was joking at first, and considered it a poor joke. Eunice was six years old. And poor Marjorie MacTavish was clearly not the type of female who could take the stage and make a audience do anything but yawn. Isabel, on the other hand . . . well, *there* was a different story.

As he glanced at her now, he saw a lovely woman of average height, although that was the only thing average about her. She had a glow to her. A radiance. And her coloring was so marvelous, too. That beautiful, thick blond hair and those smashingly gorgeous blue eyes. Somerset still hadn't hit upon a flower that did Isabel's eyes justice. A *Laurentia fluviatilis,* perhaps. Or a deep blue *Ranunculacae.* The flower of the *Borago officinalis,* maybe. Well, he'd keep thinking.

Loretta said, "Isabel Golightly is our dancer, Joe. Her family has a long history with the British theater."

Balderston seemed to have forgotten which woman was which, because his gaze was bouncing between Isabel and Marjorie when Isabel solved his puzzlement for him by speaking. Somerset could scarcely believe it. Imagine not being able to tell, upon first being introduced, that Isabel was the one who belonged in the spotlight. Balderston must be as thick as a plank. Surprising in a man who operated such a flourishing business.

"I wouldn't go that far," Isabel said, clearly embarrassed. "It's only that my aunt and uncle taught me the modern ballroom dances."

"Well, that's good, because that's exactly what we're looking for here at the Fairfield, Miss."

"Missus," murmured Isabel. "Mrs. Golightly."

"Good name for a dancer, Golightly." Balderston grinned broadly, pleased with his own attempt at humor.

"Perhaps you could explain to us exactly what a dancer at the Fairfield will be expected to do, Joe." Loretta spoke in a no-nonsense voice that took Somerset aback slightly. He'd never heard her in business mode before, although he guessed she'd have to be pretty authoritative if she managed all the causes and committees she talked about.

She went on, "Mrs. Golightly has a little girl whom you've met, Eunice here, who will be in school during the day. I presume that Isabel will be dancing at night, but she doesn't want to completely lose track of her child."

"Of course, of course. Dancing in our dining room starts at eight p.m., and continues until one o'clock in the morning. Our dancers give a dance demonstration at nine-thirty p.m. and another one at midnight, and they dance with the guests and socialize in between the demonstrations. Only occasionally, guests will need a fourth for bridge. Do you play bridge, Mrs. Golightly?"

"Bridge?" Isabel's face assumed a troubled expression. "Er . . ."

"I'll teach you," Somerset offered, surprising himself.

Balderston frowned a bit. "Our guests would prefer someone skilled in the game."

"Is knowledge of bridge a necessity?" Loretta asked sharply.

Balderston shrugged. "I don't suppose so."

"Then perhaps Isabel can learn as she dances. Surely people are more interested in dancing than playing cards. It's too dark in the dining room for a decent game of cards, anyway." Loretta sat back in her chair, as if pleased to have taken care of that obstacle.

Somerset heard Isabel clear her throat softly, and saw her sit up straighter. "I'm sure I can learn the card game, Mr. Balderston. I've always been good at cards. My uncle and aunt and I used to play whist sometimes."

"Isn't whist akin to bridge?" Somerset asked eagerly,

culling from a memory nearly lost in the convolutions of his brain. "It will be a snap to teach Mrs. Golightly bridge." Provided he could remember the game himself. Somerset wasn't much of a card-player.

Balderston nodded, as if he'd let bridge-playing slide for the nonce.

Again Isabel spoke. "What types of dances do you expect your dancers to know, Mr. Balderston?"

He waved a plump hand in the air breezily. "Oh, all the latest. The fox trot. Ragtime. Waltzes, polkas, schottisches, the usual. People have been requesting the Peabody lately, and the Lambeth Stroll, and the Castle Walk, of course. That's very popular."

Isabel nodded. "I see."

She seemed relieved, although Somerset didn't know why. He learned a second later.

"And the tango." Balderston squinted doubtfully at Isabel. "Can you tango, Mrs. Golightly? The dance has taken San Francisco by storm."

She swallowed. "Er . . . yes, I can tango."

Balderston's doubtful expression vanished. "Excellent! That's excellent. Then let us retire downstairs to the dining room. Jorge will join us there."

"And who, pray tell, is this Jorge character?" Somerset hadn't meant to ask the question in exactly that way.

"Jorge Luis Savedra," Balderston elaborated.

Loretta turned to him with a slight frown marring her vivid countenance. "I thought we already discussed that. He's the male dancer who works here."

Feeling a good deal sillier than was comfortable, Somerset sat up straighter. "Well, yes, but who *is* he? I mean, is he a gentleman of character? I'm sure you don't want to risk Mrs. Golightly's reputation."

Silence filled the luxurious office as they all stared at him. Defensively, he said, "Well, we don't, do we?"

Balderston rose from the chair behind his desk and smiled at Somerset. "Don't worry about Jorge, Mr. FitzRoy. Mrs. Golightly's reputation will be safe with him."

"Good." Somerset stood, too, and pulled his coat tails down with a jerk. He couldn't recall the last time he'd been this embarrassed. And for what?

Damned if he knew. All he knew was that suddenly, as he listened to Joseph Balderston and thought about Isabel Golightly dancing with this Jorge character—not to mention countless male guests of the Fairfield Hotel, night after night for the foreseeable future—he had felt an intense compulsion to make certain she was protected.

That, or knock somebody's block off.

Isabel was still nervous—indeed, she was even more nervous than before—when Mr. Balderston led them into his own private lift operated by his own private elevator operator and connected to his big, elegant office. She glanced down to make sure Eunice was appreciating this, her second ride in an electrical elevator, in one day.

She was. Her big brown eyes gleamed like polished agates, and her step fairly bounced. "I hope you get to work here, Mama," she whispered.

"So do I, sweetie." But she didn't, really. What she wished was that she was rich and didn't have to work anywhere at all. What she was, was scared.

"I want to be an elevator operator when I grow up," Eunice announced in a whisper.

Blessing her for providing a distraction, Isabel laughed softly. "I thought you wanted to be a journalist and a biologist."

"Those, too."

They left the elevator, and Balderston guided them down a long hallway. He pushed a door open, stepped aside, and they all entered the dining room.

Isabel tried to suppress her gasp of pleasure as she imagined herself dancing amid all of this opulence. She had just formed a mental image of herself swirling about the large dance floor in the arms of a refined gentleman with waxed mustaches to the tune of a lively waltz, when another door burst open, and a man who was the epitome of the cinematic Latin-lover type thrust himself into the room.

"Ah," cried Balderston, "there you are, Jorge."

As the two men charged towards each other and greeted one another with hearty handshakes, Balderston with a huge smile and Jorge with an insolent smirk, Isabel watched with interest tainted by apprehension. Balderston she'd already pegged as big and boisterous and rather taken with himself and his position as proprietor of this grand hotel. Isabel figured she might have to avoid his advances, but that he'd probably accept a rebuff with good humor.

Jorge was another matter entirely. The man reeked of vanity and self-importance. His wasn't a particularly imposing physique, being slender as a reed, although he was tall enough to make a decent partner for her. Isabel herself was approximately five feet, four inches tall, and she preferred dancing with men who didn't tower over her. Offhand, and at first glance, she couldn't see anything else about Savedra that inspired her to believe they'd make a comfortable couple. He didn't look the sort who would accommodate a partner readily. He'd want the limelight at all times.

But that wasn't the point. The point was that if they looked well together and didn't actually trip over each other's feet, Isabel might have found herself a job. And, what's more, it was a job doing something she enjoyed, which would be a pleasant change, especially as this was a first-rate hotel. She doubted that the male guests would be inclined to pinch her bottom, as they might do in a lower-class establishment. Of course, she didn't actually *know* that. But she had confidence in her ability to take care of herself.

Because she was making herself nervous, she left off watching Savedra and Balderston and surveyed her surroundings. They were truly something.

The place was breathtaking, even now, with chairs stacked upside down on the tables and a cleaning crew puttering about with mops and rags. A crystal chandelier glittered like the sun over the dance floor, which was polished parquet and gleamed like gold. When Uncle Charlie had been teaching Isabel the steps to various dances, she'd learned them to Uncle Charlie's singing in her own small parlor at her home in Upper Poppleton, which would fit quite nicely into this one room. The home, not the parlor.

"Our guests enjoy the finest dining and wining," Balderston said, laughing with gusto at his little witticism, as he led a surly-looking Jorge Luis Savedra up to the quintet waiting for him. Isabel noticed that Loretta, Marjorie, Eunice, Somerset, and herself had formed a huddle. Maybe she wasn't the only one who was nervous.

"And we have a first-class dance band to entertain our guests before, during, and after their meals,"

Balderston went on. "Our guests expect only the best, and that's what we deliver."

That excluded her, Isabel thought grimly. But she wouldn't let Loretta down for anything, so she vowed to do her best.

"Anyone who works for the Fairfield has to be top of the line. Our guests expect nothing less."

"I," declaimed Jorge, thumping himself on the chest, "am the best."

"You sure are, Jorge!" Balderston cried, slapping the dancer on the back and sending him staggering several steps forward. Jorge caught himself and glared at Balderston, who didn't notice.

Rubbing his hands together, Balderston said, "As soon as Hank gets here, we can begin." He turned to the huddled group. "Hank's our piano player. He doesn't generally play for the dancers. He's in the bar. But since I didn't want to get the whole band here for this audition, Hank agreed to play."

Feeling about two inches tall, Isabel tried to remain serene when Balderston pinned her with a smile that showed no mercy. She knew, because she'd seen that look on other people's faces, that he was willing to give her a chance to prove herself, but he wasn't going to hire her for friendship's sake. If she couldn't pass his test, she'd . . . she'd . . . well, she wasn't sure what she'd do. Train for a nurse, perhaps.

"I'm sure Isabel won't disappoint you," Loretta said bracingly, for Isabel's sake. Isabel appreciated it.

"Huh," said Luis with a sneer that would do a dyed-in-the-wool villain proud.

"My mother is an excellent dancer," Eunice piped up, nettled by Jorge's skepticism. Isabel took her hand, just in case.

"Is that so, little lady?" Balderston patted Eunice on

the head. Eunice stiffened. "Well, that's just swell, that is."

Isabel prayed that Eunice, who was usually well-behaved but had never been patted on the head like that before, would remain polite.

Eunice didn't have time to disappoint her mother, even if she'd had the inclination, because the door opened again and a middle-aged black man with a slight limp and a huge smile entered the room. "I'm here," he called cheerily.

Jorge's sneer got bigger.

"Good, good," bellowed Balderston.

Hank headed over to the piano without waiting to see if he'd be introduced. He didn't anticipate an introduction, Isabel saw at once. He knew his place, as she'd known hers for years until she'd made this mad dash to America, where everything she thought she knew about social positions was being knocked cock-eyed.

Her heart started hammering like crazy when Loretta reached for Eunice's hand and murmured, "Come with me, dear."

As her friends and her daughter deserted her, Isabel was left on the dance floor with Balderston and Jorge Luis Savedra. Balderston took a couple of steps back, off the parquet flooring, and Jorge, with two giant but exquisitely graceful steps, loomed in front of her. He bowed and held out a hand, and his face didn't so much as crack a grin. In fact, his expression reminded Isabel of a locked door.

"Start with a waltz, Hank," Balderston said.

"Sure thing, boss."

And as Isabel took Jorge's hand and offered him a pretty curtsy, the opening bars of "The Merry Widow Waltz" filled the room.

How appropriate, Isabel thought insanely. And then

she melted into Jorge's arms and he swirled off with her.

She was stiff at first, until she and Jorge found each other's rhythm, and then they danced as a unit. He was wonderful. So was she. Together they fairly floated across the floor. Isabel's heart rose. She knew they were meant to dance together. How strange. She didn't even like the man, yet they might have been created to dance with each other.

"Good, good!" Balderston called out after a minute or so.

Jorge whirled her one last time and they stopped. Applause rippled from their tiny audience. Isabel gave Jorge a grateful smile, but he only nodded curtly. Oh, well.

"Let's try a fox trot next," said Balderston.

Hank instantly played the opening bars of "I'm Always Chasing Rainbows." Again Jorge bowed and Isabel curtsied. And then he bounced her off in a lively fox trot.

Isabel absolutely loved to dance. That she might actually be able to dance for a living almost made her stumble, but Jorge's frown and her own ambition made her cover the mistake with a flair. She was proud of herself. A glance at her partner told her that he wasn't proud of her. Or anyone else in the world but himself. Well, that was all right. He danced like an angel, and if he was a devil instead, so be it.

Balderston ended the dance earlier this time. "Good," he said, sounding pleased. Isabel hoped she wasn't hallucinating that part. "Now how about a polka?"

From Jorge's sneer, Isabel deduced he considered the polka beneath him, but she rather enjoyed a lively polka. Jorge made her work for this one. Once Hank began playing "The Fire Brigade Polka," and they established their partnership, he led her into a series of flourishes that left her breathless.

But she enjoyed herself hugely. And that was in spite of Jorge's animosity—if that's what it was. Isabel couldn't tell. Perhaps he disdained anyone who hadn't proved herself as worthy to dance with him. She hoped she'd qualify, mainly because it would make her job more enjoyable, but she wouldn't repine if he never warmed to her. As long as they could dance this well together, all would be well. She hoped.

"Splendid!" This time Balderston clapped, too. "I'm sure you two can perform an admirable schottische. I'd like to see you do something to ragtime, though."

"I'm in my element now," Hank said with a wink for Isabel.

Now Hank, unlike Jorge, was gloriously likable. His fingers picked out the opening bars of "That Hindu Rag," and Jorge and she leaned toward each other and took off dancing. Isabel loved ragtime. The music always sounded happy, and it made her happy. It didn't seem to have the same effect on Jorge as it did on her, but she presumed he wasn't as bored as he looked. It would be difficult to be bored while dancing to a ragtime melody.

"Good, good!" Balderston called out after a minute or so. "You two look very good together. Now let's try the tango."

Oh, Lord. This was the one Isabel had been trying not to think about. The tango was so . . . so . . . sensual. So voluptuous. So . . . entangling. The dance was scandalous, was what it was, and Isabel had never even dreamed of dancing it with anyone except her paunchy uncle Charlie, who was a hundred and ninety years old if he was a day.

That, however, was not the point, she reminded her-

self once more. The point was that she had to tango
with Jorge right this minute, for the sake of herself and
her daughter. He did look the part. A good deal more
than she did, if it came to that.

Hank struck a chord and Jorge turned so that his
shoulder was to her. Isabel sucked in a deep breath and
turned so that her shoulder was aligned with his. He
took her hand in one of his and placed his other hand
on her waist—low on her waist. Practically on her hip,
for heaven's sake. Then he looked down his nose at her
as if he intended to eat her for dinner. He was absolutely perfect for the role of a Latin lover.

That being the case, and because Isabel really, really
needed this job, she gazed up at him as if she aimed to
marinate herself in chocolate in order to make his meal
more interesting. Hank hit the piano keys, beginning a
tune that Isabel later learned was "La Chitita," in an
Argentine rhythm that all but smoldered. They were off
across the dance floor, virtually pressing their bodies together and staring into each other's eyes with hot intensity.

Isabel knew that anyone watching would see two
people who looked as if they were madly in love with
each other, or at least madly lusting after each other.
Jorge was *so* good at this. She could do no less than
prove herself worthy of him. It was a pity he was such a
crosspatch. Ah, well, perhaps Somerset could dance.

Now where, she wondered, had that thought come
from?

Before she figured it out, Jorge dipped her as low as
she'd ever been dipped in her life, turned her in a tight
circle, flung her away from himself whilst maintaining
his grip on her hand, then drew her to him and pressed
her close, and then, in one last, passionate flourish,

dropped to one knee and deposited her on his leg as Hank's piano crashed to a stop.

Before Isabel had caught her breath, Jorge dumped her off his knee and tossed her hand away. "She'll do," he said.

Well, how nice.

She didn't have a chance to think about it because Balderston and all of her friends, and Eunice, leapt to their feet and roared their appreciation. Even Hank, sitting on the piano bench and grinning from ear to ear, clapped.

Balderston thundered toward her, bringing to her mind the image of a charging elephant. "Wonderful! You two are perfect together! I've never seen Jorge look better."

Jorge, who had marched off a few yards, folded his arms across his chest, and taken to staring at the far wall, glanced over his shoulder, his eyebrows drawn into a vee of disapproval. "Huh!"

"Thank you," Isabel said, short of breath. It had been a long time since she'd done that much dancing.

"You two will be the rage of San Francisco before the week's out!" declared Balderston. "When can you start?"

Loretta rushed up to her. "Oh, Isabel! I had forgotten you were so talented. You were *wonderful!*"

"Thank you," panted Isabel.

"She can't start until next week," Loretta announced.

"Next week?" Balderston frowned, but not heavily. Isabel decided to let him and Loretta battle for her time. She still had to catch her breath.

"Mama, that man dances better than Uncle Charlie."

Laughing, Isabel picked up her daughter and hugged her hard. "Yes, he does, doesn't he?"

"I must say, that was beautifully done," said Marjorie MacTavish, who had joined Isabel and the rest of them on the dance floor. "I don't believe I've ever seen a more impressive performance."

Her heart full of love for her newfound friends, even the usually stiff and aloof Marjorie, Isabel gushed, "Thank you very much, Marjorie."

The only one of her friends who didn't appear to be ecstatic for her was Somerset. He walked over to the group, but he didn't smile. She glanced at him expectantly, hoping for a compliment, although she knew she shouldn't expect one. After all, he was a *very* new friend, and a gentleman, too. Perhaps he didn't feel comfortable making flowery speeches about her audition, even though it had been spectacular, if she did say so herself. Because she wanted to know what he'd thought of her talents, she lifted her brows at him.

He cleared his throat. Isabel smiled harder.

Loretta said, "You simply must teach Marjorie and me how to dance like that, Isabel. Not that we can ever be as good as you, but I'd love to learn the steps."

"I'll be happy to," Isabel said, waiting for Somerset to speak.

"I've never danced very much before," admitted Marjorie. "It looks like an enjoyable exercise."

"Oh, it is," Isabel assured her, still waiting.

"Mama taught me how to dance," Eunice announced proudly.

"Yes, I did, and you're very graceful." Isabel hugged her daughter. And waited.

"I must say you're much better than Jorge's old partner," said Balderston.

"Thank you." Isabel felt herself blush. And she waited.

"That one," said Jorge, referring to his old partner

and flipping his hand in a dismissive gesture, "she was a spotted cow."

"Oh." Isabel didn't know what else to say to that comment, although she had a response all ready for Somerset when he bestowed his own compliments upon her.

"I wouldn't go *that* far," said Balderston. "But Mrs. Golightly is definitely better."

"Thank you." Wondering what was taking him so long, Isabel peeked at Somerset. She was surprised to find him scowling hideously. "Why, Mr. FitzRoy, whatever is the matter?"

"Nothing." Somerset still scowled, though, and he turned and took a few steps away from her.

Puzzled, Isabel put Eunice down and exchanged a glance with Loretta, who shrugged.

Suddenly Somerset turned and stared straight at Isabel. "I think you'd be better off cleaning houses."

Chapter Nine

"I'm glad you're speaking to me again."

"Don't be silly, Mr. FitzRoy. I wasn't angry with you."

"You had every right to be." Somerset gestured at a bare spot in Loretta's garden. "What about right over there?"

It was four days after Isabel's audition at the Fairfield Hotel, and Somerset had come over to study Loretta's grounds with an eye to landscape design. He had asked Isabel to help him and was surprised when she'd agreed. He had rather expected her to decline to see him. Slam the door in his face, even, because of his inappropriate comment after her audition at the Fairfield.

But dash it, he'd almost suffered a spasm—if men did things like that—when that filthy Argentinean had stared into her eyes and pulled her so close to him that they might have been glued together. The tango was a shocking dance, and Somerset didn't approve of it. Oh, he supposed it might be fine, if one were married to one's partner, but to dance like that with a stranger . . .

"I don't know," said Isabel, shading her eyes and squinting into the setting sun and interrupting Somerset's train of thought. "What exactly *is* a *Yucca brevifolia*? I don't think we have them in England."

"I'll have to show you." Somerset congratulated himself on suggesting a cactus garden. He'd pored over all of his botanical books and, while he had discovered that there was a burgeoning movement to import cacti to Great Britain, he hadn't found any references to *Yucca brevifolia* growing there. Ergo, he had decided to plant a back border of them. "We should take a day trip to Golden Gate Park. There are lots of them there."

"I'd love to see it, and I know Eunice would, too. We've driven past the park several times. It's huge."

"Perhaps we can visit the park on a Saturday afternoon."

As he expected, Isabel turned to see where her daughter was. Also as he expected, Eunice, wearing trousers this evening, and with her blond hair plaited into two long braids, sat cross-legged under a big incense cedar tree, reading a book by the light of the fast-fading sun. It wasn't just any book, either. It was *Adventures of Huckleberry Finn*. And the kid was only six years old.

"We will definitely take Miss Eunice with us. It will be an educational experience for her." Not that she needed it.

"And Miss Linden and Miss MacTavish, too? I know Miss MacTavish is interested in the park."

"Why not?" For a second or two there, Somerset had envisioned a pleasant day in the park with Isabel and Eunice. He should have known better. With a sigh, he walked a few feet farther away from Loretta's back porch. "I really am sorry about what I said at the Fairfield."

"Please don't think any more about it, Mr. FitzRoy. I

understand that the tango can seem . . . um . . . surprising when one first witnesses it being performed."

Surprising was one word for it. It wasn't the word Somerset would have chosen. Shameful, perhaps. Iniquitous. Deplorable. Fascinatingly decadent. Because he didn't want to lose her good opinion, if she had one, he refrained from saying so, contenting himself with a mere, "Ah."

He heard her sigh and wondered if it had been a happy sigh or a sorrowful one. She didn't seem particularly distressed about having to dance the tango in public with that slimy foreign fellow for pay. Rather, she seemed more pleased than anything, probably because she wasn't faced with the prospect of working as a scrubwoman.

Somerset guessed he could understand that. He didn't like it, though. In fact, if she were Somerset's sister or wife, he'd be inclined to grab her by the shoulders and shake her until her teeth rattled and her senses cleared, and then demand that she take a course in nursing or something that was at least respectable.

He supposed he had Loretta Linden to thank for the fact that Isabel found nothing innately unrespectable about dancing for a living. Damned free-thinking women. There ought to be a law.

Loosening his grip on his pencil for fear it might snap, he controlled his profound outrage and spoke mildly. "Do you think Miss Linden likes roses?" He turned another page over in his sketchbook, gazed appraisingly at the large, unbroken expanse of green grass, and tapped his teeth with the pencil, which was enduring a lot of abuse this evening.

It was difficult to dislike Loretta Linden, even though she was a bad influence on Isabel. Somerset had to admit that she seemed to be a friendly, caring person. And she was doing all she could to help her new friends. He supposed she shouldn't be held accountable if one of her friends had selected a career of which he didn't approve. The world was changing too blasted fast for his comfort, and he should probably attempt to update his attitudes. They were, after all, twelve years into the twentieth century.

As soon as he thought about modernizing his thinking, his mind's eye featured Isabel and Jorge Luis Savedra locked in the tango's scandalous embrace, and his teeth started grinding again.

"I don't know," said Isabel thoughtfully, making Somerset's brain swerve back to the matter at hand. "I should think so. I don't know anyone who doesn't like roses." Isabel rolled up the tape measure with which she'd measured space for a garden shed. "She's out tonight at a meeting, so I won't be able to ask her about it until she gets back."

"Is the woman ever at home?" Somerset asked, nettled. It was bad enough that Loretta was having such a drastic effect on Isabel; he couldn't imagine anyone with this fabulous house being so uninterested in its decoration. Especially when her frequent absences were due to such unfeminine things as attending suffrage rallies and so forth. Why, the woman even orated on street corners, for the love of God. He'd only read about people like Loretta before he met her. He'd disapprove of her even more if he didn't like her so well. She was a bad influence on Isabel, though. He was sure of it.

Isabel, however . . . well, she was a perfect woman, in Somerset's estimation. This evening she wore a plain dark plaid skirt and a white shirtwaist with a little plaid bow at the throat. Her hair had been raked away from her face and twisted into a knot that she'd pinned at the back of her head. She looked more like a school-marm than a woman who danced the tango with a strange and unwholesome foreigner for a living.

"She's quite the gadabout." Isabel laughed indulgently, again jerking Somerset's attention away from his brooding thoughts. "But she's so interested in so many things, and she never participates in anything simply for pleasure. The causes she propounds are all for the public good."

Somerset almost snorted, but turned it into a sneeze in the nick of time.

Isabel continued, "She loves her house and truly wants the grounds to be beautiful. It's only that she doesn't consider herself artistic. She's depending on you for the artistry, or so she says."

"Hmm. I guess that makes sense. Better to rely on someone you trust than to depend on your own judgment if it tends toward gold brocade and crimson velvet."

"That sounds garish."

"It is."

"I don't think Loretta's taste is that theatrical."

"Perhaps not." He was still faintly irked with Loretta, however. Somerset had been doing his very best work in the landscaping plans for her back yard and garden, but he could never find the dashed woman at home.

He'd come, thanks to a written invitation from Loretta herself, to dinner tonight with the express intention of working on his plans with her afterwards. Yet it was now afterwards, and there was no Loretta to say yea or nay to anything.

Ah, well, at least he was here with Isabel. Life could be worse. He set pencil to paper and began to draw, putting his vision for her yard down in his sketchbook.

As he drew, he continued to talk to Isabel. "Has Eunice started going to school yet?"

"Yes. Loretta has a friend, Miss Pinkney, who runs a Montessori School, and she enrolled Eunice there."

Somerset frowned over his sketch. "I've never heard of a—what did you call it?"

"A Montessori School. Named for Maria Montessori, who has developed a new and modern method of education." Isabel gestured vaguely as if she wasn't sure exactly what the new method entailed.

"Oh. Well, that's good, I guess. I've never heard of one before."

"I hadn't, either, but Eunice seems to be thriving."

"She likes it there?" he asked as he drew.

"She loves it." Isabel paused, then said, "She still has terrible nightmares, though." She shot a swift glance at her daughter, who was lost in her book. "About the sinking, you know. It has affected her profoundly."

Somerset glanced up from his drawing and shot a peek at Eunice. "I'm sorry to hear that. I have to admit that I've had a few bad moments myself ever since."

"So have I. I think even Loretta is bothered by bad dreams sometimes."

"I expect we all relive that night occasionally."

With a sigh, Isabel said, "Yes." After a short pause, she said, "But at least Eunice is enjoying school. She's made friends, too, which is very important, I think."

"Very important indeed." He wasn't sure if he'd just lied or not. There seemed to be too dashed many modern ideas floating around in this particular Russian Hill abode for his peace of mind.

"I suppose so." Isabel sighed softly. "As for me, I sometimes I wonder if I'll ever have control over my life again."

Somerset glanced sharply at her, surprised by her words. Yet, after thinking about them for only a moment, he understood. "At least Miss Linden is a kind-hearted person and doesn't expect you to do her bidding in order to earn her goodwill."

"Oh, yes. She's very generous. And it's not that I'm ungrateful . . ."

"You needn't say anything more. I know exactly what you mean. It's hard to accept help sometimes."

"You can say that again. Loretta's been an angel."

Somerset wouldn't go *that* far. "I hope she likes my plans."

"I don't know how she could not like them. They're beautiful."

That pleased him. "Thank you." He was relatively certain that Loretta would agree. She didn't seem all that interested in how the work got done or what work *was* done, as long as something happened to her grounds and the end result looked good. After having known her for a few weeks, Somerset agreed with Loretta on her artistic talents. For all her qualities that were so greatly valued by her friends—and even Somerset, if he wanted to be honest—from what he'd been able to gather thus far, she didn't have an artistic bone in her body.

All of a sudden, Isabel said, "You know what I'd really like to do?"

Again, Somerset stopped sketching and looked at her. "No," he said, praying that whatever it was didn't include dancing the tango with Jorge Savedra, "please tell me."

Color crept into Isabel's cheeks, painting them the sweet blush of one of Somerset's favorite roses, *Mme. Pierre Oger.* He caught his breath. "What I'd *really* love to do is run a dance academy where young ladies and gentlemen can come and learn the latest dance steps. Before they make their debuts into society, you know. It would be most respectable," she added, sounding adorably stuffy about it.

"My goodness." Somerset never would have guessed. Operating a respectable dance academy sounded better to him than dancing with hundreds of strange men at the Fairfield. "Let me know if there's anything I can do to help you achieve your goal, Mrs. Golightly."

Mme. Pierre Oger gave way to the deeper, more embarrassed tint of *Baronne Prèvost*. "Thank you. You're too kind to me. Everyone's too kind to me."

"Nonsense."

Somerset gestured with his sketch book, hoping to relieve Isabel's embarrassment. "I can appreciate Miss Linden's interest in saving the world from itself, but I wish she'd at least *look* at my plans one of these days."

She accepted the change of subject with good grace. "She will. Don't worry." Isabel laughed again. She had a musical laugh, and Somerset was glad he'd coaxed it out into the open. "She's a very busy person and belongs to a lot of organizations. Tonight she's at a suffrage rally at the city hall. She's hoping to be arrested."

"Dear God."

"It's for a good cause," Isabel said, sounding sure of herself.

"Do you really think so?"

"Well . . . yes, I do." She lifted her chin. "I know I'm British and not even an American citizen, but the struggle is going on in Great Britain, too. In fact, Loretta was on her way back to San Francisco from meeting with the leading British suffragists when the *Titanic* sank."

"Aha." That was noncommittal enough, Somerset hoped.

Isabel went on, "It's important for women to step up

and demand their rights as human beings on an equal footing with men."

"Of course." Good God, he wasn't going to lose her to a bunch of causes, was he? Not that he had her to lose, but . . . well, he knew what he meant. The notion of Isabel Golightly orating on street corners for women's suffrage was almost as repellent as the notion of her dancing with that dashed foreigner. "Er . . . do you go to suffrage marches and so forth with Miss Linden?"

"Not yet." Isabel lifted her perfect chin. "But I shall. As soon as I have time."

Good. Somerset relaxed. That meant she wouldn't. From his perspective, Isabel had plenty enough to do already, with her job and her motherhood. "I see."

"And I *do* think most women are every bit as smart and capable as most men." She cast another quick look at her daughter.

Somerset knew what she was thinking. It was his turn to laugh. "And some females are smarter and *more* capable·than most men."

With a shrug, Isabel said quietly, "I'll never understand it. No one else in the family is like that."

"Fluke of nature," he said. "Come here and look at this." As they'd chatted, he'd continued to draw, mainly to keep his mind from returning to the mental picture of a blushing Isabel dancing with that Argentine creature. He was happy with the result of his effort and held it out for Isabel's inspection. He watched as she examined the drawing, and was pleased when her lovely blue eyes opened wide.

"Oh, my, it's beautiful! What's this?" She pointed at a portion of the drawing of which Somerset was especially fond.

"I thought the place could use a rose arbor." He

leaned over a trifle, breathing in the faint scent of lemon and ginger. Isabel always smelled wonderful. "I thought the arbor could be a restful place with a garden path strewn with cedar chips and delineated by trellises going through it and benches set here and there."

"It sounds beautiful. Can you imagine the aroma?"

"Miss Eunice would enjoy reading in the rose arbor; I'm sure of it."

"Oh, my, yes." She shook her head, as if in wonder.

"There are some newly developed polyanthas that are excellent when grown on trellises. I think *Cecile Brunner* is a must. You can help me pick some other ones."

"I'd love to. Um . . . what's a polyantha?"

"A type of rose. It has a very strong scent and clusters of tiny flowers. *Cecile Brunner* is pink and has an absolutely perfect shape." Not unlike Isabel, as a matter of fact. "It's a gorgeous rose."

"It sounds perfect."

"We can see that one and others at the park, too. It'll take a squad of gardeners to keep up Miss Linden's grounds once they're replanted, but she told me not to think about that."

Isabel's eyebrows rose over her wonderful blue—perhaps the blue of *Anchusa capensis?*—eyes. Somerset imagined she was thinking how nice it would be to be able to afford a squad of gardeners to tend one's garden.

A disturbance at the back door caught their attention, and they both turned to look. Marjorie MacTavish, bright pink and looking frustrated enough to spit railroad spikes, burst through the door, closely followed by Dr. Jason Abernathy. Somerset grinned, knowing that Jason must have tweaked Miss MacTavish again. She made a splendid target for his sense of humor.

"Marjorie," said Isabel confidentially, watching her friends cross the porch, "is taking a refresher course in typewriting at the YWCA. That stands for Young Women's Christian Association."

Somerset thought Isabel's ignorance of the American idiom was adorable. "I thought there were YWCAs in England."

She considered it. "There might be. I don't know. I don't think there were any in Upper Poppleton."

"Probably not. Is she enjoying her job as Miss Linden's secretary?"

"I believe so. She says she finds the work satisfying."

"Ah. That's good."

"And she's teaching Eunice how to use the typewriting machine, too. Eunice wants to be a journalist, you know. Among other things." She chuckled softly.

"That's right. And an elevator operator."

"And don't forget biology."

"How could I? I remember she told me she wanted to be a biologist when we first met. It's good of Miss MacTavish to teach her." Somerset was pleased to learn that Marjorie MacTavish, who was quiet and withdrawn, except when she was furious at Jason Abernathy, had a softer side. He hadn't anticipated that she'd be good with children, even un-childlike children like Eunice Golightly, but he'd apparently been mistaken.

"She's really awfully nice," Isabel assured him, as if she knew what he'd been thinking. "She takes things very hard, and she's not used to American manners. She also . . . well, I shouldn't talk about that."

"About what?"

She eyed him for a second, then reconsidered her reluctance to speak about Marjorie's problem. "She's quite embarrassed because her ordeal with the *Titanic* has given her a great fear of the water. She's terrified of going to sea again. So, you see, she could no longer be a stewardess and she *had* to find other employment. She's awfully grateful to Loretta."

"Is that so?" Somerset's gaze went from Isabel to Marjorie, still sparring verbally with the doctor on the porch, and he frowned. "I don't think she has anything to be embarrassed about. I should think her fear is only a sensible reaction to a truly terrifying and tragic event."

"It was worse for her than for the rest of us, although Eunice does have those awful dreams, as I told you. But Marjorie lost so many friends and co-workers. She feels it dreadfully."

"I'm surprised we all aren't suffering from various mental problems after that experience. It was the worst thing I've ever been through. Perhaps Miss MacTavish has developed a . . . what do the alienists call them? Phobias? Perhaps she has a phobia."

Isabel narrowed her eyes at him. "Loretta said she had a phobia, too. Exactly what is a phobia, pray tell? Obviously, it's another one of your Latin words, but what does it mean?"

"A phobia is an exaggerated and illogical fear of something. For example, my aunt Greta has a phobia about cats. When she sees a cat, she's terrified. Starts to perspire, mouth gets dry, heart begins pounding out of control. She has to leave wherever she is if the cat stays there. She admits it's not sensible, but she can't help having an inexplicable and overpowering fear of cats."

After thinking about it for a second or two, Isabel said, "Even little house cats?"

"Even little house cats. That's what makes it illogical. But the poor woman isn't faking or joking. She's absolutely terrified of cats."

"Hmmm." Isabel plucked a dead leaf from a nearby

bush. "Well, that's interesting, all right. Overall, I'd say that Marjorie's fear—or phobia, if that's what it is—of the ocean is more logical than a fear of house cats. Lions, I could understand."

Somerset chuckled. "That's what makes it a phobia, I guess. It doesn't make sense."

"I guess." She was silent for another couple of seconds, then said, "Although if Marjorie's problem *is* a phobia, she's probably the only working-class person in the world ever to have one. Most regular people can't afford fancy problems like phobias."

His chuckle turned into a laugh. "That's all too true, I'm afraid."

"I'd better get Eunice inside. It's time for her to wash up for bed."

"Right." Somerset closed his sketch book.

"Eunice! Time to come inside now."

"Yes, Mama." Eunice stood, and Somerset saw that she wore not simple trousers, but an entire Chinese pajama set featuring a mandarin-collared top and trousers in a silky brocade. The fabric was a soft, shimmering peach color, and it flattered Eunice's coloring.

"My, but don't you look swell!" he cried.

Eunice stopped walking, tilted her head to one side, and pinned Somerset with a puzzled frown. "Why, I don't know. Do I?" Accurately interpreting the amused glint in Somerset's eyes, her own countenance cleared. "Oh, you mean I look good."

"Yes, indeed. You look very good."

"Thank you. Miss Linden said I looked like an Oriental empress. I should like to be an empress one day."

"After you finish with biology and journalism?"

"And elevator-operating," Isabel put in.

Eunice nodded. "Yes. Perhaps there's a school that teaches empressing. I should like to learn."

Forcing himself not to laugh, Somerset said, "Well, I do believe you'd be good at the job, Miss Eunice. And I think your Chinese pajamas are lovely."

"Thank you." She brightened still further and trotted up to Somerset and her mother. "Miss Linden got us each a set. Mine is peach-colored; Mama's is blue, to match her eyes; Miss MacTavish's is the color of ivory; and Miss Linden's own set is green."

"Somebody has good color sense," Somerset noted.

"Mama picked out the colors," Eunice said proudly.

"Aha."

Isabel, darling that she was, blushed again, and prompted him to write *Ispahan* in his notebook. Somerset liked the old roses.

They strolled toward the porch, and Somerset tucked his sketch pad under his arm. He could put the rose arbor in the middle of the yard just beyond the porch, and plant fruit trees in the back. That would be nice. And he'd be sure to include several rare and unusual specimens in the cactus garden.

Then, if he could talk Loretta into adding a side patio area, with a woven redwood awning, as he'd seen while visiting a lovely garden in New York City, she would have a showplace she could be proud of. Such a delightful outdoor retreat might also impress the people she invited over for her endless meetings and rallies. Politicians were far more easily swayed by displays of wealth than by fiery rhetoric, mainly because they could bank money. Words just flew into the air and were lost.

By this time, they were close enough to the porch to hear the brangle in progress between Dr. Abernathy and Miss MacTavish.

"I am *not* feeling poorly, thank you," Marjorie said, and it was obvious she was only curbing her temper with difficulty. "I'm feeling perfectly bonny."

"Are you sure? You look mighty pasty-faced to me," said the doctor, lifting his bushy eyebrows in feigned concern. He had great eyebrows for teasing people with. He moved closer to her. "Perhaps you need a thorough physical examination." He took her arm.

"Adone do! Leave off teasing me, you wretched blatherskite. You're embarrassing me."

"But I'm a doctor. I'm supposed to take care of people. I'd be delighted to take care of you." He waggled his eyebrows at her.

"Don't be daft!"

"Perhaps you need a tonic. Or maybe your beautiful, fiery red hair only makes your skin appear paler than it really is."

Her skin wasn't pale any longer. Marjorie had blushed a red that rivaled the sunset. Somerset pulled his notebook out of his pocket and wrote down *Henri Martin.*

Isabel wished the doctor wouldn't tease Marjorie so, because the poor woman never knew how to take it. Instead of giving the doctor as good as she got, she became flustered and upset.

She hurried up to the porch. "Dr. Abernathy!" She spoke loudly, in order to interrupt his flow of nonsense. "How nice to see you this evening."

Marjorie snorted. It was an indication of exactly how perturbed she was, because she was usually the most delicate and well-bred of women, the result of all that training as a White Star stewardess, Isabel felt sure. Funny how Dr. Abernathy could destroy her dignity with only a few words. Isabel suspected that the doctor had an underlying purpose, but she didn't think he was going about it the right way.

Dr. Abernathy bowed politely. "How do you do, Mrs.

Golightly? Loretta invited me over this evening to tell me all about your audition, which I understand went very well." He pulled out an engraved gold watch and squinted at it. "She said she'd be home around seven-thirty, and it's almost seven-thirty now."

"Yes, I believe she'll be home soon, if she doesn't get arrested."

"Arrested!" Dr. Abernathy threw his head back and roared with laughter. After a few moments of that, he mopped his eyes with a hastily retrieved handkerchief and said, "Good old Loretta. She never manages to get herself arrested, no matter how hard she tries, so I suppose she'll be home soon."

"I hope so," said Isabel, trying not to laugh along with him. Loretta's desire to get on the wrong side of the law could be considered amusing, she guessed, although she'd known people aplenty who couldn't *not* get arrested, no matter how hard they tried. Eunice's father sprang to mind. "And thank you, yes, the audition went very well. Marjorie, why don't we go fetch some tea, since I doubt if Li and Molly have finished up in the kitchen yet. And Eunice can run upstairs and wash up for bed."

"Aye," said Marjorie, still bright pink, "We'll do that, and leave the gentlemen to enjoy the sunset."

"Castor oil!" Dr. Abernathy called after the two women. "A dose of castor oil will fix what ails you!"

Somerset and Jason heard Marjorie growl, "Hateful fesart!" before the porch door slammed behind her.

Chapter Ten

Isabel had no idea what a "fesart" was, and she decided it would be best not to ask. She pretended she didn't hear either of them. However, when the doctor shouted, "Wait! Put these in water while you're there!" Isabel gestured for Marjorie to go inside with Eunice, and she returned to the porch to take a small bouquet of flowers from the doctor.

"How pretty," she murmured, lifting them to her nose to sniff.

"Bought 'em off a bum at the foot of Russian Hill," he said indifferently.

"That was kind of you, Dr. Abernathy."

"Hmph." He shrugged.

Isabel found it interesting that Dr. Abernathy was always dismissing his efforts at charity, yet he inevitably showed up everywhere he went after having helped some poor person. And he ran that clinic right in the middle of Chinatown, where he offered free or extremely cheap medical help to the poor people who couldn't afford to go to expensive doctors. She sus-

pected that under his teasing exterior, Dr. Abernathy's
heart was as soft as pulp.

Which meant he was very much like Marjorie, who
did her level best to behave as a proper White Star stewardess at all times, even though she wasn't one any
longer. The notion amused her. Taking the flowers, she
followed Marjorie into the house.

After kissing Eunice good-night, she caught up with
Marjorie. "I'm sure he only teases you because you react
so violently, Marjorie," she ventured delicately.

Marjorie's cheeks, which had lost their color, bloomed
anew. "Bother. How would you like it if someone goaded
you every time he saw you? The man's a haggis-headed
nyaff."

Isabel couldn't help herself. She laughed as she held
the door for Marjorie to enter the pantry before her.
She always showed deference to the former stewardess,
although she wasn't sure why. Probably leftover class
consciousness from her British upbringing. Marjorie
huffed past her into the pantry.

"What in the name of heaven is a haggis-headed
nyaff?"

Marjorie took a deep breath and looked as if she
were trying to calm down. "A very annoying person."

"He said you had beautiful hair," Isabel pointed out.

"Only so he could say I looked sick," Marjorie shot
back. "He called me pasty-faced."

Pressing her lips together so as not to giggle again,
since she didn't want Marjorie to get mad at her, Isabel
said, "I think he doesn't mean to be vile. I think he admires you."

Marjorie stopped so abruptly, Isabel bumped into her
back. "I beg your pardon," she gasped, putting a hand on
Marjorie's shoulder so she wouldn't fall down and holding
the flowers out to the side so they wouldn't get squashed.

Swirling around to look Isabel in the eye, Marjorie's face glowed fiery pink when she spoke. "He admires me, you think? He *admires* me?" She turned and stomped through the swinging door into the kitchen, where Li and Molly were just finishing up the evening-meal dishes. "I'd appreciate it if he didn't show his *admiration* in exactly that way."

In spite of Marjorie's avowed anger, Isabel smiled. Marjorie's Scottish accent became very pronounced when she was incensed, and her Scottish vocabulary popped out. Eunice, who had professed an interest in becoming a linguist one day, had begun collecting Scottish words and phrases. If there was one person guaranteed to provoke Scottishisms from Marjorie MacTavish, it was Dr. Jason Abernathy. Isabel reminded herself to offer *haggis-headed nyaff* to Eunice in the morning. She couldn't remember the other strange word Marjorie had used, unfortunately.

She shooed Li and Molly out of the kitchen when they asked if they could be of service, and put the posy in an old jelly jar she'd filled with water. Deciding the kitchen help needed some brightness in their lives, she put the jelly jar in the kitchen window. It looked pretty there.

Then she and Marjorie prepared a pot of tea. Isabel loved taking tea at Loretta's house, because she had the most beautiful tea things. Loretta's so-called everyday china was more beautiful than any Isabel had ever seen, even in the houses she used to clean in Upper Poppleton, and Loretta had special cups and saucers for when friends came over for tea. Loretta's array of friends comprised about every type of person imaginable, from the politically powerful leaders of San Francisco, to actors and actresses, to temperance workers to a priest and a couple of nuns who ran the soup kitchen Loretta helped support.

No matter who came to tea, the service was magnificent. Tonight, Isabel measured out loose, fragrant oolong tea into a vivid blue teapot with a silver dragon crouching on it. Loretta said she'd bought it in Chinatown, a section of San Francisco Isabel wanted to explore one day. She set out six beautiful blue cups with silver handles on a tray, filled the matching milk pitcher and sugar bowl, set the sugar tongs and tea strainer on the tray, and leaned against the table, waiting for the kettle to boil.

In an effort to soothe Marjorie's jangled nerves, she said, "Mr. FitzRoy's plans for Loretta's grounds are coming right along. Tonight he showed me a sketch for a rose arbor and a cactus garden."

"That sounds nice," said Marjorie in a tight voice.

Isabel looked at her sharply, but Marjorie had turned her back so that Isabel couldn't see her face. "I believe it will be." For a few moments, Isabel watched Marjorie's back. "Is anything the matter, Marjorie?"

Marjorie stood at the stove staring at the kettle and didn't answer. She gave her head a quick shake, but Isabel didn't believe her.

She licked her lips and ventured hesitantly, "Marjorie, I know it's hard, being here in America and having to start over and all."

A choked sniffle answered her, and Isabel's heart hitched. She went to the stove and put a hand on Marjorie's sleeve. "Please, Marjorie, I wish you'd talk to me. If there's anything I can do—"

"Oh, stop it!" Suddenly Marjorie wheeled around to look at Isabel, her face chalk-white, her green eyes brimming. "You're too good, Isabel Golightly! Here you are, a widow with a daughter to care for, and you're fine! I'm all alone with nobody to worry about but myself, and I'm falling apart! And that *man!* I never know what to do when he teases me, and then I feel stupid! I—I—*oh!*"

She collapsed then, right into Isabel's arms. Patting her on the back, Isabel crooned softly, feeling tremendous sympathy for the unhappy woman. "But don't you see, sweetie? That's just the thing. I do have someone, and that's why it's easier for me. If I didn't have Eunice, I'd be a wreck." She didn't actually know that for a fact, but it sounded good when she said it.

"But your life is so hard, and you have to dance at that hotel and rear your daughter and all! You've lost so much more than I have!"

"But I still have Eunice. She's the most precious thing in my life. You've lost everything."

"Codswallop. I'm just so . . . so . . . oh, I don't know. I'm adrad, Isabel. So, so fleesome."

"Um . . . what's *adrad* mean? And *fleesome?*" Isabel hated to break the rhythm, but she needed to know what the problem was is she aimed to help.

"Afraid," Marjorie sobbed. "I'm terrified, Isabel. It's because I'm useless, you see. Utterly, absolutely, useless."

Isabel was honestly shocked. "Never! Why, you're ever so much more capable than I am. You can be a secretary and typewrite and compose letters and use the telephone and do all those useful things. The only thing I'm good for is dancing and cleaning houses."

Pulling away from her as if she didn't believe she deserved being comforted, Marjorie dug in a pocket for a handkerchief, then blew her nose with ferocity. "Nonsense. You're a capable woman, Isabel Golightly, and talented, and you have a beautiful daughter with brains.

I'm . . . I don't know what I am. I'm useless without my profession, and I can't—" She stopped talking and gulped in air. "I just can't do that any longer. Go to sea." She seemed to shrink into herself, and she shivered.

"I know. I'm so sorry."

"Because I'm a worthless goff!" Marjorie said almost hysterically.

"That's not true." Isabel shook her head hard and decided she didn't need to know the exact meaning of *goff.*

"It is, too." Marjorie blew her nose again, a great, honking sound that would have been funny under other circumstances. "Anyone with an ounce of self-respect would have climbed right back aboard the next ship out."

This time it was Isabel who shuddered. "Now, I know that's not true, Marjorie MacTavish. You couldn't get me back on another one of those ocean liners with a winch and a crane."

Frowning as if she didn't believe her, Marjorie said, "Be that as it may, I feel like a piece of dandelion fluff being blown abin and aboot with no purpose or direction, and I feel particularly daft to know that I'm this way because of *fear.* It's unconscionable, the way I'm succumbing to dread of the ocean."

Isabel shook her head in dismay. She was glad that Marjorie had finally taken her into her confidence, but she felt bad that she didn't have any advice to offer. If they'd still been in England, this conversation never would have taken place. Perhaps talking about her problem might at least ease Marjorie's sense of loneliness and isolation. Isabel still felt unhelpful. "I think you're being too hard on yourself, dearie."

The kettle started to sing, and Marjorie grabbed a mitt and lifted it from the flame. Isabel removed the lid from the teapot and Marjorie poured water into it. She replaced the kettle, turned down the fire, and mopped her eyes.

"Are you well enough to return to the porch?" Isabel asked. "I wish Dr. Abernathy wouldn't tease you so, but I honestly think he does it because he fancies you."

"Codswallop. He thinks I'm a stuffy old spinster with no grit." Marjorie blew her nose yet again, stuffed the hankie back into her pocket, and straightened her shoulders. "I may be a useless, contemptible female with no direction in life, but I willna let that man get me down."

"Good," Isabel said with more heartiness than she felt. Knowing her place in the world, even if she was currently residing in America, she picked up the tea tray. She was about to march off with it when Marjorie touched her arm. She set the tray back down and glanced at her.

"Are my eyes too red? Will he be able to tell I've been having exterics?"

Figuring that exterics were probably akin to hysterics, Marjorie's question made Isabel smile. If she could worry about her looks, perhaps all wasn't completely lost. She replied with candor. "Your eyes are a trifle swollen, dearie, but the light is dimming. I doubt that he'll notice anything."

Marjorie sniffed. "He'll probably be too busy thinking of some new way to flummox me."

As she lifted the tray again and headed for the porch, Isabel thought Marjorie was probably right.

Somerset didn't have any trouble at all in persuading Loretta Linden, Marjorie MacTavish, and Dr. Jason Abernathy to accompany him to dinner at the Fairfield

Hotel the night of Isabel's debut as part of the hotel's new dancing pair, Isabel and Jorge, supposedly dancers of international renown.

"They're international, at any rate," muttered Jason.

"And they'll probably acquire some renown once people see them dance together," Loretta said brightly.

She wasn't wearing her spectacles, but had brought them with her so she'd be able to see when Isabel and Jorge took to the dance floor. She held tightly to Jason's arm so she wouldn't bump into anything. Somerset wished she'd just don the specs. She looked quite well in them, and Loretta without her eyeglasses could be dangerous. His foot still hurt where her high heel had come down on it.

"Their first demonstration begins at nine-thirty, doesn't it?" asked Marjorie.

Jason drew out his gold watch, and Somerset held his breath. He understood that Marjorie made a tempting target for his teasing, but he wished Jason would ease up on the woman. According to Isabel, Marjorie, far from being the bland wallflower she presented herself as being, was a good and sensitive soul who was more to be pitied than laughed at. He'd decided to take her word for it, even if she still seemed to him to be aloof and withdrawn.

At the moment, Marjorie gripped her evening hand-bag as if it were her one link to life and kept shooting worried glances at Jason, anticipating an attack. Somerset felt kind of sorry for her. So far, Jason had behaved.

"Yes. So that gives us an hour and a half before they perform." Jason put his watch back and didn't so much as wink at Marjorie. "Should be plenty of time to have dinner and dance a bit."

Marjorie and Loretta were looking lovely this evening. Somerset hadn't believed Marjorie could look so well, actually. Her red hair was dressed in an upsweep and shone like polished copper. Loretta's hair was also dressed prettily. She had thick, dark brown hair, and could, of course, afford to hire the best hair dressers. Somerset assumed she'd strong-armed Marjorie into accepting the services of whichever hair dresser enjoyed her custom. Or perhaps she employed a lady's maid, although that didn't sound like the Loretta Linden he'd come to know.

Their gowns, too, were quite the thing, even though Somerset wasn't quite sure how women managed to get around in the new fashions. Fortunately for an evening intended for dancing, Loretta's free-thinking tendencies had not allowed her to have her dress drawn in so tightly at the ankles that she hobbled when she walked.

Loretta's own gown was a vivid scarlet made from some shimmery fabric that appealed to Somerset's artistic soul. Marjorie, who had always seemed to Somerset a bit of a plain Jane, stood out like a swan among ducks tonight, in a sea-green gown that matched her eyes and made them seem huge. With her red hair and pale skin, she truly looked almost beautiful. Somerset was impressed. Neither Loretta nor Marjorie could hold a candle to Isabel, of course, but they were very attractive women.

The maitre d'hotel bowed low before Loretta's party—Somerset was pretty sure it was Loretta who was being honored since neither he nor Jason had quite enough money to warrant such servility—and smiled. "Your table is awaiting you, mesdames and m'sieurs." His accent was thick enough to spread on toast.

As the maitre d' headed off, followed by Loretta and Marjorie, with Somerset and Jason bringing up the rear, Jason whispered, "Do you think that guy's really French?"

Somerset shrugged. "I haven't the least idea."

Putting a hand on Somerset's arm to slow him down, Jason tipped his head toward the two women preceding them. "They both look quite lovely tonight, don't they?"

"Very. I was just thinking the same thing."

"Wonder if Miss MacTavish will be shocked when she sees Mrs. Golightly take to the floor. Loretta said she and her partner make quite a pair."

Somerset realized he'd started grinding his teeth and stopped. "Yes," he said. "They make quite a pair."

Jason's eyes were twinkling fiendishly when Somerset glanced at him. He said, "What? What's the matter."

"Not a thing, old man. Not a thing. But, you know, sometimes you have to take the bull by the horns."

Stiffening and feeling foolish, Somerset said coldly, "I haven't a notion in the world what you're talking about."

With a "tsk-tsk," Jason propelled his companion along the way, between tables, following the two women as they headed toward a table at the edge of the dance floor. "All I'm saying is that Mrs. Golightly is a lovely young widow, and she deserves better than having to dance the tango with a stranger for a living."

"I agree," Somerset said tersely.

"Then it might be wise to speed up the courtship, old man, or she's liable to be snapped up by someone else. From this night on, she's going to be in a position to be noticed."

The full horror of the doctor's statement brought Somerset to a standstill. He might have stood there gaping indefinitely, but Jason still had a grip on his arm and tugged him forward.

The man was right! Good God above, he was *right!* Not only was Isabel now in a position where she would be noticed by available single men, but she might even be noticed by available *married* men in search of fresh prey. The notion of Isabel becoming the mistress of some philandering San Francisco millionaire made his blood run cold.

"Come, come, old man. It's not that bad." Jason chuckled, as if he'd read Somerset's thoughts and found them amusing. "But I know you tend to be rather focused on your work and forget the social amenities. I don't want you to lose out on a good thing from sheer oversight."

Although Somerset wasn't sure he appreciated Jason's words, he honestly did appreciate having this salient, and heretofore unnoticed by him, fact of life pointed out to him. Therefore, he opted to be grateful and to save his wrath for another purpose. "Thanks, Doctor. I appreciate the tip."

"Thought you might."

They'd reached the table where the maitre d'hotel and Marjorie and Loretta had stopped. Somerset hurried to hold Marjorie's chair, preempting Jason's doing so for fear he might not do it without the accompaniment of a ragging comment. If Jason could abet Somerset in his love life, could Somerset do any less for Jason? He didn't honestly think that teasing a woman to death was the finest example of courtship he'd ever seen. Perhaps he'd drop a hint in the man's ear.

All through the soup course, the conversation was light and breezy. Somerset's thoughts, however, were anything but. He contemplated Isabel Golightly more fervently than he'd done since he'd met her.

During the fish course, he tried to recall every interaction they'd had, starting with that horror of a night on *Titanic*, when he was fortunate enough to be there when Isabel had stumbled. Since Somerset didn't believe in divine intervention, he chalked that circumstance up to chance, but he appreciated it.

Then he contemplated the nature of his feelings for her. He daydreamed about her constantly, true, but was this love? His nose wrinkled as he sipped a pale, dry Chardonnay from a nearby California vineyard.

"Is something the matter, Mr. FitzRoy?"

When Somerset peered at her over his wine glass, Loretta appeared concerned, although that might only be a result of near-blindness. "Not a thing, Miss Linden. In fact, the fish is delicious. So is this wine."

She leaned forward a trifle. "That's from a vineyard owned by a friend of mine, Lucy Magdalena. I had to twist Joseph's arm before he'd try it, but even he now admits that Lucy's wines are superb."

The notion of a woman operating a functioning vineyard so surprised Somerset that thoughts of Isabel slipped into the distance for a couple of seconds. "Does she run the place alone?" he asked, astounded.

Loretta lifted her chin. "Her brothers help."

"Ah." That made more sense. Somerset couldn't feature a female actually running a business. She probably kept the books or typed letters or something.

"But," Loretta said, cutting into his thoughts rather loudly, "Lucy runs the business. Tony and Sam are only the brawn."

"Oh." If Loretta was correct, that shot his assumptions about a woman running a business right out of the sky. Somerset decided not to believe her quite yet, and his mind wandered back to Isabel.

Love. Did he love Isabel?

His nose wrinkled again, but he managed to subdue it before Loretta noticed. He supposed he did, actually, although love seemed rather an unmasculine thing to succumb to.

Did love matter? He admired her tremendously. He liked her very well indeed. He found her almost too attractive. In fact, when he was in her company, his juices tended to flow a trifle too freely.

Which made him think about that filthy Argentine fellow and all the men who would be holding her in their arms this evening, and his teeth began grinding again. As luck would have it, the waiter had just served the roasted lamb, and he chewed on that while he contemplated Isabel dancing with a horde of randy strangers.

He came to the conclusion that love was an unnecessary frivolity and that he needn't think about it. Somerset had seen many happy marriages in which the partners didn't fawn over one another. His parents sprang to mind. The notion of his mother and father canoodling boggled his mind, actually, although they must have been intimate a couple of times, at least, or Somerset and his sister wouldn't have been born. Still, one could be married and preserve the proprieties.

Anyhow, Isabel had been married once. Surely if she *had* wanted the trappings of love and romance, she'd got that out of her system by this time. Somerset, who knew himself to be somewhat stodgy at times, and who also knew that he could more easily get lost in a garden than in a swashbuckling adventure story, prayed that she wasn't looking for dash, because he didn't have any.

Oh, he knew all the stories told about devil-may-care journalists who tracked down stories and got involved in exciting undertakings like wars and rebellions and so forth, but he wrote a gardening column, for God's sake. The idea of him, Somerset FitzRoy, fending off foes with sword or pistol might have made him laugh if he'd been alone. As it was, he peered around the table to make sure no one was watching him. He'd forgotten he was in company. Jason winked at him, and Somerset tried to pull his mind back to the here and now.

"This is a wonderful salad," he said, to make them think he'd been paying attention.

When Jason rolled his eyes and Marjorie and Loretta looked only confused, he guessed he'd tipped his hand. He took another bite of salad to prove that he wasn't *totally* unaware of his company and smiled generally.

"Yes," said Marjorie. "It's very tasty."

Somerset managed to get through the rest of the dinner without too many more social blunders by making a great effort to remain in the here and now. His problem, he decided, was that he was liable to go off on tangents while he was in the company of others. If he intended to ask for Isabel's hand in marriage, he needed to stop being so absent-minded.

When the dance band started playing, his heart sped up and he took out his pocket watch and squinted at it. A quarter past the hour. Only fifteen minutes left, and he'd get to see Isabel again. Hold her in his arms, even, if he could fend off the hordes of other men with similar intentions.

"Would you care to dance, Miss MacTavish?" Jason asked.

Somerset's attention immediately focused on Marjorie, who shrank back against her chair and peered at Jason as if he were the devil incarnate. This reaction only tickled Jason, of course. He said, "I promise I won't stick pins in you."

Her cheeks seemed to catch fire, and she muttered, "Don't be daft."

"Wouldn't dream of it." Jason reached over, took Marjorie's hand, and fairly dragged her out of her chair and over to the dance floor.

With a laugh, Loretta said, "Oh, dear, I hope those two will start getting along one of these days."

"I do, too." Somerset shook his head. "I'm not sure why he torments her so."

"Isabel claims it's because he fancies her. And she might be right. I've never known him to treat anyone else like that, and I've known him all my life."

Following the direction of Loretta's glance, Somerset saw that, so far, Jason and Marjorie were waltzing with great propriety and a good deal of flair. He stood and bowed over Loretta. "Why don't we join them, Miss Linden? This is a lively tune."

Loretta stood, too. "Thank you, Mr. FitzRoy. I should like very much to dance. I have so little opportunity to do so these days."

"Ah, yes. All those committee meetings and so forth."

"Absolutely." She spoke the one word as if she aimed to flatten anyone who so much as hinted at disapproval of any of her causes. Somerset knew better than to do anything so idiotic, no matter what his private thoughts might be.

They swirled off into the crowd of dancers. Loretta was quite short, but she danced well. Somerset hoped to get in as much practice as possible before Isabel took to the floor, because he wanted to be a partner she wouldn't be reluctant to dance with.

Naturally, he'd been forced to take dancing lessons as a boy, like most of the children he knew in his social class, but he hadn't really paid much attention to the art form, being more interested in the natural sciences. Since he'd met Isabel and learned how well she could dance, he'd been practicing at home alone. But at home alone wasn't the best way to practice dancing, and using a wooden chair for a partner only made things worse. He knew himself to be a trifle rusty. In actual fact, he believed he might possibly have been born with two left feet.

The band's rendition of "Fascination" lasted a little longer than Somerset thought was strictly necessary, but he enjoyed it. So, evidently, did Loretta, who applauded with zest when the music stopped. Before they reached their table, the band struck up the opening bars of a ragtime tune. Loretta stopped walking and looked up at him, and Somerset decided why not. A little more practice couldn't hurt, especially given Isabel's expertise with the various dance forms.

He lost track of the time and of Jason and Marjorie while he danced with Loretta. After the ragtime number, the band played a foxtrot, then another waltz, and then the master of ceremonies took the floor. Somerset was out of breath when he finally held Loretta's chair and she all but fell into it.

"Oh, my!" she breathed. "I haven't danced like that for years."

"Nor have I," admitted Somerset, trying to wipe his forehead with a discreetly drawn handkerchief.

"I have an announcement," said Jason, escorting Marjorie back to the table.

Loretta and Somerset both looked up at him with interest. What did the man mean? Had he taken his own advice and popped the question? Somerset understood that, if he meant to pursue Isabel, he'd best get at it before some other man beat him to it, but he didn't see any particular hurry regarding Marjorie, who wasn't exposed to so much competition on a daily basis. A glance at Loretta told him she was thinking along the same lines.

She only said, "Oh? And what is that?" Then she picked up her water glass and drained half of it.

"The ice maiden dances like an angel." Jason bowed deeply as he held Marjorie's chair.

She blushed like a forest fire as she sat. Somerset

shook his head and wondered why Jason couldn't go through one tiny little evening without ragging poor Marjorie.

Isabel fingered the bright-red fringes at her waist nervously. Loretta had paid for this frock, of course. She had paid for the other three Isabel had had made for her new job, although she'd reluctantly agreed to let Isabel pay her back a little at a time. She glanced at Jorge, who was inspecting himself in the mirror.

She didn't think she'd ever met so vain a man before. He preened more than any three women Isabel knew. She'd inspected her own makeup and decided she looked as good as she could, and that was that. Not Jorge. If he wasn't fiddling with his hat, he was fussing with the fringes on his crimson sash, all the while staring into the mirror and striking dramatic poses.

For their first number, a sizzling Argentine tango, they both wore black and red, and her hair was pulled back starkly and knotted at the nape of her neck. Isabel's gown was a black satin number with a fiery red silk scarf that draped over one shoulder and tied at her waist. The other shoulder was completely bare, and she felt terribly exposed. However, Jorge had gone so far as to lift an eyebrow and say she looked all right, so she figured she must. Jorge was only lavish when he was complimenting himself.

Mr. Benedict, the master of ceremonies, was talking, and Isabel listened closely. She didn't want to miss her cue—not that Jorge would let her.

He left off worshiping himself in the mirror, came to her side, took her hand and nodded at her. He never smiled unless a smile was required for the dance. Since this was a tango, the dance of love, and since evidently the composers of tangos all considered love a serious business, he wouldn't have to exercise his cheek muscles during this number. That was all right with her. This was her debut, and she was as nervous as a mouse in a herd of cats.

Then she heard Mr. Benedict say loudly and with extravagant enthusiasm, "And now, ladies and gentlemen, the marvelous dancing duo known and loved internationally: Isabel and Jorge!" The piano thrummed out the first sultry notes of "Ojos Negros," and Jorge took a deep breath. She did, too, and they were off.

Riotous applause greeted their entrance. Jorge was *such* a splendid dancer. He slithered here and slithered there, leading her along masterfully. This dance was interesting, because the way Jorge had choreographed it, they never once looked each other in the eye. Jorge's eyes were always looking one way, and hers the other, as if they'd had a lovers' quarrel or something.

When they performed a series of intricate twirls in the middle of the floor, she caught a glimpse of Loretta, Marjorie, Somerset and Jason seated at a table on the edge of the dance floor, and her heart gave a tremendous leap. She'd known they would be here, of course, but she hadn't realized how very glad she was to have them as her friends until that minute.

The dance ended with a crashing piano chord and with Jorge on one knee and Isabel looking as though she were pulling away from him. The reaction from the crowd was almost overwhelming. Isabel wasn't accustomed to being applauded when she danced.

But Jorge, who was in his own way an admirable instructor, had prepared her for that, too, and they took their bow as if they'd been dancing together for decades, rather than days. Then Jorge led her from the floor, and Isabel hurried behind the dressing screen to change into her dancing-with-the-customers gown, a pretty blue brocade one that, according to Eunice, matched her eyes. Now her job would entail intermingling with the paying guests until half past eleven, when she'd dress for the second dance demonstration of the night. They had a medley planned for that performance, featuring a ragtime number and a lively foxtrot.

Her heart was rattling like dice in a cup when she took a last glance at herself in the mirror and decided she was fit for company. She'd even dabbed cologne under her armpits in case she'd perspired from nervousness. She'd never had to think about things like sweat before this, her opening night as a professional dancer.

"All right," she told herself firmly. "Let's go."

Thanking her lucky stars that her friends had come and that she could start her job by socializing with them, she met Jorge, and the two of them walked out from behind the band together, each taking off in the opposite direction. That, too, had been choreographed, so that they wouldn't look like a couple once they stopped dancing together. The notion of dancing with many strange gentlemen, especially having just exposed her bare shoulder in the tango, had been giving Isabel some anxious moments, although she wasn't sure why. Surely, no gentleman would try to take advantage of her on the dance floor!

"Isabel! Isabel! Over here!"

The sound of Loretta's voice carried to her over the music of the band, and Isabel started off toward the table where she'd last seen her friends. She didn't get there. All at once a strange man loomed before her and almost made her gasp until she remembered her job. Then she smiled at him instead.

"May I have this dance?" he asked politely.

"Of course. Thank you." Was she supposed to thank gentlemen for asking her to dance? There was a lot she didn't know about this job. She wished she could take notes.

He took her in his arms and they waltzed off. He was rather graceful, although not so graceful as Jorge. And he held her a trifle too closely for her comfort. Isabel wasn't sure what she was supposed to do if a gentleman became too friendly on the dance floor.

Suddenly the man stopped dancing. Isabel was confused until she saw that another man had tapped the first man on the shoulder to cut in. Gratefully, she slipped from the too-tight embrace of the first man and into that of the new stranger.

"You're a wonder, you and your partner," this man told her. He had a friendly grin and a bouncy step.

"Thank you," Isabel said breathlessly.

"I don't think I've ever seen such grace in motion."

"Thank you."

"And you're no bigger than a minute, either. Say, is that dancer fellow your husband?"

Sweet merciful God. Wondering if it would be better to lie or tell the truth, Isabel said, "Well, actually—" and got no further, because this man, too, had been tapped on the shoulder. Her feeling of relief intensified when she realized the new man was Somerset FitzRoy. She practically fell into his arms, and he whirled her away with practiced ease.

"Thank you for rescuing me, Mr. FitzRoy. That man just asked me if Mr. Savedra and I were married! That seems rather forward to me, although I suppose my position might give people the wrong impression."

"I was afraid something like that might happen."

Isabel glanced up quickly, because Somerset had sounded grim. "I'm sure he didn't mean to be rude."

"Hmmm."

"Perhaps I should prepare answers to impertinent questions and have them handy for future use."

"Good idea. Tell 'em all you're married."

"You mean lie?"

"Why not? It'll keep them all away."

"Hmmm. That *is* a good idea."

Somerset deftly eluded a man who was poised to tap him on the shoulder, and Isabel giggled. "Very adroit of you, Mr. FitzRoy."

"Thank you." He grinned at her and went off into a series of swirls that left her breathless and laughing. "Say, I'm not bad at this sort of thing," he said, and he was laughing, too.

Later on in the evening, she got to sit with her friends for a few minutes, and they enjoyed themselves making up replies that Isabel could use to respond to questions she didn't want to answer.

"If anybody else asks if you're married to Savedra, tell 'em no, that your husband is a boxing champion," Jason suggested.

"Or a policeman," offered Loretta.

"And if he asks you to dinner, you can say it's against the rules for you to consort with customers."

They all turned to stare at Marjorie, from whom this sensible suggestion had come. Naturally, she blushed. "Well, that's what we were supposed to do when I worked for White Star."

"I'll be hornswoggled," said Jason.

"Whatever does *that* mean?" Loretta laughed.

"It means I'm betwaddled. Our own Miss MacTavish just offered a brilliant suggestion, Mrs. Golightly. Who'd have thought?"

"I would," said Isabel stoutly, smiling at Marjorie. "That *is* a brilliant suggestion, Marjorie. Thank you!"

"Oh, ta!" said Marjorie, but Isabel could tell she was pleased.

Her friends stayed through her second dance demonstration with Jorge, which was a courtesy greatly appreciated by Isabel. The exhibition went splendidly, although it wasn't quite as dramatic as the tango had been. That was all right with Isabel, who still worried about her earlier bare shoulder. For the ragtime-foxtrot number, she was fully clothed.

After she retired to the dressing room and put her dance-with-the-customers gown back on, she returned to find Loretta, Marjorie, and Jason having departed. She was delighted that Somerset remained behind.

"I thought it would be best for you to have a ride home," he told her. Isabel thought he seemed a trifle embarrassed.

"Thank you. I had planned to take a cab, but if you're willing to drive me, I'll be happy to accept."

"I'm glad you didn't think of walking at this hour of the night."

"Walking?" She blinked a couple of times, because he'd sounded testy. "I'm sure I'd be all right, but no, I promised Loretta that I wouldn't walk home from work." Besides that, even though San Francisco was an easy city to get around in, Isabel didn't particularly feel like tackling all those hills after having danced all night.

"I'm glad she thought of it."

With a trace of asperity, Isabel asked, "Did you think she wouldn't? Or that I would blithely trot into possible danger without giving a thought to what Eunice might lose should something happen to me?"

It was his turn to blink, evidently not having considered that his hints might be taken amiss. "Oh . . . why, no. I mean, I just didn't want you to have to worry about how you were going to get back to Miss Linden's house."

Relenting, Isabel said, "Thank you. It's very kind of you to care about my welfare." Plus, she'd get to see how it felt to be driven in a Maxwell sedan. She was quite taken with Loretta's Runabout, although she didn't think she'd care to drive herself, primarily because the front of the automobile looked wider than the road when one sat inside it. The Maxwell was even larger and more luxurious than the Runabout.

"Think nothing of it."

Someone asked her to dance at that point, and she didn't have another opportunity to talk to Somerset until it was time for her to change into her street clothes and go home. She accomplished this as quickly as possible so as not to make him wait. She was out of breath when she dashed to meet him. He sat at the same table he'd occupied earlier, and the cleaning crew was already sweeping up around him. As soon as he saw her, he rose politely. He was *such* a polite man. Isabel liked him so well. She thought she'd like him even if he hadn't rescued her and Eunice.

"All ready?"

He had a splendid smile, as well. And straight, white teeth. And very pretty hair that had a slight curl to it, but not so much of one that it got unruly easily. His evening costume, too, fitted him admirably. Isabel assumed he'd had it tailored especially to his measurements. Until she'd got this job, she'd always made her own clothes. And Eunice's, too.

"Yes, thank you."

He took her coat from where she'd slung it over her arm and held it out for her to don, just like a real gentleman. Well, she supposed, he was a real gentleman, for all that he was an American and the designation didn't mean the same thing here as it did in Britain.

The same went for *lady*. Which was a good thing, in her opinion, because it smashed class distinctions to blazes, where they belonged.

"I must say, Mrs. Golightly, that you dance divinely," Somerset said as he held the door for her to pass through.

So polite. So genteel. So . . . trite? Well, he wasn't usually trite.

"Thank you. My uncle Charlie was an excellent teacher."

"You were an admirable pupil."

"You should have seen Uncle Charlie and Aunt Maxine, though. They were real professionals. I guess I'll get better the more I do it, but the stage was their life." She sighed, remembering her relations back home. Her parents had died of influenza two winters before, but Uncle Charlie and Aunt Maxine were still going strong, given their ages. They'd retired in York, and Isabel wondered if they might like to come to the United States. Probably not.

Somerset gave the parking attendant a voucher, and the lad ran off to fetch his automobile. Then Somerset opened the door for her, the attendant opened the door for him, Somerset handed him a tip—it looked like a large one to Isabel—and they were off.

"Mrs. Golightly, I need to ask you something," Somerset said after they'd been tootling along for a few minutes, uphill and down, heading for Loretta's grand home on Lombard Street.

He sounded serious, and Isabel turned toward him. "What is it?" She hoped he wouldn't begin to lecture her about the way she was trying to make a living. Dancing might seem inappropriate to a man, because men could obtain employment doing anything. Women weren't so lucky. She considered herself fortunate to have found a job at all. And to have found one she enjoyed was more than she'd ever dreamed of.

After clearing his throat nervously, he said, "I've been thinking a lot about this in the past few days, and I've decided I shouldn't waste any time. After all, you'll be meeting any number of men now that you're dancing at the Fairfield, and who knows what will happen?"

She blinked, confused. Who knew what would what? "Um . . . I'm not sure I understand what you're saying, Mr. FitzRoy." His name felt sweet on her lips.

"Well . . ." he gestured with his left hand, the back of which flapped against the Isinglass window on his side. He quickly replaced it on the steering wheel. "I mean, I know you need to support yourself and Eunice."

"Yes."

"And it worries me that you have to do it by dancing at the Fairfield."

Fiddlesticks. He *was* going to lecture her. She didn't need any sermons on the evils of the performance arts. She was so grateful to have Loretta as a friend. Loretta understood that practicality took precedence over propriety. It would break her heart to be preached at by Somerset, whom she liked so well and admired so much. In truth, she adored him.

With reserve she said, "I was fortunate to have secured this position, Mr. FitzRoy. It pays ever so much more than char work."

"I know that. I'm not belittling you for having taken work that pays well, but it still worries me. You never know whom you'll meet in a place like that."

"In a place like the *Fairfield*?" She goggled at what she could see of him. Night had fallen hours before, and it wasn't much. But, honestly! The Fairfield was the most exclusive hotel in San Francisco.

"Well, what I mean is that it's still dancing, you know. With men."

"Yes. I know."

"And dancing is fine," he hurried to say. Obviously, he was becoming anxious as he fumbled around with his words.

Understanding this, Isabel took pity on him. "Why don't you just say what you want to say, Mr. FitzRoy. I'll try not to get angry." She smiled to show that she was a good sport—although if he said anything too outrageous, she might have to fight an impulse to smack him. Men had no idea how difficult it was for a woman alone to make a living.

She heard him swallow hard. Then he said, "Thank you. I will." And he stopped speaking entirely.

Isabel sighed and waited.

Finally he burst out, "I want you to marry me."

Chapter Eleven

Isabel's heart leaped even as her body froze on the luxurious bench seat of the Maxwell. She found herself unable to believe what she thought she'd heard him say. He wanted her to *what*? He couldn't be in love with her, could he? Isabel didn't have that kind of luck.

"I know this is sudden. After all, it's only been a short time since we met."

"Yes, it has." He must be joking, although it was a dreadful joke. Isabel was not amused—and that almost amused her since it would put her on a par with the late queen. Laughter was very far away from her in the moment, however.

"But something Jason said—that's Dr. Abernathy, you know—"

"Yes, I know."

She heard him swallow again and guessed she wasn't making this easy on him. That was fine with her, since it wasn't easy on her, either. He might have saved her life, and she might be secretly in love with him, but that didn't give him the right to make bad jokes at her expense.

"He reminded me that you're now in a position to meet any number of eligible men."

"Eligible men?" As she sat there, she tried to decide the appropriate word to describe her condition. Flabbergasted? Baffled? Bewildered? Confounded?

Perhaps outraged more nearly hit the mark. "Ah . . . what does meeting eligible men have to do with anything?"

She barely saw Somerset's hand lift into the air, a trifle darker than the pervading night, then fall again. She gathered this was a gesture of confusion. "You'll meet *men*. Some of them might try to sweep you off your feet!"

"Good Lord."

"It's the truth. You can't even imagine the kinds of men there are in the world, Isabel. Why, you might meet anyone!"

"Aha. And you fear that some cad in gentlemen's clothing will sweep me off to his lair and have his way with me?"

She sensed his frown. "I wouldn't put it *that* way, but . . . well . . . yes. Something like that."

"I see." Both Somerset and Jason were two exceptionally foolish men if they had such a low opinion of her. Did they honestly believe that she could be swayed by pretty words and allow some sweet-talking man to bedazzle her? Little did they know. She'd done that once, and once was too often. Isabel Golightly didn't need to be taught twice. She huffed loudly.

"Not that I think you have less than good sense or anything like that." The words almost tripped over themselves leaving Somerset's mouth, and Isabel was pleased that she'd managed to get her point across with nothing more than a huff. "But, still, you're in a difficult position—you know, having to earn your living and provide for your daughter and all."

"Yes, I'm fully aware of my position, thank you."

"And if some millionaire happened to come along and take a fancy to you—which is absolutely possible, you know. You're a beautiful woman and any man would be a fool not to want to marry you."

"Thank you." The two words sounded as if she'd poured alum on them before delivering them to her companion. Anyhow, what was wrong with marrying a millionaire? Even if she didn't like the presumed rich man much, a woman could do worse than have money to console herself with.

He swallowed again. "And I'm quite fond of you, you see, and Jason—Dr. Abernathy—he said I probably oughtn't wait too long because someone else might snap you up."

"Snap me up?"

"Yes. Because you're so beautiful and . . . and desirable, and so forth."

"Ah."

He turned and squinted through the darkness, trying to perceive her expression, she supposed. It was just as well he couldn't see it. At the moment, Isabel was fighting hysteria. She didn't know whether to burst out laughing or heave herself to the floor of the car and begin drumming her heels in a temper tantrum.

Leaving aside the fact that Isabel couldn't marry anyone, let alone Somerset, whom she adored, this so-called proposal of his absolutely galled her. The *nerve* of Somerset FitzRoy and Dr. Abernathy to talk about her as if she were . . . were . . . a commodity. A thing. A rag doll with no more motherwit than a pea. An entity with no judgment to call her own and no ability to choose for herself what was best for her to do.

"Are you angry with me?" He sounded incredulous.

Isabel took a deep breath and told herself that

Somerset was actually quite a fine man—for a man—
and that he probably hadn't meant to treat her as if she
were, say, a wind-up doll or a nitwitted puppy. After lick-
ing her lips and testing her insides to be sure there
weren't any screams lurking in there waiting to spring
forth, she said in a measured voice, "I am . . . ah . . . not
altogether pleased with you at the moment."

He jerked the steering wheel and the automobile
squealed to a stop against a curb. Fortunately, they were
on flat land, or Isabel felt sure the poor machine would
have rolled backward downhill and into the bay.

"But I just asked you to marry me!"

"I know."

"I thought ladies were supposed to be happy when
men asked them to marry them."

She took another deep breath. No sense in having a
temper fit. Obviously, Somerset had no idea he'd done
anything the least bit unkind or insulting. "I believe,"
she said after a moment's thought and with a mental
nod to *Pride and Prejudice,* "that it is customary for a
woman to thank a man for doing her the honor of asking for her hand in marriage."

He stiffened. She felt him do it. "It *is* an honor, dash
it!"

He was so perfectly unconscious of having done anything insupportable, and was so absolutely certain of
his masculine entitlements in this stupid world—and he
was now so incensed that she wasn't swooning over
him—that Isabel lost the fight to keep her indignation
in check. When she spoke again, it was with all the
venom that had been seething in her soul ever since
she'd discovered men to be liars and cheats.

"Yes, it usually is. However, I don't believe it's such a
bloody—I mean blooming—honor to be taken up like
a stray cat and rescued!" She added, because she felt

certain it was true, even though she was furious, "Although I'm sure your motives are pure. And I'll be forever grateful that you saved Eunice aboard the ship—at which time rescue was warrantable."

"That's not what I meant at all!" he cried, clearly stung.

"Isn't it? You just finished telling me that I have no judgment, no clarity of thought, no intelligence, no discernment, and no discrimination, and that you're worried lest I be led astray by a millionaire. I must say that the notion of being led anywhere by a millionaire appeals to me more than that of being married to a pauper."

"I'm not a pauper!"

"I didn't say you were."

"I'm quite well off, in fact."

"How nice for you."

"Isabel! I can't understand your attitude."

Isabel was having to exert all her energy to remain seated and not open the auto's door and march off, away from the man who had so grossly insulted her—and couldn't even be made to see that he'd done so. "And *I* can't understand why you think a woman—any woman, even me—would be grateful for being treated like a lost soul that has no sense and no means of coping. I can take care of myself! And my daughter! Without any help from you!"

"I didn't mean it that way. For the love of God, listen to reason, can't you?"

She crossed her arms over her chest and stared straight ahead into the darkness, fighting tears of rage. "Evidently not, if you're the voice of reason."

"But . . . I don't . . ." Somerset stopped trying to make sense of the situation and slumped back against the seat. He was breathing heavily, Isabel presumed from annoyance and frustration.

Well, she was frustrated too, damn it! She meant dash it. Why couldn't he understand that she was a fully functioning human being with every bit as much intelligence as any man and with the same needs, wants, and desires as any other human being in the world. The notion that she would leap to marry him because he chose to be noble and propose—evidently in spite of his better nature, or he wouldn't have brought up the dancing angle so bloody many times—made her want to yell and throw things. Damn him! "As soon as I am able, I plan to open a dance academy. It's my ambition, and I won't be swayed by men who think women are idiots."

"I didn't say that!"

"You implied it."

"Bah."

Feeling petulant and unhappy and hoping she wouldn't start crying, she said, "Would you like me to walk home from here? It's not far."

That brought him out of his slump. He sat up as if she'd goosed him. "Dash it, of course I don't want you to walk! That's why I'm driving you, for heaven's sake."

"Very well." For a few seconds she groped to think of something else to say, and didn't come up with anything. She didn't believe *then get at it, will you?* would go over too well under the circumstances.

But she was very tired and wanted to go home and get to bed. She longed to tell her daughter about her first night on the job and hoped she'd awaken before Eunice set off for school so she could do so. If Somerset didn't resume driving again soon, however, that hope was likely to be dashed.

She heard Somerset stir on his side of the automobile, and then grumble, "I'll have to crank the dashed thing again."

"Do you need me to help?" she asked politely, blatantly courting rejection.

She got it. "Of course not!" He opened his door, hurled himself out of the machine, and slammed the door behind him.

Isabel could scarcely see him stomp to the front of the automobile and lift the crank. She hoped he'd be careful. She'd feel guilty if his anger caused him to lose his concentration and break his arm—even if right was on her side, and he was a pigheaded *man*. She supposed he couldn't help the man part. The pigheadedness was another matter.

Somerset had often heard men in the *Chronicle's* press room complain about women, but he hadn't understood their point of view until this evening. Because he was a gentleman, no matter what *she* thought of him, he walked Isabel to the front door of Loretta's grand mansion and endured her polite handshake and thanks.

They were both startled when the door burst open in front of them and Marjorie MacTavish, her flaming hair in braids, and engulfed in something white that might have been a dressing gown, took Isabel's arm. "Oh, Isabel, Eunice is ever so fleid!"

Isabel didn't even glance back at Somerset when she dashed into the house. Marjorie slammed the door in Somerset's face, and he was left on the front porch, gawping at the door, and wondering how the evening could have ended so abruptly.

Then, stuffing his hands into the pockets of his natty evening trousers in a manner sure to gain him censure from his manservant, he slouched back to his machine, opened the door, climbed in, sat, and brooded. He couldn't figure out what had gone wrong. But it most certainly had gone wrong. Totally, completely, and devastatingly.

He squinted up at the house, wondering what the matter was with Miss Eunice. Was she ill? Had she been awakened by one of her nightmares? He saw lights in the upper floor, but they gave him no clue as to the problem. Huffing, he sat back against his seat and frowned through the windshield, brooding about Isabel, life, marriage, and his own persona.

He wished he could look in a mirror. Was there something wrong with him? Had he grown a second nose? Had he not shaved closely enough? Was he so ugly no woman would have him?

Somerset wasn't a vain man, but he'd never had cause to rue his looks. There were many men in the world more handsome than he, and he knew that his chosen profession wasn't always considered manly, but there was nothing inherently *wrong* with him, was there?

True, he wasn't one of those hard-drinking, hard-talking, wild-acting journalists who followed wars and criminals and were held in awe by the population. He wrote a horticultural column for the *Chronicle* and wrote books about plants. But that didn't mean he was less than a man, dash it. He'd pursued a university education in order to learn everything he could about plant life and the care and propagation of that life. He knew how important plants were to mankind, and how important they were to life in general. Was it less manly to sow new life than dodge bullets aimed at ending it?

His life's work wasn't all sweet peas and roses, either. He had a vast knowledge of trees, as well. Trees were manly, weren't they? Hell's bells, lumberjacks were about as masculine as men could get. Was it less manly to plant trees than to chop them down?

Deciding he'd best not sit in Loretta's circular drive while mulling things over lest someone come out and ask him if he needed help, he engaged the choke wire, discovered with relief that he didn't need to crank the beast again, and chugged off.

By the time he'd arrived at his own home, Somerset had come to the conclusion that Isabel's rejection of his proposal had nothing to do with her perception of him as being less than manly. Rather, she'd carped about how she had judgment and sense and didn't like his supposed presumption that she was some kind of stray that couldn't take care of herself.

He hadn't done that. Had he? As he flung his hat and overcoat onto the hall table and climbed the stairs, he puzzled over her reaction to his proposal. He couldn't understand it.

She was a woman. There was no denying that. Even Isabel couldn't dispute that. He pushed his bedroom door open, stepped inside, and looked around. Good. Calvin, his manservant, had done Somerset's bidding and not waited up for him. He pressed on the electrical light and closed the door behind himself.

All right. She was a woman. That was clear. And he was a man. That also was plain as day. Men and women needed each other, didn't they? Leastways, women needed men. It was a fact of life. A point of nature. There was no disputing that men were stronger than women and better able to survive in the world.

Women were the breeders, for God's sake. They were the nurturers. They needed to preserve their strength for having and caring for babies and for keeping house for their men. They weren't supposed to be out working at jobs and so forth. They were supposed to remain in the houses their men provided for them and keep the home fires burning!

He nearly strangled himself yanking his cravat loose, then he flung it on the bed, sat on it, and began unlacing his shoes. His feet ached from dancing so much, and he massaged them as he continued to muse about Isabel. He didn't understand how such a thing as a marriage proposal could have gone so wrong.

Maybe the problem didn't stem from something being wrong with him. Maybe it was because something was wrong with Isabel.

That was such a revolutionary thought, Somerset stopped massaging his feet and sat upright on his bed. Could *Isabel* be the problem here? Could she have some fundamental flaw that wasn't apparent on the surface? Certainly, on the surface she looked just fine. Swell, in fact.

But it was evident that she had no idea of her place in life. Not only did she believe it was her duty to go out and earn a living instead of marrying him, but she didn't even understand that when a man proposed, she was supposed to be appreciative, not indignant.

Or perhaps that wasn't the problem, either. Perhaps the problem lay in her having been married before.

Somerset began to feel the tiniest bit better. Maybe she was still mourning her lost husband, although that was carrying loyalty a trifle too far, in his opinion. How long had the man been dead, anyhow? Since before Eunice's birth, he'd gathered. Had the late Mr. Golightly been a dashed saint that his widow continued to honor his memory with such abject devotion?

Then again, women were notorious for their loyalty to the least worthy of men. Look at Penelope and Odysseus. Or that artist's model, Evelyn Nesbit, and the rakes she got herself involved with, Stanford White and Harry Thaw. Or Guinevere and Arthur . . . no, wait. In that case, it had been Guinevere who'd spoiled everything.

Still, perhaps the late Mr. Golightly hadn't been a good man at all. Perhaps he'd been a blackguard. Or maybe Isabel just needed more time. He frowned, knowing that wasn't the answer. She seemed perfectly at ease regarding the loss of her husband, and if she was grieving inside, she hid it well.

Anyhow, Isabel Golightly wasn't the only woman in the world who'd lost a spouse. And most of those women went on to remarry, if they got the chance to do so. Marrying again was the sensible thing to do, given that men were put on the earth to take care of women. This was especially true when the women had children to support. He snorted when he recalled Isabel's ambition of opening a dance academy. Women weren't supposed to operate dance academies, for God's sake!

The notion hit Somerset suddenly that the above philosophy didn't account for the millions of women who had to work at jobs away from their homes every day and still care for their young, cook for their spouses, and clean up after their families. The thought irked him, and he frowned as he unsnapped his garters and rolled his socks down. Was it his fault there were so many irresponsible men in the world? No, it was not. He was accountable only for his own actions, and he was a man of principle.

At least Isabel wouldn't have to do char work if she married Somerset. She wouldn't have to work at all. She could even have household servants if she wanted them.

And that, he thought glumly, brought him back to the start of his musings. Why in hell had she refused him? He had everything to offer her! A nice home, a father for her daughter, money, ease. Plus, he could provide very well for an enlarged family if they should have children together.

The idea of little Somersets and Isabels filling his house on Chestnut Street made him smile. The smile vanished when he considered that Isabel might possibly give birth to other little Eunices.

But no. Eunice was a trick of fate. An interesting phenomenon sent to earth to teach the rest of the world's inhabitants humility. There couldn't be more children like her in the world. And if there were . . . well, he and Isabel could cope with them together.

At least Somerset was an educated man with the wherewithal to send his children to school and see that they were properly educated and situated in life. *His* children wouldn't be sent via steerage-class to some foreign country and left unprovided for should he die.

After his socks were off and hurled in different directions, he marched over to his dressing table and stood before the mirror affixed thereto, squinting at his image. Critically. Not for Somerset FitzRoy the vanity of some of his fellow men, who expected women to swoon over them because they were handsome or wealthy or powerful or whatnot.

All in all, he had to admit he was rather satisfied with what he saw reflected in the mirror. There he was: six feet tall, well-built. Muscular, even, from doing so much manual labor, which just went to prove once more that horticulture wasn't for sissies. He had broad shoulders and firm legs. He didn't just sit around doing nothing all day long. He didn't work in a boring office lifting nothing heavier than papers. His work—the horticultural part of it, anyway—required strength. Fitness. Why, look at him. He was a healthy outdoor specimen, with tanned arms and face. True, his legs were white, but that was only to be expected. A gentleman couldn't run around without his trousers on, could he?

His face wasn't bad, either. Granted, he wasn't slimily handsome like that dashed Argentine fellow, but he had regular features, a decent nose, ears that didn't stick out, no nose or ear hairs apparent. A good head of thick hair on his head, dark brown and wavy with no unruly cowlicks. Fine dark brown eyes out of which he could see well, and perfectly serviceable thick dark eyelashes and well-arched eyebrows. Oh, he fully understood that Isabel might not consider him to be, say, an Adonis, or Romeo personified, although he sensed his physical appearance wasn't the reason she'd refused him.

The reason she'd refused him was that she was an idiot, dash it! She was a *woman!* She couldn't honestly believe that claptrap Loretta Linden was forever spouting about equality for women and votes for women and this and that and the other thing for women. Why, next they'd be agitating for equal pay for women. Preposterous. In . . . sane.

By the time he'd unbuttoned his collar studs, his annoyance had reached such a pitch that he flung his collar across the room. It hit the window with a less than satisfactory *thwack*. He removed his shirt and trousers, flopped onto his bed—which had been nicely prepared and the covers turned down by Calvin, although its looks were now slightly marred by his crumpled cravat.

To hell with Isabel. Tomorrow he would work on his book and not think about her at all. That would teach her.

* * *

Isabel didn't exactly bounce out of bed the morning following her debut as a dancer at the Fairfield, but she did manage to rise before Eunice left for school. Poor Eunice. She'd had one of her terrible nightmares last night, and her mother hadn't been home to comfort her.

Thank God for Loretta and Marjorie, who loved Eunice almost as much as Isabel herself. Loretta had held and rocked the girl, and Marjorie had made hot cocoa and kept an eye open for Isabel's return. She must have flown down the staircase and to the front door, because Somerset hadn't even had time to say more than good-night when Marjorie opened the door. It was just as well. Isabel hadn't wanted to speak to him anymore last night, anyway.

This morning, she felt sluggish and tired. She only stopped to pat cold water on her face, paying particular attention to her puffy eyes, before she ran downstairs to make sure her daughter was well enough to go to school.

Humiliating as it was, Isabel had cried herself to sleep the night before, her bosom swelling with hurt, and with rage and embarrassment roiling in her.

How dare Somerset FitzRoy offer a proposal like the one he'd offered? Had he honestly believed she would be so overcome with gratitude that she'd snap up his offer and thank him for it? He'd spoken no words of love, or even of admiration. He hadn't said *he'd* been swept off his feet, although he did mention that he feared *she'd* be swept off hers by some cad or other. Was she that pathetic in his eyes?

Evidently.

Well, that was just too bad, because Isabel Golightly was no man's pet. She stared at herself in the bathroom mirror, frowned at her still-swollen eyelids, pinched her cheeks to give them color, straightened her shoulders, threw on a dressing gown, and marched downstairs and into the kitchen, where Eunice took her breakfast before school.

Her daughter looked up and smiled with genuine pleasure when she saw her mother. "You're awake!"

Laughing gently, Isabel said, "More or less. I wanted to tell you all about my premiere last night."

"Oh, good! I want to hear about it." Eunice scooped up a spoonful of oatmeal, brown sugar, and cream and stuffed it into her mouth. Her large brown eyes sparkled like gemstones. "And I want to show you something I read in the *Chronicle.*"

Isabel loved her so much in that instant that she very nearly succumbed to tears again. It was only by the grace of God, and with a little help from Somerset and Loretta, that Eunice was eating so well. If Eunice had been living alone with her mother in this new land, she might well be starving to death, Isabel's only skills lying in the realm of the terpsichorean.

But she didn't want to think about that right now. God apparently had a plan for Eunice and her because they weren't shivering on a street corner somewhere in New York. They were here, in Loretta's magnificent home, and Eunice was eating porridge and cream and brown sugar for breakfast.

Eunice continued to eat, but she listened with gratifying attention as Isabel told her about the dances and the hotel and the glittering chandelier and everything. "And Miss Linden and Miss MacTavish and Mr. FitzRoy and Dr. Abernathy all came to lend me their support, too," she finished, buttering a piece of toast for herself that she didn't want. She was attempting to put on a brave face for her daughter.

"I knew they were going, of course," said Eunice. "It

was nice of them to stay till the end. It must have been a comfort for you to have your friends there."

"It was." Again, she had a sudden and burning urge to cry. Again, she didn't give in to it. "I think I'm going to enjoy my job. My feet hurt." She tried for a hearty laugh, although it came out sort of thin. "But I don't mind."

"I think you'll find that having your feet hurt from dancing is better than having your hands raw and bleeding from doing char work."

Ah. So Eunice remembered her mother's hands, did she? Isabel was sorry about that. "Yes, indeed. My poor hands still hurt when I think about it."

"I'm glad you don't have to do char work any longer, Mama." Eunice picked up the *Chronicle* that lay folded neatly beside her cereal bowl. "Look at this, Mama. It's about a dancing contest."

"A dancing contest?" Interested in spite of her gloomy mood, Isabel took the newspaper and began reading aloud as her daughter picked up her bowl and glass and walked to the sink to rinse her dirty dishes.

" 'Attention, ladies and gentlemen interested in the modern social dances. A contest will be held at San Francisco's famous Palace Hotel on August 15, 1912, beginning at one p.m. The winning couple will receive a $5,000 prize.' " Isabel felt her eyes widen at the amount of the prize. " 'Dances will include the foxtrot, the waltz, the schottische, and the tango. Couples must dance to the music provided.'" She stared at the announcement. "My goodness."

"I thought perhaps you and Mr. Savedra could enter. You'd have to share the prize, but it might help you in earning money, which I know you're eager to do."

"It might, indeed." Isabel's head filled with visions of a dance studio run by none other than her very own self. The Amazing Graciousness Dance Academy. Yes. That was it, all right. Amazing Graciousness. "Thank you for showing me this, Eunice. I can hardly wait to ask Mr. Savedra about it."

"You dance beautifully together, Mama. And if you danced that well when you'd never even met each other before, by the time the contest arrives, it will take a tremishously skilled couple to beat you."

"Tremishously?" Isabel asked, puzzled. "Um . . . do you mean tremendously, sweetie?"

Eunice thought about it. "I guess so, yes."

"Thank you." Isabel smiled at her daughter, wondering if it was love guiding Eunice's opinion, or if she might be right. As a rule, Eunice didn't succumb to emotion, except in the middle of the night when sleep conquered her resistence.

"I'm not only saying that, either," Eunice assured her, as if she knew what was on her mother's mind. "As you know, I don't often allow emotion to influence my opinions."

"Yes. I know it well." God bless the child. "When do you have to leave for school, sweetie?"

Eunice looked at the clock on the kitchen shelf. "In about fifteen minutes. I always try to give myself plenty of time."

She would. Little Miss Responsibility, Eunice. Didn't have a single spontaneous trait in her, which was a good thing. Spontaneity was what had led to Isabel's own downfall.

"I'm going to run upstairs and change, and I'll walk you to school. Will that be all right, dearie?"

"Oh, yes, please! That would be very nice!" Since her eyes gleamed and her smile extended from ear to ear, Isabel believed her. Sometimes, since her daughter was so unlike most children, Isabel needed concrete signs to remind herself that Eunice was, after all, only six years old.

Isabel was as good as her word. It didn't take her long to throw on a day dress and some shoes and stockings, top it with a sweater, and to wrap her hair into a knot and pin it at the back of her head. She plopped a hat on top of everything, jammed in a pin to hold it on, and when she hurried downstairs and into the kitchen again, Eunice had just received a lunch pail from Mrs. Brandeis, who always prepared a noon meal for her to take with her to school.

Eunice reached for her mother's hand, they both thanked Mrs. Brandeis, and the two Golightly ladies headed out the front door. The day was glorious, with no fog or dust in the air, and Isabel felt a sense of contentment that she hadn't expected.

If her heart ached a trifle, and if she wished Somerset FitzRoy, the hero of her life, had offered her a slightly more heroic proposal than the one he had, well, she still had Eunice. Eunice was more important than men or proposals or anything else in the world.

And she couldn't help but wish Somerset had told her that he loved her madly and couldn't live without her.

Foolish, foolish Isabel.

Chapter Twelve

"You did what?" Jason Abernathy squinted up from his cluttered desk, upon which sat several wilting bouquets of flowers that he'd bought from street urchins, and a variety of beauty creams and lotions, teas and herbs that he'd bought from different Chinese herbalists whose businesses he tried to help.

"I proposed last night." Somerset was sprawled in a hard-backed chair on the other side of Jason's desk, hands jammed into his pockets, his legs stretched out in front of him and crossed at the ankles. From the expression on Jason's face, Somerset presumed he didn't look like a happy bridegroom-to-be.

"Um . . . this is just a shot in the dark, you understand, but I get the feeling it didn't go quite as you'd planned."

"She refused me."

"She did, did she?" The good doctor didn't seem awfully surprised.

Something cynical twisted inside Somerset. In his rational brain, he knew it wasn't Jason's fault that Isabel had refused his proposal, but he felt ill-used by the man anyway. It was, after all, Jason who'd suggested Somerset be prompt in his attentions to Isabel. If he'd waited and courted her a little longer, he might have had better luck.

Then again, given his scholarly turn of mind, he'd probably have forgotten all about it and Isabel would have been wooed and won by somebody else. Somerset sighed heavily. Relationships between men and women were very confusing to him, which was the reason he'd mostly avoided them thus far in his life.

Frowning, he decided it had been the train that was at fault. If he hadn't had the time to come to know her on the stinking train, he wouldn't have this aching hollow feeling in his chest from having lost her.

"I'm sorry about that, old man. I thought for sure she fancied you."

"Apparently she does not."

"Ah . . . when did you spring this proposal on her?"

"When I drove her home last night."

"I see. And did you preface the proposal with words of love and admiration?"

Somerset sat bolt upright. "Did I what? No! Of course, I didn't do that! I barely know the woman."

"I presume you didn't get down on one knee and tell her that you would climb the highest mountain to win her or that you'd shoot yourself or join the French Foreign Legion if she didn't accept you."

"Of course not! What kind of idiot do you think I am?" He resented it when Jason rolled his eyes. "Now see here, you're the one who told me I had to hurry up and propose or I'd lose her, you know."

Very softly and slowly, as if he were instructing a particularly dull student, Jason said, "What I meant was that you might want to increase your attentions to the lonely widow, man, not that you should grab her by the hair and drag her into your cave."

"I didn't do that! My home is not a cave! What do you think I am?" His outrage propelled him out of his chair and around the room, taking large steps that were loud in the doctor's cluttered office.

"I beg your pardon," Dr. Abernathy said soothingly. "Please sit again. I didn't mean to rile you. I only meant that perhaps you were the least little bit hasty."

Somerset stood still and scowled at his friend. "I thought I was supposed to hurry things up. You said so, don't forget."

"Yes, I did. And I still believe some forward motion on your part will prove to be a good thing. I didn't think you'd take it to mean you had to propose instantly. It might be a good idea to court her a little. Take her places. Show her things. You know, perform in the time-honored way men are supposed to court women. Broaden her horizons. She hasn't been in the United States long. Show it to her. Find out what her interests are and cultivate them."

Cultivate. Good word, that. Somerset understood it. Judiciously, he said, "I suppose we must have some interests in common." He couldn't think of any offhand, but that could be remedied.

"I'm sure you must."

Somerset gazed suspiciously at Jason, but he detected no sign of sarcasm on the doctor's face.

Jason went on, "Courtship doesn't have to be a burden, Somerset. It should be enjoyable."

Great. Easy for Jason to say. Somerset hadn't a single clue as to how men courted woman. "Right," he said, since to admit the truth would be too humiliating. "You're probably right."

Jason's head tilted slightly. "Would it help if I jotted down a few suggestions for you? I know you're more accustomed to paying attention to books and the science of horticulture than to females."

Because he felt heat creeping up the back of his neck from embarrassment, Somerset turned and walked to Jason's office window. Pulling back the curtain, he gave a casual shrug. "That's not really necessary." He cleared his throat. "However, I don't suppose it would hurt."

"I don't suppose it would." The doctor's voice was dry.

Defeated by the truth, Somerset slumped and walked back to the chair he'd vacated. He sat with a whump. "I'm no good at this courtship nonsense."

"Don't be foolish, Somerset. You haven't even tried it yet. Besides, no man's good at courtship, mainly because he only gets to practice the art once or twice in his life unless he's a total cad. But I've been down that road once, and I can tell you a few of the things that my late wife found endearing when I was courting her."

Somerset's eyebrows arched. "I didn't know you'd been married."

Jason sighed deeply as he wrote. "Yes. It was a short but happy union. She died of consumption not long after we were wed."

Amazed, Somerset said, "I'm surprised you were allowed to marry. I thought they had passed laws to prevent consumptives from marrying."

He watched as the doctor's mouth thinned into a grim line. Jason didn't look up from his notations. "Not anymore, they don't. Besides, 'they' don't care what happens to the Chinese, my friend."

Even more amazed, Somerset said, "Your wife was *Chinese*?"

"Yes." No elaboration.

"Ah."

"However, people are people, no matter what color their skin, and I think that if you gave these few little suggestions a try, your luck might change." He held out the paper.

Somerset leaned toward the desk and took it. "Thank you."

"One other suggestion I have is that you include that astounding child in your courtship as much as possible. I know you probably want to spend your time with the beautiful Isabel, but there's not much hope of separating them, and you'll gain her favor much more successfully if you get along with little Miss Golightly."

Somerset felt a small surge of triumph for having figured that out on his own. His enthusiasm increased as he read down the list Jason had written. "I've already asked them to visit Golden Gate Park with me."

"Good. See? You're not completely hopeless." Somerset's quick frown made the doctor laugh.

"It's not funny, Jason. This means a lot to me."

For the first time since Somerset had met the man, the planes on Jason's face relaxed and he appeared something other than sardonic. "Of course, it does. Marriage is a big step." Eyeing him quizzically, Jason asked, "Do you love her?"

"Love?" Frowning more seriously, Somerset pondered the word. He'd pondered it before and had tried to put it out of his mind. "Do you think love is a necessary ingredient to marriage?"

"Yes. I do. I suggest you be sure you love the woman before you begin a more advanced courtship. If you don't love her, there's not much hope that you'll be happy together."

"I was under the impression that love doesn't last," Somerset said stiffly. "I should think a good, solid friendship based on shared likes and dislikes—" He stopped speaking, remembering that he and Isabel had so far not established that they shared any mutual likes or dislikes. "Well, I should think a mutual liking and respect would be more important to a happy marital union than so transitory an emotion as love."

Jason's head tilted the other way. "Have you been taking elocution lessons from Miss Eunice? I've never heard such a formal sentence filled with such infernal claptrap in my life."

After thinking about objecting and deciding not to, Somerset said, "Well, look at you. You say you loved your wife."

"Very much."

"And it's unfortunate that she died—but wait a minute." He sat up straighter and his eyebrows dipped again. "I thought it was against the law for a white man to marry a Chinese."

Jason shrugged. "It isn't, although some people wish it were. However, even if it were, some laws are bad and need to be ignored."

A short pause preceded Somerset's next words. "I don't wonder that you and Miss Linden are such good friends."

With a broad grin, Jason agreed. "Absolutely."

Determining not to lose track of his purpose, Somerset said, "But do you honestly believe that you and your Chinese wife would have been happy if she had lived?"

"Blissfully."

That was short and sweet. "You don't think that your dissimilar backgrounds would have led to eventual misunderstandings and, perhaps, unhappiness?"

"Have you ever read Jane Austen, Somerset?"

"What does Jane Austen have to do with anything?"

"Have you?"

"No."

"According to Miss Austen, happiness in marriage is largely a matter of chance. But no, I don't believe that Mai and I would have been unhappy. I can't imagine it. There's a difference between short, passionate attraction and deep and abiding love, Somerset. Love is what you have left when you've soared into the atmosphere and been thrown to earth with a crash. It's what's left after the infatuation fades. After the initial fever cools, if you have love left, you'll be a happy man."

Somerset couldn't think of a thing to say to that. He regretted having reminded Jason of sad times. Although . . . He pondered whether or not to ask what he'd just thought about, and then decided why not? Jason was prying into the most intimate aspects of his own life; why not return the favor?

"What about Miss MacTavish?"

Jason's eyebrows soared above his glittering blue eyes. "What about her?"

"It seems to me that there might be more to a successful courtship than constant teasing."

A grin once more spread itself across Jason's face, giving him a devilish aspect. "Oh, the type of courtship depends on the people involved and their intentions. Don't you think so?"

"What do you mean by that?" Somerset demanded. "I had until now presumed your intentions were honorable."

Spreading a hand on his chest, Jason said, "My intentions are *always* honorable, old fellow."

"Oh?"

"Miss MacTavish needs to learn to open up to life. I'm only trying to help her do that."

"I doubt that she appreciates your way of doing so."

"Not yet, she doesn't, but I know there's a sense of humor and warmth under that prim facade. I can tell."

Somerset couldn't, but he didn't argue. Anyhow, he didn't care that much. He had his own problems to deal with.

A knock sounded on the door, and Somerset turned in his chair to see Jason's Chinese nurse, a young man in dark blue pajamas and a long pigtail, poke his head in. "Sorry to interrupt, Dr. Abernathy, but there's an emergency out here."

Jason stood instantly. "What's the matter, Lo Sing?"

"The tongs are at it again, it looks like." He gestured at Jason's desk, and Somerset saw a red paper lying on it, covered in Chinese characters.

"Damn. I had thought the red sheet was some kind of joke." He picked up the paper and slammed it back onto his desk in a gesture of total disgust.

"Apparently not. There are several bad injuries."

Confused, Somerset asked, "What are tongs? What are red sheets?"

As Jason rose and hurried to the rack by the door, to retrieve a white coat, he said, "Tongs are Chinese social organizations. Unfortunately, some of them have turned into criminal societies. Red sheets are murder orders posted on Chinatown walls offering rewards for killing certain people."

"Good God! How can they get away with such overt advertisements?"

Jason shot him a cynical grin. "Do you read Chinese?"

"Uh . . . no."

"Neither do our elected officials." Jason stuffed his arms into his coat and picked up his black bag. Right before he dashed out the door, he said, "I'll see you later, Somerset. Let me know how it goes."

"I will. Thank you." Somerset watched the doctor rush away, his nurse on his heels. With a sigh, he snagged his own hat from the rack, plopped it on his head, and ambled out the door. He was going to the library now, to look up some information he needed to know for his book.

Later he'd resume thinking about Isabel. Of course, in order to do that, he'd have to forget about her first.

Impossible.

"This is a pleasant walk, Eunice." Isabel and Eunice started out at the top of Russian Hill and walked down a steep zigzag path built out of what seemed like a million bricks. From this position, she could see all of San Francisco and the ocean beyond. There was a great deal of construction going on here and there to remind everyone of the 1906 earthquake, but the view was still impressive. San Francisco was quite a place. She liked it ever so much better than the little she'd seen of New York, which hemmed one in on all sides.

"Yes. I believe I like the panamas here better than those I remember of Upper Poppleton."

Isabel stared down at her daughter's head, covered this morning with a pretty straw hat. "Panamas?"

Eunice looked up at her. "Isn't a panama a vista?"

"Oh. I think you mean panoramas, sweetie."

"Ah. Thank you."

"You're welcome."

"So you like the looks of San Francisco better than those of Upper Poppleton?"

"I think so."

"Well, then, I'm glad we're here."

Eunice gave a little skip. "Me, too."

As for herself, Isabel missed so many things about

her former home, she could scarcely bear to think about them. It was nice to have fallen into a generous rich person's life and to be taken care of and to have new friends and all, but Isabel still missed her homeland and her old friends. The food. The way she'd been used to doing things. The familiar broad Yorkshire accent—the same accent she'd worked so hard to overcome with the help of her uncle Charlie and aunt Maxine.

Now, today, this minute, she thought she might just cry from homesickness as she mentally told herself that what she and Eunice were doing was walking "doon brick step on hill." She heaved a huge sigh as she contemplated the loss of her native Yorkshire's articles. Nobody ever said "the" in Yorkshire. "I miss Upper Poppleton a lot."

"I understand that," Eunice said seriously. "Since you're considerably older than I, and because you lived so many, many years—"

"Not *that* many," said Isabel, her sense of humor returning.

As ever, Eunice didn't understand the joke. Isabel sighed again.

"Well, because you lived there your whole life, and you're quite old now, you must miss things that I don't."

Quite old, was she? "Yes, I suppose so." She'd been seventeen when Eunice was born. She was only twenty-three years old now. A young woman still. After a fashion. How strange it seemed that she'd never felt young until recently.

When they arrived at Eunice's Montessori School on Montgomery Street, Isabel was pleased when two little girls, spotting them, ran over to greet Eunice. Now this never would have happened in Upper Poppleton. Truth to tell, most of the people Isabel knew in her homeland considered Eunice too strange to be comfortable with, even if they didn't hold the accident of her birth against her—and most of them did. She was glad to know that her daughter's intelligence wasn't feared here, in this particular school.

Eunice dragged her mother over to meet her friends. "Mama, please let me introduce you to Lilian Blyley."

A little blond girl with big blue eyes curtseyed politely. Tickled, Isabel held out her hand and said, "Delighted to meet you, Miss Blyley."

"Lilian," Eunice confided, "is a mathematical genius."

Isabel felt her eyebrows lift. "My goodness. I wish I were."

"It's not so great a gift for a girl," Lilian told her with a hefty sigh. "If I were a boy, it would be much more useful."

Isabel thought about protesting, but recognized the truth when she heard it. And Lilian, apparently a lot like Eunice, was probably sick of soothing lies. "Yes. I'm sorry about that, dear. It's not fair at all, is it?"

Lilian subsided with another sigh and a shake of her head as Eunice turned to her other companion, a pretty child with dark brown braids, a serious mien, and small, wire-framed glasses.

"And this is Rebecca Steinberg. Rebecca is a scientific genius." In an undertone, Eunice confided, "She's also of Hebrew heritage."

Good heavens. Isabel hardly knew what to say. Shaking the girl's hand, she offered, "Is that a problem?"

"Oh, it might be, Mama," Eunice declared. " 'Cause lots of places don't hire women and lots more don't hire Hebrews."

"I'm sorry to hear that. I'm very pleased to meet you, Rebecca. Perhaps by the time you grow up, times will be better for women and—and Hebrews."

"Thank you, ma'am," the little sobersides said. "Perhaps you know already that Eunice is our linguistic genius. She's excellently good with words. And she's learning German, too."

"German?" Eunice's mother stared at her child, mystified.

"Miss Pinkney is teaching me," Eunice said with a grin.

Beaming upon her daughter, Isabel said, "My goodness. That's wonderful, dearie." Including the other two girls in her smile, she added, "It sounds to me as if you have all your bases covered."

To a girl, they looked confused.

"That's an American baseball term, I think," elucidated Isabel. "It means that the three of you together have all the skills you need. Perhaps you can go into business together when you get older. I'm sure that together, you can overcome most of the obstacles the world will present."

They looked pleased at this assessment of their worth and future, and Isabel heard them talking about it as they walked into the school's grounds together. That had been perhaps the most incredible conversation of her life so far. The fact that it had been conducted between her and three six-year-old girls made her laugh out loud. She felt much better as she walked home than she had when she'd awakened that morning.

Isabel and Jorge performed their tango number again that night for their first demonstration. As had been the case the night before, thunderous applause erupted the moment the hot thrumming stopped and Isabel leaned away from Jorge. This time, Isabel pressed the back of her wrist to her forehead to make an even more dramatic statement, and was both surprised and pleased when Jorge commended her for it in the dressing room.

"You've got a . . ." He flicked a hand carelessly in the air. ". . . a flair for this drama."

Isabel glanced at him over her shoulder. She was at the dressing table, plucking red plumes out of her hair and toning down her makeup in preparation for dancing with the customers. "Thank you." She added, "You're wonderfully dramatic."

He shrugged, as if accepting a mere truth. "You keep working, you be good, too."

How encouraging. "Thank you." She didn't smile and was proud of herself. No sense in riling her partner. He was the senior member here, after all, and if he took a dislike to her, Isabel felt sure he could make her life difficult and her job impossible and perhaps even gone.

Picking up her red feathers and the black band which affixed them to her head during their tango number, she went behind her dressing screen, hung up her tango gown, and selected a pretty cream-colored silk evening gown with a high waist emphasized by a not too tight light pink cummerbund (there was an art to looking fashionable while working as a dancer). The cummerbund had a darker pink rosette attached, and the dress had a ruched bodice and embroidered cap sleeves. Isabel had nearly gone blind embroidering them, but the effect was beautiful. Loretta hadn't helped any by persisting in making her laugh over her labors. Loretta, needless to say, had never embroidered a sleeve, cap or otherwise, in her life, having had no need to do anything of the sort.

"You could be coming with me to a women's suffrage march, Isabel!" she'd cried when she spied Isabel at her labors. "That's ever so much more useful in the long run than embroidery!"

"I'm sure you're right," Isabel had said with a smile, "but marching for women's suffrage won't pay for my daughter's education."

"Pooh!" scoffed Loretta, as Isabel had known she would. "You needn't worry about Eunice's education. I'm more than happy to take care of that."

With a suppressed sigh, Isabel, forever trying to make Loretta understand without hurting her feelings, said, "I know it. But you're doing more than you should already. You're probably the first genuinely good-hearted person I've ever met in my life, Loretta, but I would be shirking my own responsibility by allowing you to take on the entire burden of my daughter's education."

Leaving behind a trail of her usual assortment of *piffles* and *balderdashes,* Loretta had left her to her embroidery. Isabel could never think of Loretta Linden without smiling. She was the most charming, annoying, troublemaking female Isabel had ever met. As much as Isabel loved her, she was sometimes grateful that there weren't more Lorettas in the world. Her goodness and generosity could be almost oppressive at times.

Now, as she tugged on various articles of clothing, her heart sped up and she said, "Jorge, are you interested in participating in a dance contest with me?"

"A contest? Dancing is no sport. Dancing is *art.* "

"Well, of course, but it might be fun to enter a contest." Isabel held her breath. Since she'd read that article in the newspaper, she'd been spinning daydreams about winning it and opening up her dance academy.

"Fun? Dance is not *fun.* Dance is magic. Music. Art."

Damn the man for his artistic temperament. Isabel wanted to scream at him that art wouldn't pay for her academy, but she tried to sound reasonable. Then she remembered that she hadn't mentioned the money. Even artists like Jorge could use money. "Yes, I know, but this contest pays five thousand dollars to the winning couple."

A pause. Isabel hoped the amount of the prize would reach him. "Five thousand dollars? American?"

No. Japanese. Rolling her eyes, Isabel said, "Yes."

"Hmmm."

"Does that mean you'll think about it?"

"I don't know. Art is not a contest."

Isabel wanted to deck him. Recollecting his pride— and how she could have forgotten so enormous an entity, she had no idea—she said, "Well ... I suppose that's so, but it would be a shame if someone else won the money, when you're the best."

Another pause, this one longer than the last. "Yes," he said musingly. "I *am* the best."

"Indeed, you are. And the world ought to know it. It would help if you won the contest, don't you think? Then your name would be in the newspaper and everyone would know who you are."

"Everybody already know who I am. Still ..."

"So you *will* think about it?" Isabel didn't want to press him, since he could be terribly temperamental, but the contest had come to matter to her. A lot.

"No. I not think."

Isabel's heart sank.

"I do it."

Her heart soared like a lark.

"Thank you! The contest dances are those we do all the time, but I suppose we'll need to practice anyhow."

"Yes. We practice."

When she emerged from behind her screen, he was waiting for her. As soon as he saw her, he cocked his elbow and jerked his head toward the entrance to the dance floor. Isabel presumed this was either an invitation or an order to take his arm and allow him to lead her out. Or allow herself to be led out by him, she guessed would be more accurate.

Oh, well, why not? She was pleased, in a way, to be accepted by her partner as worthy of his . . . elbow? But he'd agreed to enter the contest with her, bless his heart . . . if he had one.

As soon as they emerged from behind the curtain shielding the dance band from the dressing rooms, Jorge allowed his elbow to straighten gradually, until Isabel was holding on merely to the tips of his gloved fingers. Then he released even that token of a grip, and she understood that he'd just choreographed their entrance onto their own little stage in a way that would never have occurred to her.

She regretted that her uncle Charlie would never have the opportunity to meet Jorge Luis Savedra. It was probably true that Jorge would scorn her uncle, but they were both, in their own unique ways, masters of their art forms.

And he'd agreed to enter the contest with her!

The band had struck up a foxtrot and dancers were already thick on the floor. As soon as Somerset cut in front of another man in order to stand before her, bow, and take her hand, she realized he must have been keenly awaiting her arrival.

After what had passed between them the preceding night, she wasn't sure how to react to him. He *had* proposed, after all. That he had done so in a manner both insulting and infuriating to her, she wasn't sure he even understood. Since she was on the job, she smiled her usual be-nice-to-the-customers smile. "Good evening, Mr. FitzRoy."

"Good evening, Mrs. Golightly."

So much for that. As he trotted her off to mingle with the other dancers, Isabel considered whether or not to bring up last night's conversation. She decided to let him do it. She was at work.

He cleared his throat. "Um, Isabel, I apologize for the mess I made of what I said last night."

Hmm. Interesting. He wasn't even going to admit to having proposed. Icy fingers tapped on her heart, and she said, "Think nothing of it."

He wasn't as good a dancer as Jorge. That notion made her feel superior for a second.

On the other hand, she liked Somerset and she didn't like Jorge, so what did dancing matter? Or, say rather, she *had* liked Somerset. She wasn't sure any longer.

"How can I think nothing of it?" he asked with a little laugh. "I annoyed you, and that was the farthest intention from my mind."

Damn your mind, Isabel thought furiously. She wanted his *heart.*

Good heavens. Did she mean that? Oh, Lord, she wished he hadn't come tonight. Or . . . she *knew* she didn't mean that.

"I'm sure that's so," she said soothingly, wishing they could talk about something else.

He cleared his throat again. Must be nervous. Well, good, because she was, too.

"By way of making amends, I wondered if you and Miss Eunice would be interested in visiting the vaudeville some afternoon. I understand that you work at nights and that Miss Eunice is at school during the morning hours, but I thought perhaps we could find an agreeable time."

"The vaudeville?" Oh, my, she hadn't been to a musical comedy house since the last time she'd visited Uncle Charlie's. It sounded like such fun. Although . . . during that particular show, there had been one or two bawdy pieces that weren't at all suitable for children. On the other hand, that was in England, and perhaps music houses in America were different. "Would the show be appropriate for Eunice?"

"The show I've earmarked is set for Sunday afternoon at the Orpheum, and it's intended for children. There's a Chinese acrobatic act and a children's chorus, a strong man, some trained animals and lots of singing and dancing."

"Sunday afternoon . . ." Isabel hesitated. Her first impulse was to throw her arms around Somerset and tell him yes to everything he'd asked her thus far in this life. She knew that was the spontaneous, unsound, romantic side to her character rearing its ugly head—the one that had caused her so much trouble thus far in her life—and that it needed to be trod underfoot firmly and with great vigor. "It sounds like it would be entertaining," she said cautiously. "May I let you know after discussing it with Eunice?"

"Certainly."

Did she hear a sigh of relief come from her dancing partner? Isabel wasn't sure.

"In fact," he went on, as if attempting to sweeten the pot, "does Miss Eunice have any little friends from school that she might like to ask?"

In spite of her state of nerves, Isabel chuckled under her breath. She recounted the morning's conversation to Somerset as the music stopped and they applauded politely. She was amused by how hard he tried to hide his state of concern and how miserably he failed. "They're really only children," she said gently.

He eyed her slantways, making her heart skip. He didn't look like a horticulturist, particularly. He looked like an extremely handsome, desirable man. And he was her hero. She had the sudden and idiotic wish that he'd propose to her again tonight. This instant, in fact.

"You think so?"

She laughed, mentally taking herself by the shoulders and shaking herself silly. "Yes, I do. They may be smarter than other children, but they're still children and need to be treated as children sometimes. All the time, really. You only have to keep in mind that they understand more than most, but they still only have their own short life experiences."

He nodded. "Insightful."

"I've had years of practice."

Another gentleman claimed her hand, and Isabel was swept away in a waltz.

And so it went.

Somerset was as good as his word and invited not only Isabel and Eunice to the vaudeville show, but also Jason and Miss MacTavish and Lilian Blyley and Rebecca Steinberg.

Isabel was sure he invited the two other adults because he was nervous about being more or less alone with three little-girl "geniuses." She thought that was both sweet and sensible of him. The girls had a marvelous time, and Somerset took everyone to eat ice cream afterwards.

Isabel wasn't certain, but she deduced from his pallor and his state of exhaustion that he probably had a headache when he finally took them all home that evening. She didn't feel unwell at all. In fact, she felt simply splendid when she finally tucked Eunice into her bed and lay down to sleep in her own.

* * *

At three o'clock, the sound of soft sobbing gently invaded a dream in which she'd been dancing with Somerset. Knowing instantly what the noise meant, Isabel sat up in bed. "Eunice?"

"Oh, mama!" The little girl threw herself into her mother's arms. "I had a horrid dream!"

Isabel's arms wrapped around her daughter, and she held her close. "It's all right, sweetie. Everything is all right now."

"Why can't I stop dreaming about the ship, Mama? I saw all those dead bodies floating in the ocean. It was . . . it was . . ." Tears flooded her words.

"It was awful, wasn't it, dearie?" Six-year-old children, no matter how intelligent, shouldn't have memories like that one, Isabel thought, pain stabbing her in the heart.

Eunice nodded miserably.

"I'm so sorry, Eunice. I imagine that the dreams will lessen over time. It's not unusual for people to have bad dreams after such a terrible experience. I know Miss MacTavish does."

Settling more comfortably on her mother's lap, Eunice asked, "Do you have dreams about it, Mama?"

Recalling her fast-fading dream and wishing she were still in Somerset's arms, Isabel said, "Yes, I do. It's probably the worst thing that will ever happen in your life, sweetie. And I'll always be here when you dream bad dreams."

"You weren't here the last time," Eunice said, not accusingly. She was merely stating a fact.

Guilt speared Isabel. "I'm sorry, sweetie. I was at work."

Nodding, Eunice said, "Yes, I know. But Miss Linden and Miss MacTavish were very kind to me."

"They're very nice ladies."

"I wanted you, though."

Sometimes, Isabel thought as she gently rocked her daughter in her arms, life just sneaked up on you and grabbed you by the throat. Damn life, anyhow.

Chapter Thirteen

By the end of July, Somerset was willing to admit to himself that he loved Isabel. He was also beginning to wonder if he had a chance in hell with her. She was so excited about her upcoming dance contest, she could scarcely talk about anything else. Neither could the rest of the people who so often populated Loretta Linden's Russian Hill mansion. He knew, because he spent as much time in their company as was humanly possible for a man with other responsibilities to attend to.

Isabel and Jorge practiced for the contest as often as they could—and that was besides dancing together every night except Sundays and Mondays. It drove Somerset to distraction that they were so often together. *Dancing* together. In each other's dashed *arms*.

He'd never concurred with those stuffy souls who deplored dancing as sinful . . . until now. At the moment, he would cheerfully consign Vernon and Irene Castle and every other proponent of the healthful benefits of dancing to perdition. Except Isabel. He wanted to keep

Isabel around until she realized he was the only man in the world for her.

However, his wishing they wouldn't didn't affect the fact that Jorge and Isabel practiced all the blasted time. Except when they danced at the Fairfield, they practiced primarily in Loretta's ballroom, sometimes using Loretta's Victrola or her player piano, but more often using Marjorie MacTavish. Damned if the former stewardess, whom Somerset had scarcely pegged as human, much less musical, didn't play the piano as if she'd been born to it.

Eunice, always happy to help, manned the metronome, primarily as an aid to Loretta, who lost track of the beat more easily than the rest of them. Somerset FitzRoy, whom Isabel had forgiven—at least, he thought she had, since she was speaking to him again—and Jason Abernathy, whom Marjorie would probably never forgive, came to watch and to participate. Especially on Sunday afternoons, since Isabel and Jorge didn't have to work at the Fairfield and nobody else had to work at all, they gathered in Loretta's gigantic ballroom.

"Loretta's making me do this," Jason said pettishly, wiping his sweating brow with his white handkerchief. He'd bought a dozen of the Chinese-embroidered handkerchiefs from a street vendor and given half of them to Somerset who had no use for them, but accepted them because he approved of Jason's practical charity. "She says I have to learn how to dance better."

"You dance very well, Dr. Abernathy," Isabel said kindly.

"Better than I do," Somerset grumbled.

"You dance better than I do, too," Loretta said, laughing. "I mainly need you here to partner me."

"Indeed," agreed Isabel. "You're both coordinated and graceful, and your partners need never fear for their lives or the lives of their feet when they dance with you." She tactfully refrained from mentioning all the times Loretta had danced on Jason's toes.

Jorge snorted derisively, but they all ignored him. It was much the best way to deal with Jorge.

Isabel went on, "You, Mr. FitzRoy, only need more confidence to be truly superb. Watch Jorge here."

Somerset didn't want to watch Jorge. Jorge gave him a pain in a portion of his anatomy no gentleman should mention.

"Jorge is always confident when he dances," Isabel said. "Look at this."

Somerset looked. He didn't like what he saw. As Marjorie's hands skimmed over the piano keys and her fingers plunked out the merry melody to "Alexander's Ragtime Band," Jorge and Isabel danced together as if they'd been crafted out of cloud fluff and then animated. They didn't even appear to be working at it, although Somerset knew how dashed much energy dancing like that took.

They smiled and flirted with each other, and if he didn't know better—or hope better, perhaps—he'd have thought they were madly in love with each other. Then they turned a series of those tight little turns as if they'd been glued together before the beginning of time, their feet in perfect rhythm, neither of them ever getting in the other's way. He'd tried that move in front of his mirror and had tripped—and that was without a partner.

He couldn't dance like that in a million years. But he hated the notion of Isabel entering the dashed dance contest with Jorge. As much as he wished it could be he with whom Isabel won the funds to start her dashed dance academy, still more did he understand that Jorge was by far the better dancer. But the dashed woman had flatly refused his offer of funds to start up her academy. She wouldn't even accept his money as a loan. Said she'd already taken too much from people. Bah.

In short, the whole thing made him sick. Nevertheless, because he recognized jealousy when it attacked him, he joined Jason and Loretta in applauding the dancers when they twirled to a stop.

"You see?" Isabel said, only slightly out of breath and her cheeks flushed with exercise. "Jorge never looks as if he's trying to think of the steps or the choreography or anything other than having a good time."

Jorge buffed his fingernails on his lapel and appeared bored. Somerset exerted all of his self-control and didn't pop him one. "Yes," he said, hoping it didn't sound like a growl. "But I fear Jorge's had more practice than I." Somerset had more important work to do than dancing his life away.

"You don't need to practice dancing to portray confidence," Isabel declared. "Here. Let me show you." And she went over to him and held up her arms.

With mixed emotions, Somerset took her in his arms. Not that he didn't like having her there; he did. But he had trouble controlling his baser urges when he held Isabel. He had to fight the impulse to pick her up, march upstairs to her bedroom, and ravish her. He didn't know which bedroom was hers, true, but that didn't matter.

However, as long as he had her there, and as long as ravishing her was out of the question, he aimed to enjoy the experience of dancing. Turning his head toward the grand piano, he said, "A waltz if you please, Miss MacTavish." He wanted a slow waltz, but couldn't quite make himself say so.

Fortunately for him, Marjorie seemed to be in a slow-waltz mood at that particular moment. The lilting introduction to "Listen to the Mocking Bird" floated out over the ballroom, and Somerset set out with Isabel, for the first time wishing the contest would never arrive so they could keep practicing together forever.

He held her firmly but loosely, as he'd been instructed, and tried to become as one with the music. He couldn't do it. He was too desperately aware of Isabel in his arms. As the music lilted them across the polished parquet flooring, Somerset decided that she felt as if she belonged there always, as if God had intended this pairing.

Ass, he told himself. *God helps him who helps himself.* Which reminded him of Jason Abernathy's advice, which brought him back to reality.

Glancing down at Isabel, he noticed her eyes had drifted shut and she had a dreamy expression on her face. "Isabel?" he said softly.

With a small start, she opened her eyes and glanced up at him. She licked her lips, as if her mouth had gone dry. He knew his own mouth was longing for a taste of hers, but he didn't suppose her problem was the same as his. Unfortunately.

"There," said Isabel, giving herself a tiny shake that Somerset barely felt. "See? You dance beautifully. Gloriously, in fact. But you need to lift your chin and look down at me as if we were the only two people on earth."

He thought that was what he'd been doing. "That shouldn't be any trouble at all." Or it wouldn't be if he had a gun. Not that he'd ever do violence to Loretta or Jason or Eunice, but he didn't feel the same qualms about Jorge. Besides, it would be nice to be alone with Isabel.

Did she blush ever so slightly, as if she understood

the meaning behind his words? Somerset wasn't sure, but he tried to appear confident. It would, of course, help if he *felt* confident. He didn't.

His ambience was the earth and its loamy soil and the plant life that grew therein, not the dance floor. He could plan out a garden like nobody's business and grow roses that could win prizes at any rose contest in the United States. If you showed him a plant, he could tell you what it was called in three different countries and add the Latin botanical name, to boot.

"You're very smooth," Isabel said softly. "I mean, your moves are smooth. I mean . . . Oh, dear."

She was blushing. "Thank you." She was the most adorable woman he'd ever met in his life. Why the deuce wouldn't she marry him?

"What I meant was that you really do dance well," she said, trying to recover her composure. Somerset danced her away from their friends, to the far corner of the ballroom. "All you need is to project more . . . more— Oh!" Her smile nearly sent him reeling. "I know *exactly* what it is. And it's something Jorge has in abundance. Overabundance, actually. You need to portray arrogance!"

Arrogance. Good word for Jorge, all right. Somerset's erratic thoughts left the bedroom and returned to the dance floor. "Arrogance. Of course. Why didn't I think of that?"

"Because you're too sensible to be arrogant," Isabel said, laughing. "But arrogance is what you need to portray as you dance. You've seen Jorge and me at the Fairfield. Now, on a daily basis, I'm not a dramatic person, but I am on the dance floor. Jorge, on the other hand, is arrogant all the time, but you can see that acting can be just as good as the real thing. At least, I think so. I mean, I do think Jorge and I make a good dance team, and I'm always acting when I dance with him."

"You're an excellent dance team." And, Somerset's pangs of jealousy aside, it sounded as if that's all they were. He decided to be bold and ask. "Ah . . . you don't fancy Jorge as anything more than that?"

Her eyes grew huge. "What do you mean?"

"Well . . . I mean . . ." Damnation, she hadn't married *him*, Somerset FitzRoy. Did she want that smoldering popinjay Jorge Luis Savedra instead? "I mean, well, you don't fancy *Jorge* as a husband, do you?"

She made a false step in the waltz, and they very nearly crashed into a wall. Somerset had strong muscles, however—from hurling trees around, dash it—and he prevented a serious accident.

"Jorge?" Her voice squeaked the name out. "Whatever made you think that?"

He couldn't tell if she was amused or irate. "Just wondered." His still-festering sense of injury made him add, "I mean, you refused my proposal. I thought perhaps it was because your feelings were engaged elsewhere. With Mr. Savedra, perhaps." And that was another thing: she called that greasy Argentine by his Christian name, yet she persisted in calling him *Mr. FitzRoy*. Bah.

"Dear God." She didn't say anything else for several seconds, and Somerset wondered if he'd offended her. If he had, it was the second time he'd managed to do so without any conscious help from his own brain. He supposed he agreed with popular opinion: women were unfathomable.

At last she said, "No, Mr. FitzRoy, my feelings are not engaged elsewhere. Especially not with Jorge. My refusal of your proposal had nothing to do with . . . with feelings. It was based on something else entirely."

The odd note in her voice made him frown. Peering down at her, he realized she had her own head lowered, so he couldn't read her expression. Swell. True, even when he was staring straight into her eyes, he hadn't a clue to her thoughts, but looking at her face might help. "Ah . . . would you like to tell me what your refusal was based on?" Miss Grimble, his third-grade teacher, would have smacked the back of his hand with a ruler if he'd used that sentence structure in her classroom.

She lifted her head, and he saw that she was chewing on her lower lip. What's more, she appeared flustered and a little sad. His heart lurched. "I'm sorry, Isabel. I had absolutely no intention of stirring up unhappy memories. Or anything. I mean . . . I didn't . . ."

"I know what you mean," she said, rescuing him from a pit of jumbled words. "But I can't . . . well, let's just say I don't think I can talk about it."

"Oh." What did this mean? Was she still so madly in love with her damned dead husband that she wouldn't even *talk* about him? It didn't make any sense to Somerset. Trying to be fair, he mentally acknowledged that he'd never known a love as great as all that. His few flings had been fun and physical. His feelings hadn't been engaged.

Until now. At this moment, he was relatively certain that if Isabel should vanish from his life, he'd never be able to fill up the gaping hole her absence would create. Dashed uncomfortable emotion, love. He wished it hadn't hit him.

"I'd prefer not to discuss it any longer," Isabel said in a stifled voice. "If you don't mind."

He did mind, actually, but he couldn't, as a gentleman, argue with her, especially not in Loretta Linden's ballroom with the whole world watching. "Not at all," he lied, and he waltzed her back to the piano.

* * *

As Isabel prepared to take to the Fairfield's polished parquet dance floor two evenings later, she contemplated Somerset FitzRoy. Never one to assume things—she'd done that once and it had nearly cost her everything, including her life—she went over the conversation they'd had in Loretta's ballroom. She thought, although she wasn't positive, that Somerset sounded as if he still wanted to marry her.

She knew for a certified fact that she couldn't marry him without telling him her story. She cared too much for him to lie to him, and not confessing would be every bit as bad as a telling an outright lie. Isabel feared that her unhappy past might be an insurmountable obstacle to achieving any kind of pleasant future. Offhand, she couldn't think of anyone she'd sooner live out that future with than Somerset FitzRoy. Bother.

Could she possibly tell him the truth about herself? She tried to envision the scene in her mind, but her mind wouldn't cooperate. It balked at the mere notion of confessing to Somerset FitzRoy, the one person on earth whose good opinion truly mattered to her. Well, besides Eunice.

Anyhow, Jorge and she were going to win the dance contest, and then her troubles would be over, because she'd be able to get rich San Franciscans to send their debutantes and sons to her dance academy. She'd still be able to see Somerset and all her friends. She knew she wanted more than friendship from Somerset but decided not to think about it right now. There were more important goals to achieve before she could solve the problem of what and how much to tell Somerset. She and Jorge *had* to win the contest. Isabel wouldn't—couldn't—settle for anything less.

"Isabel!"

Jorge's peremptory voice jerked her out of her blue mood. "One moment, please!"

Oh, Lord, she'd been mooning over Somerset and her past sins and poor Eunice, and she wasn't ready. Jorge could become very unpleasant when Isabel kept him waiting. Jabbing a red feather into her headband, she peered in the mirror and readjusted the black ribbon about her neck. Then she tugged at her left sleeve, and decided she was almost ready to face Jorge and a roomful of happy diners.

"Beautiful," a sultry Argentine voice behind her said. "Excellent."

Catching Jorge's eye in the mirror, Isabel smiled and said, "Thank you." Returning to her toilette, she stabbed one last red feather into her black headband and rose from the dressing bench. "I'm ready," she said brightly.

Jorge took her hand and glided them both toward the curtain. His movements were so lithe, they sometimes made Isabel feel clumsy, as if she were a little girl trying to keep up with an older brother. He was certainly the consummate tango dancer. That was a good thing. Even when Isabel made the occasional misstep, Jorge was perfect enough to keep the both of them going.

At the moment, as they waited for their cue, he had his arm around her and was holding her close. A little too close for her comfort, but she didn't object. Jorge knew what he was doing, and he certainly didn't mean anything by it. Jorge had no interest in her as a woman, but only as a dance partner.

She heard the announcement of their first demonstration number, a so-called "steamy Latin dance called the tango," the band slithered into the first couple of bars, and Jorge oozed them both out from behind the curtain. Isabel's heart bounced slightly when she caught sight of Somerset and Dr. Abernathy in the audience.

As Jorge flung her here and there during the dance, doing his version of a modified French "Apache" dance, Isabel kept an eye on Somerset. With a sigh, she decided that Somerset appeared the very epitome of a handsome knight come to rescue her from a dismal and solitary future.

Ah, but what about the dance academy?

Dance academies were all good and well, she told herself, but she still might end up alone and lonely. Besides, she had to win the contest first.

You will win the contest. With Jorge as your partner, you can't lose. Then you'll be able to establish your dance academy and become the toast of San Francisco's dance teachers.

And you'll still be alone.

Bother.

If there were any justice in the universe, people's hearts would behave sensibly instead of tilting one way one day and another way the next and keeping one constantly confused with their vagaries and inconsistencies. On the other hand, if hearts behaved like brains, there would be no use for both organs. And that would be fine with her.

Before the dance ended, she'd just about convinced herself that her confused emotions had sent her 'round the bend. Then, when Jorge led her offstage amid a clamor of applause, sat her down on the dressing bench, and said, "And now, we marry, you and me," she knew it for a cold fact.

She stared up at him, her mind a blank. "I . . . I beg your pardon?"

He pointed insolently from himself to her. "We marry now. We must. You are wasted on any other man." He buffed his fingernails on his lapel.

He wanted to *marry* her? Isabel could scarcely believe him. He'd never given her the slightest indication that he cared for her. Never. Not once.

Yet it wasn't like Jorge to make jokes.

She decided to take him seriously, although she still had trouble believing he'd actually proposed to her. "But . . . but . . . Jorge, I'm flattered, really, but . . ." She saw his eyes narrow and realized his temper was beginning to smolder; Lord knew she'd had enough practice in recognizing the symptoms. She'd managed not to aggravate him very often since they'd been partners, but keeping on his good side was a touch-and-go proposition.

"We marry," he insisted. "It's a matter of sense."

A matter of sense, was it? Isabel felt a headache beginning to nibble at the corners of her brain and thought that if there was one thing on earth she needed less than she needed Jorge's proposal right now, she couldn't think what it might be.

"But . . . do you love me?" The question came out in a squeak, and Isabel felt silly. But, honestly, wasn't love supposed to enter into marriage somewhere?

"Love? Love?" He stared at her as if she were crazy, which made sense to her, since she thought she must be. "Love is no matter. We belong together."

"Oh." Good heavens. Isabel guessed she was grateful he wasn't attempting to make passionate love to her, but . . .

"We marry," Jorge repeated. "We be a team always."

Terrifying thought. Isabel frantically searched for some words that would dissuade but not enrage Jorge. "But really, Jorge, we can't marry," she said, feeling weak and irresolute and ill-equipped to fight a battle with the man upon whom she was relying for her entire future. It sounded bad when she put it like that.

"Why not?" He stood upright before her, stamped his foot, and glared down at her, his fists on his lean hips.

"Because—because—" She was at a loss for words. She couldn't very well tell him that she considered him vain and ridiculous and good for nothing except dancing. Then she recalled a line Somerset had spoken to her. "Because my affections are already engaged elsewhere." Bowing her head, she tried to look demure.

"What?" Jorge exclaimed. "What that mean? Your affections are engaged? What do you mean?"

"I mean that I care for another gentleman, Jorge. Your proposal means the world to me, really," she hurried on, lying through her teeth. "I appreciate it ever so much, but you see, I can't marry you if I care for another gentleman."

Jorge held onto his savage frown for a few seconds, then grunted, "Huh!" and marched off. Watching his back, Isabel considered what that might mean. Nothing good to her, she was sure.

As she wandered behind her dressing screen, unhooking her neck ribbon and twirling her red feather in her fingers, she wondered how many other proposals she was going to get this evening. At least Jorge had offered her marriage. Most of the men who asked similar questions while they danced with her had other arrangements in mind.

She feared it was going to be a long night. The only bright spot in it that she'd discovered so far was the image of Somerset FitzRoy sitting at a supper table on the edge of the dance floor. An impulse to throw herself into his arms and beg him to have his way with her followed her through her costume change and clear out to the dance floor on Jorge's arm.

* * *

"Now that," declared Jason Abernathy with vibrant approval in his voice, clapping for all he was worth, "was one spectacular dance number."

"Hmm, yes. It was." Somerset didn't like it, either. It didn't seem right that Isabel and that Argentinean fairy should dance so well together. "She plans to win the contest with him, of course."

"Of course."

He heard Jason chuckle and turned to frown at him.

Jason held up a hand. "Don't get jealous, Somerset. I'm sure Mrs. Golightly hasn't a bit of interest in the fellow except as a dance partner."

Jealous? Outrageous! "I'm not jealous," he said loudly, embarrassing himself. He looked around, but no one else was paying any attention to their table. The music was loud, and they were all chatting and dancing.

"Oh. I see."

Damn the man. He didn't believe him.

Unfortunately, Somerset didn't believe himself, either. He was unbelievably jealous of Jorge Savedra, and that was the unvarnished, unpalatable truth. In fact, when he boiled everything down to its essence, he, Somerset FitzRoy, a man who'd never even believed in the softer emotions, a man who'd given himself over to scholarship of a high order and who was now writing the definitive book on native American plants and their uses, was head over heels in love with Isabel Golightly, a woman who evidently didn't care for him except as a friend.

It was a discouraging thought. Worse, he didn't know what to do about it. She'd rejected his proposal of marriage already. He would be a cad to pursue the matter after she'd made her wishes known on the subject.

How degrading.

Somerset had been staring at his empty wine glass,

but he knew when Isabel reappeared to dance with the customers. He had some sort of magnetic reaction to her presence. Whenever she was in his vicinity, he knew it. Turning his head, he discovered he was right. She and Jorge were just emerging from behind the curtain.

She looked stunning, as usual. Clad in a blue dress crafted of a feathery-light fabric, with a high waist cinched by a darker blue cummerbund, the hem was uneven, showing a good deal of her perfectly shaped ankles. Somerset's heart felt heavy with the knowledge that he couldn't possess that brilliant creature. Not that he wanted to *possess* her. Exactly. But he wanted her. Badly.

"Ask the lady to dance, Somerset," Jason said under his breath. "Are you waiting until a dozen other men snatch her up? Get along with you!"

No further urging was required. Somerset popped up from his chair and made a dash at Isabel, trying to appear dignified even in his hurry. As he approached, he searched her face. She seemed to be upset or worried about something. He hoped Eunice hadn't taken ill or anything. One of Isabel's most endearing qualities was her devotion to her daughter, as odd as Eunice was. Not that he believed parents should shun odd children, but . . . oh, hang it, he knew what he meant.

As soon as she saw him heading her way, she altered her course to intercept him. Somerset took this as a favorable signal. He appreciated her wan smile, too, although he might have wished it wasn't quite *so* wan. He took her hand and leaned closer to her. "Is something the matter, Isabel? Are you feeling quite the thing?"

"Oh, dear." She laughed one of her silvery, tinkling laughs. "Do I look that bad?"

"You could never look bad." He grinned, feeling more than a little sappy, but he was under her influence and couldn't seem to help himself "But you don't look as at ease with the world as you usually do. Is anything the matter with Miss Eunice?"

"Eunice? Why, no. What should be the matter with Eunice?"

"Er . . . I don't know."

"Oh."

Clumsy ass. Taking a deep breath, Somerset attempted to redress his question. "Not that you could ever appear anything less than utterly charming and beautiful, but I sense a certain . . . ah . . . disquiet about you tonight." Mentally kicking himself in the head, Somerset bitterly wondered if he might be better off if he continued the conversation in Latin. Latin couldn't possibly be more formal and unromantic than that stupid speech had been.

The band struck up a waltz, bless it, since that was his best dance, and he took Isabel in his arms. She fitted beautifully there. She was as graceful as a willow tree, as slender as an iris stalk and as perfect as a rose. Her skin was as smooth and delicate as magnolia blossoms, and her eyes were as blue as—hang it, he still hadn't come up with the right blue for her eyes. Ageratum came close, although they were a little on the purple side. Isabel's eyes tended toward the gray, not the purple. He'd keep working on it.

"You're very perceptive, Mr. FitzRoy. Something just happened that . . . unsettled me."

"I'm sorry to hear it." He took another breath and a chance. "Ah . . . would you like to talk about it? I may not be much of a dancer, but I listen quite well." He smiled at her, throwing all his good wishes and any charm he might possess into the expression.

She gave him a lovely smile in return. "You dance

beautifully. You needn't ever apologize for your dancing skills."

"No need for flattery. I know I'm no Mr. Savedra."

This produced a huge sigh. "No, thank God, you're not. He proposed marriage to me this evening."

Somerset stopped dead in the middle of the dance floor, causing quite a pile-up. "He *what?*"

Isabel tugged him gently by the arm, and they set off waltzing again, garnering only a couple of glares and half a dozen grins for having interrupted the smooth flow of the dancing couples. "There's no need for alarm, but that's why I'm a little upset now. He said it only made sense that we marry, and that I'd be wasted on any other man."

"Good God."

Somerset didn't like this. He didn't like it at all. He thought he'd imagined all the possible proposals and propositions Isabel might have to fend off in her career as a dancer, but he'd never even considered Jorge Luis Savedra as a rival. The dashed little fairy. Only, apparently he wasn't a fairy. Damn, damn, damn. This was bad.

She sighed again, and he tightened his arms around her slightly. "I refused him, of course." She actually managed a little laugh. "Can you imagine a marriage to Jorge Luis Savedra?"

"No. The thought boggles my mind." Although the urge to hug her and kiss her soundly was so strong, he fairly trembled while suppressing it, Somerset didn't dare become too forward in his attentions. It was his intention not to seduce her, but to marry her. She needed to know that he, of all the men in her new world, respected her and held only honorable intentions toward her.

Which made him think about Jorge. Isabel was with the man all the time. He could conceivably become ugly about her refusal. He could even, heaven forbid, take forced advantage of her. The notion made him see red.

"Listen, Mrs. Golightly, if that man offers you any insult, I'll be more than happy to—"

"Oh, no! No, please. It wasn't an insult. It was an . . . well, it was a proposal of marriage. That's not insulting." She didn't sound sure of herself.

"I suppose not." It galled him that she might be lumping Savedra's proposal and his own under the same category in her mind: Not insulting. A tepid classification at best. "But do you think he'll accept your refusal with equanimity?"

Yet another sigh. "Unfortunately, Jorge doesn't accept anything with equanimity. His entire personality is . . . well, unequanimous. If there is such a word."

"Perhaps you should ask Eunice." This little quip produced a small laugh from her, and Somerset congratulated himself. He surreptitiously rubbed his cheek against her soft, sweetly scented hair. "Do you think he'll continue to bother you?"

"Probably not. I'm mainly worried about the dance contest. If he becomes angry with me, he might not enter the contest with me, and that would be dreadful."

"Does the contest matter that much to you?"

"Oh, yes!" She gazed up into his eyes with fervent intensity. "It means *everything* to me. It's how I plan to earn money to start my dance academy."

"Hmmm. I don't suppose you'd reconsider my offer of a loan to start your academy, would you?"

She gave him such a wonderful smile, his knees nearly buckled. "I don't suppose I would, but I do thank you. You're such a very kind man."

Kind, was he? Well, it was better than unequanimous, he supposed. It still didn't sound as if she were considering him for a permanent place in her life. Weren't women supposed to fall for cads and roués? Somerset was afraid he didn't qualify as either of those things.

Somerset and Isabel clapped politely when the band ended their number, and Somerset said, "Come over to the table and say hello to Dr. Abernathy. We dined here tonight in order to discuss some business, and decided to stay and dance a little, too."

"Gladly."

He led her to their table. Jason rose and bowed, and she smiled and gave him her gloved hand to shake. "It's good to see you, Dr. Abernathy."

"Likewise, Mrs. Golightly. I have something here for Miss Eunice." He reached into his coat pocket and withdrew a small wrapped package. "It's jasmine soap. One of my patients makes it." His face clouded momentarily, and Somerset wondered why. He didn't pursue the matter.

"Thank you so much. Eunice loves the soaps and lotions you give her. She's never had such exquisite toiletries before." Isabel lifted the small bar to her nose and sniffed delicately. "It smells heavenly. She'll be ever so grateful."

"My pleasure. Do you have a minute to talk, or do you need to get back to your work?"

"I'd better be available to dance with the customers. I'll try to come back and chat after a few more dances."

"Your tango number is spectacular," Jason told her with a wicked grin. Somerset wanted to level him.

Blushing prettily, Isabel said, "That's Jorge. He's such a dramatic choreographer."

"I must agree if he choreographed that one. It was brilliant."

"Thank you." She hurried off, tucking the soap into her cummerbund.

Somerset sank with a sigh into his chair and stared after her. "*Jorge* proposed marriage to her this evening." He gave Jorge's name the emphasis he felt it deserved.

"My God, did he really?" Jason chuckled.

"Yes. She's afraid he won't enter the contest with her because she refused him." Somerset didn't feel the slightest inclination to chuckle.

His fingers drummed on the table as he watched Isabel dance. And dance and dance and dance. And all the men she danced with, he wanted to murder. This was terrible. He didn't know what to do about it.

"I doubt she has to worry about the contest," Jason said after a moment or two.

"Really?" Somerset left off wishing all the other men in the room were dead and glanced at Jason. "Why not? He's a weasely little scoundrel. I wouldn't put it past him to bow out of the contest because he's peeved with her."

"Ah," said Jason, "but you're forgetting the money angle of the thing, Somerset. I seriously doubt that he'll be willing to walk out on twenty-five hundred dollars for the sake of peevishness."

Somerset brightened. "You're right! I'd forgotten about the money."

"I doubt that Mr. Savedra has."

That was the first good thing Somerset had ever heard said about Jorge Savedra, other than that he was a swell dancer.

Chapter Fourteen

Isabel began to grow nervous as the time approached for her to leave the dance floor and get ready for her next number. What would Jorge do? Would he be angry? Would he pout? What she feared most was that he'd storm off in a huff and never come back.

But that was silly. He needed his job almost as much as she needed hers. She bit her lower lip, and the words to the tune now playing fluttered through her head. The song spoke of a woman who'd married an old man for money, and who now regretted doing it. While she seemed happy and carefree, she wasn't. Isabel doubted that. Marrying for money seemed much more sensible this evening than it usually did.

The music ended at last, and she could no longer put off facing Jorge. She dreaded this. But she had to change into her costume for the ragtime demonstration with which she and Jorge were going to thrill the audience.

Slipping backstage, she stopped, closed her eyes, sucked in about three gallons of air, and wished she were already rich and in control of her very own dance academy. She wished so even harder when she opened her eyes to see Jorge awaiting her, fists on hips, scowl in place. She sighed deeply and braced herself.

"What do you do with your husband?"

Isabel blinked. "What do I do with him? What do you mean, Jorge? I don't have a husband."

"What do you do with this . . . this man you affection? You marry with him?"

"Er . . . yes. I mean, I hope to marry him. One day."

Jorge sneered. He had a superb sneer. "He not ask you yet? Huh! He not ask you yet. I know. But you affectionate him. Bah! He is not the one for you. I—" he pounded himself on the chest. "I am the one."

No, he wasn't. "I'm sorry, Jorge. I'm not sure what will happen, but I do know that I dearly love the other man. I . . . I'll have to talk to you later about it."

"Who is he?"

"Who?" Good question. She'd like to say *Somerset FitzRoy*, but she wasn't sure he really gave a rap about her. "Uh . . . I don't think . . ." Her words trailed off.

"Huh." He stalked behind his changing screen. "I know how to take care of this. In Argentina, we *know* what to do in this cases."

Isabel, behind her own screen, felt her eyes grow wide and her heart thud painfully. Holding on to the edge of the screen, she peered out from behind it, but she couldn't see Jorge. "What do you mean? How do you take care of these things?"

"We have our ways," Jorge said ominously.

Alarmed, Isabel said, "Don't you dare do anything to anybody, Jorge. I haven't even told you who it is. And I won't, either, if you threaten to do anything to him."

"There is no one," Jorge said smugly. "I know it."

"There is, too!"

"No. You won't tell me, so I know you lie."

"I'm not either lying!"

"Huh. You only shy for me. You not be shy long. I know how to treat a woman."

Good Lord! Isabel felt panic beginning to snatch at her nerves. "No! I mean, I'm not shy. I love another man, Jorge!"

"Huh."

She could hear him smirk from clear across the room. "It's the truth!"

"Huh. You can't tell me the name, because he *has* no name. He nobody."

Almost beside herself, Isabel blurted out, "It's Mr. FitzRoy!"

Silence issued from Jorge. Isabel could have kicked herself.

After a moment, Jorge said, "FitzRoy."

Isabel, her heart hammering, said, "Yes."

He said, "Huh" again.

Beginning to worry about Somerset, Isabel said hotly, "I mean it, Jorge. Don't you dare do anything to Mr. FitzRoy."

"Huh."

"Jorge?"

"What?"

"I mean it."

"Huh."

"Jorge!"

The dancer flipped his hand in the airy gesture he made when he wanted things to go away and stop bothering him. "Huh."

Isabel figured that was about as much assurance as she was liable to get from that source this evening. Lord, Lord, *why* has she mentioned Somerset's name? Why hadn't she made up a name? Oh, what did it mat-

ter, as long as Jorge believed her. She was so stupid
sometimes, she could scarcely believe it.

When she got home that night, she had terrible
dreams in which Somerset FitzRoy showed up at
Loretta's front door with a knife in his back. It was she,
and not Eunice, who woke, trembling and teary-eyed,
in the middle of the night.

Somerset sat at the desk in his library, working on a
plan for a garden he'd been hired to landscape, but his
mind wasn't on his work. The hour was approaching
eight in the evening, past the time he usually ate dinner, and he was contemplating dining at the Fairfield.
He'd already told his housekeeper he'd be dining out,
but he hadn't decided where to do it yet.

The Fairfield seemed to call to him, sort of like
Lorelei calling to a poor, bemused boatman on the
Rhine. The Fairfield was where he *wanted* to dine. The
problem was that Isabel might get the wrong idea if he
ate there every dashed night. Or she'd get the right
idea, which might be worse. Or, then again, it might be
better.

It would help if Somerset had a single clue as to how
she felt about him. He'd tell her he loved her in a second, if he thought he had a snowball's chance in hell of
her loving him back. But he wasn't fond of rejection or
humiliation.

If he was madly in love with her and she only faintly
liked him, he didn't really want to know it. He didn't
think his ego, which wasn't nearly as large as Jorge
Savedra's, could stand the pain.

Suddenly, he lifted his head at the sound of someone
hammering on his front door. Whoever it was must be
pounding hard, because his house had thick walls and

he couldn't ordinarily hear people when they knocked. He stepped to the door of his office and peered out in time to see his housekeeper, Mrs. Prendergast, hurry to open it. He was as flabbergasted as she when he beheld Isabel Golightly standing on his front porch, looking agitated.

She cried out when she saw him, "Oh! Thank God! You're here! And you're alive!"

Whatever that meant. "Isabel!" He cried, rushing out to see what was wrong. Recalling his manners, he said, "I mean, Mrs. Golightly."

"Oh, I don't care what you call me!" she cried. Glancing at Mrs. Prendergast, she asked, "May I come in? Something dreadful has happened!"

Resuming control of himself and his household, he smiled at Mrs. Prendergast. "I'll take care of this, Mrs. Prendergast. Thank you."

The housekeeper sniffed once, then turned and headed back to wherever she spent her waking hours. Somerset didn't know. The keeping of his house was a mystery to him. "Yes, please, Mrs. Golightly, come in. You seem to be upset."

"Upset? Upset! I've never been more upset in my life!" She sucked in a deep breath and passed her hand over her porcelain brow. "No, that's not true. I was more upset than this when I thought Eunice and I were going to drown."

"I'm sorry you're distressed." *Stuffy, Somerset. Unbend, will you?*

"I'm better now that I've seen you. I'm so *glad* you're well."

Confused but gratified, Somerset said, "Thank you." He squinted at the clock in the hallway. "But aren't you supposed to be working right now?"

"Yes!" She shrilled the word, then passed her hand

over her forehead again. "I'm sorry, I didn't mean to shout."

"Come into the parlor," Somerset suggested. He'd never pegged Isabel Golightly as the hysterical type, but perhaps he'd been mistaken. And why had she expected him not to be well? "Let me pour you a sherry or a bit of brandy to calm your nerves."

"*Nothing* will calm my nerves," Isabel avowed as if she were pronouncing a death sentence on herself.

Somerset led her into his parlor and guided her to the inglenook. There, two chairs had been artistically arranged before the fireplace with a table between them, the detective novel he'd been reading residing there at an angle pleasing to his eye. He switched on the table lamp he'd bought at Tiffany and Company in New York City. The shade was a masterpiece of stained-glass irises, and the light from it glowed in soft colors that brought out the richness of the black-cherry wood from which the chairs were crafted.

Gesturing at one of the chairs, he said, "Please take a seat, and tell me about it. Perhaps we can solve your problem between us." He gave her a smile that he hoped would encourage her to unburden herself. He didn't know what had happened to upset her, but he wanted to slay it for her, whatever it was.

She took off her hat, flung it onto a window seat nearby, and was about to sit down, when she took note of the room into which Somerset had led her. With one hand on the arm of the chair and the other clutching a small handbag to her bosom, she said, startled, "My goodness, what a beautiful room!"

Beaming with genuine pleasure, Somerset lifted a decanter and poured some sherry into a tiny cut-crystal stemmed glass. "Thank you. I'm glad you like it. I designed the house, you know, and furnished it myself."

He was proud of this house. Not only had he designed it and the grounds himself, but he'd had it furnished in the Craftsman Mission style, and it was both
uncluttered and elegant. None of your Victorian frou-
frou for him. Strictly Stickley, had been his motto when
selecting furnishings. He'd wanted to be able to live in
harmony with his choices for years to come, and he
loved the rich woods Stickley used. All the furniture
complemented the polished cedar floors, Oriental and
Indian rugs, and the clean lines of the house.

Isabel sat slowly, her eyes huge as they surveyed her
surroundings. "I didn't know that. You did a beautiful
job. I don't believe I've ever seen a room that . . . that . . .
appeals to me so much."

Aha. If she wouldn't marry him for himself, perhaps
she'd marry him for his house. It was a thought, anyhow. He handed her the glass. "Why don't you sip this
and tell me what happened to put you in such a state."
Not that he minded particularly. Whatever it was that
had upset her had brought her here, to him, and
Somerset considered that a very good thing.

She sipped a tiny bit of the honey-colored liqueur
and wrinkled her nose. Exercising great restraint,
Somerset didn't grab her, tuck her under his arm, and
run upstairs with her. She'd never know what she did to
him. Well . . . if he was lucky, she'd find out someday.
Smiling at her fondly, he said, "It's supposed to be excellent sherry. It shouldn't produce nose wrinkles."

"What?" She looked at her glass, then looked at
Somerset and laughed. Good sign, he decided. "Oh, I
didn't mean to wrinkle my nose at your sherry. I guess
I'm not accustomed to drinking wine. Or anything else
of an alcoholic nature, for that matter."

"Perhaps it will help soothe your nerves," he ventured, wondering if she'd ever tell him what the matter

was. Not that he cared, particularly, as long as she stayed here, with him.

Her delicate eyebrows tilted down over her beautiful blue eyes. They were the color of—dash it, he still didn't know exactly which flower did them justice. Perhaps he'd have to hybridize one for her himself. "I'm sorry I barged in on you, Mr. FitzRoy—"

"Please call me Somerset. I think we're well enough acquainted by now to use first names."

Her cheeks, warmed by the glow of light from the stained glass lampshade, bloomed a pretty pink. "Thank you. Please call me Isabel."

"Gladly. You have a lovely name, Isabel."

"Thank you." She took another sip of sherry in an attempt to drown her embarrassment. Then she took a deep breath and blurted out, "Jorge has disappeared."

Taken aback, Somerset paused in the act of pouring himself some sherry. He turned to stare at her. "He what?"

"He's disappeared. Vanished. Mr. Balderston has sent some of his people out to look at him, but I fear he may not come back."

Puzzled, although not especially worried, about this state of affairs—in truth, he felt rather like applauding—Somerset took his sherry and sat in the chair next to Isabel's. "I'm not sure I understand."

Isabel put her glass down on the table, making sure she placed a coaster on the shining wooden surface first. "I don't understand, either. All I know is that he didn't show up for work tonight. I thought perhaps he was miffed with me because I'd refused his proposal." She gave him a quick glance. "Not that I believe I broke his heart or anything, but you know how big his head is."

"Yes, I'd noticed that about him." He hoped the son

of a dog had drowned in the San Francisco Bay, although he'd never say so, since he understood how upset Isabel was.

"And I . . . well, I thought I'd ask you if you'd seen him."

"I?" Confused, Somerset paused with his sherry glass halfway to his lips. "Why did you think I might have seen him?"

"Because . . . because . . ." She stood abruptly. "Oh, it's all insane!"

She started pacing in front of the two chairs. She looked quite charming there, stamping back and forth on his imported Bokhara rug. Fitted right in, in fact. Somerset approved.

But that didn't answer his question. He shook his head in an effort to clear it of irrelevancies. "Did he state an intention of coming here?" he suggested, perplexed.

"No." Isabel strode to another table, where she picked up Somerset's first published book, *Flora of San Francisco.* He was proud of that book, as he was proud of his house. The colored plates were gorgeous, too. "My goodness, did you write this book?"

"Yes, indeed. My first effort. I drew the illustrations as well." He hoped he sounded modest and unassuming. The truth was that about the only things he was proud of were his work and his house.

"I had no idea," Isabel whispered. "Why, you're truly an expert in your field, aren't you?"

"I suppose I am." Even more modestly. He was in danger of fading into the woodwork if this kept up. Deciding to assert himself a bit, he said, "I am considered an expert on the flora of my adopted state, and especially that of San Francisco and vicinity. I give lectures at the university sometimes."

"My goodness." She turned and gazed, wide-eyed, at him.

It took some effort, but he managed to remain seated and didn't leap up and take her in his arms. Trying to get the conversation back to some sort of manageable state, he brought up Jorge again. If anything could dampen his ardor, it was the slick Argentine. "But why did you think he might come here, Isabel? We aren't exactly close friends or anything." He had to fight the impulse to strangle the fellow most of the time.

She gestured wildly, "Because of something I said! Oh, it's so stupid! And it's all my fault!"

Isabel had seldom felt this helpless. Evidently, Jorge hadn't come after Somerset with a dagger or a gun or anything. And now Somerset wanted to know why she believed he might have done so. She couldn't tell him it was because she'd told Jorge she was going to marry him. The whole situation was insane.

But she had to confess. Somerset needed to know so he could watch his back, in case Jorge truly was going to try to kill him. The entire mess was too mortifying for words.

However, Isabel had never shirked a duty in her life. She'd made plenty of mistakes, some of which, like this one, she owed to her impulsive nature, but at least she knew when and how to face the consequences. With a deep, unhappy sigh, she sank into the perfectly magnificent chair she'd vacated a minute or two earlier.

Somerset smiled encouragingly. He was *so* kind. Isabel loved him madly. Passionately. She wished she'd accepted his proposal when he'd offered it, even if he hadn't accompanied it with words of love.

Staring into her lap, she murmured, "When I refused his proposal, I told him it was because I was going to marry you."

From the corner of her eye, she saw him jerk in his chair, spilling a few droplets of sherry onto his tweed trousers. Oh, dear.

"Uh . . . I beg your pardon?" He made a couple of tentative swipes at his trousers, but didn't seem concerned that the sherry might stain them. He appeared too astonished to think about it, actually.

Daring to look him in the face—after all, if she was going to be responsible for his dastardly murder, she ought at least to face him when she warned him about it—she said, "I'm so sorry, Somerset. When I refused Jorge's proposal of marriage, he demanded to know why. I tried to put him off with vague references to someone else, but he demanded to know whom. When I couldn't tolerate his pestering another minute, I said it was you."

"Me?"

She nodded.

His smile grew larger. That's because he still didn't understand. Isabel worried her lower lip between her teeth. "I'm so sorry."

"Please don't be sorry. If only you meant it, I'd be the happiest man on earth."

She blinked at him. "You would?"

"Yes. I want to marry you, Isabel. I already told you that."

"But . . . you were only being nice to me." Remembering the problem at issue here, she waved her hand as if to clean the slate between them. Although she longed to pursue the other subject, it was Somerset's imminent demise that was important now. "Anyhow, that's not the problem. The problem is that Jorge threatened to kill the man who had engaged my affections."

"Good God."

"Yes! So don't you see? I practically threw you to the wolves, Somerset! I'm so, so sorry! I didn't even think when I mentioned your name that Jorge might kill you!" Again, guilt and worry overwhelmed her and she rose from her chair to pace. "He claims that's what people do in the Argentine."

"Good God."

"It's all my fault," she went on. "It's because I'm so concerned about that contest and the money. I wanted him to enter the contest with me, and I was afraid when I refused to marry him that he wouldn't. When he kept after me about it, I thought that if he knew it was you, he'd understand and still be willing to be in the contest with me." She whirled around and threw out her arms. "I've endangered your life for the sake of a contest! Oh, Somerset, I'm *so* sorry!"

He rose from his chair and came to her. She expected him to start pacing along with her, but he didn't. Isabel gasped when he threw his arms around her and hugged her hard.

"Stop worrying about it, Isabel. I doubt that Jorge will do anything at all to me. Not that you aren't worth a murder or two, but I expect he was only blowing off steam."

Because she couldn't help herself, she hugged him back. She fought the impulse to close her eyes and melt into his arms. They were so strong and he was so big, and she felt so good there. Protected. Cared for. Loved.

Loved?

Well, a girl could dream, couldn't she?

"Do you really think so?"

"I'm sure of it. Please don't give it another thought."

"I can't not give it another thought! He frightened the life out of me when he threatened you."

"Were you really worried about me?"

She sensed that he'd lifted his head, which had been resting on her hair, and she nodded. She wished she could stay in his arms forever. Since she couldn't do that, she tilted her head back and looked up at him. She loved him *so* much.

"I think it's nice of you to worry about me, Isabel." His voice was gentle, seductive. It reminded Isabel of velvet and eiderdown and rabbit fur and all the soft things in the world.

"It's my fault anybody has to worry," she whispered. Her senses began to quicken, and she was suddenly aware of her body and how it yearned to be snuggled and fondled and stroked. Merciful heavens, she hadn't felt like this in years. She hadn't dared.

"Nobody has to worry about anything," he assured her, his voice a caress she felt through her whole being.

"You think not?" She swallowed, yearning for more, yet afraid of what she thought this embrace might lead to.

"I think so."

She was right about the leading-to part. Somerset bent his head, Isabel lifted hers, and their lips met in a kiss. It was light at first. Then, as hunger sped through both of them, it became harder, deeper, more urgent. Isabel moaned a little and wasn't even embarrassed. She pressed against him, feeling the evidence of his arousal against her stomach, and was ever so grateful that the nature of her job precluded her wearing tight corsets and stays. She wanted to feel everything there was to feel for however long this lasted.

"You're so beautiful," Somerset murmured, his lips tracing the line of her jaw.

"Mmmm."

He found a deliciously sensitive spot beneath her ear and kissed her there, then feathered his way to the pulse at the base of her throat. Isabel was glad she'd decided to wear her gray silk dress today, since it had a lower neckline than her other gowns. Somerset's lips were soft and delightfully warm against her skin. She sighed and wished he'd continue doing that for an hour or two.

"I've been wanting to see your hair down, Isabel," he murmured, nuzzling her neck. "You have beautiful hair."

"Mmmm," said Isabel. And, since he'd reminded her, she lifted one of her hands to the nape of his neck and allowed her fingers to burrow into his own thick, brown curls. He had perfectly glorious hair. She wondered if he'd go bald eventually and decided she didn't care. "You have a perfect head, Somerset."

"Thank you."

She felt him chuckle and guessed he'd never considered the shape of his head before this. "Some men's heads aren't as well-shaped as yours," she said by way of explanation. "My uncle Charlie was interested in phrenology."

"Ah. Well, I think your head is absolutely beautiful, Isabel."

"Thank you."

His hands lifted to her waist and a little higher, until they spanned her back and barely touched the undersides of her breasts. She hoped he didn't hear her quick intake of breath, because she didn't want him to stop what he was doing.

"You're so little," he whispered. "My hands can almost fit around your waist."

"Mmmm." To the devil with her waist. She wanted his

hands on her breasts. The word *abandoned* filtered into her head, and Isabel tried to shove it out again. It wouldn't go.

Very well, then, she was an abandoned woman, just like they all used to whisper behind her back in Upper Poppleton. At this moment she didn't give a curse, which probably confirmed everyone's opinion.

A pounding at the front door made them both start and leap away from each other. Somerset stared at Isabel, who stared back at him. Isabel thought he looked approximately as stunned as she felt, and was glad. She didn't want to be the only one. Another racket at the front door brought Somerset out of his stupor, although Isabel still felt like a limp rag. An unfulfilled limp rag.

He said, "I . . . I . . ." He shook his head hard. "I'd better see who's at the door. I think Mrs. Prendergast is—"

"The door!" Isabel cried, the last vestiges of her lust vanishing in a wave of terror. "No! Don't go! Let me get it!"

"But . . ."

Without allowing him to finish his sentence, Isabel dashed through the parlor doorway and barreled to the front door. She nearly upended Mrs. Prendergast, who hadn't done whatever Somerset had feared she'd done and was heading to do her duty by answering the door.

Afraid with all her heart that Jorge had discovered Somerset's address and was standing outside his house with a loaded revolver or a saber or a big rock or something, Isabel beat the housekeeper to it. She flung the door open, ready—no, eager—to take the knife or bullet or pounding meant for Somerset. It was her fault he was in danger, after all. Her senses raged at a fever pitch, her emotions roiled, and it took her a second to reconcile the person standing at the door to her mental image of her knife-wielding, revolver-toting, or rock-brandishing Argentine dancing partner.

She blinked. "Marcus?"

"We found out what happened to him, Mrs. Golightly," said the little man standing at the door, holding his soft cap in his hands and grinning at Isabel with teeth that resembled a tumble-down picket fence that hadn't been painted in a few years.

"To . . . to . . ." Isabel gave herself a mental slap and commanded herself to pay attention. "I beg your pardon, Marcus. Won't you . . ."

Remembering that this wasn't her home and that it wasn't her place to invite people inside, she looked back to see if Mrs. Prendergast was still in the hall. She wasn't, but Somerset was.

"What's going on?" he asked mildly.

Isabel noted with alarm that she'd seriously mussed his hair. She hoped his housekeeper hadn't noticed or that, if she had, she could think of some way other than a heated embrace that had made it so. She cleared her throat. "Somerset—" Isabel gave herself another hard mental slap. "I mean, Mr. FitzRoy, this is Marcus McKnight. He works for Mr. Balderston, and he says they've discovered Jorge's whereabouts."

"Well, now, Mrs. Golightly," said Marcus. "I didn't rightly say that."

She stared at him, then, confused, turned back to Somerset. "Er . . . may Mr. McKnight come in and tell us about it?"

Lord, she hoped her own hair didn't look like that. Somerset had commented upon it. Had he pulled out any pins? She couldn't remember. She wished she could pat it and check, but didn't want to call attention to it if it was disheveled.

"I beg your pardon?" Somerset, too, blinked at the small man waiting patiently at his front door. After a moment of apparent stupefaction, he shook himself. "Of course! Come right in, Mr. McKnight. Mrs. Golightly has been very worried about Mr. Savedra."

"I reckon we all was," said Marcus, stumping into the house. "Grand place you got here, Mr. FitzRoy."

"Thank you." Somerset looked at Isabel, who looked back at him, wishing Marcus to hell. Then he said, "Er, won't you . . . um . . . hang up your cap there?" He gestured at a hat rack next to the door.

"Thankee." Marcus complied.

"Why don't you come into the parlor here and tell us what you've discovered." With a gesture, Somerset indicated which room was the parlor.

"Thankee, thankee." With a knowing grin—Isabel wished she could trip him—Marcus followed Somerset's lead into the parlor.

"Take a seat, Mr. McKnight," said Somerset, regaining his composure at last.

Isabel wished hers would come back. She felt as though Marcus had found her and Somerset in *flagrante delicto*, when the unhappy truth was that he had interrupted a torrid embrace that hadn't even gone so far as removal of a single piece of clothing.

"Would you care for a glass of sherry?" Somerset offered. "Or perhaps you'd prefer brandy?" He poured out a hefty tot of brandy and downed it before turning to see if Marcus aimed to accept his offer.

"Brandy would be swell, thankee." Marcus sat on a sofa that matched the chairs. Isabel adored Somerset's furniture, although Marcus looked somewhat out of place on it.

Somerset poured out another glass and glanced at Isabel. "Mrs. Golightly?"

She shook her head and murmured, "No, thank you." Because she felt ostentatious standing in the middle of the room, she went to the chair she'd occupied earlier and sat.

After pouring another for himself, Somerset brought Marcus's brandy to him. Taking the chair next to Isabel, he said, smiling as if nothing of a passionate nature had transpired in the room only minutes earlier. "There, now, Mr. McKnight. Tell us what happened to Mr. Savedra, if you will."

"Glad to." Marcus took a healthy swig of his brandy. "Danged if the ferrin devil waren't shanghaied."

Chapter Fifteen

"Shanghaied?" Somerset's mouth fell open.

Isabel glanced from Somerset to Marcus and back again. "I . . . I . . ." She swallowed. "I don't understand."

Marcus tried to enlighten her. "He were shanghaied. Took. 'Pressed. Kidnaped. Seized."

Totally perplexed, Isabel looked to Somerset for help.

"According to Mr. McKnight, Mr. Savedra was impressed into military or merchant service of one sort or another." He squinted at Marcus. "I didn't know they still did that. You know, impress people into the merchant marine or the navy or whatever."

"Good Lord." Isabel stared at Somerset, flabbergasted. "Jorge?" She wanted to ask *who'd want him?* but it sounded rude, so she didn't.

Marcus shrugged. "He's a ferriner. I guess they got their own rules. Accordin' to Jake, it was an Argentine steamer took him. Jack watched it. Couldn't stop 'em, 'cause there was too many of 'em. But Jorge, he was drunk as a sailor. Never saw him drunk before, neither, but accordin' to Jake, he was drunker'n a skunk."

Isabel pressed a hand to her cheek. Had her refusal of his marriage proposal pushed Jorge to drink? Guilt slithered up her spine like a venomous snake.

"He was drinkin' at a bar down to the Barbary Coast and I guess he was singin' up a storm. Jake saw a couple o' Chinks along with some bully-boys come in and take him off. Just like that." Marcus snapped his fingers. "Drug him up the gangplank, pulled it in after him, and the last Jake seen of him, he was trying to teach them same two Chinks how to dance the tango, and they was starin' at him as if they thought he was loony." He laughed. "Dang, I wish I coulda seen it."

Unable to think of a single thing to say, Isabel only sat there, her gaze ricocheting between Marcus and Somerset, her brain a jumble of incoherent thoughts. Primary among them was the idea that she had caused Jorge's descent into the peril of drink, leading him directly to the hands of the Argentine sailors. Which brought her up short for a moment.

Her attention fastening on Marcus, she said, "I thought you said it was an Argentine vessel. Why did Chinese people take him?"

Marcus shrugged. "Reckon they work fer the Argentines. Them sailors, they come from all over."

"Oh." She glanced helplessly at Somerset.

"Interesting," he said, and downed the rest of his brandy.

"Interesting? But we have to get him back! We can't let him be snatched from American soil and made to work aboard a horrid ship!"

"Offhand, I don't know what we can do about it."

"But—but . . . Oh, my Lord, can you imagine Jorge as a *sailor?*"

"No."

Somerset didn't seem nearly as upset by this dreadful incident as he should, in Isabel's opinion. She said sharply, "I don't know, either, but we must think of something! We can't allow this—this—kidnaping to take place. Why, it's unchristian! It must be against the law."

Frowning, Somerset said, "I don't know if it is or not. I know they used to shanghai people all the time off the Barbary Coast. In the old days. Didn't know the practice was still done. I suppose I can call the police and find out."

Isabel brightened. "Oh, yes, please do! Thank you, Somer—er—Mr. FitzRoy."

With a sigh, Somerset rose to his feet. "The telephone's in a room off the hall." He made a vague gesture eastward. "I'll be right back."

Isabel sat and fidgeted while Somerset was out of the room. Marcus sat, drank, and took in the luxury and exquisite tastefulness surrounding him. "Swell place," he muttered after a while.

"Yes," said Isabel, sparing a glance for the furnishings. "It's beautiful, isn't it?"

With a sly squint, Marcus said, "I didn't rightly expect to find you answerin' the door here, Mrs. Golightly. Mr. Balderston called up a couple of folks, and one of 'em said for me to come here, but I didn't expect you to *be* here."

Blast the man. And blast Loretta or whomever it had been who'd thought she might be at Somerset's house. "Yes, well, Mr. Savedra had said something that made me think he might have gone to Mr. Somerset's house, so I came here hoping to find him."

"Uh." Marcus nodded, still looking sly.

He didn't believe her. Bloody hell. Isabel didn't

bother to correct her mental profanity, believing she deserved a few curse words at this time. Hoping to get Marcus's mind to veer in a different direction, she said, "I can't believe Jorge has been taken like that. I had no idea such things were done in this modern day and age. For heaven's sake, it's the twentieth century."

Her ploy succeeded. Nodding energetically, Marcus said, "Yup. Use't be a lot o' shanghai-in' done in the old days." He grinned in fond remembrance. "I like to be took once myself. Ain't drunk much ever since then, 'cause it skeered me so bad."

Isabel, for the first time considering joining Loretta's Temperance League, murmured, "Then, in your case, I guess everything turned out for the best."

"I expect so. I ain't much never liked the sea."

A sudden memory of a black, icy ocean, made Isabel shudder. "No. I'm not fond of the sea, either."

Marcus stopped grinning. "Sorry, ma'am. I fergot about you bein' on that ship what sunk. That was a turrible thing. Turrible."

"Yes," she said, striving to drive out the mental images. "It was."

"But I expect Jorge'll be all right. I think that ship he was on was headin' straight to Argenteeny, so mebbe he can get it all straightened out when he gets there."

"I hope so. I can't really feature Jorge as a sailor."

Marcus shook his head. "No, ma'am. Nuther can I. I never seen nobody acted less like a sailor than that feller. Sure could dance, though."

"Yes, he sure could." Isabel sighed, her mind returning to the dance contest as a person's tongue will probe a sore tooth. The contest would be upon her in another two weeks, and then what? Would Jorge's troubles be solved by then? Even if the ship went straight to

Argentina, would he be able to get back to San Francisco in two weeks' time?

Of course not. Isabel told herself not to be a dreamer and a fool. There was no hope for winning that contest money now.

Suppressing a sudden urge to sob out loud, she thought savagely that she ought to have accepted Jorge's proposal. Even if she'd had to break the engagement later—and she would be boiled in oil before she'd marry a man like Jorge Savedra—she'd still have been able to enter the contest and win the money to start up her dance studio. Of course, Jorge would probably shoot, stab, or bash *her* then, but at least she could have tried to establish herself.

Now . . . Well, now she was doomed, was what.

Somerset entered the room, and Isabel glanced up to see if he'd fixed his hair. He hadn't, but he looked calm and in control of himself once more. She guessed that was a good thing.

"I told the police department what happened, and they said they'd look into it. I don't know if they'll be able to do anything, though. The ship is already on the water and probably beyond the United States' three-mile limit by this time."

Isabel slumped in the chair. "Oh, dear." She shook her head and wrung her hands, feeling simply awful.

Somerset sat down in the chair next to her, reached across the table, and took her hands in his. "Try not to worry about him, Isabel. I'll keep on top of the situation with the police, and I'll let you know as soon as I hear something."

She felt foolish when tears flooded her eyes. "Thank you. You're very kind."

They both jumped when Marcus cleared his throat.

Isabel didn't know about Somerset, but she'd forgotten all about Marcus. "Well, then, I reckon I'll go back to the Fairfield, folks." He rose and grinned at them. Isabel snatched her hands from Somerset's grasp and rose, too. "You comin' back to the hotel, Mrs. Golightly?"

"I . . ." Good Lord, she didn't know *what* to do. "I don't know."

Like the gentleman he was, Somerset came to her rescue. "Mrs. Golightly can't return to the Fairfield this evening, Mr. McKnight. I'm sure Mr. Balderston will understand that she's upset by this news. Besides, the other half of her act is on his way to Argentina."

Marcus scratched his stubbly chin. "You got a point there, Mr. FitzRoy."

"Oh, dear." Bleakness began crawling through Isabel, chilling her. Where, only minutes earlier, she'd been in the throes of romantic ecstasy, now she felt alone and bereft. "I just don't know what to do."

Somerset stood up, too, and patted her shoulder in a brotherly fashion. She'd have worried about that if she weren't already worrying about so many other things. "I'll help you, Isabel. I'm sure that between us, we can figure out what to do."

"But the act at the Fairfield," she whispered unhappily. "Without Jorge, there's no more act."

"We'll work something out," Somerset said.

She gazed at him and wanted to shout *how?* but knew that was only her nerves reacting. Perhaps he really would think of some way to salvage her job at the hotel. Or perhaps she'd be scrubbing floors in other people's houses soon. Or training for a nurse. That would be better than char work.

"I'll be on my way, then," said Marcus. He shook

Somerset's hand and gave Isabel a little bow. "Reckon I'll be seeing you, Mrs. Golightly."

Isabel said, "Yes," uncertainly. "Thank you for coming, Marcus."

She and Somerset followed the little man to the front door, and Somerset opened it for him. They both watched him march jauntily off. Isabel presumed he was headed for the cable car line that would take him back to Nob Hill and the Fairfield Hotel. She started when Somerset shut the door, cutting off her view of Marcus's back.

"How the devil did he know that he'd find you here?" He took her arm and guided her back to the parlor.

Isabel rather hoped he'd take her in his arms again and offer her the comfort of his large, warm body, but he didn't. With a sigh, she sank back into the chair she'd begun to think of as hers. "He said Mr. Balderston telephoned several people. I suppose Loretta or Marjorie suggested he look for me here."

"Ah."

They gazed at each other for several seconds. Isabel didn't know what to say, and she assumed Somerset was in the same condition.

Finally it was Somerset who broke the deadlock. "This rather blows a hole in your hopes for that contest, doesn't it?"

She sighed gloomily. "Yes, it does. Not to mention my job."

His eyes narrowed. "I don't know about that. Perhaps we can find someone to take over for Mr. Savedra. I understand that Miss Linden numbers several people with . . . ah . . . unusual occupations among her friends."

Sitting up straighter, Isabel cried, "Of course! Why

didn't I think of Loretta? She knows positively *dozens* of strange people!"

Somerset's mouth tilted into a small smile. Isabel caught her breath. She loved his smile. "I didn't mean strange," she said, backpedaling furiously. "I meant that she knows lots of actors and singers and people like that. She *must* know a dancer or two who needs a job. They all need jobs."

"Yes, Dr. Abernathy told me the same thing. Of course, that leaves the contest."

She sagged again. "Yes. It does." Swallowing the lump that threatened to produce more tears, she went on, "I was so confident that we'd win it, too."

Oh, bother, she was going to cry. How embarrassing. But she'd pinned *so* many hopes on that bloody contest. She grabbed the small handbag she'd consigned to the table earlier in the evening and fumbled for a handkerchief. "I'm sorry, Somerset. I'm being foolish."

"Not at all," he said in a consoling voice. And why the devil didn't he rush to take her into his arms and comfort her, was what Isabel wanted to know? "I know how much you were depending on that contest."

She sniffled and blew her nose. She tried to do so discreetly, but blowing one's nose is never discreet. When she was through, she said, "You probably think I was stupid to believe so ardently that Jorge and I could win the contest, don't you?"

"Not at all," he assured her. "I observed most of your rehearsals, remember. I can't imagine that another couple could honestly compete against you. I know how good the two of you were."

Were. Yes. That was the word, all right. Isabel sighed again. "That's all over now, I guess. I'd so hoped I'd be able to open a dance academy, but my hopes have been dashed for good and all now."

"Not necessarily."

She smiled at him sadly. "I won't accept money from you, Somerset. Not even as a loan."

"I wasn't thinking of a loan—not that I'd ever make you repay any money I gave you, or—" He shook his head hard. "But that's not what I meant."

She looked up sharply. "What *do* you mean? If you're thinking one of Loretta's friends can learn the contest dances and choreography in two weeks, I'm afraid you don't quite understand the level of expertise necessary for—"

He cut her off. "No. I'm not thinking about one of Miss Linden's friends. I'm sure you'll be able to find one of them who can dance at the Fairfield, and in time, will probably be a decent partner for you, but I was thinking of someone else for the contest."

"You were?"

"I was."

"Who?" Or should that be whom? Bother. It didn't matter.

"Me."

Isabel stared at him, shocked. *"You?"*

Isabel and Loretta were in Loretta's kitchen, making tea. Marjorie had gone out to run an errand, Mrs. Brandeis was doing something housekeeperish with the grocer's man, and the two maidservants were about their daily duties. For the first time since she'd moved into Loretta's Russian Hill abode, Isabel scarcely noticed the beauty of her tea service. She was feeling guilty.

"Oh, Loretta, I know I shouldn't have laughed, but his suggestion caught me off guard."

With a broad grin of her own, Loretta poured boiling water from the tea kettle into the teapot. "It was all I could do to keep a straight face when you told me, too, Isabel. Don't feel guilty."

"I can't help it. He's been so kind to me, and I laughed at him. He didn't like it, either."

"He'll get over it."

Loretta set the tea kettle back on the stove lid with a crash that made Isabel wince. She didn't think she'd ever get used to the nonchalant attitude Loretta had about her possessions. Yet another difference between the Lorettas and the Isabels of the world, she supposed. The Lorettas didn't bother being careful with their things because they could just go out and buy others if they broke. "But he was so stiff and cold when he drove me home." She nibbled on a knuckle.

"He won't hold it against you for long, dear," Loretta assured her. "He's quite taken with you."

Isabel stopped gnawing on her knuckle and stared at her friend. "He's what?"

"He's taken with you. In fact, I do believe he's quite in love with you."

Unable to respond, Isabel continued to stare.

"Don't look at me like that," Loretta said, laughing. "It's the truth. I don't understand how you could not know it yourself."

"My word." Sensations flooded Isabel's body in remembrance of the afternoon's heated embrace. She felt her face flush. "He did . . . kiss me," she said in a tiny voice.

"Aha! There, you see?" Loretta dropped a teacup. Isabel hastened to fetch the broom and dustpan. "Fiddlesticks. I'm so clumsy. Give me that broom, Isabel. I'm the one who broke it. I should be the one to clean it up."

Equality was too new to her. Isabel couldn't just hand

over the broom to a rich woman. Besides, she needed to do something to quell her embarrassment. "Nonsense," she said, sweeping like mad.

For several seconds, the only sound in the kitchen was the scrape of the broom against the linoleum floor. Then Loretta spoke again.

"Tell me, Isabel, you've . . . er . . . had experience. And Mr. FitzRoy kissed you this afternoon. What is it like? I mean, is it wonderful? I've heard two sides of the physical-love issue, but I want to know from someone who isn't a free-thinking actress with a reputation as a hellion to uphold. I mean, you're normal. You ought to be able to tell me."

Isabel stood so abruptly, the dustpan tipped and pieces of broken teacup dropped to the floor, splintering into even smaller fragments. "I beg your pardon?"

"You heard me." Loretta's tone was dry. "I really want to know."

"But . . . don't you know?" Isabel's flush turned into a full-blown blush. She felt it. "I mean . . . well, I mean, you believe in free love and all that, don't you?"

Even more dryly, Loretta said, "Just because I believe in something doesn't mean I've experienced it. I . . . well, I'm not the sort of woman men cherish, I guess. I'm too outspoken. Too independent. Too . . . well . . . unfeminine."

Isabel gaped at the woman who had been her salvation. "That's bloody damned nonsense, Loretta Linden! You're a beautiful, warm, wonderful woman!"

"Fudge. Just answer my question, will you?"

Because it sounded to Isabel as if Loretta was becoming peeved with her, and because Isabel would die before she did anything to upset Loretta, she decided to answer the question.

That didn't preclude her feeling of embarrassment

when she obliged her friend. "I still think you ought to find out for yourself, and it's nonsense to say you're not cherishable, but I must say that . . ." She paused to relish the recollection of the afternoon's embrace. "It felt absolutely delicious to be in Somerset's arms."

There. She's said it out loud. She paid for it, too, when her cheeks positively caught fire. Pressing her palms against them, she admitted, "I wanted it to go on and on and . . . and lead to other things." After taking a deep, sustaining breath, she said, "There. Now you know. I guess I'm an abandoned woman."

"Fiddlesticks." Loretta gazed at her with envy for a moment, then sighed lustily. "I wish somebody would want to kiss me like that."

Isabel put the teapot on a silver tray and goggled at Loretta. "Whatever do you mean by that? I'm sure many men would love to kiss you!"

"Ha! That shows how much you know about my life." Loretta made a move to go to the cupboard and fetch another teacup, and stepped on the shards of the broken one.

Isabel jumped and began sweeping again. "That's nonsense, Loretta. Why, you're a very pretty woman. It's true that you're a woman of strong opinions and high moral standards and that you're an outspoken proponent of many causes some men fear, but there are hundreds of other men to whom those characteristics would be unimportant—or even attractive. You wouldn't want a fussy old reactionary, anyhow, would you?"

With a sigh, Loretta returned with the teacup and set it, and the others, on the silver tray. "No, but I wouldn't mind if *somebody* loved me."

"What about Dr. Abernathy? You and he are the best of friends. *He* thinks you're wonderful."

"*He* thinks of me as his kid sister."

Oh. Well, pooh. Isabel wasn't sure what to say to encourage her friend. When one only *looked* at Loretta, one saw a lively, charming woman with beautiful dark hair and huge dark eyes and a figure that any man would want to explore by hand.

Loretta's problem, Isabel decided bitterly, was that she was too bloody smart, and most men were scared to death of smart women. She feared her own daughter would encounter such prejudice in years to come. Because she truly believed it, even if she could provide no evidence, she said, "There's someone for you in the world, Loretta Linden. I know it."

"Hmmm," said Loretta. She picked up the tray and headed for the parlor, where Somerset FitzRoy and Jason Abernathy awaited the ladies. "I hope you're right, because I'm about ready to snatch someone off the street, just to see what it feels like."

Isabel stared after her, her mouth open, for several seconds, before she dashed after her to open the door.

Once Isabel had stopped laughing at Somerset's suggestion that he fill in for Jorge in the dance contest, she'd begun to realize that, in actual fact, Somerset was her only hope.

It would help if he wasn't so dratted stiff when he danced with her. That afternoon's rehearsal hadn't gone well, and Somerset had left in something of a huff. She hoped he'd forgive her for laughing at him and making suggestions about his dancing technique— and soon—because they had at least to *look* as if they got along while they danced in the contest.

And if she was really lucky, he'd kiss her again.

* * *

Isabel woke with a jerk when Eunice threw herself onto her bed, sobbing as if her heart were broken, at about two-thirty the following morning.

"Sweetheart! Whatever is the matter? Did you have another bad dream about the ship?"

"Y-yes!"

Eunice hugged her mother so tightly, Isabel feared she might strangle. Attempting to sit up while holding Eunice and, at the same time, move her into a less life-threatening hold, she blinked away sleep. "I'm so sorry, dearie. Do you want to tell me about it?"

Ahh. That was better. Isabel had managed to maneuver herself into a sitting position against the headboard with the pillows propped at her back.

"Yes. No. Yes." Eunice took a huge, shuddering breath. "I guess so."

Stroking her daughter's pretty blond hair, Isabel's heart ached for the little girl. Poor Eunice had enough to face in this life without the ghastly memories of the *Titanic* to plague her, too. "Take your time, sweetie. Just take your time. Remember that it was only a dream."

"I know." Eunice sniffled and gulped. Her sobs had calmed into occasional hiccups. "I know it *now*. But I don't know I'm dreaming when I'm dreaming. I wish I could."

"Yes," agreed her mother. "That would help, wouldn't it? I wonder if it's possible to make yourself understand that you're dreaming while you're dreaming." That sounded idiotic and Isabel was sorry she'd said it because Eunice didn't care for idiocy, even from her mother.

To her surprise, Eunice drew away and looked at her as if she'd uttered something insightful. "What a good idea!" Her little face was tear-streaked and blotchy, and she swiped at her tears with the back of her hand. "I wonder if it *is* possible. Perhaps I can find a book about dreams. I've heard that a doctor in Austria named Freud is studying dreams, and that he claims a person can, in some way, maniculize them. Maybe he's published something on the subject."

Blinking at her brilliant child, Isabel said, "Um . . . maniculize them?"

Eunice wiped away more tears and looked thoughtfully at her mother. "Doesn't that mean to control or change?"

"Oh. Manipulate, is the word you want, I think."

"Manipulate. Of course. Anyhow, he's written a book about dreams."

"The Austrian?"

"Yes. Dr. Freud."

"Wouldn't it be written in German, though?"

"That wouldn't matter. I'm learning German."

Dear God. "That's right. You are," Isabel said doubtfully.

"I hate these bad dreams, Mama. This one had my best friends, Rebecca and Lillian, in the water, calling for me to rescue them. I tried to reach them and couldn't." She sniffled pathetically.

Isabel rocked her in her arms, her rhythm gentle.

"I wish the dreams would stop," Eunice said woefully. "I wish I could wake up before they get bad."

"I wish you could, too, sweetie."

"Hmmm." Eunice's tone turned contemplative. "I wonder if there's a way to do that."

"Do what, sweetheart?"

"Make me know I'm dreaming when I'm dreaming."

Isabel squinted down at her daughter, wishing she could fathom the convolutions of Eunice's thinking processes. "Um . . . I beg your pardon?"

"I bet there's a way." Eunice settled more comfortably on her mother's lap. "Maybe I can find it in that book."

"Oh." Well, if anyone could, it would be Eunice. "Would you like to sleep here for the rest of the night?" She thought suddenly that it was a good thing she *couldn't* marry Somerset, should he ask her again, because three in a bed was one too many.

"Yes. Thank you, Mama." Eunice burrowed under the covers, and Isabel handed her one of the pillows.

Eunice went to sleep with her mother's arm around her. Isabel lay awake for a long, long time after her daughter slept, wondering what was to become of them both.

Chapter Sixteen

"Am I looking confident enough?" Somerset refrained from adding the *for you* dancing on his tongue. He was mighty tired of Isabel constantly carping on how he didn't seem confident, though. Damn it all, he was more of a man than Jorge Savedra could ever even dream of being, wasn't he? Yes, he was, curse Jorge and Isabel both.

And besides all that, they'd been dancing so hard for so long that his feet hurt, his head ached, and he feared his back was broken, or the next thing to it. This dancing nonsense was hard work.

"Almost."

Somerset ground his teeth but remained silent. It would do no good to object. Besides, he'd probably only look like a sniveling fusspot if he did.

It was the Sunday before the contest was to be held, and he and Isabel had been dancing since noon. Isabel probably would have made them start earlier, but she was diligent about taking Eunice to Sunday School and church at the nearby Presbyterian church, and they couldn't get started until after lunchtime. At least, Somerset thought sourly, Isabel had allowed him to eat lunch before she commenced torturing him.

Now Eunice was upstairs taking a nap—which sounded like a very good idea to Somerset—Loretta was out somewhere stirring up mischief, and Marjorie was catching up on correspondence in her room. Isabel frowned as she sorted through piano rolls. "Would you mind going over 'Bird in a Gilded Cage' again? We've almost got the choreography down."

And that was another thing. According to Isabel, Somerset's taller, more manly form required changes in the choreography that she'd been practicing with that little fruit, Jorge. With exquisite—and silent—sarcasm, he reminded himself that *Jorge* wasn't the fruit. *Jorge* was only a pain in the ass. Isabel's new Fairfield dance partner, Geoffrey Gardner, found among the riffraff littering Loretta's life, was the fruit. His jaw began to ache, so he unclenched his teeth. "I don't mind at all."

Smiling brightly, Isabel took Somerset's left hand. "Ready? We've almost got it."

It took a good deal of effort, but Somerset managed to pry his jaws apart. "Do you really think so?" He couldn't help himself, and added, "Even given my level of incompetence and lack of confidence?"

"Now, now, now, Somerset. You're neither incompetent nor do you lack confidence. You do seem just a little stiff still, though."

He was stiff, all right, only not in the place Isabel meant. It was hell, dancing this close to her and not being able to rip her clothes off and do all the things he'd been dreaming about doing to her. Soon, though. He was going to get the woman to marry him or die trying.

The introduction to "Bird" filled the room, and

Somerset forced himself to relax. Their entrance in this one required a smooth, but tightly choreographed, series of twirls to get them into the ballroom and in position to dance before the judges.

When done right, it was amazingly effective, with him strong and tall and looking as though he was in command—what a laugh—and Isabel small, wispy and dainty, with her ball gown's skirt billowing out behind her.

Somerset knew for a fact how impressive their entrance was, because Loretta Linden had gone out and bought herself a motion-picture camera, of all things, and two tall electrical lamps like those used by the flicker-makers. She'd been filming almost all of their dance rehearsals, and he'd had to sit and watch the films every night after Isabel got home from dancing at the Fairfield, and listen to her critique his performance. It was never right, of course. She didn't say it like that, but he knew what she meant.

He didn't know how she did it, dancing all day and dancing all night, but she was determined to win that dashed contest. That she was liable to kill them both as she went about it didn't seem to matter to her. If he was about to drop dead from exhaustion—and he was—he didn't understand how she could keep going.

"You're still a little stiff," Isabel said softly. "Relax."

"How the devil can I relax?" he demanded. "Every time I try to do anything, you tell me I'm too stiff."

"Oh, dear, I'm sorry, Somerset. I don't mean to carp at you. I'm only concerned about the contest."

"I am too, dash it."

Damn. They were arguing, and they weren't even lovers yet. He knew better than to start a fight with a woman he wanted to marry. After he married her, he could fight with her all he wanted. Not before.

But, dash it, he was tired of being criticized. He said, "I beg your pardon, Isabel." His voice was as stiff as she claimed his body was.

"Please don't," Isabel said. She sounded discouraged. "You're right. I'm too particular." She brought them to a stop, went over to the piano, and the music stopped, too.

Somerset took Isabel's arm and led her to a corner away from the piano. He was beginning to think of the dashed piano as an enemy. "Let's talk about this, Isabel. Do you really think I'm too stiff? I'm trying very hard not to be, you know. Maybe it's only that my style is different from Jorge's."

She shook her head. "I'm sorry, Somerset. I know it's difficult to hear someone criticize you over and over again, but . . . well . . ." She took a deep breath. "No, it's not just a difference in style. It's a level of relaxation. You know all the steps, and your technical ability is as good as Jorge's." She shrugged helplessly. "I don't know the answer."

Well, damn. Maybe he just wasn't cut out to be a dancer. He said, "Then I'm afraid I don't, either. I'm not good at reading minds." He said it stiffly, and cursed himself as an ass.

After a few moments of silence, during which Somerset took note of Isabel's furrowed brow and assumed she was thinking of more things that were wrong with his dancing style, her shoulders became slightly less tense, and she said, "I have an idea."

That's more than he had. Striving for a congenial tone, he said, "Yes?"

She looked up at him with those huge blue eyes, and Somerset almost lost track of the conversation. "Do you remember when I told you about Eunice's bad dreams?"

"Yes." What in God's name did the kid and her dreams have to do with this?

"Well, she said something that rather alarmed me last night after another nightmare."

"Oh?"

"She said she was going to look in some psychology books in order to try to make herself wake up or recognize that she was dreaming the next time she had a nightmare."

Isabel Golightly had a very strange child in Eunice. Somerset only offered her another, "Oh?"

She gave a self-deprecating laugh. "I don't know anything about alienists or psychology books."

Somerset was glad to hear it, since he considered alienists only slightly less ridiculous than astrologers.

Isabel went on, "The only psychology books I could think of were the ones written by Sigmund Freud, and I didn't want her even touching those."

Momentarily shocked out of his black mood, Somerset said, "I should hope not!"

With a grin, Isabel said, "I checked into the books in Loretta's library. She had Dr. Freud's book, so I took it upstairs and hid it. However, I glanced into it first."

His gaze narrowed, and his frustration returned in waves. If she was going to start spouting psychology at him, he might just have to throw a fit. "I'm not sure I go along with all the new theories those alienist fellows are cooking up," he said, trying to sound reasonable, rather than humorless and stodgy.

"No, I'm not, either, but I did find something rather interesting that might help us in this instance."

Somerset doubted it. He didn't say so.

"According to Dr. Freud, the more a person consciously tries to do something, the more aware he is when he achieves anything less than perfection. Even though it's only natural to begin to do something less than perfectly, rather than assuming he'll conquer whatever it is with more practice, he'll be discouraged and think of himself as a failure. Therefore, because he thinks of himself—or herself, of course—"

"Of course," grumbled Somerset, feeling like a schoolboy being lectured by a professor.

"Well, then, I mean, if a person thinks he—or she—is a failure, they'll believe they're unable to correct their errors and their conscious minds will live up to their expectations." She frowned briefly. "At least, that's what I got out of it. It was more complicated than that, but it made sense. In a way."

It didn't make any sense at all to Somerset, and he didn't know what to say. His first impulse was to stamp out of the room and leave Isabel to dance with herself, but he knew that was only his sense of futility climbing. "And is there a point to this?" he said at last, then wished he hadn't because it sounded rude.

Isabel didn't seem to notice. She said, "Actually, yes, there is. If I understood the book correctly, what Dr. Freud would suggest in this instance is that you stop even thinking about the steps and the choreography."

"Stop even—" Somerset shut his mouth, since he'd spoken rather loudly. Striving to remain civil, he went on in a harsh whisper, "What do you mean, stop thinking about them? I've done nothing *but* think about them for the past ten days!"

Taking his arm in both of hers and looking up at him pleadingly, Isabel said, "I didn't mean it that way. Please don't be angry."

Easy for her to say. She wasn't the one being picked on constantly.

"What I mean is that you don't *need* to think about

the steps and choreography any longer. You know them. They've become a part of you." She searched his face. "Oh, dear, I'm saying this all wrong."

Somerset couldn't argue. He feared, in fact, that he'd begun glaring at her.

"What I mean is . . . Well, have you ever seen Vernon and Irene Castle on the screen? They've been in a couple of motion pictures."

"Yes. I've seen them."

"Well, the Castles don't appear to give a single thought to the rules of the dances. Rather, they look as if they're only enjoying themselves." She stopped talking, thought, frowned, and said, "Well, except for the tango, which *I* think is a deliberately self-conscious dance. You *have* to think about what you're doing when you dance the tango. But, except for the tango, maybe you should just think about having fun."

For approximately five seconds, Somerset feared he was going to explode. Then Isabel's words slipped past the roadblocks his vexation had erected, and he heard them. He wasn't sure he believed them. Dubiously, he said, "Having fun?"

With a shrug, Isabel said, "Well . . . yes. Dancing is an art form, true, but it's really more fun than anything else."

Not for him, it wasn't. They stood in the corner of the ballroom, staring at each other, for what seemed like an hour. Finally, after a furious spate of thought, Somerset said, "Hmmm. That actually sounds logical. In a way." He hated to admit it.

"I'm sorry if I've been too picky."

He shook his head. "You're depending on this contest. I understand that. And I understand that you want us to be the best we can be." Making a huge effort, he managed to overstep his resentment and actually smile at her. He held out his hand. "Do you want to give it another try? This time for fun?"

Tears brimmed in her eyes. Somerset almost gave in to the urge to take her in his arms and kiss the daylights out of her.

Making a quick swipe of her wrist to catch the tears, Isabel smiled back. "Yes. Thank you."

"And, as long as we're dancing for fun, why don't you pick out a fun dance."

Flashing him a glorious smile, Isabel said, "Thank you. I will." And she tripped back over to the piano to look at the piano rolls as if her own feet didn't ache as much as his did, although they must.

Shaking his head, Somerset limped over to join her.

She showed him a roll. "How about 'Alexander's Ragtime Band.' "

"Sounds good to me." So Isabel put the roll into the piano, cranked the handle, set the needle onto the roll, and the first few bars of the ragtime number hit the air.

And then Somerset decided that, if he was supposed to be having fun with this dancing nonsense, he'd dashed well have fun the way *he* wanted to. Therefore, he grabbed Isabel around the waist and twirled her to the middle of the dance floor. Surprised, she laughed, throwing her head back and making Somerset want to continue twirling out the door, up the stairs, and into bed.

Unfortunately, Somerset was a gentleman, even when he didn't want to be, so he didn't do that. He also didn't worry about the steps or the choreography. He just danced. It felt good, and by God, he actually began to relax. For the first time that day, he didn't think about what Isabel might be finding to criticize in his movements. Her smile was radiant. He smiled back and realized he was enjoying himself.

When the music ended, Somerset stopped, and he

and Isabel stood in the middle of the dance floor, staring at each other. All of a sudden, Isabel threw her arms around him, laughing. "That was *wonderful!*"

His arms closed around her, and finally he felt as though he was doing something completely right. "Yes," he said. "It was."

She heaved a huge sigh and subsided into his arms, as if she was as weary as he and relished this closeness as much as he did. He held his breath, as he held her, and prayed that they could stay wrapped in each other's arms for a decade or two.

Peering down, Somerset saw her eyes shining with pleasure, and he felt the tension leave her body. She seemed to melt into him. Her eyelids fluttered, closed, and time stopped still.

All at once her eyes flew open again. Her body tensed. Damn.

"Well." Her laugh sounded strained. "That was *much* better." She drew away slightly. "I think we're going to be fine."

He let her go with the greatest reluctance.

Isabel and Somerset danced until dinnertime, then Loretta came home and insisted they eat something. So Somerset stayed for dinner, then Isabel dragged him back to the ballroom. Eunice was in bed by that time, and Isabel felt a tiny bit of constraint at first.

She hadn't meant to hug him earlier. It had certainly felt good, but it was a bold thing to have done. Somerset hadn't seemed shocked; in fact, he seemed to have enjoyed it, but Isabel didn't want to appear loose.

Or did she? She supposed that once he knew the truth about her, he wouldn't want to marry her any longer, but . . .

She told herself to concentrate on dancing and forget everything else. They'd have to use the Victrola this evening, because the piano was too loud, and Isabel didn't want to disturb Eunice's sleep.

Because she was a little nervous, she put on her brightest smile and spoke in her heartiest voice. In truth, she was so exhausted, she could have dropped dead on the spot, and her feet hurt so badly, she was sure the bottoms must be bruised. Then there were her arms, which were about to fall from her shoulders in fatigue.

The contest meant too much for her to fail now, though, so she persevered.

"We're doing ever so much better now." Although she'd been skeptical that a book written by Sigmund Freud might really offer some practical advice, she had to admit that he'd been right about trying too hard.

"I'm actually having fun," Somerset admitted.

"I'm so glad." Isabel had been worried earlier that day, because he had seemed to be getting stiffer and stiffer the more they practiced. No longer. Now he actually looked as if he was enjoying the dance. Maybe he was simply too tired to be stiff.

"I have to admit that my feet are starting to hurt, however."

Isabel paused with the cylinder for "In the Good Old Summertime" poised over the Victrola. She'd been driving him very hard. She'd been driving herself hard, too, but she had more at stake in the contest than did Somerset, who was partnering her out of the goodness of his heart. As much as she hated to do it, she supposed she ought to let the poor man rest. And herself. Her poor feet were crying out in agony, and her eyes were so gritty, they felt as if someone had thrown sand into them.

"I'm sorry, Somerset. I guess I've become a little obsessed about this." She offered him a quavery smile. "I wonder what Dr. Freud would say about that."

He laughed. Isabel loved his laugh. She loved everything about him, actually. "I doubt that you'd want to know what the good doctor has to say."

She laughed, too, although she didn't feel much like it. Her nerves were jumping and she was so on edge, she was sure she'd be unable to sleep that night, as she'd been unable to sleep more than an hour or two at a time for days now. She knew she was putting too many of her life's hopes and dreams on the upcoming contest, but she couldn't seem to help herself. "But he was right, wasn't he, about not trying so hard?"

"Absolutely."

He had drawn closer to her. Isabel held her breath, hoping that he would hold her again. She knew she must be a total wanton, but she wanted even more than that from Somerset FitzRoy. She might not be able to marry him, but perhaps, if she was very lucky, she might know his love once or twice. Was that too much to ask of the fates?

"You seem to be rather tense, Isabel."

Her laugh was genuine, if sardonic, this time. She rolled her shoulders, for the first time realizing how much they hurt. "I am tense. My shoulder muscles are in knots, and I haven't been sleeping. Too nervous about the contest, I suppose."

He shook his head. "You should try to relax." He grinned. "Although I know from experience that relaxing is easier said than done."

"Yes." Noticing the Victrola cylinder in her hands,

she put it down. "I suppose I've driven us both enough for one day."

"Turn around, Isabel. Let me see if I can get the knots out of your shoulders. I go to a Turkish bath every now and then just to get a massage."

She turned obediently. As soon as his hands touched her shoulders, shock waves of want careened through her. She wasn't sure this was the best way to relax, although she could think of something else the two of them could do that would probably work.

Lord, she truly *was* an abandoned creature. Her only saving grace was that she really didn't want to be one. She'd love to marry this wonderful man. But in order to do that, she'd have to confess her terrible secret. The only person on this side of the ocean to whom she'd confided was Loretta Linden, the one person on earth she trusted not to cast her off when the truth was known.

"Does that feel good?" Somerset's voice was soft, and it slid through her like warm honey.

She allowed her head to fall forward slightly. "It feels perfectly wonderful." If she were to tell the whole truth, she'd have to confess that his touch made Isabel feel sensations she hadn't felt in years . . . since long before Eunice's birth.

They were both silent for a few minutes. Somerset's hands worked wonders on Isabel's shoulders, then they slid down her arms. Isabel's breath caught. This wasn't massage anymore.

"I wish you'd marry me, Isabel," Somerset said, his lips brushing the skin at the back of her neck and making shivers rocket through her body.

"I . . . I wish I could," she whispered.

He turned her around and held her at arms' distance away from himself, frowning. "Why can't you?"

"I . . ." Isabel swallowed. A million thoughts and

thought fragments raced through her brain, until she willed them away. Then, making a decision she was almost sure to regret, she decided to take a chance. If he hated her after he learned about her background, she'd face that later. In fact, she wouldn't even tell him until after the contest. She was being sly and cunning, two traits that were opposed to her generally open nature, but she didn't care at the moment. She wanted Somerset so much, she burned for his touch. At last she blurted out, "I will!"

His eyes widened. He had perfectly gorgeous eyes. "You will? You'll marry me?"

"Yes." She flung her arms around his neck. "Oh, Somerset, I love you so much!" There. She's said it. She was pretty sure she'd pay for it later, but again, she didn't care.

He hugged her hard. "You've made me the happiest of men, Isabel."

And then, as Isabel had hoped he would, he kissed her. Because she didn't anticipate this heaven to occur more than once or twice, Isabel wasted no time in deepening the kiss. Shamelessly, she pressed against him, feeling his arousal against her and longing for more.

"Be careful," Somerset said, his voice gravelly. "I've been waiting for a long time. I don't know how well I'll be able to control myself."

"I don't want you to control yourself," announced Isabel without a blush. "I want you to come upstairs with me now."

She feared she'd gone too far when she heard Somerset gulp and then say nothing. But, oh, she needed him. Badly. Her nipples were dimpled and aching, the pressure between her thighs was so great, she felt as if she'd die unless it were relieved, and she had gooseflesh everywhere.

Before she could apologize or scream or run from the room in shame, Somerset shocked her nearly into a faint by scooping her right up from the floor. She clung to his strong shoulders with a soaring heart. He was going to do it! Somerset FitzRoy, the man of her dreams, was going to succumb to passion and bed her before they were married. Isabel considered that an extremely fortunate circumstance, since they most likely wouldn't be married at all.

"Which way to the stairs?"

Isabel considered it a good sign that he sounded as eager—or perhaps desperate was a better word—as she felt. "Out the door and straight ahead."

He took off, walking fast. "Are we liable to run into anyone? I don't want you to be embarrassed."

"No. Everyone's gone to bed long ago except Loretta and Marjorie, and they're at a concert and won't be back until after midnight."

"Good." He strode to the staircase and climbed, taking the stairs two at a time.

"You're very strong, Somerset," Isabel murmured, enjoying the sensation of being carried in this dramatic, knight-in-shining-armor fashion.

"It's from all the tree-planting I do," he said, beginning to be a trifle short of breath. "Which room is yours?"

"Down the hall and to the right. My room is the second door. It's not locked."

"Good." He didn't speak again until they got to her door. Then he faced a dilemma.

Isabel solved it for him. "Turn me around and I'll open the door."

"Good idea." He did as she'd suggested, and so did she, and Somerset marched her through the door and into her bedroom. Then he stopped and looked around. "Nice place Loretta has here."

"It's like a palace," Isabel agreed. "But I like your house better. It . . . it touches something in me."

"I'm glad to hear that. I'm hoping to do the same, very soon."

She chuckled softly, glad he hadn't misplaced his sense of humor during this moment of high passion. "If you'll put me down, I'll lock the door connecting my room to Eunice's. Every now and then she has nightmares. Well, I told you about them."

"Yes. I'm sorry about that." He set her gently on her feet. "I had nightmares for the first few weeks, but haven't had any for a month or so."

Isabel kicked off her shoes before going to Eunice's door. Her room boasted a thick carpet, thanks to Loretta's generosity, but Isabel didn't want to take any chances that she'd make noise. She turned the key, feeling guilty, then told herself that if Eunice had a bad dream, she could knock. Isabel would hear her.

She returned to Somerset and took his hand. Peering into his beautiful eyes, she said, "I still have bad dreams sometimes. I expect we're not the only ones."

"No. I'm sure we're not." He lifted her hands and kissed her palms, one at a time. "Are you sure about this, Isabel? If you've changed your mind, I'll understand." With a strained smile, he added, "It'll probably kill me, but I'd certainly understand and respect your wishes."

He was the most wonderful man in the world. Isabel shook her head. "I haven't changed my mind. I only hope you won't believe me to be abandoned beyond redemption."

"Lord, no!" Again, he picked her up. This time he

took her straight to the four-poster bed decorated with a lovely blue counterpane. "I've been wanting to do this forever, Isabel. Since that awful night on the ship, believe it or not."

In spite of herself, Isabel felt her eyes fill with tears. "I was so upset because I hadn't asked your name, Somerset. I wanted to pray for you, but I didn't know your name."

"You'll share it soon."

"Yes." She didn't want to think about that, since she knew he was incorrect on that score. Instead, she said, "Will you help me with my buttons? My shirtwaist buttons down the back."

"Gladly."

They undressed each other. Isabel was glad she danced for a living, because her employment precluded corsets and stays. Therefore, undressing was a much less cumbersome procedure than it might have been.

They both took their time at first, savoring the discovery of each other's bodies. Isabel felt as if she were melting into the sheets sometimes, Somerset's tender caresses were so inspiring. As need climbed in both of them, their movements became quicker.

Panting, Isabel said, "Let me unbutton your shirt, Somerset."

"Gladly. I'll just slip these straps off your shoulders and . . ." His words trailed off as he gazed at the swell of Isabel's breast, revealed when she shrugged off her unbuttoned shirtwaist and he first glimpsed her upper torso. He licked his lips. "You're beautiful, Isabel. I knew you would be."

"Thank you." Her fingers trembled slightly, but she managed to unbutton the last of his shirt buttons. With a yank, she pulled the shirt down until the sleeves caught because the cuffs were still buttoned. She briefly cursed her stupidity before becoming enchanted by his musculature. "Oh, my, so are you."

Somerset didn't bother with his cuff buttons. He tore his shirt off, popping buttons off both cuffs, then flung it aside. Reaching for Isabel, he pulled her to his chest, and for the first time, Isabel felt him without layers and layers of fabric between the two of them.

There was, however, one layer left, and she aimed to correct that problem at once. "Just a minute," she whispered, pulling slightly away from him.

"Hey," he said, but didn't continue his protest when he realized what she planned.

With one sinuous movement, Isabel rose to her knees, whipped off her lace-trimmed petticoat. Then she knelt before him, bare but for her black silk stockings, tied this evening with plain white garters. If she'd known this was going to happen, she'd have worn more exciting garters.

Somerset didn't seem to mind. His eyes examined her from the top of her head to her knees. She saw him swallow. He said, "My God. I've been longing for this moment ever since I first laid eyes on you, Isabel. I love you."

He loved her? Isabel stared at him, amazed. "You do? You didn't say so before."

"Didn't I?" He swallowed again and reached for her right garter. "I meant to. At least, I think I did. I do love you. That's why I want to marry you. I mean . . . Oh, hell."

And with that, he flung away her right garter, untied her left and consigned it to the floor, then tore off his own undershirt and wrapped her in his arms. Isabel would have cried out in rapture, except for Eunice being sound asleep in the other room.

She had craved this for so long. It had been years since she'd lain with a man, and then it hadn't been like this. Then, it had been hurried and fumbling, and it had left Isabel craving fulfillment. Not this time. This time she was with a man who cared about her. Loved her. Wanted to please her as much as he wanted to be pleased. His big rough hands stroked her back, making tingles dance through her. He was so big, and so warm, and so wonderful. Isabel felt cherished for the first time in her life.

Her breasts felt as if they were on fire, pressed against his chest as they were. She wanted to run her fingers through his chest hair. She wanted to feel him, to caress the silky length of his sex, to kiss him everywhere.

Very gently, Somerset laid her back on the bed, then stood, unbuttoned his trousers, and pushed them off, along with his drawers. Before Isabel could fully appreciate how very large he was—in every way—he joined her on the bed. "Don't be frightened, Isabel," he whispered.

Frightened? Was he teasing her? But no. He was worried lest she fear his possession of her body. She'd heard so many stories about women who fled from the marriage bed. She wasn't one of them. She had considered this a flaw in her nature until this minute. "I'm not frightened, Somerset."

He smiled as his hand cupped her breast. Isabel thought she might die from the pleasure of his touch. "Good. That's right, you've been married before. You know what to expect."

No, she didn't. She'd never felt like this. And he wanted to marry her. Isabel felt truly blessed, and only wished the condition would last. Since it wouldn't—

couldn't—she aimed to enjoy this experience to the full.

Since he was paying attention to her breasts, bless him, she decided to do some exploring of her own. Tentatively, she reached down and found his shaft. It was hot and silky, hard as stone, and much larger than she'd expected. Goodness, maybe she was afraid—a little. He moaned softly, and Isabel forgot about worrying if he'd fit. Gently, gently, she stroked him. With his hand still on her breast, he buried his head in a pillow, as if in an ecstasy of arousal. Good.

"That feels so good," came, muffled, from beside her.

Isabel turned a little and kissed the back of his neck. He was as hot as a cannon barrel. "I'm glad."

Suddenly, he lifted his head and turned over, taking Isabel with him until she was on top of him. "But I can't take much more of that, because I'm about to explode."

"No? Well, then, perhaps we should move on." She knew she was ready. She'd never felt this kind of pressure before, this longing for release.

Somerset caught his breath. "Are you sure?"

"I'm sure." Leaning over, she kissed him hard as she reached to guide him home. She slid over him as if they'd been made to fit together. Somerset closed his eyes, threw his head back, and groaned.

Slowly at first, Isabel rode him. She hadn't believed she could be so brazen, but it felt too good to stop. As the pressure inside her grew, she speeded up, until she felt as if she were riding a storm.

And then, all at once, everything inside her first clenched and then shattered into a million sparks. She gasped, cried, "Somerset!" softly, then collapsed on top of him as shudders and tremors shook her body.

"Ah, God, Isabel. That was so good." He turned over, taking her with him, until he was poised above her, braced with his bulging arms. "You're so beautiful. So beautiful."

Before Isabel had recovered from her own release, Somerset began moving in her. He wasn't gentle this time, and Isabel was on the verge of climaxing a second time when his release came, taking her with him into another crescendo of sensation.

A few minutes later, Somerset's arms enfolded her, and Isabel felt as if she'd finally found a safe haven from life's storms. It was an illusion, but such a pleasant one she opted not to worry about the truth for a couple of hours.

Chapter Seventeen

If the world were a kind and just place, Somerset thought as he lay next to Isabel, exhausted and totally content, he would be able to remain with her all night long and no one would bat an eye. The world being what it was, he knew he'd have to drive himself home, and soon, or her reputation would be in tatters.

She stirred, and he turned onto his side, marveling at her body, perfect in every way. "Dancing must be good for you, Isabel. You're beautiful everywhere."

Her smile was dreamy. "Thank you. You are, too." Then she blushed and hid her face in the pillow.

With a laugh, and although he didn't want to do it, Somerset swung his legs over the side of the bed. "I suppose I have to go home?" His voice lifted at the end of the sentence to make it a question, although he already knew the answer.

She heaved a huge sigh. "Yes. I suppose so."

Sitting on the bed next to her, he took her hand and kissed it. "You know, Isabel, I've been trying since the day we met to decide what color your eyes are."

Opening those spectacular eyes in surprise, she stared at him. "They're blue."

He grinned. "Yes, but they're not just any old ordinary blue. And they're not *Dampiera diversifolia* blue or *Exacum affine* blue, and they're not the blue of *Consolida ambigua* or the blue of the sky or of *Catananche caerulea*.

With a laugh, she hugged him. He returned the hug with interest. "You really have thought about this, haven't you?"

"You bet." Since they were already in each other's arms, he decided a kiss wouldn't be amiss, so he kissed her. He didn't dare allow his lips to linger for fear he wouldn't be able to stop. With a gasp, he drew away, wishing he didn't have to. "I've seen a *Violaceae—Viola sororia*—that's almost the blue of your eyes." Judging from the look in those eyes that she had no idea what he was talking about, he elaborated. "That's a gray-blue pansy."

"I'm very fond of pansies."

"And a certain wild flower I saw in New Hampshire comes close. I have a specimen but I haven't identified it yet. It's probably some kind of anchusa."

"I love you, Somerset."

"I love you, Isabel. I don't know what I ever did to deserve you."

Her grin broadened. "You saved Eunice's life and drew a picture of a weed."

He laughed and stood up, looking at the floor and hoping he'd be able to find all of his clothes.

"There's a bathroom right over there, if you want to wash up." Isabel pointed and yawned. Small wonder, considering her schedule for the past several days.

"I won't be long," he promised.

"Don't be loud, either. There's nobody in the room on the other side of the bathroom, but it's probably best not to tempt the fates." With a sigh, she, too, got up from the bed.

"Good idea. I'll be very quiet."

They both froze when the doorknob on the door connecting Isabel's room with Eunice's rattled. Isabel said, "Oh, dear."

Somerset said, "Let me grab my things."

"I'll help."

Stark naked, they both scrambled around the room, picking up discarded clothing. Isabel thrust his shoes into his arm and hissed, "You'll have to leave from the door leading from the bathroom to the hall."

"Mama? Mama, I had another dream." Eunice sounded sleepy but not terribly distressed. Perhaps this wasn't one of her nightmares, but only a dream that had awakened her.

"Bloody hell," Isabel whispered, then slapped a hand over her mouth.

But Somerset only grinned. "I love you, Isabel." He leaned down and kissed her.

"I love you, too, Somerset." If only she could marry him.

"Mama?"

"Oh, dear." Isabel raced to her dresser and opened a drawer. Somerset watched appreciatively and decided clothing was highly overrated. "I'll be right there, sweetie!"

"I guess I have to go, then," Somerset said upon a sigh. "Do I have everything?"

"I hope so." Drawing on a dressing gown, Isabel searched the room, looking frantic.

"Don't worry about it. If I've left anything, I can get it later."

"But I don't want Eunice to see!"

Right. Somerset took another quick look around the

room, determined that he had everything he'd flung
off in such haste, and decided that the next time they
did this, they'd do it at his house.

He could hardly wait.

Isabel hastily pushed her hair out of her face,
glanced in the mirror, hoped Eunice wouldn't be as discerning as she normally was, and went to the door.
Taking a deep breath, she unlocked it and drew it open.
"Come in, sweetie. I'm sorry I took so long."

Eunice frowned at her, puzzled. "Why did you lock
the door, Mama? Do you not like me to come into your
room at night?"

Guilt gnawed at Isabel's heart as her ears tried to
hear the sounds of Somerset using the washing facili-
ties. She picked her daughter up and hugged her hard.
"Good heavens, no, sweetheart. I don't mind at all
when you come into my room at night." Before Eunice
could ask another question or demand that Isabel answer the first of her original ones, she went on, "Did you
have another bad dream, sweetie? I'm so sorry."

She carried her to the bed, noticed a telltale wet
spot, cursed herself for forgetting to pull up the sheets
earlier, and did so before Eunice saw anything out of
the ordinary. Then she sat, settling her daughter on her
lap.

"Yes," said Eunice, scanning the room in, Isabel presumed, an effort to ascertain why her mother was behaving so strangely. Fortunately for Isabel, mention of
the dream distracted her. "Oh, but I have to tell you,
Mama, that Dr. Freud was right."

So far from her daughter's problems had Isabel
drifted during the past hours that at first Eunice's reference to Dr. Freud didn't register in its proper context.

She looked at her daughter in horror, recollecting some of the things she'd read in Dr. Freud's book. "I thought I'd hidden that!"

Eunice frowned slightly. "Why did you hide it? Anyhow, you couldn't hide this one because it was at school. Miss Pinkney lent it me."

"Oh." Isabel remember that her daughter had only been interested in dreams and relaxed slightly. "You mean you . . ." But Isabel couldn't remember what Eunice had planned to do with her dreams. What a terrible mother she was!

"Yes!" Eunice said in triumph, evidently not worried about her mother's parental worth at the moment. "I had another dream about the ship sinking, only instead of Rebecca and Lilian, the people in the ocean whom I was trying to save were you and Mr. FitzRoy."

Isabel heard a clunk from the bathroom, and presumed that Somerset had dropped a shoe. She pretended she hadn't heard it. "I'm very sorry, sweetheart. It must have been frightening to see your mother and Mr. FitzRoy in the water."

After a brief glance at the bathroom door, Eunice seemed to lose interest in the errant noise. She nodded. "It was awful. But before I went to sleep, I did what the book suggested and told myself that if I had a bad dream, I would remember it was only a dream and wake up. The book calls it lucid dreaming."

"Lucid dreaming?"

Eunice nodded. "I'm sure the word was lucid because I had to look it up in Miss Pinkney's dictionary."

"My goodness." By this time Isabel herself had almost forgotten about the bathroom, so intrigued was she by her young daughter's mental ability. "And it worked? You still woke up."

"Yes," Eunice agreed. "I woke up, but that was by way

of rescue. Once I realized I was dreaming and that the dream was one that would only terrify me, it woke me up. I was scared, but not so badly as usual." She gazed pensively at the wall. "Maybe I can train myself to interrupt the dreams as they're happening and turn them into happy dreams so I won't wake up. I could get more sleep that way."

Although her daughter was probably the most extraordinary person Isabel had ever met in her life and she didn't understand her or how she ever could have given birth to her, Isabel only murmured, "Er . . . yes."

"Children need lots of sleep," said Eunice soberly. "Miss Pinkney said so."

Isabel hugged her hard. "If anyone can do it, you can, dearie."

Eunice's little forehead furrowed. "It smells funny in here, Mama."

Good Lord. Isabel felt another strong surge of guilt. "Uh, yes. I . . . uh . . . noticed it, too. I don't know what it is."

"Hmmm. Maybe you ought to sprinkle some cologne around your room. That's what Miss MacTavish does."

Did she, indeed? Interesting. Isabel never would have guessed. "Good idea. Here, sweetie, let me carry you to your bed."

Eunice consented, Isabel thanked God that she hadn't had a nightmare that would induce her to want to spend the rest of the night in her mother's bed, and took her back into her own room.

She deposited her gently on the bed, and Eunice pulled the covers up to her chin. "I hope I have another dream," said she with an elfin grin. "I want to see if I can direct them."

"I hope you succeed, sweetie." Laughing softly, Isabel kissed her daughter's forehead. "Sleep well, Eunice."

"Thank you, Mama."

"I love you, dearie."

"I love you, too, Mama."

Isabel contemplated the nature of love as she returned to her room and closed, but did not lock, the door connecting it to Eunice's. Then she tiptoed to the bathroom, discovered that Somerset had unlocked it, and peeked inside. But he was gone. With a deep sigh, she went back to bed, and wished she could be like Eunice—only instead of directing her dreams the way she wanted them to go, she wanted to direct her entire *life*. It was a dirty shame she didn't have a magic wand or something.

Isabel didn't know whether to be overjoyed or frightened when Somerset invited the whole gang—Loretta, Marjorie, and Dr. Abernathy—to dine at the Fairfield the next night. He announced to them all that he and Isabel were to be wed, and there was quite a celebration. Isabel felt like the meanest of traitors when they toasted her after her first number with her new partner, Geoffrey Gardener.

Geoffrey, on the other hand, was ecstatic when he heard the news. Clasping his hands to his breast, he said, "What fun! Isabel, *darling*, I had no idea you'd snagged such a gorgeous man!"

Embarrassed, Isabel smiled and tried to look as if she were as ecstatic as he. "Yes. I'm a very lucky woman."

"And he's a lucky man." Dr. Abernathy lifted his glass and winked at her.

"I'm so happy for you both." Loretta drew out a hankie and had to wipe tears from her eyes.

"I am, too. Tis a verra brilliant match." Marjorie, too, appeared somewhat misty-eyed.

Isabel stared at her. She'd come to like and appreciate Marjorie, who wasn't nearly as aloof as Isabel had at first believed. Still, she hadn't dreamed the woman would ever overcome her class consciousness enough to consider a marriage between the low-born Isabel Golightly to the upper-crust Somerset FitzRoy a "brilliant" match. Smiling fondly upon her friends, she said, "Thank you all very much. I wish I deserved your good wishes."

They all rushed to correct her assessment of herself. Only Isabel knew why she felt like a cheater and a fake, and that the feeling was fully justified. She also knew that Somerset would hate her when he learned the truth. She already hated herself.

Nevertheless, she allowed herself to pretend that all was well, and she enjoyed dancing with Somerset that evening. He was ever so much better a dancer than Geoffrey. In fact—Isabel hoped she wasn't deceiving herself—he had become so confident in himself and his skill, and so relaxed in his presentation, that he would be a match for Jorge Savedra himself, should Jorge ever return to San Francisco.

Isabel spared a pang of remorse for Jorge. She hoped that, wherever he was, he was able to tango with a partner worthy of him.

As for herself, she couldn't remember the last time she'd felt so wretched.

The day of the contest dawned foggy and drippy. The weather matched Isabel's mood. The only good thing about the mess she'd gotten herself in to was that she honestly believed that she and Somerset had a good chance of winning the dance contest. If they did, she'd be able to support herself when all of her friends turned against her. She and he moved together beautifully, and they had choreographed special maneuvers for every type of dance they'd have to do, no matter what the music turned out to be.

She hadn't had the chance to be alone with him since the night they'd made love, but she guessed that was for the best. The more she allowed herself to succumb to her love for him, the harder and more painful their eventual parting would be.

Of course, there was a chance that Somerset would turn out to possess a forgiving nature, but Isabel knew better than to count on it. So few men did. She stared out the parlor window, wondering what it would feel like to be dead. Then she chided herself for being a defeatist and a coward. Whatever happened, she would survive, and so would Eunice. And if Somerset couldn't tolerate the truth, so be it.

She glanced at her daughter, who was curled up on a chair, her nose in *Wuthering Heights*. She'd been concerned about Eunice reading such sensational literature, but Miss Pinkney had assured her that Eunice was up to the challenge and that such books as Miss Bronte's and Mr. Freud's wouldn't warp her brain. Isabel imagined the good woman was right. If anyone could survive such reading material, it was Eunice.

Loretta clattered down the front staircase, stabbing a pin into a cunning confection of a hat. "Are you ready, Isabel? Is Jason here yet? Where's Somerset?"

Laughing a little, Isabel said, "It's early yet, Loretta. Somerset is on his way. He telephoned a few minutes ago." It seemed odd to her that she should have already become accustomed to such luxuries as the telephone, but she had.

Next to rush down the staircase was Marjorie Mac-Tavish. She was brandishing something Isabel couldn't see clearly, although it appeared to be a piece of jewelry. "You mun wear this, Isabel! It's a lucky piece I got in China when I worked with White Star." Panting, she thrust the item at Isabel, who took it slowly, astonished that the conventional Marjorie would offer such a whimsical token as a good-luck charm.

"You're all too good to me." She peered at the lucky piece. "This is beautiful, Marjorie." A small carved ivory fish hung on a silver chain. The workmanship was splendid. "It's so delicate. I'm afraid to wear it. It might break."

"Dinna be daft," said Marjorie, back to being her pragmatic self. "Wear it under your gown if you don't want it to bounce up and down while you dance. It's codswallop, of course, to believe in lucky charms, but I thought of it when I was getting dressed." With a grin the likes of which Isabel had never thought to see on that face, she added with a shrug, "It canna hurt."

"It's awfully pretty," Eunice observed, peering over her book. She, too, was dressed up today, in a pretty blue frock, black patent-leather Mary Janes, and with blue ribbons tied around her blond braids.

"Yes it is." Isabel impulsively leaned over and kissed Marjorie on her cheek. "Thank you so much." She fastened the chain's clasp and decided she liked the looks of the pendant against her black organdy gown. "I'll wear it out, if you don't mind."

"It's grand with me."

Isabel had opted for simplicity, comfort, and ease of movement in her gown for the contest. The one she'd chosen featured a wrap-over bodice that formed elbow-length sleeves, a high waist circled by a not-too-tight organdy cummerbund, and a hip-length overskirt. She'd already worn it once, in what she'd thought of as the dress rehearsal, the evening before, and it had performed as well as she had, which was the whole point.

"This is charming, Marjorie." Loretta lifted the fish and squinted at it. "I'll have to wear my spectacles at the contest. I don't want to miss anything."

A knock came at the door. Mrs. Brandeis answered it, and Jason Abernathy marched straight to the parlor. As soon as Marjorie saw him, she headed for the other side of the room. Isabel sighed and wished Marjorie weren't so shy.

"Are we ready?" Jason asked in his booming voice. He rubbed his hands and looked Isabel up and down. "You appear to be ready. Where's your partner?"

"He'll be here in a minute," Isabel assured him.

Sure enough, not five minutes later, Somerset showed up at Loretta's front door. He carried four corsages, one for each lady and Eunice. "Sorry I didn't get here sooner. I saw a flower vendor on the corner and couldn't resist."

"Oh, my," murmured Marjorie. Then she shot a suspicious glance at Jason. When he didn't look as if he aimed to say anything that he would consider humorous, she took the pretty white chrysanthemum corsage from Somerset. "Thank you."

"You're more than welcome." Somerset beamed upon his companions. "I thought we might as well look festive." He sported a boutonniere in his lapel.

Isabel loved him passionately. "Thank you, Somerset."

He pinned a white orchid to the shoulder of her gown. "Do you think we'll squash it while we dance?"

"I don't think so. It's just lovely." Again succumbing to impulse, she got up on her tiptoes and kissed him. It was a chaste kiss on his cheek, but she noticed her friends all smiling at her afterwards.

"What a splendid idea," Loretta said. "Thank you, Mr. FitzRoy. Will someone pin this on me?"

"I'll help you," Marjorie volunteered at once. "Then you can help me with mine." She pointedly ignored Jason, who chuckled.

"Here, Miss Eunice," said Somerset. "Allow me." Eunice obediently trotted over to him, *Wuthering Heights* tucked under her arm, and he pinned a pretty corsage to her shoulder. "There. That looks very nice," he said, standing back and smiling down at her.

"I've never had a corsage before," Eunice said, trying to see the flower on her shoulder. "Thank you very much, Mr. FitzRoy." She stuck out her hand, and Somerset shook it gravely.

"You're very welcome, Miss Eunice."

Somerset, Eunice, and Isabel rode in Somerset's Maxwell to the Palace. Loretta, Marjorie, and Jason braved Loretta's Runabout.

"Marjorie doesn't look very happy," Isabel said as she watched the woman climb into the Runabout's front seat. "At least she won't have to sit next to Dr. Abernathy."

"I asked him why he likes to tease her, and he said it's because she needs to loosen up."

"Hmmm," said Isabel. "I doubt that will work."

"It sounds crazy to me," agreed Somerset.

"It might work," mused Eunice, again entering into the conversation as if she were an adult talking to the other adults. "Miss MacTavish really does have a sense of human."

"A sense of humor, sweetie?"

"That's what I meant. Humor. It's just hard to find most of the time."

"I've noticed that." Somerset's voice was dry.

"She's a lovely person, really," said Isabel. "She's only shy. I get the feeling she liked being a stewardess because she knew all the rules. America is so new and different, she's not sure what to do."

"That could be," murmured Somerset.

Isabel sensed he wasn't much interested in Jason and Marjorie. "Are you nervous, Somerset?"

"A little. You?"

"Very."

He glanced at her. "I'm surprised to hear it. You're such a superb dancer. I can't imagine any other lady holding a candle to you. Providing, of course, your partner doesn't stumble or fall down."

"Thank you." She gave him a smile she hoped conveyed her love and appreciation.

"There *might* be other profane—profuse—I mean professional dancers in the contest." Eunice was staring out the Maxwell's window, observing with interest the hustle and bustle of San Francisco's busy Geary Street.

Isabel and Somerset exchanged a glance. "I hadn't thought about that," admitted Isabel. "I suppose it is possible."

"Daunting idea," said Somerset dryly.

Isabel got the impression that he'd be just as happy if Eunice had stayed at home today. "We can only do our best," she said, trying to sound optimistic.

"You're awfully good," Eunice said. "I think it would take a very good couple or one who's very lucky to win any contest with you in it."

"Hope you're right," Somerset muttered. "I probably should have bribed a judge or something."

"Somerset!" Isabel glanced sharply at her daughter to see if she had an opinion on bribery, but Eunice's face was impassive. Just to make sure, she said, "He was only joking, Eunice."

Somerset said, "Hmm."

Eunice eyed her mother. "Yes," she said noncommitally.

Isabel's heart crunched a little when Somerset pulled up the Palace's drive and stopped the Maxwell in front of the grand entrance. A uniformed attendant rushed over to help the ladies alight. Somerset handed over his key and some coins, and shepherded the ladies into the hotel.

Geoffrey met them at the door. Isabel was glad to see him and gave him a peck on the cheek. "Thank you so much for coming, Geoffrey."

"I had to come," he said in his breathless voice. "I just *know* you're going to win."

"I hope you're right."

They waited in the magnificent lobby for Loretta and the others to arrive. "I hope she didn't hit anything," Isabel said under her breath. She'd started fidgeting with her gloves, and commanded herself to stop it at once. There was no reason in the world for her to be so nervous. She danced virtually every day of her life, and Somerset and she had established a perfect and graceful unity in motion. A glance at Geoffrey informed her that he was every bit as nervous as she. What's more, he didn't try to hide the fact.

Telling herself not to fret didn't work, so she was glad when Loretta screeched the Runabout to a halt in front of the entrance, scattering a couple who were walking across the drive, and terrifying the attendant into jumping up onto the curb. Oblivious, Loretta bounded out of the machine, happy as a lark. Marjorie opened her eyes, her face as white as the proverbial sheet, and allowed the attendant, who had recovered himself, to open her door for her. Jason Abernathy, who had, Isabel presumed, long since become accustomed to Loretta's driving, got out of the tonneau, laughing. He took both ladies' arms and guided them into the hotel.

Spotting Somerset, Isabel, Eunice, and Geoffrey, he cried heartily, "Here we are, unscathed and only slightly daunted."

Loretta smacked him on the arm. "I don't know why you're always carrying on about my driving, Jason. I've never once had an accident."

"Thanks to the sharp eyes of the other drivers on San Francisco's streets," Jason told her with a wink.

"Fiddlesticks." Loretta patted her hat back into place—the wild ride had knocked it askew—and said, "Where do we go now?"

"The grand ballroom, according to the announcement." Isabel took a deep breath. "I guess we're ready." Casting a questioning glance at Somerset, she lifted an eyebrow.

"The grand ballroom it is," he said heartily. "Away with us."

He took Eunice's hand, Isabel placed hers on his other arm, and they set off to their doom. No, no. Isabel meant to their certain victory.

She only wished she believed it.

Chapter Eighteen

"There are a lot of people in here," Somerset said, sounding as if he were trying not to convey disappointment or worry.

"Yes," agreed Isabel. "There certainly are."

"Are they all contestants?" Loretta wondered in a bewildered voice.

"I hope not," grumbled Somerset.

"You'll outshine them all," said Geoffrey, sounding as if he didn't quite trust his assessment.

"I think there are as many spectacles as dancers," Eunice piped up.

They all turned to look at her. Isabel said doubtfully, "Spectators, do you mean?"

Eunice nodded. "All the other dancers probably brought friends and family along, just like you did." She smiled brightly at her mother.

Jason said, "You're probably right." He started suddenly. "Hey! I forgot something." Whipping a packet out of his coat pocket, he presented it to Eunice with a flourish. "For you, my dear. I believe they're bath salts."

Eunice's bright eyes shone. "Thank you ever so much, Dr. Abernathy." She sniffed the packet. "Oh, it smells so good."

"Honeysuckle," said the good doctor. "One of—"

Loretta finished the sentence for him—"his patients gave it to him in payment for his medical services."

Somerset chuckled. "You're going to go broke if you keep doing that, Jason."

Jason shrugged. "At least my friends will smell good."

"It's very kind of you to offer your services for such payment, Dr. Abernathy. I believe every one of us should be humiliated by your goodness."

They all turned to look at Eunice, who had uttered the pompous sentiment. Isabel cleared her throat. "Um . . . do you mean humbled, dearie?"

Eunice squinted at her mother for a moment, then nodded. "Do I?"

Isabel smiled. "I think so, dearie."

"Well, then, yes. Humbled." She bestowed another shining smile on Jason.

Isabel said, "You're absolutely right, Eunice. You're too good, Dr. Abernathy."

They all murmured their assent. Even Marjorie went so far as to nod her head and smile shyly at the doctor.

Jason said, "Fudge," but he looked pleased.

A harried voice called out, "All contestants up front, please."

Somerset and Isabel shared a glance. Somerset said, "I guess this is it."

"I guess so." Isabel gave him what she hoped was a dazzling smile. "Let's go."

"Good luck, Mama and Mr. FitzRoy," Eunice said.

Isabel bent to kiss her. "Thank you, dearie."

"You'll do beautifully," Geoffrey assured them, slightly marring his declaration by gasping and pressing his hand to his heart as if he were suffering from palpitations.

Somerset shook the little girl's hand again. "Thank you, Miss Eunice."

"Good luck," the rest of their friends called out as Somerset took Isabel's hand, and the two of them walked to the front of the ballroom.

A small orchestra had assembled. Isabel recognized Hank, the pianist who had played for her audition at the Fairfield. She nodded at him, wondering if he'd remember her. He seemed to, because he grinned back and nodded. Although she knew it was ridiculous of her, her confidence rose, knowing Hank was there.

"All contestants up front!" the voice called out again. Isabel saw the owner of the voice, a short, portly fellow in a loud checked suit, long side whiskers and a big waxed moustache. She and Somerset obediently moved closer to him.

Counting couples, Isabel came up with thirteen. That seemed like an awful lot of competition to her. Nevertheless, she was a professional. And Somerset was a natural. Unless all the others were either professionals or naturals, they might have a chance. No, they *did* have a chance. A good chance. A great chance, even.

Lord, she was scared.

The order in which the couples were to perform was determined by pulling numbers out of a hat. There was a grand total of fourteen couples. When Somerset insisted that Isabel pick their number, she shut her eyes and grabbed. Her fingers trembled when she unfolded the paper. "Thirteen." It sounded an inauspicious number to her.

"Good." Somerset was obviously not a superstitious gentleman. "That's almost at the end. If we do well, people will remember us."

They'd remember them if they made an egregious mistake, too, but Isabel didn't point that out. She knew they were good together—in more ways than one.

The first couple of pairs lightened her mood considerably. Oh, they were good, but they were good in an ordinary way, as if they enjoyed dancing together but hadn't bothered to choreograph anything special for the contest. The third pair was better, but nothing spectacular. Isabel began feeling quite encouraged as the fourth, fifth and sixth couple took to the floor.

And then came number seven. As they started waltzing, Isabel's newly engendered optimism began to fade. She whispered to Somerset, "They're good."

He whispered back, "We're better."

Were they? Isabel eyed the seventh couple appraisingly, endeavoring to keep her personal feelings from coloring her opinion. Now that fashions had lifted ladies' hems so that their ankles could be seen, footwork was much easier to assess. So Isabel fastened upon the couples' feet, and wonder of wonders, she discovered Somerset was right. The couple had the steps down flat, but without the measure of grace that Isabel knew both she and Somerset possessed in abundance. She only hoped the judges' eyes were as discerning as hers.

"There's nothing you can do about the judges," Somerset whispered then, as if he'd been reading her mind.

He was right, of course. Isabel had the wicked thought that she wished he *had* bribed a judge or two.

Couples eight and nine weren't awfully good, and couple number ten made a big mistake. Isabel decided that if their only real competition came from couple number seven, their chances of winning were good, if not superb.

Then couple number ten took to the floor. Isabel watched in growing worry as the pair whirled off in the waltz, adding several dazzling twirls. Were they as dazzling as those she and Somerset had choreographed? The lady's dress wasn't as full as Isabel's, and that was nominally encouraging, since her own skirt billowed out artistically as they turned. She knew, and prayed that the judges did, too, that presentation was almost as important as skill and grace.

Couple number ten's ragtime number was excellent, too. Isabel began chewing the finger of her glove. Somerset put a hand over hers to stop her.

"Quit worrying," he said. "We're every bit as good as they are, and if the judges like your dress or our choreography better than theirs, we'll win."

Unless couples eleven, twelve and fourteen are as good as they are, Isabel thought, but she knew that to say so would only serve to undermine their chances. Better that Somerset honestly believe they were the best, even if Isabel herself was unsure.

She survived watching couple number ten. She was almost, but not quite, positive that she and Somerset danced the Castle Walk better than they did. She hoped so. So far, none of the couples did the tango with the flair she and Somerset put into it, thanks to Jorge Savedra. Until this minute, Isabel hadn't known how much she'd learned from Jorge. She offered up another prayer for his safety.

Couples eleven and twelve were good, but not spectacular. And then it was their turn.

"Couple number thirteen!" called the portly man in the tasteless suit. "Come forward, please."

Isabel glanced at her friends and daughter for luck, then looked at Hank, who winked at her and gave her a thumbs-up sign. Taking that as a signal of Hank's belief in her, she took a deep breath and looked up at Somerset.

Dr. Freud's advice had done wonders for Somerset's presence on the dance floor. Isabel hoped it would carry him through the contest, which she was finding a nerve-wracking experience. And she was a professional.

"Start with the waltz," the portly gent called out.

The orchestra, which had prepared a variety of musical offerings for the contest, played the opening bars to "Valse Maurice," which had been composed for the wonderful French dancer Maurice Mouvet by Sylvester Belmonte. Isabel had been holding her breath, hoping to get a good tune. She let it out and smiled at Somerset. "Maurice" wasn't a particular favorite of hers, but they waltzed well together, and she knew they would look beautiful dancing to the number.

Wild applause broke out when the music ended. Somerset had added a flourish of his own, in a move Jorge would have approved. He'd timed it to perfection, too, when, as the orchestra sailed into the last notes, he'd twirled Isabel outward, then drew her in, and they ended the number with them both facing the audience, and with Isabel's back held against his chest by his right arm.

They took a short bow, then the announcer called out, "The Castle Walk."

Isabel barely had time to catch her breath before the orchestra started playing "Too Much Mustard." The music pleased her, since it wasn't the same old thing. She and Somerset shared a huge smile—a choreographed smile, but genuine for all that—and took off. It was a fun dance, a modified foxtrot, made popular by Vernon and Irene Castle, and Isabel was pleased to note that Somerset appeared to be enjoying himself hugely. She'd known for years, thanks to Uncle Charlie, that what he called "stage presence" counted as much as, if not more than, knowledge and skill. They ended "Too Much Mustard" with another flourish, only this one didn't catch Isabel by surprise.

More applause greeted them. Isabel tried to judge the level of noise generated by the audience. Were they getting more applause than the first twelve couples? Her head was so full of tension, she couldn't make a valid determination.

"Ragtime!" the announcer shouted next, and the orchestra launched into the "Honeysuckle Rag." Given the bath salts Dr. Abernathy had recently presented Eunice, Isabel decided to take this as a good omen.

"We're perfect today, darling," Somerset murmured as they danced. "You'll get your dance academy in no time flat."

It was an encouraging comment, especially in light of Isabel's expectations for their supposed engagement. Ah, well. As long as she could support herself and Eunice, she wouldn't repine. Yet. Because she loved him so much and so appreciated his optimistic words, she gave him a spectacular smile and kept dancing.

"Honeysuckle Rag" was a happy, lively tune, and Isabel and Somerset gave it their best. Their best was superb, to judge by the reception from the audience when they finished.

"Foxtrot," shouted the announcer. Isabel was beginning to think of him as Mr. Checkers.

The foxtrot and the Castle Walk were similar, but the Castle Walk was a little faster and more syncopated. Isabel was pleased when the orchestra dove into "I'm Always Chasing Rainbows." It reminded her of her own life, and she put everything she had into the number, including the showy gestures she and Somerset had worked out, featuring twirls and a portion of the dance where they were only connected by holding hands and dancing side-by-side. Isabel heard gasps from the audience and a scattering of applause. She suspected nobody had ever seen a move like that before. Again, she had Jorge to thank for the innovative choreography.

And then, last, and only after the audience had calmed down from their flattering reception of their foxtrot, came the tango. Isabel was a trifle worried about this one, because Somerset, no matter how relaxed he got, wasn't as comfortable with the tango as he might be. Small wonder. The tango required a man who could at least emulate Jorge's level of arrogance if he didn't have it to begin with, and Somerset didn't. He was too kind for the tango. The notion struck Isabel as amusing, although she wished she'd waited to have it until after they'd finished dancing.

"I hope we get one of the tunes we've practiced to," she whispered to Somerset as they took their places on the floor. Their beginning, no matter what music the orchestra played, was dramatic, with Isabel and Somerset holding hands and facing away from each other at arms' length. After that, it depended on which number the orchestra played.

Isabel's heart quavered when she heard the opening bars of the "Brazilian Tango," sometimes called the "Tango del Maurice," another tune written for Maurice Mouvet. Mouvet was one of the most innovative and popular modern dancers of the day, and the few times Isabel had seen him at the cinema, she'd been impressed. The problem with dancing to music composed for him was that, depending on the dancers, they looked either magnificent or ghastly. She and Somerset had practiced to this very music, thanks to Loretta's Victrola, but it wasn't one of Somerset's best dances. He wasn't extravagant or arrogant enough.

They could but do their best, however, and when Somerset pulled her to him, put his arm around her as if she were a possession he didn't intend to relinquish no matter how many male dancers tried to wrest her away from him, she perked up. For the very first time, Somerset put on a show. He'd been embarrassed to do so in Loretta's ballroom but, thank God, he overcame his misgivings now, when it mattered.

Except for the orchestra and their own feet, Isabel didn't hear a sound. Apparently, the audience was captivated. She hoped she wasn't imagining it. There was one slightly tricky part to this tango since she'd modified Jorge's choreography. When they got to the end, Somerset was supposed to fling her away from him and then yank her back. Isabel would end in his arms, gazing up at him, while he glared down at her. His coloring didn't exactly shout *Latin Lover*, but he could smolder when he wanted to. Isabel knew it for a fact.

It was almost over. The pounding strains of the music was reaching its crescendo. She and Somerset locked gazes. Isabel took a deep breath in preparation.

And the strap on her left black satin pump broke.

Somerset, of course, didn't know what had happened. But Isabel didn't wobble. She was a professional. She told herself that when Somerset flung her with unusual vigor away from him. When she landed on her left foot, her ankle, with no strap to hold it, buckled. She heard a crunch, and a shock of pain almost knocked her over.

She didn't even wince. Holding in her cry of agony and her alarm—if she'd broken her ankle, God alone knew what would happen to her and her daughter— she twirled back to Somerset when he tugged at her, and she ended up without a limp, being held in his embrace. Her left black satin pump lay about five feet away from them, on its side, looking like a fallen soldier.

Nobody noticed the shoe but Isabel. After holding their final pose for approximately ten seconds, Somerset lifted Isabel right off the dance floor and whirled her around and around, as the audience went mad.

He didn't put her down until Loretta, Eunice, Marjorie, Geoffrey, and Jason had rushed up to congratulate them. When he did, Isabel uttered a sharp, *"Ow!"* and collapsed.

"Good God!" Somerset cried, instantly stooping to pick her up again.

"Isabel!" Loretta said, shocked.

"Och, what happened?" Marjorie exclaimed.

"What's the matter?" echoed Jason.

It was Eunice who, as might have been expected, solved the problem. A black satin shoe dangling from her small gloved hand, she said, "I think Mama's shoe strap broke. She probably splayed her ankle."

"Good God," Somerset repeated. He had Isabel in his arms by this time. He carried her to the sidelines as the announcer called for the last couple to take the floor. "Are you all right, darling?"

"I think Eunice is right," she said. "Except I do believe my ankle is sprained and not splayed."

"I'll have Jason look at it right away." Somerset sounded much more worried about her ankle than he ever had about the dance contest.

"No. Please. Wait until the last couple finishes and the announcer tells who won."

"Well . . ."

"Please, Somerset. This is important."

"Not as important as your health."

Isabel wasn't sure about that. "Please?"

"All right." He turned around and craned his neck to see the last couple dancing.

Isabel couldn't have watched him if she'd wanted to, since her friends and her daughter were all hovering around her, blocking her view of the dance floor.

Only when the music stopped and the announcer called out, "And the winners are . . ." did all fussing cease. So did all the noise in the ballroom. Isabel, Somerset, Eunice, and their friends turned toward Mr. Checkers. In Somerset's arms, Isabel held her breath. Her ankle throbbed like mad.

"You, you, you," she heard Loretta chant under her breath. Isabel fervently prayed she was right.

"That looks bad," observed Dr. Abernathy. When Isabel glanced at him, startled, she realized he was talking about her ankle, at which he was staring with professional interest.

"Mr. and Mrs. Somerset FitzRoy!"

The audience exploded in cheers and applause. Eunice, acting like a little girl for once in her life, laughed out loud as she clapped and jumped up and down. Geoffrey joined her. Loretta threw her arms around Isabel and Somerset both—she couldn't do anything else and still get the job done—and Marjorie actually whooped. Jason cheered. Isabel already had her arms around Somerset's neck, so she squeezed him hard. He buried his face in her hair and laughed and laughed.

It took them a long time to get out of the ballroom, and when they did it was past dinnertime. "I suggest we retire to Loretta's house before we dine. I intend to take a look at that ankle, Mrs. Golightly."

"Good idea," said Loretta. She smiled broadly. "Isn't it funny that the announcer had the two of you married already?"

"Smart man," said Somerset. His mood was high as the sky.

Isabel wished hers was. But she was determined to let the truth out tonight, at Loretta's house. And she'd tell them as a group. In her heart, she knew it was the only way to make amends for tricking them all. Even Geoffrey. Given his own proclivities, he was the only one besides Loretta whom Isabel trusted to remain her friend after the truth was revealed.

Because she was in great pain, she decided to allow Dr. Abernathy to bind her ankle before confessing. That was probably only one more indication that she possessed a weak character. So be it. At least she could start her new life if not whole, at least bandaged.

Geoffrey rode with her and Eunice in Somerset's Maxwell. She was tired. It was a good tired, except for her ankle and her agonized anticipation of the confession to come. But they'd done *so* well. If she hadn't been too much of a coward to tell Somerset her true condition before they began rehearsing for the contest, she would have been totally content.

As it was . . . well, she hoped two thousand five hundred dollars would be enough to open her academy, because she expected she and Eunice would be on their own again soon. Very soon.

Somerset couldn't recall the last time he'd been this happy and excited. Actually, when he thought about it, he guessed he never had been. His had been a solitary life, horticulture his passion, and he hadn't socialized a whole lot. The notion of entering a dance contest wouldn't have occurred to him in a hundred years if he hadn't met Isabel Golightly.

Now, thanks to her, he'd not only found love, but he'd

discovered the joys of dancing. It occurred to him that he and Isabel actually had an interest in common at last, and he almost laughed out loud. He was a very happy man.

He pulled the Maxwell to a stop in front of Loretta's house. "Let me carry you indoors, Isabel. I don't want you walking on that ankle."

"Thank you. I don't want to walk on it, either. It's been weak ever since that mad scramble to get to the lifeboats on the *Titanic.*"

"How awful," whispered Geoffrey, who had delicate sensibilities.

"It was," agreed Somerset. "I'll certainly never forget it." He exited the car, opened the door to the tonneau so that Geoffrey and Eunice could get out, and went to Isabel's door. She was so lovely. So perfect in every way. And she would soon be his. He could hardly wait.

She smiled up at him. "It really does hurt. I hope it's not broken."

"I read somewhere," said Eunice, watching with interest as Somerset lifted her mother and balanced her in his arms, "that sprains are often slower to heal than clean breaks. I think it's because the tentacles—" She stopped speaking and thought hard for a second. "I mean tendons get torn during a sprain and not when a bone is broken."

Geoffrey said, "Ew," and looked at Eunice as if she were the demon's spawn.

Somerset said, "You may be right, Miss Eunice. Let's go ask the good doctor."

Eunice skipped up to the porch steps. "When I grow up, I want to be a doctor."

Both Somerset and Eunice's mother chuckled.

Loretta and her passengers had arrived ahead of them. Somerset had anticipated this circumstance, since Loretta drove like a fiend and he had taken it easy out of consideration for Isabel's injury.

"He's awfully nice to look after it for me," murmured Isabel.

"It's his job," said Somerset.

"But I don't have any honeysuckle bath salts to give him in payment." She grinned.

"Maybe he'll accept money."

"That would be nice." She snuggled close, clutching him tightly. Somerset thought it was almost as if she feared they were going to be separated. Silly woman. He'd never let her go.

The door was flung open before they'd all climbed the porch stairs, and Loretta called out, "Bring the invalid into the front parlor. I have Mrs. Brandeis opening champagne so that we can celebrate properly."

"Champagne!" Isabel laughed. "Thank you, Loretta. I didn't know you'd planned on champagne."

Somerset carried her through the door and down the hall, Geoffrey, Eunice, and Loretta trailing. Loretta said, "Oh, my, yes. I figured we could use it either in celebration or condolence. I'd planned on a celebration, of course."

"You're too good to me," Isabel murmured.

"Where do you want the patient?" Somerset asked Dr. Abernathy, who stood before the unlighted fireplace, stroking his chin. Marjorie, who was similarly occupied, stood across the room from him. They both slanted glances at each other from time to time, but no teasing had commenced yet. Somerset could only be glad of it.

"That chair will be fine," Jason said, pointing.

Somerset deposited his precious burden in the chair. "I'll just prop your foot up on this ottoman."

"Thank you," Isabel said with a grimace of pain. "It does hurt a lot."

"Put this cushion under her heel," suggested Marjorie, handing Somerset a pillow. So he did.

"Thank you." Isabel settled her foot on the cushion.

"Let me take a look at it." Dr. Abernathy walked over and knelt beside Isabel's chair. "You're going to have to remove that stocking. We'll turn our backs. Do you need help?"

Isabel's cheeks turned bright red. "I don't think so."

"All right, then. About face, gentlemen."

Somerset, Jason, and Geoffrey turned their backs. Somerset thought Geoffrey probably didn't need to, since it would take more than a naked leg to get him interested in a female, but he didn't say so.

He heard a few rustles as Isabel lifted her gown's skirt and untied her garter. He pictured her rolling down her stocking, and his juices started to flow with a vengeance.

Because he didn't want to make a spectacle of himself, he turned his mind away from Isabel's lovely legs and began contemplating where they should hold their wedding ceremony. He wanted to be married as soon as could be, and Isabel had been married before, so he imagined she wouldn't care about a huge church wedding. He'd like to hold the ceremony in his house, actually.

"I'm ready," came Isabel's voice from behind them, interrupting his chain of thought.

He turned, saw the purple, swollen ankle Isabel had propped on the cushion, and gasped. "My God, Isabel! That looks awful. It must hurt like crazy."

She gave him a tender smile. "It does. But it won't last forever." Looking at her ankle, she added, "It's ugly, though, isn't it?"

"Yes." Somerset's heart ached for his beloved and her pain. He wished he could take it away and bear it himself.

"Och," murmured Marjorie. "That looks worse than the last time, when you sprained it on the ship."

"Yes," said Eunice, staring at her mother's ankle with rapt fascination. "It does. It's very ugly, Mama."

"I'm afraid it is," agreed Isabel. "My ankle went over sideways."

"Well, Jason will fix it up for you," said Loretta.

"I heard an awful crunch when it happened," Isabel added ruefully.

Geoffrey fainted.

They all turned to look at him. Jason sighed. "I don't think there's really anything wrong with him. He just doesn't like the sight of bruised flesh."

"Maybe I should get him a pillow and a glass of water," Eunice suggested.

"Good idea." Jason gave her an approving smile.

"But I want to see what you do to Mama's ankle."

Loretta took over. "I'll ring for Mrs. Brandeis. Here. Put this cushion under his head, Eunice. Then you can watch the operation."

"Thank you, Miss Linden." Eunice, efficient as a woman ten times her age, did as Loretta had bidden her while Loretta rang for her housekeeper. Then the little girl walked over to the chair and stood by her mother's side. "If you need to hold my hand, Mama, I'm right here."

Her offer tickled Somerset, but he didn't laugh, knowing that Eunice was deadly serious. He was also irked with himself for not thinking of offering his own hand.

"Thank you, sweetie. I'll take you up on your offer." She reached for her daughter's hand and smiled. Eunice, on the other hand, was as sober as a judge.

"All right, let's see this mangled member."

Jason gently lifted Isabel's foot and pressed and palpated and twisted it until Somerset wanted to punch him in the jaw for hurting her. His hands fisted, but he held them at his sides, knowing he was being irrational. He told himself that Jason wasn't really fondling his darling's foot and ogling it, but examining it in order to determine the best course of action to take.

After what seemed to him like an unconscionably long time, the doctor said, still eyeing the ankle, "It's a bad sprain, all right. I don't feel any broken bones. It's going to take a long time to heal, though, and I'm afraid you won't be able to resume your work at the Fairfield for at least a month. Perhaps more, depending on how well you treat it in the meantime." He left off staring at her unclad leg and peered at Isabel's face. "You need to stay off it for at least a week. I'll ice it and bind it and then I'll check it daily, but I don't want you walking on it."

"But . . ." Isabel was shocked. "But I need to work! I can't stay away from my job for a week, much less a month!"

"Nonsense," said Loretta firmly. "You will stay right here with that foot elevated and you won't stir from this house. I'll see to it." She nodded at Jason to emphasize her decision.

"No!" cried Isabel. "I can't. You don't understand."

"I know what we'll do," Somerset, who didn't want anyone else taking care of Isabel, said. "I'll call a preacher or a judge, and we'll get married right here, right now. Then *I* can take care of you, Isabel! You won't have to go back to the Fairfield, and you can open your dance academy when you're well again." He thought it was a splendid idea.

His suggestion brought the clamor to an abrupt halt. Everyone gazed at him for several silent seconds.

A slow smile spread across Loretta's face. "What a good idea."

"Indeed," concurred Marjorie. She, too, smiled broadly. Somerset was amazed. One didn't often see a smile brighten that particular countenance.

Eunice said, "Really?" She grinned like an imp and clasped her hands in front of her. "Oh, Mama, how bully! Mr. FitzRoy, I'm so glad you're going to marry my mother!"

"Thank you, Eunice." Somerset was genuinely touched by the child's approbation.

"Good man," affirmed Dr. Abernathy, grinning from ear to ear.

Isabel swallowed hard and said, "Wait."

Everyone's attention swerved from Somerset to her. She looked wretched.

Baffled, Somerset said, "Wait? But I thought . . ."

Isabel bowed her head. "I know. But I need to tell you something first." She glanced up and looked at everyone in the room, one by one, including her daughter. "I need to tell everyone. You may not want to marry me once you know the truth."

"Isabel, do you think—"

But Isabel held up a hand, and Loretta stopped talking. "Everyone deserves to know the truth, especially Somerset."

"The truth?" Where only seconds before joy had possessed Somerset's entire being, apprehension was rapidly taking over. He didn't like this. It boded ill.

"The truth?" Eunice, clearly befuddled, remained beside her mother, holding her hand and looking as if she'd stand by her no matter what the problem turned out to be.

"The truth?" echoed Marjorie, puzzled. "You're daft, Isabel. What can possibly be so bad that Somerset won't want to marry you?"

"Nothing." Loretta's brow furrowed. Somerset was alarmed to note that she was adopting her militant-agitator demeanor, ready to do battle for her friend. "Not a single thing."

"Better spill the beans," Dr. Abernathy said. He was the only one who sounded natural.

"Yes, I shall," Isabel said, and she swallowed again. "I should have told you—all of you—long ago. I was . . . afraid that you wouldn't want anything to do with me if you knew the truth."

"That's silly, Mama. These people are your friends. If you made a mistake . . . well, everyone makes mistakes sometimes. Friends are people who stand by you when you need them."

Isabel burst into tears. Somerset handed her his handkerchief. She whispered brokenly, "Thank you, Eunice. Thank you, Somerset. This is a very bad thing I did, though, sweetie. It's something many people can't forgive, even if they're your friends."

Eunice's little eyebrows dipped over her pretty brown eyes. She looked as if she couldn't think of anything *that* bad barring, perhaps, cold-blooded murder. After giving the problem a moment's thought, she said, "It isn't because you weren't married to my father, is it?"

Chapter Nineteen

Everyone in the room who wasn't Eunice gasped, including Eunice's mother and Geoffrey, who had recovered from his swoon and was sitting on the floor, watching the goings-on.

Isabel screeched, *"How did you know that?"*

Eunice shrugged. "Some of the children in the village used to call me a bastard, so I looked it up in great-Uncle Charlie's dictionary."

"Oh, my God." Isabel threw her arms around Eunice and drew her onto her lap. Burying her face in her daughter's hair, she sobbed, "I'm so sorry, darling. I'm so sorry. I never wanted you to suffer for my sins."

"I didn't suffer, Mama, and I don't think it's much of a sin." Eunice seemed slightly uncomfortable with her mother's naked emotions. She glanced up at Somerset. "Does it matter to you, Mr. FitzRoy? That my mother wasn't married to my father, I mean? I'm sure it wasn't her fault. She's ever so good a person, really. I think my father must have seduced and abandoned her."

Another screech from Isabel, who jerked her head up from Eunice's hair. *"What?* What did you say?"

Eunice shrugged again. "I only said that I think my father must have seduced—"

"No! Don't say it again," begged Isabel.

Suddenly Loretta burst out laughing. "Eunice Golightly, if you aren't the most perfect child I've ever met, I don't know who is! You have *exactly* the right attitude." She turned on Somerset like a tiger. "And if you don't agree with her, Mr. FitzRoy, you'll kindly take your leave and never darken my door again."

Stunned, first by Eunice's matter-of-fact announcement of what her mother had considered a confession worthy of abandonment by him, then by Isabel's horror that Eunice even knew, and then by Loretta's unprovoked attack upon him, Somerset staggered back a step and stuck out a hand to steady himself on a nearby sofa. "You mean you weren't married to Eunice's father?"

Unable to speak, Isabel only nodded. Tears pooled in her beautiful blue eyes as she watched him.

As a matter of fact, everyone seemed to be watching him. How embarrassing. He'd much rather have done this in private. Ah, well, so be it. If Isabel was brave enough to confess to what might conceivably—so to speak—be considered a black sin in front of all her friends and God almighty, could Somerset be less?

He walked over to her chair, got down on one knee, and took the twined hands of Isabel and Eunice in his. He spoke to Eunice first. "Miss Eunice, you are, without a doubt, exactly what Miss Linden called you. And the person who made you thus is your mother, whom I love with all my heart."

Isabel gasped.

He transferred his gaze to Isabel. "I'm sorry you didn't trust me enough to tell me about this before, darling. But believe me, it doesn't matter a whit and I'll never, ever hold your sad circumstances against you."

She looked as if he'd socked her in the jaw, as he'd wanted to do Jason. "You . . . you . . ." She had to stop and swallow again.

"I think he means that he still wants to marry you, Mama," Eunice explained. She smiled at Somerset. "I knew you weren't a stuffy old prig, Mr. FitzRoy."

"Thank you very much, Miss Eunice."

"I can't believe it!" Isabel buried her face in her hands and sobbed as if her heart were breaking. Eunice tried to struggle off her lap, couldn't do it, and brushed at the wrinkles in her skirt.

"Here," said Somerset, uneasy by this reaction, "what's all this? Don't you want to marry me? I thought you said you loved me."

Still sobbing, Isabel said, "I do. Oh, I love you so much!"

Relieved, he said, "Well, then, that's all I need to hear. But my knee hurts. Do you mind if I stand?"

Before he could do so, Isabel flung herself along with her daughter, who was still on her lap, at Somerset. Fortunately, he had braced himself with his knee, so he didn't fall over backwards.

"Hurrah!" shouted Loretta. Then she gestured at her friends to join in. "Three cheers for the happy couple!"

So they all of them, even Marjorie, yelled, "Hurrah! Hurrah! Hurrah!"

Later that night, after Loretta, who had many powerful friends in the city of San Francisco, had called upon a judge of her acquaintance; and after a brief ceremony uniting Isabel Golightly and Somerset FitzRoy in holy matrimony; and after Mrs. Brandeis had prepared a supper to go with the champagne (Isabel's ankle was too badly hurt for them to go out to supper); and after toasts had been drunk and a sleepy Eunice put to bed and everyone else had either departed or gone to bed, Isabel and Somerset lay in her bed, happy and exhausted from a delightful bout of lovemaking.

"I'm glad Dr. Abernathy bound my ankle tightly. I don't think it would have survived all that if it weren't bound." Isabel had her arms around Somerset and decided she'd just keep them there for a while. She never wanted to let him go, although she figured she'd have to release him someday, if only so that he could help her pack.

"I am, too." Somerset was still panting slightly. His grin told her that he'd enjoyed their recent exercise a lot and that he believed he'd done a good job. So did she. He didn't seem inclined to make her let him go, either. Isabel considered that a good sign.

"It was lovely of Loretta to make her judge friend come over here and marry us."

With a laugh, Somerset said, "It's probably a good idea that you and Eunice will be moving into my house. If you stayed here, God alone knows what would become of you."

"Loretta is a wonderful person," Isabel said. "She's my very best friend in the whole world. Why, if it hadn't been for her, Eunice and I would have drowned along with all those other people on the *Titanic.*"

That sobered Somerset instantly. "In that case, I think I'll have a statue erected in her honor. There's probably a park somewhere in the city that can use a good statue."

"Don't be silly." But she giggled.

Contentment captured them both, and they lay

silent for several minutes. At last Somerset spoke. "Did Eunice's father really seduce and abandon you?"

Isabel's heart crunched. She'd been afraid he'd ask. It was his right to know. "Well . . . yes. I hate to talk about it, because I was so stupid. But . . . well, I believed him when he told me he loved me. But as soon as . . . as I knew I was expecting Eunice and I told him, he lit out for America. With his wife. I didn't know he was married until after he left."

"Good God, what a rotter."

"Yes." Isabel hoped that would be the end of that particular conversation, but she was disappointed.

"Is that why you left for America? To find him?"

"Good Lord, no! I never want to see the man again as long as I live. I don't even know if I'd recognize him, it was so long ago. I only feel sorry for his wife."

"Yes. He doesn't sound very much like a man of good character."

"That's an understatement. But so far, Eunice isn't at all like him."

"I should hope not."

Isabel was glad to see him grin. He had been looking quite somber and serious. She didn't want a somber and serious wedding night. She wanted joy to prevail tonight and forever. She said, "In fact, I can't think of anyone in my family after whom Eunice *does* take. My uncle Charlie is smart, but nothing like Eunice. And my mother and father were bright, but not any brighter than most people. And God knows, I'm not."

"You're my bright and shining star, Isabel," Somerset told her.

"Thank you. I never thought I'd ever meet a man like you, Somerset. I love you ever so much."

"Good. That's good."

They shared a kiss that started out sweet, turned hot,

then passionate, and finally ended with Somerset again delving into Isabel's sweet, velvety secrets, which she lifted to meet him. As they rocked together in the timeless rhythm of love, Somerset gazed into her eyes, and she offered up a silent prayer of thanks for sending him to her. And in such an amazing way.

He lowered his head and captured his lips with hers as they loved each other. The pressure built in Isabel until at last she tumbled over the precipice into a shattering, rippling explosion of pleasure. Somerset joined her shortly afterwards.

Isabel had never been so happy as when she lay, spent, in her husband's embrace. Her eyes closed, she relished the sweet languor stealing over her body. She loved and was loved, and life was and would remain good. From now on. She'd have Amazing Graciousness, her dance studio, and she'd have her daughter and her husband—and who knew? Perhaps there would be more little ones. She'd like that.

"I'd like to adopt Eunice." His remark startled her out of her lethargy.

Her eyes popped open. "You would?"

"Yes. I love the little girl. She's rather frightening, but I think I can stand it." He chuckled.

Isabel didn't. She tightened her arms around him and wept softly against his chest. "Thank you, Somerset. That's the most marvelous thing you could ever do for us."

"Is it? It only seems natural to me."

"That's what's so wonderful about you. You think of yourself as only natural, when you're actually superb. Perfect. Precious. Oh, I can't even come up with enough superlatives to describe you."

"Careful. I'm liable to get a swelled head."

She gave a watery chuckle. "Impossible."

Suddenly, Somerset scared the wits out of Isabel by crying, "I have it!"

After uttering a small, sharp cry of alarm, Isabel commanded her heart to quit racing and said, "You have what?"

"The color of your eyes."

"Good heavens."

"They're the blue of *Myosotis!*" He smacked his forehead with the palm of his hand. "How could I not have come up with the comparison before?"

"I don't know."

"I knew they weren't gentian, because *Gentiana acaulis* is too purple. They're almost the color of *Lobeliaceae*, but not quite. *Catananche caerulea* come close, but aren't quite perfect. But *Myosotis* . . ." He sighed happily. "Now why, I wonder, didn't I think of that until right this minute?"

"Since I have no idea what *Myosotis* is, I can't answer that."

Somerset laughed and hugged her. "I'm sorry. I keep forgetting you don't speak Latin. Forget-me-nots. Your eyes are the exact color of forget-me-nots. Forget-me-nots are perfect."

Isabel thought that having eyes like forget-me-nots sounded like a very good thing. She also knew that nothing about her was perfect. But Somerset . . . well, Somerset FitzRoy was absolutely, stunningly perfect.

Isabel and Somerset had been married for three months. She and Eunice had moved into his Craftsman-style house on Chestnut the day after they were wed, and Isabel had never been happier in her life.

Somerset was a loving husband, an attentive father, and he and Eunice had even started playing baseball together, Eunice having decided she wanted to be a base-ball player when she grew up. Since he didn't know anything more about the game than she did, they had fun making up the rules as they went along.

Isabel's ankle had healed nicely, and she'd taken a lease on some office space that she aimed to turn into a dance studio. Thanks to Somerset's artistic leanings and deep pockets, she'd even started redecorating it. The mirrors and new glass windows were being installed the next day, and she was busy in the back parlor of her new home, sewing curtains for the Amazing Graciousness Dance Academy's windows.

She'd been so engrossed in her sewing—Somerset had bought her a brand-new, side-pedal Singer sewing machine, and she was having fun using it—that when Mrs. Brandeis entered the room and cleared her throat, she jumped a little in her chair. "Yes, Mrs. Brandeis?" She wasn't yet comfortable having servants, but Somerset had told her she'd just have to *get* comfortable, because he wasn't going to let her do all the housework.

"A gentleman to see you, ma'am."

Mrs. Brandeis had a strange expression on her face; Isabel couldn't find a word for it, but she rose from her chair and hurried after the housekeeper, a little worried.

"I put him in the front parlor, Mrs. FitzRoy."

"Thank you, Mrs. Brandeis. Er . . . did he give you a card?"

"No, ma'am. Nor did he give me his name."

"Oh."

When Isabel entered the front parlor, she beheld a man, all right, but he was totally unfamiliar to her. She was sure she'd never seen him before. Of medium height, with black hair, what she could see of him was tanned to a fare-thee-well. He wore a suit of foreign cut.

He also had his back to her and seemed to be staring into the fireplace.

Unsure of herself, and of him, she said, "May I help you?"

And then he turned around.

For only a second, Isabel's mouth dropped open and she stared. Then she cried, *"Jorge!"* and ran over to throw her arms around him.

"I return," he said, returning her embrace without enthusiasm, but with great strength.

It was Jorge's voice, all right: arrogant, supercilious, condescending, and heavily accented.

"We didn't know what had happened to you!"

Although Jorge didn't seem inclined to let her go, Isabel pulled herself out of his arms, remembering as she did so one of the reasons she'd never cared much for Jorge.

"I was took," Jorge said with a dramatic gesture so wide it nearly knocked over a lamp. "Right off the dock, I was took."

"We heard you'd been shanghaied," Isabel said. "But let me ring for refreshments. Sit down, Jorge! Sit down!"

So Jorge sat. He did so with the same old flair.

"You look so tanned and healthy," Isabel said, after giving instructions to Li, who had answered her ring. "The sailor's life must have agreed with you."

"Huh," said Jorge. "I'm an *artist,* not a sailor."

"Of course you are," Isabel said soothingly.

They were still talking when Somerset came home. He didn't look awfully pleased when he entered the front parlor and found Jorge Luis Savedra lounging on his sofa and chatting with his wife. But he cheered up when Isabel instantly rose from her chair and greeted him with a kiss.

"And guess what, Somerset?" Isabel was terribly excited.

"What?" Somerset himself looked slightly dubious.

"Jorge has agreed to be the dancing master at the Amazing Graciousness Dance Academy for Young Ladies and Gentlemen!"

Somerset said, "Gmmph!"

Peering at him closely, Isabel decided he was suppressing laughter.

"I," Jorge said, knocking his thin chest with his fist, "am the best."

Isabel grinned at Somerset, and Somerset, after swallowing his mirth, smiled back at her. He reached for her hand. She gave it gladly. Somerset said, "You might be the best, but I won the contest."

Isabel squeezed his hand, loving him madly. "It was the second time you saved my life, Somerset."

He grinned and turned back to Jorge. "And, as you can see, I also won the girl."

Jorge, scowling and with his arms crossed over his chest, said, "Huh!"